TYCHE'S FLIGHT

A SPACE OPERA ADVENTURE EPIC

EZEROC WARS
BOOK 1

RICHARD PARRY

CONTENTS

TYCHE'S DECEIT

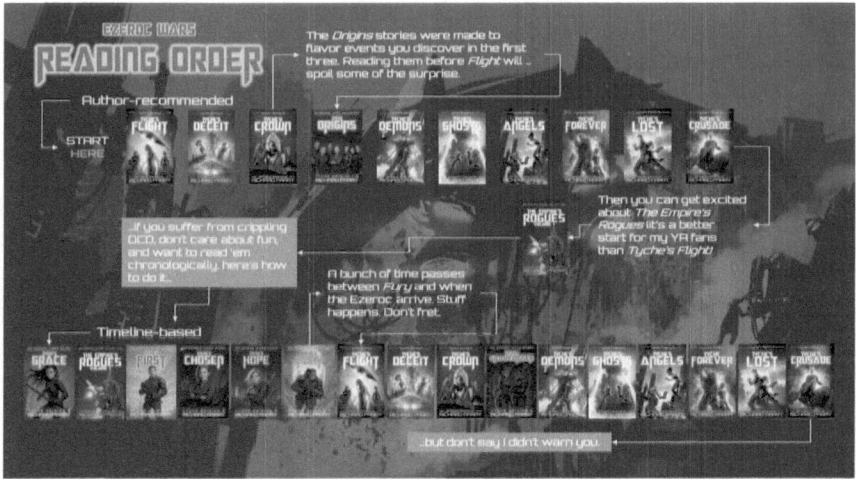

TYCHE'S FLIGHT
A COLONY HAS FALLEN. THE REPUBLIC IS NEXT.

Nathan Chevell captains the free trader *Tyche*, an **ex-military heavy lifter** now flying under merchant colors. He's no pirate, but he's no white knight either. **There's no business in helping strays.**

Grace Gushiken is a liar, a thief, and an esper—one of the Republic's most wanted. But when she stows away aboard *Tyche*, Nate finds himself dragged into something far worse than a smuggling job.

The doomed colony of Absalom Delta is deserted. The insect-like Ezeroc didn't come to talk. **They came to consume.** The Republic Navy tried to stop them and got **torn apart.**

Now, *Tyche* is caught in the crossfire. Outgunned, outnumbered, and light-years from help, **Nate and Grace have two choices: run, or fight a war they can't win.**

Because the Ezeroc don't stop. They don't reason. They don't fear. **They just feed.** And if Nate and Grace can't stop them here, **there won't be a next time.**

Tyche's Flight is the first book in Richard Parry's explosive *Ezeroc Wars* series. If you love **high-stakes space opera** with sharp dialogue, heart-pounding action, and a war that could end humanity, read it today!

YOU'RE AWESOME

You could have picked any book, but you chose this one. That means a lot.

Your support keeps independent authors like me forging ahead, writing the stories we love (and hopefully, the ones you love too). Whether you're here for the characters, the worldbuilding, or just a little escapism, thank you for being part of this journey.

You. Kick. Ass.

ROLL FOR NARRATIVE
WHERE WORLDBUILDING AND
OVERTHINKING COLLIDE

Love stories that linger in your brain long after The End? Ever wonder why some books hit like a natural 20 and others critically fail their way into the 1-star abyss?

Join *Roll for Narrative*, my hub for sci-fi and fantasy lovers. I explore storytelling like a rogue casing a dungeon, review movies, books, and games, and dish out writing tips like a chaotic-good bard with a grudge against bad prose. No spam, just good stuff.

Join the quest:
https://rollfornarrative.parrydox.com

For my Rae, because you asked for it.

AN EASY MARK

GRACE HAD A DAY TO LIVE.

Oh, sure. She might stretch it to a day and a half. But what's twelve hours against your lifetime?

Not a lot. Her room at the hotel was burned. The only thing she had left was her stash with her sword and a few Republic coins for emergencies. She hadn't expected to be on this particular crust for this long. She hadn't expected to be here at all. When Grace got caught, she'd die. Simple as that. Not getting caught? Harder by the minute.

The Republic were getting close to her now. She could almost smell their hounds on her heels.

Grace could certainly *feel* them. The *excitement/chase/hunger* of their pursuit; it was all around her. She stood in the warm air of Enia Alpha, a yellow star overhead, an easy 0.9Gs under her feet, and felt the coarseness of the silk material under her fingers. The holo said *Genuine Earth Silk!* This, like much of life, was a lie. Grace was used to lying, except she liked to think she was better at it than the merchant. To make a lie believable, there needed to be at least a hint of truth. The silks cost nowhere near enough good Republic coin to be from Earth; the price was low enough it called into question whether it was silk at all. A bigger price and the lie of the silks would, almost naturally, become truth. It didn't have to *be* true; it needed to *feel* true.

The only good thing about the bad lie in front of her was that it was like a disguise. The Republic guards behind her were hunting an esper, not a shopper of silks. An esper would run, not bargain for material by the meter. The Republic soldiers would have been told about the devils they hunted. *Espers, they'll take your kids in the night.* Or, *espers, they can make you* do *things.* The first was an exaggeration, because espers only took other espers, but the second? That was truth. And because it sounded horrible, they expected the people doing it to *look* horrible. With a peg leg, or a scar across the face. They didn't expect them to look ... *ordinary.*

The problem with the Republic — *one of them anyway, right Grace?* — was that they were used to being on top. A good ten years had passed since the Old Empire had fallen. Ten years was a long time for people to forget about the good, holding on to the bad. Folk remembered the Intelligencers as the first of these devils to walk among them. They wanted them to be the last, so — almost naturally, like the changing of seasons — came the witch hunts, where anyone with the smell of the gift was fair game. Cheat at cards? An esper. Lucky break in the markets? Esper. Your kid fall in with a bad crowd? Espers, all of 'em. The reach of the Republic was far, and their boot — made from fear and strength — was heavy. Fear and strength was why she'd chosen the mark she had.

Her mark knew the feel of that boot on his neck. Nathan Chevell, captain of the free trader *Tyche*. If *captain* was even the right word for the owner of an aging rust-bucket. He hadn't been on the winning side of the war. Not to say he was on the losing, either; her research said he was out the door before the real fighting started. Maybe a coward. Even if he wasn't, he'd be easy to play; either the *hero* card or the *guilt* card would work. The important part was that this Nathan Chevell was good at his job; he ran a free starship outside of Guild constraints. She needed to sign on as crew. Find an empty spot to fill, or make a spot empty if all berths were full. He didn't have an Assessor, and that was her path in. Assessors lied about little things like they mattered, and Grace had been lying for more than the ten years the Old Empire had been rubble.

She knew — courtesy of last night's tryst with a talkative Navy officer, proud of his rank, uniform, and alcohol choices in equal measure — that Nathan Chevell would be sent out to the back of the hard black by the Republic themselves. Because this Nathan Chevell didn't like the press of the boot on his neck, he would argue about it, so she needed to give him a nudge. Make sure he took the job, and her with it. Then she could enjoy the trip, and the irony of being sent away by the very Republic that hunted her.

Grace Gushiken let the silks fall. She needed her sword. It was time to get to work.

CHAPTER ONE

HE WOULD ALWAYS REMEMBER the first time she lied to him.

Nate was sitting in a spacer bar — not that it had signs saying *Spacer Bar* or *Drunk Crew Welcome*. It was the way it smelled more than anything, old engine oil overlaid with the unmistakable tang of ozone that came from working heavy machines or plasma cannons. Beer, vat-grown because out here that was the best way to get consistent results. Still, you never knew if some strain of modified soy was being used on-planet for your drink. There was also the smell of sweat, and sometimes, of anger.

That last was typical. *Drunk Crew Welcome* wasn't always a good thing.

"Captain Chevell," said the man across from him, Republic uniform starched so crisp you could shave yourself with the collar. It was a dress uniform, lieutenant's insignia on the shoulders, wings on the breast, a bunch of other medals Nate was too bored to take in. The ID tag said *Evans*, which might even be his name. Nate didn't care about that either, because this man was a piece of a great machine, and the machine didn't care about names, only results. The uniform went nicely with dress hands, folded in front of the lieutenant. Fingers that hadn't seen a blaster since basic training, not a callus anywhere. This man was content behind a desk, and probably good at it too. The Navy hat was on the table to the man's right, almost like a barrier. Possibly a necessary barrier — the other man seated across from Nate with Evans wasn't an officer. Not even close. He had muscles, and was wearing dress fatigues that said *I'm always on duty, even in your Spacer Bar.* He wouldn't have finished that with *asshole* because Republic Marines were always polite, but he would have meant it. So yeah, that hat was a good barrier between the two: on the same side, but different points of view. "Are you the captain of the *Tyche?*" Evans said it like *Teach.*

"Certainly not," said Nate.

"You're … not?"

"No," said Nate. "I'm the captain of the starship *Tyche.*" He pronounced it like Lady Luck intended: Tie-Key. "Say it with me. *Tyche.*"

"Tie. Key," said Evans, face blank.

"Good work," said Nate. "You were going somewhere with that, right?"

"Captain Chevell," Lieutenant Evans said again, "it would be nice to hear your perspective."

"My perspective?" said Nate. "I'm not sure it needs a perspective. You're talking cash money for a milk run."

"Exactly the kind of perspective I was hoping for," said Evans. He brightened. "Are you willing to take on the job?"

"Hold up," said Nate.

Evans looked a little lost. "You said 'cash money for a milk run.' I'm not sure—"

"Where there is milk, and it's cash money, there's always a fly in it," said Nate. "Always."

"A fly?" said Evans. The Marine next to him hadn't even looked sideways at Nate, not once, eyes straight ahead, jaw clenched. Or, Nate thought, perhaps it wasn't clenched — the man might have had a jaw made of rocks and rubble. It would be nice if Kohl was here, because Kohl spoke that kind of language. But Kohl was off getting drunk or laid or a hundred other things he wasn't being paid for, which left Nate here, alone, in a *Spacer Bar* that smelled of anger and *Drunk Crew*, ass hanging out, trying to negotiate with the Republic. A Republic who didn't negotiate, which made it fun, and crazy at the same time, and if Nate was being his honest authentic self, like that holo kept telling him he should be, it was why he was pulling the tiger's tail.

Time to pull harder. "You've listed a fee, payable on delivery of an unspecified object, that is frankly astonishing," said Nate.

"Yes," said Evans, "that's—"

"Hold on to your drink," said Nate, watching as Evans' eyes went to the empty space in front of him. *No drink*, because a man like that didn't drink on duty. "Or, hell, watch me hold mine." Nate took an exploratory sip of his beer, which the bartender — a cute young thing with braids that glowed green in the dark interior of the bar — had assured him was vat-grown as he'd dropped Republic coins in front of her. It didn't taste half bad, but the other half wasn't great. *Whatever*. At least it didn't taste like soy beer. Evans was watching him drink, or was watching Nate's hand holding the beer. One of Nate's hands, like one of his legs, was metal: all shiny gold and precision metal and gleaming gears. It was that metal hand, or rather how Nate had … acquired it, that made him cautious when dealing with the Republic. "An astonishing fee means astonishing danger," he said, "or it means you'll fuck me. And I don't mean a nice, cozy fuck, full of gentle whispers and soft kisses. I mean a—"

"I understand what you're saying," said Evans, his lips pulling tighter.

Good Goddamn, but is that Marine smiling? There was something in the way the mound of muscle's face had twitched that made Nate proud. "An astonishing fee means you don't mean to pay it. And getting paid is of high importance to me and mine, if you know what I mean. So here's what'll happen. We'll talk *terms*."

"The terms are clear," said Evans. "Five hundred thousand Republic credits, payable on delivery."

"Do I," said Nate, "look like a stupid man to you, Lieutenant?"

Evans paused. "Not ... particularly, Captain."

"Perhaps green, young, unused to the rigors of command?" Nate raised his eyebrows.

"No. I would say not."

"Then why are you treating me like a gullible child?" said Nate. "I need three things from you."

"Three?"

"Three," said Nate, giving the Marine a glance. Nope, the man still wasn't moving. Like a sphinx, that one, about as readable as a rock. Nate hoped they wouldn't get into any trouble, because without Kohl, it would not be fun business, not for Nate. The Marine would have fun. He held up his gold hand, digits clicking as he extended his fingers. "First, you'll pay me twenty percent up front. This isn't a number that horrifies you. It's a rounding error in your budgets. Not enough for me and mine to run, but enough for us to know there's a higher chance of you paying the rest rather than spacing us all. Two," and a second metal digit clicked up, "you'll tell us what the cargo is. You'll tell us because of what happened two years ago, when I took Republic cargo, and then was *raided by the Republic*, and your clowns tried to charge me for hauling contraband. Took months to work through that, you assholes tried to stiff me on my completion bonus, and I was in jail. A *jail*, Lieutenant. Third, you'll hand over a load of torpedoes. Nothing fancy, no crust-crackers, just some simple ship to ship nukes, because I'm fresh out, and the only place to get nukes is from the Republic Navy. Sort of."

"Sort of?" said Evans.

"Sort of," agreed Nate. "The thing we're dealing with here is *trust*, Lieutenant. Trust can be bought. I'm offering to sell you mine, for a twenty percent advance, knowledge of the cargo, and thirty-six ship to ship nukes. How's that sound?"

The lieutenant thought about it. Nate watched the man's eyes scan the room, the rough crowd giving them a circle of calm because nothing said *stupid* like picking a fight with the Republic Navy. "You're aware," he said, after a suitable period of reflection, "that we could seize your ship, kill your crew, and do the job ourselves?"

"Sure," said Nate, "you could *try* doing that."

"We are the Republic Navy," said Evans.

"Like I said," said Nate, "you could try. There's a couple of problems. First, you'll have to scare up someone who knows how to fly my baby. Not a common ship, not anymore. Those Endless Drives are a thing of wonder and beauty, and the flight systems behind them take a loving touch, Lieutenant. My crew has a loving touch. The *Tyche*, she's our home, our palace, our playground, and our friend. She'll fly true for us, and she'll crash and burn for you and yours."

Evans was watching him. "You said two reasons."

"I did," said Nate. "The second reason is because you're the *good* guys, Lieutenant. You don't raid a peaceful freighter, kill the entire crew, and then steal their ship. No. In this instance, you're trying to pay top dollar because you don't have an Endless ship on hand, you want a dedicated crew, and you want a package delivered. I'm your man. But with those three stipulations."

"Also," said a woman, slipping into the booth next to Nate, "you'll surrender right of salvage. Fourth condition. Or stipulation. Call it something that makes you happy, like 'finder's fee.'"

Evans, Nate, and even the Marine turned to look at the woman. Casual clothes, lots of black, except for her shirt, which was white. Ruffled collar, making Nate think *pirate* before he almost laughed at himself — if there was a pirate here, it was him, with his modern version of a hook hand and peg leg. Her arm, from exposed elbow to wrist, was etched in an ancient-style black tattoo, no dynamic colors switching with her mood. Not *this* one, no sir. She tabled a sword in a scabbard in front of them all with a casual toss, a similar casual toss of her hair — short-cropped, dead straight, black, just long enough to touch her chin, not long enough to get her into trouble — following. White teeth in a smile that made Nate take immediate interest, despite his better judgement, because nothing said *trouble* in quite the same way as a smile like that — Nate had a similar smile of his own. And nothing said *run* in quite the same way as a stranger knowing your business.

Because she was a stranger. He'd never seen this woman before in his life, and that made him uncomfortable. "Hi," said Nate.

"Hi," said the woman, a flash of that smile again peeking out from around her hair. "Been looking for you. For *hours*."

"Captain," said Evans, "who is this—"

"Grace Gushiken," said the woman, "and I'm the *Tyche's* Assessor."

"You are?" said Nate. "I mean, yes, you are."

This wasn't when she lied to him. She was lying to *them*, and Nate could get behind lying to the Republic Navy. It was just more pulling of the tiger's tail, and that lent a certain air of charm to her right away.

"And," said Grace, "the captain shouldn't have been talking to you without me."

"He shouldn't?" said Evans.

"I shouldn't?" said Nate, but he wasn't sure if he was asking a question or not.

"Because the captain," said Grace, "is not an Assessor. He knows ships, and he knows people, and he knows bars," and here, a chuckle, too natural to not be rehearsed, "just fine. What he doesn't know is the value of good salvage. You're sending him out to a place where there's a downed transmitter."

"How did you know—" said Evans.

"The thing about downed transmitters," said Grace, "is that sometimes they're downed, and sometimes they're up and everyone's dead. In the second instance, there's salvage, and we want it. It'll make the trip worthwhile even if you try and stiff us on the other eighty percent." Grace looked at Nate. "You went for the standard eighty-twenty we talked about?"

"I ... did," said Nate, thinking *well fuck me, but roll with it.* He turned back to Evans, turning on his own smile. "I did."

"How did you know—" said Evans, again.

"Everyone knows," said Grace. "This bar is full of people who know. They know your precious Bridge is down, and that you don't have any Endless ships to spare, and that there's a colony out there ripe for piracy at the other end of that Bridge. We," and she jerked a thumb at her chest, "have an Endless ship. We have an Endless ship with a cargo bay large enough to hold a new transmitter. Also got an Engineer who can bolt that right on the side of your gate, fire it up, and get things working again, even if everyone's dead."

"Why would everyone be dead?" said Evans, blinking.

"Pirates," said Grace. "We were just talking about that."

"And we need," said Nate, slipping into the silence like it was made for him, "those ship-to-ship nukes. For the *pirates*. Who may have killed everyone. Not our first rodeo, Lieutenant. Not our first salvage run either. Grace here will take what's lawful salvage and leave the rest. You know our records. You know how we work."

"Yes," said Evans, looking like he was downing cheap tequila, salt, and lime, except without the salt or lime. "We know your records, which is why there will be no Avenger-class weapons given over. Not only is it illegal to provide these to civilian ships, it would cause me to lose sleep at night."

Fair enough. Nate frowned, but had to admit he wouldn't put nukes in the hands of the *Tyche's* crew either. Not after that incident back on Century Gamma. Unlucky for everyone, kind of a lose-lose, but less lose for the people with the nukes, which had been the *Tyche.* "So, Lieutenant," said Nate. "We know what we're hauling now — transmitter. We can live without the nukes. But we can't live without the twenty percent."

"I could," said the Marine, speaking for the first time, and astonishing everyone, and not least of which because his voice was gentle in a way not common with the Marines, "rough him up a little."

"You could," said October Kohl, coming up behind the Marine, leaning close enough to kiss, and nuzzling a blaster next to the man's neck, "not live past the next five minutes." He looked up at Nate. "Captain. I could rough *him* up a little." Kohl looked and smelled drunk, which was a standard state of affairs, but his eyes were bright. Like the Marine, he was a solid mound of muscle. Unlike the Marine, he had scars, a bad set of locks in dire need of washing or trimming or just burning, and what Nate was sure was an unhealthy desire to kill people. Which was why he was useful. The Marine's eyes had gone wide, his posture stiff in a way that suggested he knew the kind of man who had a gun to the side of his head.

"I think we've about established how this will work," said Nate to Evans. "Would you agree?"

"I would agree," said Evans. "I'll be in touch with the *Tyche* to arrange the details."

"Great," said Nate. "You want to be talking to El. She's our Helm." He gave a glance to Kohl. "You could..." He waved his hand, the one still made of flesh and blood.

"Kill this asshole?"

"No," said Nate. "Let him go."

Kohl looked like he was thinking about it, *really* thinking about it, about whether this was the time he would push the limits of his contract. He relaxed, letting the Marine go, and slapped a hand on the other man's shoulder. "Sorry about that. No hard feelings."

The Marine rubbed the side of his neck where the blaster had been. "Sure," he said, because there wasn't much else to say when there was a man right behind you with a blaster in his hand and murder in his heart.

The Marine and the lieutenant slipped out of the booth, leaving the bar, the Marine glancing over his shoulder, Kohl giving the man a friendly wave before slipping into the booth across from Nate and Grace. He looked at Nate. "Who's this?"

"I'm Grace," said Grace, flashing that smile.

"Was I," said Kohl, "fucking talking to you?" He was slurring a little. He seemed to see the sword on the table for the first time. "Nice sword."

"Thank you," said Grace. "I'm—"

"Still not," said Kohl, "talking to you." He blinked, coughed, and looked at Nate. "Captain?"

"Kohl raises a good question," said Nate. "Who the fuck are you?"

"Grace Gushiken," said Grace, "your new Assessor."

"Hell of a way to interview for a job," said Nate, "but we're full. And we don't need an Assessor."

"Yes you do," said Grace. "Be honest, Nate—"

"Captain Chevell," said Nate. "Let's start with that."

"Captain Chevell," said Grace, still a hint of a smile about her, "those men wouldn't tell you anything. Not about the cargo. Not about the transmitter. And sure as stars, not about what's going on at Absalom Delta." She looked at his metal hand. "You look like you might know what the Republic lying to you feels like."

Nate's eyes moved to the door of the bar, a couple walking in. They were laughing, her hand on his. He bent to whisper in her ear, and they moved to the bar. The bartender with the glowing green braids put a couple of drinks in front of them, sweeping Republic coins away like they'd never existed, like it was a magic trick to make things disappear before your eyes. Nate watched Grace Gushiken watch those two enter, watched her watch them move to the bar, and then he watched as she pretended she wasn't watching them. "So, Grace," he said. "You seem to know the Republic pretty well yourself."

"Better than you know," she said, relaxing into her seat, which — not coincidentally, Nate thought — lowered her from view.

"And why should I take you on my crew?" he said.

"Because you need me," she said.

"And because you need me," said Nate, looking at the couple at the bar. They were still laughing, and talking, but their eyes were scanning the crowd. "Why?"

"I need to get off this rock," she said. "An Assessor doesn't make coin sitting in a spacer bar."

That, right there, was the first time she lied to him. Not about her name, as near as Nate could tell, but about what she was. Not that she wasn't a great Assessor; she may well have been. It was impossible to tell from the vantage of this fine spacer bar. Didn't matter: it's that she was so much more. Nate could feel it, feel it like he could sometimes feel the old pain where his left arm and leg had been burned away in cleansing fire. Feel it like warm sun on his face when they were on a beautiful planet like this Enia Alpha, a gentle 0.9Gs tugging at him, a yellow sun in the sky above. But he could also feel that there was something about her. She had tugged that tiger by the tail like she owned the damn tail, and Nate felt an instant like for anyone who could stick it to the Republic.

Nate looked at October. "Kohl," he said, "do you want to fight?"

Kohl thought about it. "I don't know, Captain. You and me? It'll be hard for you to give orders without your teeth."

"Not me," said Nate. "Those two at the bar."

Kohl turned around, the faux leather booth seat creaking under his weight. He turned back. "How much you want 'em hurt?"

"I want 'em hurt enough to let us get to our ship without being followed."

"Great," said Kohl, rising.

"Could you," said Nate, "wait for us to go? You know how I love watching you work, but—"

"But you want 'em distracted as you go, so I can get 'em from behind," said Kohl. "It doesn't seem fair. I like it."

Grace was already slipping from the booth seat, a dancer's flow in her movements. She gathered the sword from the table like it weighed nothing, slung the scabbard's belt over her shoulder, and gave Nate a glance. Something fearful behind the play. "You ready?"

"I'm ready," said Nate, but this time he was lying to himself. Not that he knew it. None of them knew what was coming.

CHAPTER TWO

OCTOBER KOHL WAS DRUNK. He knew it. That asshole who was eyeing him up knew it. The bartender knew it. The proprietor of the brothel he'd just been thrown out of knew it. The question — then — was not whether he was drunk, but whether it would hold him up any. He put a hand out in front of him, looking at the way it drifted in space.

It wasn't waving all over the place, but it wasn't steady as a rock either. That meant no guns, because Kohl wanted to drink here again, and shooting people who weren't supposed to be shot was one of the best ways to never get back in. As Nate had explained to him, there were rules, and polite people didn't shoot people who didn't deserve it.

Kohl rose, taking a look around the bar. There were people here who deserved it, sure as ships flew, but he could already feel the look Nate would give him. So, no guns. He made sure his blaster was holstered, nice and secure, clip fastened over the top. It took him a try or two but he got there in the end. When he looked up, that asshole who'd been eyeing him up was right in front of him. Big asshole too, bunch of ink down one side of his neck, none of that glowy shit popular out here on the rim worlds, straight black needled right under the skin. Had a rivet in his forehead — a goddamn *rivet*, for fuck's sake — planted above the guy's right eye. Could be cosmetic, or could be because he had a bunch of metal in his head and that was the best way of solving the problem.

"Coins," said the asshole.

Kohl swayed, put a hand on the side of the booth that Nate and wossername, Grace, *Grace*, that was it, had just left. Looked the asshole in the eye. "Fuck off," he said.

"I—"

"No," said Kohl, "really. Look," and here, he realized he was slurring more than he'd expected, "I'm trying to work."

"Work?" The asshole looked a little surprised.

"Yeah," said Kohl. "I need to punch some fools."

"I think you're too drunk to—" started the asshole, before Kohl slammed a fist into his stomach. The guy, coughed, tried to stand, and that was just a bad move, because you should stay down when you're outmatched, but not everybody worked that way. So Kohl grabbed fistfuls of the asshole's jacket, and yanked the man forward into a headbutt. The impact was hard, but not too hard, which meant that rivet was cosmetic. He let the asshole slump to the floor, out like a cheap drive from Venus, and stepped over him en route to the bar.

Joni was behind the bar, those green braids of hers glowing like a set of emergency beacons, and she saw Kohl on his way over. "October," she said, "no."

Kohl locked on to those green braids like lights guiding him in to land in a storm. The couple Nate had asked him to delay were already looking over, which was fine, because this wasn't surprise work. He made it to the bar, jostling hard against the woman, knocking her a little sideways into the man and spilling her drink. Kohl got a good look at them. Trim and fit. Drinks untouched, holding right at the top of the water line from when they'd bought them. Dressed in dark spacer overalls, which meant they weren't spacers at all, because no crew Kohl knew of kept their damn jump-suits on when they were shoreside. It was like they'd seen a holo about spacer bars before going into this particular one, which meant two things.

First, because of how they were dressed, they were not spacers. No crime against that, rich people sometimes wanted to rub against the dirt, and Kohl was no particular judge on how people got their thrills.

Second, because of their untouched drinks, they were trying to keep sharp, because they wanted trouble, or because they were on duty, or both. That there meant the captain was right in wanting to delay them. Could be wrong too, if they were Republic agents of one shape or another, but Kohl didn't much care.

"Hey," said the woman. "Hey!"

"Hey," agreed Kohl, and counted Republic coins onto the bar.

"October Kohl, *no*." Joni tried to push them back at him. "Kohl? Are you listening to me? Not tonight. Not again."

"It's okay," said the man, holding a hand up to Joni. "Man just wants to buy us a drink to apologize."

"That's not it," said Joni. "*October Kohl, you stop right now.*"

"Sorry, Joni," said Kohl. "Captain's orders." He examined the pile of coins, then tossed another on for good measure. "There."

"Your captain wanted you to buy us a drink?" said the man, not understanding despite being more sober than Kohl. Could well have been all the way sober as Kohl figured things.

"That's not it," said Kohl. "Captain's gone. This is for damage to the bar."

The man gave a glance over to the booth where Nate had been, said something that sounded like *shit*, and tried to push past Kohl towards the exit. Kohl put an arm against the man's chest and gave a gentle push. The man stumbled back against the bar, knocking into the woman, spilling her drink again. She really should put that thing down.

Joni gave Kohl a last, angry glare, then slammed her hand under the bar. There was a rattle, and metal shutters slid down over the top of the bar, locking her in. The lights in the bar came up, causing Kohl to squint, which was why the man's fist caught him in the side of the face. It wasn't that he was drunk — he might still have worn a fist to the face, but he would have seen the damn thing coming.

That's how he landed on his back, staring at the ceiling, those damn bright lights above him. The woman was saying something to the man, using words like *move* and *backup* and *kill him*, which were all the wrong words for a bar fight. And the man was pulling out some kind of communicator, a slick little thing that had black ops written all over it. It wasn't that it was slick and black, it was that green lazed out of it, falling in quick raindrops of colored light over the interior of the bar. It made Kohl laugh.

They both paused and looked down at Kohl. He pushed himself up on an elbow, held up a hand to forestall being punched in the face a second time, then levered himself to his feet. Pointed at the communicator. "That's not very discrete," he said.

The man looked at the communicator, then at his fist, no doubt wondering at its lack of effect. "I—"

"Because," said Kohl, "it's got black ops written all over it, little toy like that. What's it doing, taking our pictures and getting backup?"

"That's the size of it," said the woman.

Kohl turned his neck to the left, then the right, rewarded with a series of pops. "Last time I was in a situation like this, the backup wanted to kill everyone."

"They—" said the man.

"I don't care," said Kohl.

"You don't?" said the man.

"No," said Kohl. "You do what you need to, right? Right? I'm here as a, what would you call it, a delaying tactic. Also, I owe you one." With that, he slammed his fist into the side of the man's face. The guy tumbled back against the bar, kind of loose in the limbs like he wasn't piloting anymore, which turned out to be the case as he slumped to the floor. The woman looked at this, then smashed her glass against the bar, holding up the broken stem, and trying to stab Kohl in the face with it.

That'd be why she kept holding that damn drink, thought Kohl. He caught her arm, the broken stem spinning out across the bar, and he punched her in the face for good measure. She hit the deck right next to her partner.

Kohl was about to give himself a virtual pat on the back for a job well done when two things happened.

First, someone hit him in the back with a chair. This was supposed to hit Kohl in the back of the head, but misjudged timing or the second thing skewed the aim and all it did was hurt, but a lot, dropping him to one knee amidst the woman's spilled drink and shards from her broken glass.

Second, a bunch of *other* assholes burst in the front of the bar, and fired into the room. The person who'd hit Kohl in the back with a chair — turned out, it was the *first* asshole with the rivet in his head — got caught in a fusillade of plasma. The plasma picked him up, tossed the body across the room, and what landed was in pieces and on fire.

So it was good, in a way, that Kohl had been hit in the back and dropped like a dress on prom night, not that he'd been to a prom, but he'd heard *stories*. Because being dropped meant he hadn't turned into human-shaped charcoal, and it gave him a moment of quiet, or quiet*er*, reflection on the floor of the bar as what looked and sounded like a small-scale war broke out. Spacers were drawing down on the newcomers and firing back, and all that was fine, but one thing was bothering Kohl.

Joni.

Because she was behind some shutters and the wood paneling of the bar, rated for broken glass and bad language, not blaster fire, and if she was back there then bad things could happen to her. Kohl wasn't troubled on a day to day basis by his conscience, but she'd tried to warn him, or at least it had felt like that, and people who warned you were worth keeping on team.

"Joni!" he yelled. "Joni, you alive back there?"

"Fuck you, October Kohl!" she screamed back at him, her voice sounding like it was coming from the same floor-level height he was at. Tricky to tell, but it was a good start.

"Later!" said Kohl. "Joni, I'll come in there and get you out." He unclipped the strap over the top of his blaster, pulled the weapon out, and pointed it up. Not at the shutters, because that was too high to climb right now, but the let's-call-it-wood next to his head. And after a moment's reflection, a little to the right. He pulled the trigger, a bright stab of plasma punching a hole through the paneling of the bar. He fired a couple more times, figuring that because he wasn't firing at the front of the bar he wasn't drawing much attention, because in his experience soldiers — if that's what they were — liked to shoot at people shooting at *them*. Everything else scanned in at a lower priority. It was the kind of oversight that killed more soldiers than was necessary.

He scrabbled over broken pieces of veneer and ceramicrete and melted plastic, crawling behind the bar. Joni helped him through, then tried to hit him in the face. She made a poor job with the first swing, because of the angle, and a better job with the second swing. Joni was looking like she wanted to go for a third, so Kohl held up a hand, wincing. "Two seems fair."

"God dammit Kohl," said Joni. "I said *no*."

"How was I supposed to know they were some kind of secret black ops assholes with secret black ops backup?" he said, then ducked as plasma fire burned a hole through the shutters above them and incinerated top-shelf liquor in a haze of steam.

"I knew," she said. "*I* knew, Kohl."

"Yeah," said Kohl, after a moment. "Sorry. Captain's orders."

"Fuck Nate," said Joni, but with no real urgency.

"Back door," he said, pleased he wasn't slurring so much. It could also have been the sharp sound of plasma weapons being discharged that covered it up; either way was fine. "Back door."

She nodded, moving on all fours through broken pieces of the bar, her glowing green hair lighting the way. Kohl got a view of her rear, which was a nice rear as these things went, which made him wonder if he was sobering up like he thought. He followed her as she pushed through a door, into a kitchen area, empty of people. Kohl got himself up into a low crouch and pointed at a door on the far side of the room. "That it?"

"That's it," said Joni. She moved towards it.

Kohl grabbed her arm. "Not so fast," he said.

She shook him off. "October Kohl, if you touch me again—"

"There will be five guys out there wanting to kill you," he said, hoping that would explain things enough in the heat of the moment.

Kohl led the way across the kitchen, still keeping low. The crackle of plasma discharge was becoming intermittent from behind them, which meant someone was winning, or both sides were just running out of people to keep pulling triggers. Kohl readied his blaster, got to the door, stood up, kicked it open, and shot the man standing there in the middle of the chest. The man spun back, smoke pouring from the hole in his chest, and Kohl turned to the left and shot the man standing there too. He spun to the right, and fired twice more into the woman standing there.

They all hit the ground in the little alley out the back in a clatter of rifles.

Kohl looked over his shoulder at Joni. "Wait here a second," he said. He slipped out into the alley. No one else here, which wasn't what he expected. Five was a better number for this, and for there to be only three spoke of budget cuts or incompetence. He bent over, checking bodies. No ID, no insignia, no tags of any kind. Not even a fashion label on their underwear. *Huh.* Well, that didn't matter much; the captain didn't want intel, he wanted a quick getaway. He hefted the bodies out of sight behind a dumpster, the side of it sporting a bright *Thank you for being a tidy citizen!* He yanked the door to the bar back open. Joni was still there.

"Kohl," said Joni. "Kohl? I'll be going now."

"Okay," said Kohl. "Maybe don't come to work for a couple of days."

"What work?" she said, head jerking behind her.

"Right," said Kohl. He cocked his head, looking up. No drones, which was odd in itself. No sirens, which was odder still. He palmed his communicator, tapping the screen. No signal. *Huh*, again. "Maybe you want to let me go first."

"Maybe I do," said Joni, her own communicator slipping back into a pocket of her pants. "What's going on, October?"

"Above my pay grade," said Kohl. "I'm a deck hand."

She laughed at him, all jangled nervousness. "You are *not* a deck hand."

He shrugged, holstered the blaster, and walked to the end of the alley. To the left, the main entrance to the bar. Smoke, a few bodies. Holo stage was out, leaving just a blank hole. Not many folk milling around, because smart money said *run* when people started firing. He crouched low, shuffled to the entrance to the bar, and took a look inside. Just a couple of soldiers or whatever they were walking around inside the charred wreckage. The coins he'd counted on the bar wouldn't cover this, but to be fair, *this* wasn't a typical event at a bar. This was what happened when black ops wanted something, and wanted it bad. That Navy lieutenant had been hiring Nate for a job, and it looked to Kohl like that contract was one that black ops didn't want fulfilled.

He'd have to tell the captain about this.

As October Kohl left the smoking bar, Joni hurrying in the opposite direction, he was left with a perplexing thought. He rarely spent a lot of time thinking about things, because why bother, the universe kept on turning about the core no matter what you did, but in this case it seemed worthwhile. The thought he couldn't shake was that if black ops didn't want the job fulfilled, there were better paths. They could send someone with a fruit salad on their chest right into the Naval office here on Enia Alpha, knock on a couple of doors, and say: *Yo. We are all on the same side and this is bad.* And then the Navy would get upset, but they'd stop, because Republic black ops were not people with whom you wanted to fuck.

Yeah. He'd have to tell the captain about this.

CHAPTER THREE

NATE AND GRACE were walking along one of the beautiful tree-lined avenues of Arlington. Nate was aiming for a stride with a little more speed, a little less rush. You didn't want to look like you were trying to get away when you were ... trying to get away. It took practice, but he'd had a lot of that.

Arlington was the spaceport on Enia Alpha that Nate had docked the *Tyche* at two days ago to deliver cargo, refuel, and get another job. He had the feeling he'd got the job just *fine*, but it came with strings. The damn Republic never let things happen easy. They always wanted an upper hand, a control in something, and that's why he liked pulling the tiger's tail so much.

That, and they'd destroyed the Empire. That was a thing that would never sit well with him.

He had his thumbs tucked into his belt — one gold-plated, the other flesh — as a bunch of soldiers ran past him, back towards the bar. At that point, his feeling about *strings* solidified. The feeling became uncomfortable, because he was certain one string was walking at his side with an athletic stride he couldn't hope to match with his metal leg. Sure, the prosthetic was fine, it had good feeling and range. The Empire had paid top credits to put him back on his feet, but it always felt to Nate like something was missing. Which was true: he was missing his left arm below the elbow and left leg below the knee. Top credits meant top work, but top work didn't mean *just like you were born with*. They were good enough, just no longer good enough for government work, which was why he was here, and not dead along with most of the other people he'd known. Since the Mercury Accords there was no AI left around to give a helping hand to the movement of his limbs. Which was a blessing; without the Guild's intercession, the AI would have killed them all. You didn't want a computer devil living in your arm or leg.

"A coin," said Grace, "for your thoughts."

"Republic?" said Nate.

"Of course," said Grace. "Be worthless otherwise."

Nate paused as a hovercar roared over the top of them, and he turned to watch it slew to a stop close to the bar they'd just come out of. Holo signage was still promising *cheapest drinks in Arlington* and *Spacers Welcome!* as men and women holding rifles poured from the car and stormed the bar. *Now there is something you do not see every day.* "Uh," he said, and turned back to see Grace already sprinting away, a hand steadying her scabbard as she ran.

Now there's a good plan.

First things first. He flipped out his communicator. "El?"

There was a moment of silence from the communicator before his Helm answered. "What's up, Cap? You get yourself in trouble again?"

Nate looked at the men and women storming the bar, listened to the sound of blasters, and then looked down at the communicator. "What would make you ask that?"

"No reason," said El, her voice coming through crystal clear on the comm. The good part about the damn Republic? Everything *worked*, even comm links on ass-end edge worlds like Enia Alpha. They probably figured that it was difficult to suck all the hope, joy, and free will out of people if you couldn't shout at them first.

Although that might have just been the phantom ache in his leg talking for him.

"Here's the thing," said Nate. He paused. "We need to be ready to dust off in, I don't know, let's call it an hour."

There was a pause from the comm, and then — again, crystal clear — El's voice came through, this time with a tone that could only be called a shriek. "An *hour?* Have you *lost your fucking mind?*" And then, when he didn't answer, she finished it with, "Captain."

"Still got that," said Nate. "I'll need you to get in touch with the Republic. They've got a crate for us, and that crate needs to be on my ship in less than one hour. Did Hope get those repairs done?"

"You say that," said El, "like fixing the cascade generator on an Endless Drive is an easy thing to do."

"I say that," said Nate, "like a Captain who doesn't want his entire ship's crew to be in jail in one hour and ten minutes."

The communicator clicked, then Hope's voice: "She'll fly true, Captain."

"Were you listening in?" said Nate.

"No," said Hope.

"Good," said Nate.

"Just the last bit," said Hope. "And maybe the first bit too. But not everything."

Nate sighed, pocketed the communicator, and walked in the direction Grace had run. The thing about firefights, and not getting shot, was to be good at not drawing attention to yourself. There were some good ways to do that. Just off the top of his head, do not point a blaster at anyone. Don't shoot a blaster. Do not shout. And never, no matter what, should you run. That kind of thing just drew the eye, caused all manner of mischief to rain down on wherever you were, wherever you'd been, and wherever you were going. This worked well for him as a general rule because he didn't like running on his leg, and he figured he'd mastered a good *saunter*.

The streets of Arlington were emptying, water down a drain, and it gave him a few moments to admire the layout of the place. Tall, thin residences stretched up out of smaller, squat businesses around them, relishing the freedom that 0.9G gave them. Trees. Everywhere, trees, growing taller, leaner than a standard Earth gravity would allow. He'd hoped they'd be able to stay on this crust a while longer; a lighter step meant a lighter heart, even if the Republic were stuck in here like a bunch of ticks. He had no quarrel with them, not anymore, but that didn't mean their boot stepped light when it found itself accidentally on your neck.

Like that bar behind him. That was the tread of a heavy boot, make no mistake. If it wasn't the Republic, they'd sanctioned it, that's just the way it was. Didn't make it right — in Nate's view, it made it far from right, and that's why he kept grabbing at the tiger's tail. Speaking of, he spied a flash of straight black hair from a doorway ahead, Grace's face ducking out for a quick glance back his way. Or back at the firefight in the bar. She waved a *come here* at him, movements short with anger or fear or both.

He kept up his saunter. No need to spoil the effect as he approached the finish line. He ducked into the doorway next to her. "Hi."

"Let's go," she said.

"Let's not," he said. He leaned into the alcove, a nook that felt like it was tailor-made for just this kind of conversation. "We haven't discussed terms. We haven't discussed where we're going. The most important thing we haven't discussed is," and here he paused as a particularly loud fusillade of plasma fire from down the street cut him off, "how on Earth, her mighty heavens, the stars we travel across, and the Senate of our true and beloved Republic, you knew me, those Navy boys, or where they want us to go. And all of those things are of interest to me before we keep walking down this fine, tree-lined boulevard."

He was watching her face as he spoke, looking for tells. She was good, maybe even great at hiding them, but this wasn't his first rodeo. Nate saw the emotions chase each other in quick succession. First there was *irritation*, then there was *anger*, and that was followed by something he'd call *incredulousness* for want of a better stake in the quicksand. Finally, a kind of *astonishment* mixed with something that might become, in just a few moments, *acceptance*. She pursed her lips, pushed her scabbard behind her on its shoulder strap, and said, "I need a ride."

Probably not a lie. "Okay," he said.

"And," she said, "there are people after me." She touched his arm, just a gentle touch, but he knew the drill and ignored it.

Still. What she'd said probably wasn't a lie either, hand on his arm or not. "Okay," he said again.

"I can help you," she said.

That there was one mother*fucking* lie. It wasn't that what she said was untrue: it's that what she said was about two percent of the truth, and that made Nate uncomfortable. He didn't like people lying to him, but he was used to it. What he couldn't tolerate was people lying to him about his *ship*. "Thing is," said Nate, "we don't need help. The *Tyche*, you see, well. We've got ourselves a crew, and that there's—"

"They'll kill me," said Grace, "if I stay here."

Nate thought about that. Okay. *That* didn't feel like a lie at all. He felt like she'd just pushed his *sucker* button and fought the urge to white knight this all the way. Because that sword behind her, and the way she walked, said she wasn't after a white knight, despite pushing the *sucker* button hard. "You," he said, "are trying to play me. Find another ride." And he turned to see a soldier, dressed in black standing in front of them. Blaster pointed at Nate. Faceless black visor. And here he was, flat-footed, his own weapon still in its holster because of his stupid damn rules about not drawing attention.

Grace moved, steel hissing out of the scabbard. Her drawing strike brought the blade out from behind her and around, slicing through the side of the soldier's chest plate. Grace's second strike left the cold whisper of air next to Nate's face as her sword reversed direction, moving through the other side of the soldier's armor, the front falling away. Her third stroke cut the soldier's gun in half, and then she was moving out from the alcove, the blade moving up the man's chest, cutting through clothing and flesh like neither of them were any bother at all. The sword's edge met the man's neck as she made the street, and then she was behind him, spinning in place, her sword an arc of white and red. She stopped, facing away from Nate, back to back with the soldier. The moment held, then the soldier's head toppled from his body, gun halves clattering to the ground, the body slumping a half second after.

She spun the sword through the air twice, blood slicking from the blade, before slipping it in the scabbard behind her.

Nate's own sword was back on the *Tyche*, but he hadn't drawn a blade in the ten years since the Empire fell, and doubted he'd be able to swing it like that even if it was resting comfortable by his side. "That," he said, "was some impressive shit."

She turned and looked at the fallen soldier, then at Nate. "I still need that ride, flyboy." Her look said *and you owe me one.*

"You," he said, "are fucking *hired.* But from here on out? It's Captain."

"Copy that, Captain," said Grace Gushiken, reaching her hand out.

He shook it, then opened his communicator again. "El?"

"There's a city-wide state of emergency," said his Helm's voice from the comm. "What did you do?" Then, "Captain."

"*I* didn't do anything," said Nate. "Clean out the spare room. We're taking on one more."

There was a pause, before El said, "Okay. What did *she* do?"

"Nothing," said Nate before pocketing the comm. He wished he'd known he was lying to himself.

CHAPTER FOUR

ELSPETH ROUSSEL SAT in the Helm's chair — *her* chair — on the Tyche's bridge. It wasn't much of a bridge, not like what she was used to from her days flying frigates for the Empire, but the captain had given her a paying job and didn't mind she'd flown for the losing side. And she was still Helm of something.

Even a small lifter like the *Tyche*. The ship was a flying wing design, like an A or V when viewed from above depending on whether you were a glass-half-full kind of woman. The *Tyche* had three decks and weighed a paltry 150 tonnes, but El liked to think she flew like a much lighter ship. Under her fingers, the *Tyche* was a nimble fighter. El reached out a hand to the console in front of her, kept clean despite the age of it. "My good girl," she said.

"What was that?" Hope's voice came from behind and below, where the Engineer was working on something below the deck grating. There was a shower of sparks, the *crack* of electricity, and the *Tyche's* console went dark.

"What," said El, "did you do?"

"I thought you said something." Hope's head came up from where she was crouched, the rig strapped to her making her look like an insect. Articulator arms reached out from behind her back, smoke still trailing from the end of a plasma torch. Her face was hidden behind the blank metal of the rig's faceplate before it flipped up, revealing a face El had always thought far too young to be the Engineer of a ship, even like their little *Tyche*. Still, you couldn't argue with results, and Hope got those results, pink hair and youthful looks aside. The captain seemed to have a way with picking up strays that were useful. It was hard to admit: strays like El herself.

"I thought you were fixing the ship," said El.

"I am fixing the ship," said Hope. "It is literally what I am doing down in this cramped compartment."

"Hope, Captain says we need to be in the air. Will she fly?" She patted the console again. "Will my baby fly?"

"She'll fly," said Hope. "You worry about the cargo. I'll worry about getting the magic smoke back inside these components." The rig's faceplate slid shut, and Hope vanished back below the deck. The crackle of arc welding started back up.

"Copy that," said El, feeling herself smile. She wasn't worried about Hope getting the *Tyche* back online; the Engineer knew the ship better than she knew her own damn self. El was more worried about where their cargo was, and where their deck hand was, because the captain didn't pay El to lift heavy things. He paid her to fly the ship. She turned back to the console, lights already coming back on. She tapped in Dock Control, flicked the comm switch on, and said, "Dock Control, this is *Tyche*. Seeking confirmation of cargo delivery and launch clearance. Please advise, over."

The communicator sat silent for a second before a man's voice spoke. "*Tyche*, we have you on lockdown. No ships, in or out. Over."

El sighed. One of *those* assholes. "Dock Control, this is *Tyche*. Please repeat your last. I thought I heard you say we were on lockdown. We have Republic clearance to launch. Repeat, *Republic clearance*. Over."

"*Tyche*, I don't care if you've got clearance from the Senate themselves. Your ship is on lockdown." Then, after a pause, "Over."

El drummed her fingers against the comm for a second. "Dock Control, let's park that for a moment. Do you have a status on our cargo? Over."

"*Tyche*, your cargo is waiting lifting of the lockdown. Over."

"Dock Control, I'd like to understand what the relationship between lawful cargo being loaded onto my ship and your unlawful lockdown is. Please advise. Over." El looked at the comm, waiting.

She didn't have to wait long. "We feel you might try and escape lockdown, *Tyche*. Over."

El laughed, keeping the comm on. "Dock Control, your feelings don't come into it. We have lawful, I repeat *lawful* Navy cargo to come on board our vessel. Do not bring us into your family counseling session with the Navy."

"*Tyche*—"

"Did I fucking say 'over,' Dock Control? No, I didn't. What I said was, give us our fucking cargo, or by God the heavens will open up and shell you and your miserable tower with the unholy vengeance of the Navy's best and brightest lawyers." She tapped the comm again, then said, "Over."

There was a long pause. "Copy that, *Tyche*. Cargo has been released for your receipt. Over."

"Thank you, Dock Control. Over and out." El flicked off the comm, feeling the warm rose glow that could only come from putting a minor bureaucrat in their place. The *Tyche* seemed to share her feelings, the console coming alive under her hands. "My good girl," she said, again.

EL WAS WAITING at the open doors of the cargo bay as the Dock's automated loader brought the Navy's cargo towards them. It wasn't moving very fast, which felt a lot like Dock Control was still fucking with her. But it was okay: she felt the wind on her face, closing her eyes for a second. God, she loved flying, but she also loved fresh air and the sound of birds. Hard to get the latter with the former these days. Too much time inside a hull out in the hard black, not enough time with her boots on the ground. The captain — *Nate* — had promised shore leave. Two days did not shore leave make. She'd seen the inside of the dock, got wind on her face, and that's it. Not that the dock wasn't nice as far as concrete jungles went. The *Tyche* sat on a pad, open sky above her. The painted logo under her wings — a woman's face, winking at you like she knew the secrets of the void — made El smile just like it always did. The *Tyche* herself? Older than her looks allowed, the sweep of her A-frame still elegant, the twin drives at her rear looking like they could still pound out nuclear fire as good as the day she rolled out of the shipyards.

A silver tube connected the Tyche's docking area with the spaceport proper a couple klicks away. The tube was part of a network of walkways like any other spaceport, filled with confused, meandering passengers and ship's crew in a constant hurry. Perhaps missing the inside of that wasn't such a bad thing. *Tyche's* pad was like a hundred others on Arlington, a collection of bays of different sizes for different ships. There were a lot of ships here, but that wasn't too surprising. Despite Enia Alpha being close to the end of the Republic's reach, it was a successful mining world. That attracted business, and interest, and even tourists.

El turned to look out across the docks, the ships clustered there, many with noses pointed at the sky. *Tyche* didn't need to point; unlike those other ships she had more than fusion rockets at her rear to get her going. The Endless Drive could tease reality into looking the other way, sure, but it had to do that through physics El would never understand. Hope might, but she might not as well, because being a good Engineer wasn't about theory, it was about practice. El would take Hope's practical knowledge every day of the week, even Sundays, because she kept the *Tyche* flying right.

It's just that not knowing how it worked *itched*, in a way El couldn't scratch. She'd read the literature, talk about configurable energy density fields being able to ... *create*, if that was the right word

... negative space. Anti-matter to interact with matter. Throw in a little dark matter for gravitational lensing, and it'd suck a ship through space like water syphoned through a hose. Manipulate all that for traversing the universe? Sure. The same tricks could be used for lifting the *Tyche*, or giving the ship artificial gravity. It worked, which was important, but she'd like to know *why*. Or maybe understand *how*.

Why or *how* aside, the artificial gravity was nice. Freighters often packed some of the tech in an Endless Drive. Enough to get some gravitational lensing belowdecks for artificial gravity. Not enough for jumps, because most captains were happy to pay the Guild their extortionate rates to use their Bridges. The Navy still used Endless Drives in their frigates, but there were fewer of those to go around as the prevalence of Guild Bridges made travel between the stars faster and safer. Faster and safer was fine as far as El was concerned, but it took some of the fun out of things.

There was a *crump* of a far-off explosion. El looked towards the city center. Smoke was pushing dark cotton balls against the blue skyline. Arlington was far away from where the serious business of mining occurred, so it wasn't mining charges, even if they'd been stupid enough to use rock-ape tech like that to punch a hole. Could be an industrial accident, but that wouldn't explain why the port was on lock down.

The silver tube connecting the rest of the spaceport to the *Tyche* opened to reveal the swagger of October Kohl. As he walked towards the *Tyche*, she saw he had what looked like blood on him, which didn't bode well, because — and this wasn't errant conjecture, this was *October Kohl* she was thinking of — it meant the explosion in the distance was probably his fault. But she said nothing about that.

Instead, she said, "You're just in time."

"I am?" he said.

"Yes," she said, pointing with her chin at the automated loader. "Cargo time."

"You load the cargo," said Kohl. "I need to go clean up."

"You load the cargo," disagreed El, "because you're our deck hand."

Kohl gave her what was meant to be a murderous stare, but he looked to also be a little drunk, so the effect was spoiled by being lopsided. He grunted. "Fine."

"You'll get dirty anyway," she said, "and have to clean up again."

"I said it was fine," said Kohl.

El smiled, and waited for the loader to arrive. Kohl would get their cargo loaded, and while he did that she would enjoy the air for a little bit longer. Or maybe a lot longer, if Hope couldn't release that lockdown.

Hell, it was Hope. Of *course* she'd be able to release the lockdown. El smiled, enjoying just a little more air that didn't come out of a bottle.

"WHAT DO YOU MEAN, you can't release the lockdown?" Nate's voice was stressed by two things: distance (he was at the bottom of the ladder leading to Engineering) and actual realized anxiety (the *Tyche* was on a pad, burning up docking credits, and they had a cargo that needed to be *elsewhere* like, *yesterday*). 'Ladder' might have been a stretch, it was more of a preamble to the airlock that sealed Engineering away from everything flammable.

Hope wiped her hands on the rag she had tucked into her belt. Ran a still-oily hand through her now less-than-pink hair and sighed. "I mean, it's a lockdown, Cap. They have locked us. Down. There wouldn't be much of a lock in the down if the lock could be broken."

"What do you mean ... look, I'm coming in." She heard his hands on the railing.

"Please don't," she said, and then he was there. Head looking around Engineering, eyes widening.

"What have you done to my ship?" he said.

It wasn't fair, and he knew it. He'd said they'd be boots-down for a week at least, maybe two. Get some R&R. They both knew she couldn't leave the ship on a Republic world, what with the law after

her for debts incurred when she'd made mistakes. Mistakes that cost
her a Guild title and her wife. But by the stars: R&R wasn't always
about leaving the ship. It was about getting all the jobs done she'd put
off for weeks while they were under sail, the little things nagging at
her mind, the things that couldn't get done when he was hollering at
her for *more speed* or asking *why have my turrets stopped firing*. Sure,
sure, people said it was about relaxing, but the *Tyche* was her ship,
more than it was the captain's, more than it was El's. It made her
relaxed to have the ship in good trim. It made her relaxed to work on
things without being so goddamn *rushed* all the time. Having access
to a few spare parts wouldn't hurt either.

"Nate—"

"Captain."

"Nate, you said *two weeks*—"

"I said a week, *maybe* two—"

"It's been two days!" She jerked an angry arm at the exposed
machinery on one of the fusion drives, the cowl stacked up against
the opposite wall. Wires. Pipes. A little smoke — now where the *hell*
was that coming from, that wasn't supposed to happen — and above it
all, the status panel. Not enough lights green, too many red. "I took
her apart because I had two weeks!"

"A week!"

"It's been two days!" She crossed her arms, glaring at him. "I
don't understand what's so urgent."

"Got a cargo," he said.

"A cargo," said Hope, "can wait another hour."

"Got in some trouble, too," he said.

She tensed. "Republic trouble?"

"Could be," he said. "I don't know."

"You don't know," she said, "or you don't want to say?"

Nate crossed his own arms, blew out a lungful of air, and looked
at his feet. Nice boots, planted strong on the decking like he owned
the place. Which he did, just not here. Not in Engineering. This was
her space, despite the empty spot on the wall where a Guild Engi-

neer would hang her Shingle. Hope didn't have a Shingle, not anymore. "Does it matter? Really. Either way. If it's trouble, one way or another it'll end up being Republic trouble." He frowned, scuffed one of those nice boots across the metal decking, then looked at her. "Will she fly?"

What he'd said was true enough. There wasn't any trouble that the Republic didn't *make* their business. Not at the Core, not here at the slippery edge, and not anywhere in between. "She'll fly true," said Hope.

"Then what's this problem with the lockdown?" Nate was still frowning at her.

"I wanted an hour," she said. "One hour. Just one."

"You can't have an hour," he said. He caught her expression, held up a hand. "Not because I'm trying to be an asshole. It's because the city is, at this moment, on fire. There are people with weapons shooting each other. In an hour, there will be soldiers crawling all over everything that can climb up that gravity well," and here, he pointed up, "because they're after something. Someone."

"Me?" said Hope.

"Hell no," said Nate. "No." He frowned again. His face looked better when it was smiling; like it was born to be happy, but had learned the hard way how to do unpleasant work. "Probably not."

"Well, which is it?" she said. "Yes or no?"

"No," he said, but like he didn't mean it. "Look, Hope, you owe money. Hell, we all owe a little money—"

"Not like this," she said.

"I'll grant that's a true story," he said. "But you do not shoot up a bar where good Republic Citizens are going about their lawful business to call in a debt."

"Spacer bar?" she said.

"Yeah."

"Hardly lawful," she said.

"Also a true story," he said, "but the spirit of the conversation remains the same. I've never seen anything like it. Or, not since, you know, the war."

"Okay," said Hope. "Okay."

"Okay you'll get my ship in the air, or okay we're all going to jail?" He had his Captain Face on, impassive, waiting for the bad news, but she'd known him the longest of anyone on this ship, and she could see the hope there. Hope they'd made it out of this one. Hope that he wouldn't let *her* down, because he was kind of stupid that way.

"I'll get my ship in the air," she said.

"Wait," he said. "Whose ship is this?"

"And," said Hope, ignoring the question and pointing at the drive cowling, "I need you to move that."

"Why?"

"Because it's heavy," she said. It was. When the *Tyche* was shiny new, all her parts had been minted with the latest and best technology the Old Empire had available. The drive's cowling was no exception. It was a ceramic, a printed material with polytopes at its core. It wouldn't dent or bend, and if it did somehow crack, the fractures wouldn't travel. By today's standards it was old tech, but it worked well enough. Despite being mostly air, and what wasn't air was an amalgam of powder and a few metals for good measure, it was heavy enough to be annoying, and she was already annoyed enough as it was.

Nate nodded at her, then turned and hollered down the ladder. "Kohl? Kohl! Get your ass to Engineering."

October's voice came back muted by two things: distance and annoyance. "Why?"

"Something heavy needs moving," said Nate. He winked at Hope.

She sighed. Time to get to work.

HOPE KICKED back in her chair, the acceleration couch feeling like an old glove. Soft in all the right places, strong where it was needed, a little faded here and there. The gimbals at the base let her spin around, the room turning about her as she thought about the lockdown. The problem with the lockdown was the way it worked — convincing the *Tyche* that Dock Control was, uh, in control, and not the *Tyche's* own Helm.

She'd broken a couple of lockdowns before, but not a Republic one. There was one ace in the hole, a thing that could get them off this perch and into the air where they belonged. The *Tyche*, she was ex-Empire. Retrofitted with all the right codes, transponder all legal and above board, but the coupling between the transponder and the real *Tyche*, well that was a complex mix of wires. The tech who'd installed it had looked flustered most of the time he'd been working on it, always talking under his breath about *fuck they got me doing this shit for* and *well it doesn't say* that *in the manual.* She'd watched over his shoulder, a thing she knew hadn't helped his state of mind, but his Republic uniform hadn't helped hers, so Hope felt that made them even.

She put a foot down on the deck, slowing her spin. Hope reached out her hands to the console in front of her and typed. The systems responded to her touch, engineering specs and console windows popping up on the holo. She rubbed a thumb across her jaw, not knowing (or caring) if it left a grease smudge on her face. An alert from the console, a bright and angry red, flashed as she violated a few protocols supposed to be inviolate. It didn't describe what she was doing right now in the manual.

Kohl leaned next to her. "What you doing?"

She gave him a glance, then turned back to the console. "Fixing things."

"Fixing," he said. "What're all the alarms for?"

"Things that aren't fixed yet," she said. She paused. "Kohl?"

"Yeah."

"I'm working, Kohl."

"Okay," he said.

"And," she said, "you being here is not helping me work." It wasn't just that he was a distraction. It was that he hated her. She knew it, he knew it. Everyone knew it. She felt ... *judged* by him. By this bad man full of bad habits. Even that wasn't the real problem; the problem was that she didn't blame him for hating her. Not really. Not after what she'd done. Hope had run out on her wife to get out from under the heel of the law, and it'd been a problem everywhere the *Tyche* went. It didn't matter that the captain had said *no way this was your fault* and busted her out from a cell he'd shared with her one night. If you believed the Republic propaganda, it was deviants like her that led to the fall of the Empire. They weren't wrong. They weren't right. But Kohl thought they were, and she understood.

So, she needed him to not be here. Because thinking about all that, thinking about *Reiko*, was not helping Hope solve the lockdown situation.

He sniffed, coughed, leaned back. She heard *clicks* from his spine. "Okay," he said. "Cowl's back in place. Need anything else?"

She considered a new alarm that popped up on the display floating in the air in front of them both. "No," she said. *Not from you.* "Thanks."

"Sure," he said. "Sure." He turned away, swung onto the handrails leading down from Engineering, and slipped from view.

Hope typed a little more. Saw what could be a deal-breaker here. While she could convince the *Tyche*, bless her heart, to ignore the Republic's lockdown, there was a corresponding coupling on the docking platform. A series of clamps held the ship in place. Nothing too serious; a couple of hours with a cutting torch would see them gone, if they had a couple of hours to burn. They could just fire up the engines, tear themselves away, but that would leave damage, and damage to landing gear led to questions, and the questions led to inspections, and inspections led to jail. The clamps on the docking platform were under Dock Control, which meant Republic fingers were holding her ship on the ground.

She stood up, grabbing her rig. She slung it over her back, felt it reach around to hug her, protective plates sliding into place down her front. The four actuator arms whined, spun, and then locked in place behind her. The rig's HUD blinked into life, first the top right corner with power indicator, systems check, status of the actuators — *lower left arm's gonna need work, second elbow is sticking* — and then the other corners blinked up. Top left, slots for status of a work crew she didn't have. Bottom right, a blank pane blinked, then filled with some of the schematic details she'd been working on at the *Tyche's* console. Bottom left, a series of comms and other systems details that were useless right now.

The HUD was reassuring for two reasons: because systems were green across the board, and because the visor that slipped over her face would hide it from view. The Republic had facial recognition everywhere. Spaceports. Public transit zones. Hell, even the damn toilets on these border worlds watched your face, scanned your irises, even checked your skin for blood flow changes that would indicate distress. While some of that was useful for good, law-abiding Republic Citizens, she was neither law-abiding nor a citizen. And she was about to get less law abiding.

"HOPE," said Nate's voice. "How's our status?"

"It's good, Captain," she said, as she looked at the docking control system on the *Tyche's* landing pad. She was *outside*. On the platform. Hope wasn't breathing good Arlington air on account of the visor's airtight seal, but the illusion was good enough. Sun. Open space. Smoke.

Wait. Smoke?

She could see the smoke rising from the city in the distance — Nate was right, that wasn't a happy thing.

"We're still in lockdown," he said.

"Working on it," said Hope.

"How much longer?" he said.

She made a growl low in her throat, then coughed to cover it. "Captain?"

"Yes, Engineer." No matter she wasn't a proper Engineer anymore. He called her that because it's what she *did*. But there was a smile in his voice as well, because he didn't much like Guild titles or Guild rules.

"Do you find when you're under a lot of pressure, you know, when things are really urgent? In those situations, do you find it helps to be interrupted and asked how things are going?" Hope pulled together a couple of programs, the rig's actuators reaching out from behind her to grasp the housing of the docking control system. There was a whine, a series of *pops*, and rivets fell from the housing like metal rain. "Because I don't find it helpful. I find it distracting, and I work slower when I'm distracted." The actuators were moving fast, pulling away the housing, dropping the ceramic and metal to the ground at her feet. Inside, treasure: the glowing heart of the docking control system.

"Wait a second," said Nate's voice. "Where are you?"

"It's better if you don't know," said Hope. The actuators reached into the systems in front her, and she initiated a new program. There was an old-style optical computer — border worlds always got hand-me-down tech — and one actuator *snicked* into place against the diagnostic port. The bottom left of her HUD lit up, that section of the display now showing her what the little machine was thinking. She could imagine that it was passionate about its one duty, which was *hold onto the Tyche until I'm told to stop*.

There was a trick to this. She could tell it to stop. That was the easy part. What she needed to do was a) tell it to stop, b) for a specific period, c) without telling Dock Control, d) and then forget everything afterwards. She could rivet the control system back together, walk away without visible evidence, but the visible evidence wasn't important. Digital thumbprints were likely to get them blockaded faster than a couple of missing *rivets*.

"Are you ... *outside?*"

Hope looked up at the *Tyche's* rear. Big drives dark and cold. Docking bay open to atmosphere, their cargo inside, roped down like a rodeo bull. A little carbon scoring here and there from planet crashing so often. The *Tyche's* smiling face painted on the hull. Hope always found the winking woman on the side held up in her mind's eye to what the ship *should* look like if she were a person. She could imagine Nate up in the cockpit, looking outside. He wouldn't be able to see her — ship was facing away from her — but that would just make matters worse. "No, Cap. I'm in Engineering. Where else would I be?"

"If you were outside," said Nate over the comm, "you could be identified." He didn't say, *and arrested.*

"If I wasn't wearing a helmet, that might be true," she said. "In this hypothetical future you've invented where I left the ship on a Republic world, that is."

"Your rig has codes, Hope," he said. "It can be identified."

She made a *pfft* sound. Then a happier one, as she got what she needed. If she suborned the comm controller, she could install a timer in that to talk to the clamp controller. Make it look like a fault. She got the rig to prepare the program then flicked it across the diagnostic interface and into the live system. "My suit is in Engineering with the rest of me."

"No it's not," said Nate.

She turned the visor of her rig towards the *Tyche*. Watched as the docking clamps disengaged, *clanking* open across all three points of contact, and smiled to herself. The rig picked up fallen panels, two arms holding in place, one fitting rivets in the sockets. She watched it work, thinking, *thirty seconds and we're off this rock.* "Why do you say that?"

"Because I'm in Engineering," said Nate. "There is no Hope, and Hope's rig is also not here."

Shit. Shit, shit, shit. "I had to pee," she said, then cringed. That was lame. *L. A. M. E.*

"That was ... is that the best you've got?"

The last panel in place, the last rivet fired home, and she was running, rig jostling around her, breath loud in her ears. *Damn, I need more cardio.* Boots on the ramp up into the cargo bay. She turned her visor around to look outside. One last look at the spaceport, all ships still held in place. All except her ship, because the *Tyche* was born to fly. Born to be free. Hope looked out farther at the cityscape of Arlington. Where she could have been, for two days. If she hadn't made mistakes, she too could fly. She could be free.

She slapped a hand against the door controls, and a red light spun in the top of the bay. An automated voice warned that *the docking bay doors are closing, please stand clear*. She looked around the bay, at the Republic cargo tied down, at the metal walls of the *Tyche*. Her ship. Her home. Probably for a long time. She didn't like thinking too much about the future, because there was nothing but anxiety and more questions down that path, but she knew the *Tyche* was likely to be her home for maybe forever.

"It's the best I've got," she said over the comm. It was okay. They were okay. They would get off Arlington, away from the Republic standing on all their necks, and back into the freedom space. And that was the best thing for everyone.

Wasn't it?

CHAPTER SIX

THEY WERE ALL AFRAID.

Grace was in the common area. These lifters were built to a spec, military design giving nothing away to comfort. But the *Tyche* wasn't military anymore, and she'd had an overhaul. Or an underhaul. It wasn't like the environment was built of lacquered wood, or even faux wood. The glass between them and the atmosphere outside as they climbed wasn't diamond silicate, just an efficient polymer that sat a little on the dull side while still being strong. Not that *dull* would matter once atmosphere fell away. Out in the hard black, the heavens took most people's breath away regardless of how you saw them.

She could always feel their awe, those who crawled up a gravity well for the first time. It was nice, that feeling, one of the few *nice* things she got from other people. It wasn't what she was getting from the crew now.

The common area sat aft of the flight deck. In the flight deck, the captain—

Nate.

—and his Helm were side by side, coaxing the *Tyche* to reach for the stars. There wasn't a lot of chatter between them, all efficient, like they'd done this before. She could feel the confidence off them, but also the fear. That fear bled back into the common area. To where the thug October Kohl sat, strapped into his acceleration couch like an angry sack. Angry, because he was scared too. And that fear from him bounced around, off the captain, and his Helm, back to October again, and washed over her. Fear was like that; even normals sensed it on each other. It might have been the sweat smell. For Grace it was pure feeling, her nerves vibrating with it, making her heart beat faster, her breath quicken, her eyes widen. She was sure her face would have been pale, and she could feel her fingers gripping the arms of the acceleration couch like the claws of an eagle. She tried to relax, to take in what was around her. So: no faux wood. Just some acceleration couches, a small galley, some windows that looked outside. Airlock doors: one leading forward to the cockpit, one aft to the crew, cargo, and engineering areas of the ship. There was a table in the middle of this room, not military spec. It had been welded to the floor; to Grace's eye the welds looked neat, efficient, practiced. Not military spec, but not a back-alley conversion: someone had put that table there because they cared what happened on the table. Which meant this was where the crew ate, if they ate together. Back when it was Empire Navy, this area would have been for crew brief-ing, downtime, and being both bored and terrified about the next mission.

Maybe the military and civilian lives weren't so different.

If she focused, she could feel the fear of the Engineer behind and above them. Fear and excitement, because she'd done something she shouldn't have, and got away with it. Grace would have to remember that, try and work out how to use it, once they got away from this rock with its Republic rot to the core of it. It had been a long time since Grace had been on a ship with someone else who was being hunted, and things like that could be useful. If the hammer hit the anvil, she could throw Hope to the wolves and run in the aftermath of the noise it would make in her wake. She'd done it before. It got easier each time, and it wasn't like they didn't deserve it. Each of them desperate, each running from a crime. Except Grace's only crime had been being born, and she'd been running for as long as she'd known how.

Because she had her own fear, packed away inside. It wasn't like she needed their fear like an extra side of gravy. But she got it anyway. She couldn't help it.

The thug was watching her, his fear making him nasty. Or just bringing the nasty out. "First time in space, huh." The steady 2.5Gs pushing at them flattened his face a little, making it uglier than it would otherwise have been. Grace was sure her own face would have been stretched or pulled. A near-solid G from Enia Alpha, plus the 1.5Gs from thrust, meant this was uncomfortable. If the fear hadn't made her want to pee already the pressure on her bladder would have done the trick.

"No," she said. "First time in space on a ship that's about to explode, though."

He gave a short, angry laugh. Angry, because he was afraid. "The *Tyche* won't explode." There was a yawning, creaking groan from the ship, the noise coming from the belly of it where their cargo sat. It was a groan of metal and ceramic stressed too many times, unhappy with its lot, ready to let go its grip and tumble them into the hard black. "Uh. That noise? Happens a lot."

She laughed, the sound higher pitched than she would have liked. Time for some conversation. Time to get to know them. "So … you're a deck hand?" Grace had to raise her voice a little, the massive roar of the fusion drives muted by the hull, but something of their power vibrated its way inside anyway.

Kohl looked at her like she was stupid. "No."

"But—"

"Ship's manifest says I'm a deck hand," he said. "Ship's manifest says our Engineer is ex-Guild. Ship's manifest says you're an Assessor. Way I see it, none of those things are true."

"I'm an Assessor," she said. "It's what I do." *And I'm assessing you right now.* "I know the stuff that's valuable. The things that are—"

"I know how to lift heavy shit," said Kohl. "Doesn't make me a deck hand."

Okay. "What is it you do?" Grace closed her eyes for a moment. *Don't feel their fear. Don't be their fear. Let it wash over you like the endless tides of space. It is nothing.* She opened her eyes again. "I mean, aside from lifting shit that is heavy. There are loaders for that kind of thing."

"That there are," he agreed.

The silence sat between them for a while. "And?" she prompted.

"And," said the thug, "when the captain figures you need to know what I'm here for, you'll know."

His fear was ebbing away. Which was not a usual thing. This man might have been many things — a deck hand, some kind of enforcer, maybe even a passable card player — but he wasn't scared by the ship taking off. No. He'd been scared by not knowing *her*, and now he thought he did.

She could work with that.

GRACE DIDN'T HAVE long to wait for more fear. More anxiety. From the cockpit, she heard the chatter of the comm.

"*Tyche*, this is the Republic Navy destroyer *Torrington*. We have you exiting a lawful lockdown of Arlington space port. Please cease thrust and prepare to be boarded."

Grace's head jerked towards the cockpit. She wanted to shout something, maybe *run!* or *we need to leave, just leave*, but it wouldn't help. The Navy would be waiting for them at a blockade somewhere else. And it would be worse, because they wouldn't be leaving a lock-down; they'd have refused a boarding order from the Navy.

"*Torrington*, this is *Tyche*." Grace could hear the Helm's voice — El — as calm, professional. She knew this music. "Our ship was released from the lockdown. We are carrying cargo on spec for the Republic Navy, destination Absalom Delta. Transmitting flight plan."

There was a pause. "*Tyche*, this is *Torrington* actual. Lieutenant Evans sends his regards. Please cease thrust and prepare to be boarded."

"Well, fuck," said Nate. Grace could feel what sounded like tension and relief warring in his tone. Like this was good and bad at once. *If only he knew how bad.* "I guess we best cease thrust and prepare to be boarded. Hope, you listening?"

"I'm listening," she said. No relief there, just pure tension.

"You going to be okay?" The *Tyche's* acceleration was easing off, the ship rotating in space as the *Torrington* negotiated docking protocols. Artificial gravity from the deck below made this feel like a gentle rollercoaster. Like it was something fun, and something she shouldn't be afraid of.

"You said *probably*," said Hope. Her voice cracked a little. "That they *probably* weren't after me."

Kohl chuckled, the sound nasty. He turned his head towards the ceiling as he spoke, as if Hope were the ship itself. "You fucking criminals, all the same. You want a free ride on the system, the same system that's looking after us, putting people back on top again, and—"

"Secure your mouth," said Nate, standing at the airlock leading to the flight deck. "It's making noises again."

Kohl gave him a glare, looked like he would finish a series of thoughts verbally that would lead to uncomfortable words and possible violence. Grace could tell the man was picking at an old wound, something that bothered him right to his core, and right here might well be the hill he would die on. Because outside their ship was the *Torrington*, and the *Torrington* was Navy, and Navy meant the law, and the law meant Hope would be put in a box and taken somewhere to mine salt until she died.

At least if they caught Grace they'd kill her quick.

Neither fate was a great one, and some quick mental math showed that if this was the time she threw Hope to the wolves to buy an escape, it wouldn't work. First, because if the Republic found one criminal on board, they'd look for another. Second, because Hope was the one who knew how the engines worked, and on a ship that made horrible sounds as it was taking off, that was a prize asset.

Putting your neck out was not a thing that was sensible, but it could make friends. And she needed these people to like her, right until she found another ride somewhere else. She cleared her throat before Kohl could start on his road to the nuclear option, and said, "I've got an idea."

Kohl and the captain both looked surprised as they looked at her. Nate spoke first. "We can't cut them down with that fancy sword of yours—"

"She's got a sword?" said Kohl. Something about him said *interested/fascinated/challenged*, and none of those were good, but they were problems for another time.

"You updated the manifest yet?" said Grace.

"Uh, no," said Nate. "You know. Time. Breaking the lockdown occupied my thoughts. You understand."

"I understand," said Grace. "Here's what we'll do."

"Wait," said Nate. "Why does everyone but me try and give orders on my ship?"

"Because in this particular circumstance," said Grace, "I have done this before. We don't have much time."

"You've got about a minute and a half," said El's voice, from ahead of them.

"Then listen," said Grace, "and be amazed."

THE *CLANG* as the *Torrington* coupled with the *Tyche* rang through the hull like a bell. Grace looked out from Engineering at the gangway below, metal looking back at her. Nothing out of place, nothing to worry about. *Good.* She turned back to Engineering, took in the cowls of the drives to the sides of the room, the empty acceleration couch where Hope should have been, and felt the warm glow of the reactor above her.

Warm. Now that wasn't good. The thing should have been insulated, should have felt no warmer than the air around them. But *warm* was good enough for now.

Be the Engineer. Be the room. Be what they expect. Be what they want to see.

She slapped the console on, pulled up some screens. *Doesn't matter what they are. It matters that they look like they should be there.* A couple of diagnostics alongside some schematics would do. She looked at the wall opposite the console, saw the tools tidied away. That wouldn't do: while Hope was supposed to be ex-Guild, she was *ex* for a reason. Grace grabbed something that looked like a cutting laser, placed it on the deck near one of the fusion cowls. She grabbed another tool — no clue what this one was, but it looked impressive, a mechanized head attached to a power pack that had real weight. She tossed that next to the cutting laser.

Quick glance down. Overalls, faded, worn. A little tight, because Hope was smaller than her. But that was okay, because no one expected Engineers to dress well. Hell, they expected Engineers to dress like vagrants. It was in the cultural meme of every world Grace had put boots on. *Drunk Spacers* went right alongside *Gruff Engineers With Bad Taste.*

If the shoe fits ... Grace ran a hand along the edge of one of the engine cowls, her fingers coming away with a layer of grease. She rubbed her hands together, dashed some against her face, and then pulled her fingers through her hair. Grace needed to look the part. She needed to *be* the part. Cultural memes aside, no Engineers did their job without getting grease under their nails.

"Hope?" Nate's voice came up to her from the ladder. "You ready for inspection?"

Showtime. "I don't know," she yelled back. She tried to put a little more spaceport, a little less cocktail bar, in her voice. "You ready to get under my feet and fuck up my day?"

There was a pause. "Uh, yeah," said Nate. "These nice Navy officers would like to come and see we do not have contraband or stowaways in Engineering."

"Great," she said, low enough it should sound like a mutter, loud enough to be heard down the ladder. "The *Navy* want to get under my feet and fuck up my day. That's *no problem*, because it's the *Navy*."

A head came through the airlock, cap on, uniform showing. Some kind of junior officer, and she knew an Engineer wouldn't care. "Excuse me, Engineer—"

She pointed a finger at the officer. "You touch one fucking thing and break it, you're getting the bill."

"I—"

"Oh, I know," said Grace. "You won't break anything! That's what the last circus clown who came up here said. Right before he broke something. Do you," and she fixed the terrified man with a hard stare, "know what you are doing?"

"I'm in training as an Engineer," said the officer. "I'm—"

"Well that's *okay* then," said Grace. "You're in *training*. We're all going to be *saved*." She folded her arms across her chest.

Nate came up the ladder behind the officer. "Hope? Hope, this is Ensign Savidge. Savidge is here because ... well, you know why."

"Yeah," said Grace. "He's here to get under my feet and fuck up my day."

"Uh," said Ensign Savidge.

"Well, get on with it," said Grace. "I assume you know what an engine looks like?"

"I—"

"It's those things over there," said Grace, pointing an angry jab at each of the fusion cowls. "They make the ship go, when we're not hauled aside for lawful shipment of lawful cargo."

"Uh," said Ensign Savidge. He turned pleading eyes on Nate. "Is there some other place we could start?"

"What?" said Nate. "Hell no, son. You've got people crawling all over the *Tyche*. You're here, in Engineering. Time is money. Let's go." He clapped his hands.

Savidge, to his credit, got going. He walked around Grace like she was a pit viper, turning himself sideways so she wouldn't be out of his line of sight. He didn't realize he was doing it. Grace could feel the anxiety pouring off the officer in waves, could imagine his stomach clenched like a fist, his heart beating faster, and felt herself wanting to give a feral smile. She held it in, because this wasn't a victory lap. Not yet. This was still the show, and the show wasn't over.

"Excuse me, Engineer Baedeker," said Savidge. "Can I—"

"Who the fuck," said Grace, "is Engineer Baedeker?"

"Uh," said the ensign. He held up his tablet, consulting it. "It said on the manifest—"

"Engineer Baedeker is not an Engineer," said Grace. "She left the Guild. It's just Baedeker. My friends call me Hope, which means you should call me Ms. Baedeker. Or just Baedeker, because Lord knows we don't have the *time* to waste on ceremony. You know, *time* you're wasting. You get me?"

"I get you," said Savidge. "It's just that—"

"Sweet Christ," said Grace, sighing. "If you're here to tell me that the reactor's running a little hot, I *know*. I know, okay? I know. I work here. With no parts, because this asshole," and she jerked a thumb at Nate, "is always running late, meaning no completion bonuses. Do you know why he's always running late?"

Savidge swallowed. "No," he said.

"Take a guess."

"Because," said Savidge, as cautiously as a man might if he were about to put a toe on a landmine, "of inspections?"

"You got it!" said Grace. "Look, I got shit to do. This reactor will not stop exploding by itself."

"It'll explode?" said Savidge.

"No," said Grace, "or at least, not if I get time to stop it exploding. Are you done getting under my feet and fucking up my day?"

"Yes ma'am," said Savidge.

"It's just Baedeker," said Grace. "Now get the fuck out of my engine room."

The ensign scurried back down the ramp. Nate watched him go, started after, then paused. He looked back over his shoulder at Grace. "Asshole?"

"Definitely," said Grace. "Seriously. This reactor? It should not be warm to the touch."

"Best we get an Engineer on that," said Nate. He flashed her a smile, and she felt warm — not because of that smile, but because of what Nate was feeling. It was *gratitude/thanks/friend* all at once. It was just what she needed him to feel.

She hated herself for it.

CHAPTER SEVEN

"WHILE I THINK this whole experience has been enlightening —
for you, for me, for my crew, and for the great Republic under which
we sail — I can't help but wonder why you're here," said Nate. He
was leaning against the cargo, plastic covering the components inside.
For a change, he'd left his blaster in his cabin, not because he didn't
want to shoot someone, but because he *did*. And that wouldn't end
well; the *Tyche* was a nimble spirit, but the *Torrington* was a ship of
war. While not a carrier behemoth, the *Torrington* was loaded for
bear. Scans had shown all manner of unpleasantness waiting to come
their way if they didn't fly steady. Particle cannons. PDCs. Torpedo
tubes. They probably had a railgun or two tucked away for special
occasions. Assuming they could overpower the boarding party —
which they couldn't, not even if Kohl was all the way sober — and
break the docking locks, they'd need to punch the Endless drive so
hard their brains would pop out the side of their skulls. If they didn't,
the *Torrington* would turn them into an expanding cloud of atoms,
some of them carbon.

So, no gun.

"Captain," said the officer in front of him, offering him a smile like someone would offer a tray of chocolates. "It's a routine inspection."

"Fuck off," said Nate, but amiably enough.

"I beg your pardon?" said the officer. This one was a Lieutenant, just like Evans, except this one had a different name: *Karkoski*. She had a face that looked like it would have a nice smile, if they'd met under different circumstances.

"I mean, I appreciate the cover," said Nate. "I appreciate you coming on board with a scanning crew, crawling into every nook and cranny that the *Tyche's* got. Some of those compartments haven't been opened in *years*, Lieutenant. You got the dust out, and for that I thank you. My *crew* thanks you, because they sure hate cleaning. I tell you! I try and scrape up a cleaning detail, and it's like the *Tyche's* a ghost ship. You get me?"

"I," said Karkoski, then stopped.

Nate pushed off from the cargo with an elbow, turned towards it, and frowned. "It makes you wonder, don't it?" He glanced in Karkoski's direction, and as she was about to say something, he said, "No, no. I understand. You can't tell me what this is all about. But I know you're delaying this shipment. This *Republic* shipment. This *time sensitive* cargo. This cargo, as I understand it, will bring light, hope, and messages from far-flung relatives to the settlers of Absalom Delta." He paused, sucking air through his teeth, still looking at the cargo. "The thing is, this cargo was given to me by the Republic Navy. The very same navy that protects us from God-knows-what since there's no war, but also the same navy you serve as an officer of some distinction." He gave her a glance. "I mean, I'm assuming you serve with distinction. Right?"

"Right," said Karkoski. Then, "Sir? Sir. My service record—"

"You can't talk about that either, I know," said Nate. "I *know*. What can you do?" He gave her a smile. "What I'd like to know is whether you guys have got a mix-up back at the Admiralty, or if you've got special instructions I need to know about. I'm good either way, but what I don't need, not today, is you to yank on my chain to see whether it's got bells on it. It doesn't. It's got anger and spite and a bunch of bad attitude, because you'll affect my completion bonus. Time is money, Lieutenant. Time is money."

Karkoski considered him for a long, slow moment. "You're quite direct, sir."

"It's stopped my rise in politics, but it works well enough out here in the hard black. Cuts to the point. Stops people dying. That kind of thing." He stretched, leaned back against the cargo. "This thing going to blow my ship apart? Is it a bomb?"

"No," said Karkoski. "It's not a bomb." She paused as the scanning crew entered the cargo bay — two techs. One was some rank-and-file junior with a skinny frame who'd done all the crawling where crawling was needed. The other was the ensign Nate had taken to Engineering. Poor man was still sweating from his encounter with Grace-as-Hope; Nate had taken pity on him and let him talk with El. She was ex-Navy too, despite being from the other side; El knew the language, knew the rules. A softer target, something to take the edge off before he wrote a report damning them all to hell.

Grace. That one had done something quite special. Quite ... *unusual* for a new crew member. She'd put herself in harm's way. She'd defused the heat that might have come their way for harboring Hope, taken it and put it in a little box the ensign would take home and remember forever. But the kind of experience that young officer had had? His report would be *crystal* clear. It would say the Engineer of the *Tyche* was a striking cobra, a danger to all unprotected souls, but it wouldn't have any of Hope's real attributes. It'd *advise caution* or *encourage restraint* when dealing with her in the future, but it wouldn't say *she is a wanted criminal with a bounty on her head.* It was the kind of report that would be pinned to walls in tired hard-copy, shared on tablets, hell even fired around the internal skunkworks comms of the Navy's engineering teams. That kind of thing was against protocol, but it would happen. Sure enough, Grace had bought Hope a reprieve for a time. While that was a welcome kindness, it bothered Nate.

It bothered him because people didn't do stuff for free.

Not in the Core worlds, not out here in the hard black. Not anywhere. Especially not stuff that was dangerous, could get you killed, either in front of a firing squad, or just ejected out into space without a suit. While Grace had done them all a kindness, she'd done it for reasons. Nate didn't understand those reasons, and needed to find them out.

Later.

Right now, he needed to get Karkoski and her scanning crew off his ship. Karkoski looked at her crew, selected Ensign Savidge with her eyes, and said, "Report."

"Ma'am," said Savidge, crisping a salute. "Manifest is accurate. Cargo, crew, transponder codes, all in order." He frowned, like he wanted to add something, but stopped himself.

"Very good," said Karkoski. "Dismissed."

There was a thing to watch: two members of the Navy, leaving his cargo hold like they were good posture trying to slink away and hide. Nate wondered what had happened to the skinny one. Maybe he'd found Kohl's ... *literature* collection. He watched them slide on by, out the airlock, and into the safety of the *Torrington*. Nate said nothing, waiting for Karkoski.

He didn't have to wait long. "There is nothing wrong with the cargo," she said. "The cargo is what Lieutenant Evans described to you. It's a transmitter. Get it to the Bridge at Absalom Delta, bolt it to the side, and comms are back up. You get your bonus, we get to talk to our colony, and the colonists get their sims and holo shows on a regular drip again. Nothing special about any of that."

"Sure," said Nate, like he was agreeing. "Nothing special. Except for you scanning my crew."

"Your ship," said Karkoski.

"My what?"

"Your ship," said Karkoski. "Not your crew. Look, Captain—"

"Nate. Call me Nate." He offered another smile.

She didn't give him one back. "Captain Chevell," she said, "the

Navy is prepared to overlook your small indiscretion of breaking lockdown."

"Hey, now," said Nate. "The clamps were lifted. We got out. Completion bonus, remember?"

She considered that, and he could see the wheels spinning in her head. Trying to work out if this was the important conversation she wanted to have, working her way from *this guy is an asshole* all the way to *there are bigger problems*. *Bigger problems* were things that worried Nate too. Karkoski turned away from him, faced the cargo. "You know, these things don't fail."

Odd thing to say. "Clearly they do."

"No," she said. "It's not Old Empire tech. These are Guild made. *Guild* made, Captain. The Guild stopped the AIs. The Guild made FTL possible. A spiced-up communicator? Trust me. They don't break. They're a lifeline to the hundreds of worlds we have scattered over space. They *can't* break. A downed transmitter is as likely as humans surviving a zero-time Endless jump. Can't happen."

"Okay," said Nate, thinking, *Well, shit just got real.* "Can't happen. So why is this one here?"

Karkoski frowned. "Maybe I'm being too strong. They have been known to *fail*. Some fool fiddles with them. Messes up the timing. Asteroids. There has been — and I checked — exactly one instance of systems failure. Solar collector burned out, not the transmitter itself." She sighed. "Doesn't matter. What matters is that the one at Absalom Delta's Bridge has gone dark. It's not sending to us, not on schedule. The Gate at our side opens, but nothing comes through. That is a situation that makes us nervous. It makes us nervous because of what happened on Arlington."

"Huh," said Nate, because his brain was saying *what the hell does what happened on Arlington have to do with Absalom Delta?*

"I'd bet you're wondering," said Karkoski, "what Arlington and the Absalom system have in common."

"Thought crossed my mind," agreed Nate.

"Nothing," said Karkoski, "*yet.*" She looked at Nate like she was waiting for him to say something clever.

"Normally I'd have something to offer here like, 'This sounds a lot like the usual sorts of military intelligence,' but I'm expecting you to shower me with fine Republic wisdom," said Nate. "I am here, waiting for my shower."

She sniffed, wrinkled her nose. "Yes, I can see why."

"Hey—"

"There was an esper on Arlington," she said.

That stopped Nate. *Espers.* It was the fucking Emperor's Intelligencers that had cost him a good left hand and an equally good left foot. He wondered for a hot second about Grace Gushiken, then pushed that thought aside. Espers were evil, and Grace might have been many things — liar chief among them — but she didn't carry the Intelligencer reek. Their arrogance was hard to miss. "Those assholes," he said, with some feeling. He clenched his metal hand.

She noticed the motion. "Something personal, Captain?"

"Could be," he said.

The silence stretched, and when she realized he wouldn't fill it with the story behind his metal hand, she turned away. Karkoski spoke to the cargo bay like it was a person, not looking at him. "You can understand why we're interested in any ship leaving Arlington."

"Well, shit," he said. "You could have just opened with that. I'd have laid on a welcome party. A few beers. We could have looked around together." He felt the ache in his missing arm, rubbed at the metal like it would make the pain stop. "People who can read minds are a cancer, Lieutenant."

"Yes," she said. "But if we'd warned you, and there was an esper on your ship, they might have rabbited. Or cored out your minds and left you drooling in your chairs. Hell," and here she sighed, "they could have jumped ships, got on the *Torrington.*"

"They can't core out minds," said Nate, thinking, *a fucking esper.*

"Sure," said Karkoski. "Sure."

"Well," said Nate. "I appreciate the heads-up. But what about Absalom Delta?"

"When a world goes dark," said Karkoski, "it's usually pirates. If it's not pirates, it's an uprising. We still have a Navy, despite there not being a war on, because of those two things. But an uprising would be worse. An uprising led by an esper? That would be disaster. So. Be careful. Report back. I hope it's a faulty solar collector. I really do. But if it's pirates, we'll send in the cavalry. If it's an uprising, we'll send *all* the cavalry." She considered him a moment longer, then turned towards the airlock. Hand on the sill, she paused. "Captain."

"Yes, Lieutenant."

"It's a hard life out here in the black. Be sure you fly straight. An uprising? That can benefit the casual trader. Turn privateer, maybe pirate, and you can make real coin. But you'll never win. The Empire didn't." And with that, she was gone, the airlock *thunk*ing closed behind her.

Nate considered the sealed lock, waiting for the *clanks* from the hull as the *Torrington* disengaged. He rubbed his chin, fingers rasping on day-old stubble. Nate thought about being on the losing side. He'd been there once before.

He wouldn't be again.

NATE WATCHED the bulk of the *Torrington* pull away. She was huge, no mistake. Ten decks, 5,000,000 tonnes depending on configuration, almost two klicks long, railguns, lasers, particle cannons, torpedoes, drop ships, oh my. Multiple reactors. PDCs and sensor arrays studding her entire length. The Republic had sent that to talk to the little *Tyche*. Because they were afraid of an esper on board.

He tugged on the straps holding him into the acceleration couch, a habit he'd picked up about the time he'd been tossed from one and lost an arm and a leg. "You always hear about them being sleek," he said.

"What?" said El, from the Helm's chair. Her voice was distracted as she worked her console, getting the computer ready for the Endless jump they were about to make.

The flight deck was cozy, enough room to stand up, move around the holo of the Enia system spinning in the air between them. Enough room to walk to the windows, look out at the *Torrington*, take in the view of the blue-green paradise of Arlington. He sometimes liked to call it the *bridge*, because it made him feel like the *Tyche* was big, important, wonderful. A dream made metal and ceramic, diamond hull to protect the soft souls inside from the harsh reality of space. But she was a heavy lifter, atmosphere-capable. She was also their home.

The holo of the Enia system showed Enia Alpha — Arlington's world — orbiting a star. Alpha was the first planet from its sun, another three colder worlds stretching out behind it. The holo showed all the usual space junk around a world, satellites and rocks and whatever else hadn't tumbled back down Enia Alpha's gravity well. A dot marked out the *Tyche*, floating above Enia Alpha — he wouldn't call that an orbit, more like a temporary abeyance of the natural order of things. A dot for the *Torrington*, markers showing the ship's class, velocity, direction. Nothing unusual. Except there was an esper too damn close, and that wouldn't show up on the system view.

He shook his head. All this talk about espers had got him unfocused. "The *Torrington*. Looks like a barge."

El laughed. "She does. Gets the job done, though."

Nate picked up something a little defensive in that. El had flown ships like that, before. Not now. Probably never again. "I didn't ... well. You've got to admit. Bit of a sow."

She looked at him, the glow from the holo tinging her face with orange. "We're all good, Captain. Navy, they make their ships to get a job done. The *Tyche*, she's got a little more class. Like a dancer."

Maybe when El was Helm that was true. She could fly the *Tyche* through a storm and come out without a drop on the hull. Real talent, and he was pleased to have her at the controls. Hell, when he was on the stick, the *Tyche* would move, but she wouldn't *dance*. She only danced for one person. "How we doing with those jump calculations?"

"I figure us at seven to be safe," she said. She tapped on the console, and the holo shifted in the air, cleared, then became a star chart. Six systems lit up between Enia and Absalom, seven jumps to take them there. Strictly speaking, you could jump the whole way in a single shot, but that was risky because you weren't always operating with the latest data. You didn't know if a star had shifted, or an asteroid had popped up somewhere. So you jumped a little at a time, scanned the stars, picked up the view from a new point in the sky. And, strictly speaking, you didn't need to jump to a planet — but that was just good thinking. If something went wrong, it was helpful if it went wrong in common, agreed locations. There was a lot of space to get lost in, and sticking to systems increased — if only marginally — being picked up if you were in distress.

It also increased — more than marginally — your chances of being eaten by pirates. Gobbled up, left as a few trace elements floating next to the burned-out husk of your ship. Those fuckers waited for ships to jump in. Sometimes by a Bridge, if the pirates were well-prepared, sometimes farther out if they were a lone skiff. Preyed on the few smaller ships still using Endless Drives.

Well, that's a depressing-as-fuck line of thinking. "You happy with that, Helm?"

"I'm happy with that, Captain," she said. "Clear for jump?"

"Clear for jump," he said. Nate felt the thrill. He'd jumped a hundred, a *thousand* times before, but it never got old. He'd been on a rollercoaster on some frontier world, an attraction with mag sleds and high G. It couldn't touch the feeling of a jump, and he'd once wondered for a hot second whether he should get in the business of taking people on pleasure trips for the rush. Then discarded the idea, because that meant passengers, and passengers meant people, and hell was other people.

El clicked the comm controls on the dash. "Helm to *Tyche*. Jump in thirty seconds." She checked the display, then said, "Hope, get your ass in a crash couch."

The comm clicked back. "They're gone?" Hope's voice sounded hollow, because she was hiding under the cowling of one of the fusion drives.

"They're gone, kid," said El. "Get out of that damn engine."

Nate caught her smile, felt it on his own face. He pressed his own comm controls. "You best say a nice thank-you to Grace," he said. "Also, talk to the *Tyche* about why the reactor's warm."

"Will do, Cap," said Hope, and then a click as she signed off. No doubt scrambling for her acceleration couch.

"Captain to *Tyche*. Captain to *Tyche*. Helm is clear for jump. Confirm readiness." He drummed his fingers on the console.

Grace's voice came first. "Ready, *Tyche*."

Hope: "Good to go, Cap."

Kohl's voice came last. "Fuck's sake. Fly, already."

Nate smiled, clicked the comm off. Looked at El. "Helm, you are clear for Jump."

"Aye, Captain," said El. Nate watched her hands reach for the sticks, felt the grumble of the *Tyche's* engines through his chair. The soft hand of acceleration pressed against his back, became a firm hand as the holo display shifted again, delta-v from Enia Alpha sidling next to absolute velocity. The hand turned into a strong arm, his head pressing against the back of his couch. "Burn is good, 3Gs, locked in." El's voice was strained now, because 3Gs wasn't like a walk in the park. It was a lot more than the flimsy 0.9G of Enia Alpha, and Nate felt his joints complain. *Goddamn. We should have stayed for two weeks.* While the Endless Drive didn't need velocity as a push start, the distance between them and the gravity well of Enia Alpha would stop the Endless Drive from exploding. After a moment, the holo stage cleared, then words filled the space: *CLEAR FOR JUMP.*

"Negative space bow wave forming," said El. "All hands, bow wave is stable. Route is green. In three." Accompanying her words, the big number 3 lit the air between them. "Two." The number shifted to a big 2, this time flashing.

Kohl's voice, from the comm, half a holler, half a cheer. All whoop, all adrenaline. Because this was a jump, and jumps were ... *jumps*.

"One," said El. "Jumping."

Space in front of the window stretched, pulled, and Nate felt—

His hair, every fiber of it. The skin of his body, a soft glove for all his essence. His arm and leg, whole again, no longer metal. No pain. The pure thrill of acceleration, impossible, unbelievable acceleration. He couldn't feel it. He was it. He was everything. He was the universe.

Stars stretched, made points of light that streaked past the *Tyche's* cockpit.

They jumped.

CHAPTER EIGHT

THE AIR FELT HOT, charged, like a storm was coming. Nate told himself it was just the after-effects of the jumps. Three down. Four to go. Jumps in quick succession played hell with your view of life. He'd been briefed a long time ago — a long, long time, when he still had two flesh and blood hands that served the Emperor — that it was something to do with human consciousness. About how time was *intrinsic to the human condition* and that faster than light travel broke all the perceptions of time. The problem, a sergeant with too much attitude and too little love for his squad had explained, was this: going between two points instantaneously was *easy*. Having sane people on the other side of that jump? Impossible.

The sergeant had gone on to yell at other people, while Nate had gone on to the Emperor's Black. But the sergeant wasn't wrong, he was just an asshole. Humans spent all their time breaking the laws of the universe, but they couldn't break the rules that governed themselves.

"Jump was clean," said El. She looked at him sideways, hands still on the controls. "Air feel hot to you?"

"I thought it was just post-jump blues," said Nate.

"No, air's hot," she said. Tapped at the console, the holo between them changing. Systems reports cascaded across the display. Life support, green. Hull, green. Fusion drives, green. Minor systems like the auto galley, green. Endless Drive, green and mean, chafing at the stars for another bite at them. Reactor, not green.

Reactor: yellow.

"Hope," said El. "Hope, we're reading yellow on the reactor. What's the situation where you are?"

The comm burst with static — a thing in itself inherently bad — and then Hope's voice came back to them, worry clear even with the noise on the channel. "Reactor's not happy. Reactor is *un*happy. Also, it's really hot in here."

"We get the temperature shift too," said El. "I've got green across the board everywhere else, but that doesn't mean shit if we can't muster the juice to make another jump."

"I got you," said Hope. "Give me five."

"You got five. Take all the time you need," said El, clicking the comm off.

Nate clicked on his own console. Time to find out where in the universe they were. Three jumps in put them in a shitty backwater system, nothing here but hunks of rock floating around a binary star. It had been tagged and bagged, dismissed as useless except to miners, and low value to them, the rocks holding junk iron and some silicates. Hell, the system was near valueless, no high value metals like platinum or fissionables on record. The rocks weren't even that big. Nothing you could call a planet, nothing with an atmosphere. Terraforming was good business, they'd turned the toxic sludge of Earth's oceans back to a brilliant blue, but you needed something to work with. Air, for one. You could make your own air, but that took more time than was profitable for the quick-wins corp mindset. None of these rocks were big enough to hold their own air. Sure, they were big enough to hammer the *Tyche* flat like a bent nail, just not big enough to set up a mining rig on. It'd be ships out here, mining lasers, inflatable sails to catch the debris. And that was low value work, for low value crews. Hell, it'd be great if no one was here at all.

Which is what it looked like. Not a soul.

Except ... *Tyche* chattered to herself for a spell, then the holo cleared, replaced with a system view. There, all those rocks orbiting their binary star. And drifting in the chunky soup, a transponder code. *Tyche* made the necessary inquiries, came back with some details.

"Well, I'll be damned," said Nate. "There's another ship here."

Helium-class ship. A lot bigger than *Tyche*, more of a boxy cargo freighter. Something the size of that could resupply a colony. Not atmosphere capable, kind of like a big brick floating through space. The transponder said her name was *Ravana*, which was a curious name to give a ship that hauled other people's luggage for a living. You might be able to park the *Tyche* inside, but unless they'd done exactly that there wouldn't be a bunch of spare parts inside. The *Ravana* was big enough she'd have a crew, some supplies they could barter or beg for, and — with any luck — send a message for help. Hope'd know what parts they needed, the *Tyche* had plenty of supplies, and things would be just fine.

The comm clicked. "Cap," said Hope. "Cap, we've got a problem."

Nate sighed, rubbed his face with a hand. *Why can't anything just go smooth?* "What's up, Engineer?"

"Reactor's more unhappy than I'd like."

"What do you mean by, 'unhappy?'"

"Well, the laser's not firing right. It's distorting the yields from the fuel pellets. We want a nice clean compressed pellet in there, and we're not getting that. We're getting a ... well, hell. How much do you know about ICF reactors, Cap?"

Nate sighed. "Hope? Hope, we've talked about this. I know *nothing* about reactors. That's why you're here. What I need to know is whether we're at the 'Oh God, we're all going to die,' phase, or whether we're at the, 'This is inconvenient but we can shore up for repairs at the next spaceport.'"

"You want a summary?"

"I want a summary," agreed Nate.

"We're all going to die," said Hope, "in about three days."

"Shit," said Kohl, voice behind Nate. "Three days? I guess I've got some whisky."

Nate turned, saw the big man at the door to the flight deck, hand on the sill, frown on his face. "Kohl, we're not going to die."

"We're all going to die," said Kohl, "eventually. For us? Three days, she said. Although I guess if she could fuck up her life so bad she has to fly with us, she could get this wrong too."

"You're making noises again," said Nate, "and those noises don't sound good. Why don't you go check on your cabin? See if the Navy took anything."

"Already checked," said Kohl. "I think I scared the skinny one. He was looking under my bunk."

"Check again," said Nate. "Keep checking until your mouth stops making noises."

Kohl gave him a glare. "One day, she'll bring the hellfire of the Republic down on all of us."

"One day, she might," said Nate. "Until then, she's on my crew. Just like you."

Kohl grunted, shrugged, and walked away.

"I don't know why you keep him on the ship," said El, her voice quiet, but hard.

"He serves a useful purpose," said Nate. "That purpose might get exercised soon. Hope, you still with us?"

There was a pause from the comm, then, "Yeah, Cap. Look, about what he said—"

"Three days, Hope. Until then, how we looking?"

"Worse and worse as the time rolls on. You've got power for a bit of maneuvering, life support will keep us alive until we explode, we can still make coffee. Don't use the Endless Drive, because nothing good will happen. Bad things are almost certain to happen. Like exploding." The comm clicked off.

"Want me to fly us there?" El pointed at the *Ravana's* icon on the holo. Her hands were already moving on the controls, the gentle hand of thrust pushing Nate back in his chair. The *Tyche* shifted in space, the usual rumble of her sounding regular, ordinary. Not like she would explode in three days.

"Yeah," said Nate. "At least she's not moving. We'll cosy on alongside, try and beg some help." *Three days.* That wasn't a lot of time. He could offload the crew to the *Ravana*, ask for a ride, but the thought of the *Tyche* drifting out here, just waiting for someone to claim salvage rights didn't sit well with him. So he'd stay, ask them to get help. It'd work. He toggled the comm. "*Ravana*, this is the *Tyche*. We are en route to your location, seeking assistance. Please respond."

Nothing.

He tried again. "*Ravana*, this is the *Tyche*. We are facing main reactor failure, seeking assistance. Please respond."

"That sounds like a lot of dead air," said El.

It made little sense. *Ravana's* transponder was operating fine, ship's computers were online, nothing in the automated comm negotiation from the *Tyche* suggested anything was wrong. And while pirates might be out here, there was no place for them to hide and this wasn't a popular route — it wasn't likely to be a trap.

"I've got nothing on scans," said El. "There's nothing else out there."

"It's not pirates," said Nate.

"Didn't say it was," she said. "I said it was nothing." After a moment she said, "But why *would* it be pirates?"

"It's not pirates," said Nate, again. He clicked the comm again. "*Ravana*, this is the *Tyche*. We are approaching and will dock with your vessel in," and here, he checked the display, "about thirteen minutes. Please do not shoot us all when we come through your airlock. Please respond."

Nothing. Not even the courtesy of static.

He tapped on the console, coaxing the *Tyche's* imaging systems into life. High-detail cameras gave a visual shadow, but it was so damn dark out here that they got nothing but a silhouette, the backwash of light near worthless. But the *Tyche*, she had military in her family tree, sass right to the core, and she saw with more than human eyes. LIDAR reached out across the void, painting the *Ravana* in detail. "C'mon girl, show me what's in front of us." The lasers painted the *Ravana's* location, building up a picture up in the holo. The outline of the *Ravana* took shape, details filled in fast and smooth as the *Tyche* touched the other ship with light as gentle as a lover's hand.

Yep: Helium-class freighter. No obvious damage. Floating there, like a leaf on a pond. Slight spin, nothing that would make docking difficult. Hell, even Nate could do that; he could give El the night off. Under better circumstances, he might have.

"She's just ... *floating*," said El. "What kind of Helm lets their ship drift like that?"

"One that's dead," said Grace, her voice behind them. Nate and El turned to face her.

Like Kohl before her, she was at the door to the flight deck, hand on the sill. She had none of Kohl's attitude; if Nate was any judge, he reckoned her to be *concerned*. "Uh," said Nate. "That's a little fatalistic."

"Don't dock with that ship," said Grace. "Everyone on it is dead already." She looked down at the deck, then back at Nate. She held his gaze. "What would kill an entire ship full of people?"

"Virus," said El. "Radiation. Bad food. Hull breach. Buffer failure."

Nate shot her a look. "That's not helping. Also, it's not true." He pointed to the holo. "Nothing wrong with her. The *Ravana's* ... fine. She's fine. Transponder gives the all clear. No distress calls. Nothing."

"Don't say I didn't warn you," said Grace.

"We don't have a choice," said Nate.

"Three days," said Grace. "We've got some time." She turned, walked away.

"Captain?" said El. "We still docking?"

"Of course," said Nate, shaking his head. "Besides. If everyone's dead, we get salvage rights. Could be a reactor in it for us."

"We don't get that kind of luck," said El.

"Of course we do," said Nate. "*Tyche* is the Goddess of Luck." He thought for a second. "Still, I'm in favor of manufacturing a little of our own luck." He toggled the comm again. "Kohl."

"What you want?" Not *what is it sir* or *can I help*, but that wasn't Kohl's style. He wasn't on the ship for his personality.

Nate leaned forward. "I got something heavy that needs lifting."

"Fuck off," said Kohl, his voice hard on the comm.

"Also," said Nate, "there might be people that need killing."

"Pirates?" said Kohl.

"Could be."

"I'll suit up," said Kohl.

THE DOCK COUPLED, locked with a *clang*, and then ... silence. Nate checked the seal on his helmet, then pressed the console by the airlock, stepped inside with Kohl, and shut it behind them. He looked back through the window, saw Grace's face looking out at him. Her expression was *don't say I didn't warn you*, but there wasn't anything belligerent in the way she held her shoulders. Like she was weary of something that hadn't happened yet.

Nate turned, opening the outer lock. He knocked three times on the *Ravana's* lock.

Nothing.

"Well, let's go," said Nate.

Kohl looked at him, face obscured by his power armor's helmet. "I hope it's pirates," he said, then turned back to the airlock. He tapped on the external controls. The *Ravana* opened, revealing an empty airlock. Well-lit. No plasma burns. No cracks in the glass of the inner airlock. Atmosphere.

Nate and Kohl shared a look, then both shrugged at the same time. Kohl led the way into the airlock, hefting his plasma rifle. It was an ugly thing, bigger than was necessary unless you wanted to bore a hole in a tank, but Kohl had said to him one time *what if there was a tank* and Nate had stopped bothering him after that. There was no foothold for an argument there.

They shut the airlock behind them, then opened *Ravana's* interior airlock. A small bay, lined with suits, all orderly, none missing. Kohl lead the way with his rifle. *Ravana* was a freighter, her cargo bay aft of where they'd docked. Gravity was still on, which meant the Endless Drive onboard could still generate positive energy fields — and by inference, negative ones too; she wasn't drifting because she couldn't fly.

Nate said, "You take cargo, I'll take the flight deck."

"What if there's people who want to shoot you on the flight deck?" Kohl frowned. "That's the whole reason I put my suit on."

"To watch me get shot?"

"No ... well, sure, I'll watch that," said Kohl. "But if there's a fight, I want to be in it."

"I'll be sure to let you know," said Nate, "if anyone tries to shoot me."

"You do that, Cap," said Kohl, and clanked off down toward the cargo bay at the aft of the ship. Nate turned and walked to the *Ravana's* fore, the deck plates under his feet making no noise, not even a squeak. Well-maintained, everything in order. He kept his helmet on in case El's prediction of *virus* was right — you could never be too careful — but he'd have expected to see *something* amiss. A body or two. Maybe signs of a fight. Hell, even a broken cup.

Nothing. Whoever the *Ravana's* captain was, they ran a clean ship. An empty one as well.

Nate passed the crew quarters, not as spacious as *Tyche's*. *Tyche* had a bunk to a cabin, each cabin doubling as an escape pod; *Ravana* kept the escape-pod double model standard across most starships, but there were two bunks in each. Four crew to a cabin. No privacy. A tidy ship, but a thrifty one too.

All, also, empty.

What the actual fuck is going on? He should have found something by now, some reason for this fully-functional ship to be floating out here. Some crew should have accosted him.

He arrived at a sealed door. He'd never crewed on a Helium-class ship before, but if the design was like other similar ships, behind this would be a room with acceleration couches, and beyond that, the flight deck. This room would be where the crew would be when the *Ravana* was under sail. He rested his hand on the door controls. *Here goes nothing.* He keyed it, the door sliding out of sight.

All the acceleration couches were full. The crew was all here, but ... *not.* Blank eyes stared at the ceiling. Slack limbs fell by sides. All strapped to their acceleration couches. Nate walked in, checking the nearest body. A young man, a gentle rise-and-fall of his chest saying his body was still alive. But his eyes didn't track Nate's hand as he waved it in front of the young man's face.

Nate looked towards the flight deck. He knew what he would find. He walked towards it, opening the airlock anyway, because he needed to be sure.

The door slid out of sight, revealing a larger flight deck than the *Tyche*, four people in acceleration couches. All like the rest of the *Ravana's* crew, all ... *gone.* The holo at the front of the flight deck flickered with red text. *FLIGHT TIME BUFFER COMPRESSED BEYOND TOLERANCE.*

Yeah. That'd do it.

He walked the room until he found it: an open port, circuitry exposed. Someone had jacked into the *Ravana's* systems, overriding the safeties. They'd pulled out the hard stops that said *not too fast* and just let the ship jump as fast as she could. Everyone knew that was suicide; you would arrive at the other end without a mind. Your brain couldn't take life without the fiction of time; it couldn't take the idea that space could be travelled in an instant. If you went too fast, you'd get a headache. A little faster, you'd forget things, or remember things that had never happened. Too much beyond that, psychotic breaks, full-on reality distortion, that kind of thing. A whisker more, and you'd just ... *stop*. Linear time defines human existence; break the rules, stop existing.

What would make a crew try and subvert the safety controls? Running from something? To something?

He keyed his comm. "Kohl."

"Captain," said Kohl, "you're not going to believe what I've found down here."

"You're probably right," said Nate. "You're not going to believe what I found up here either."

"Can I go first?" said Kohl.

"Sure," said Nate, still looking at the bodies around him. *What's the protocol for this? Do you jettison the meat overboard? Let it wind down like an old clock?* "Shoot."

"There's one thing in the cargo bay," said Kohl.

"Ship this big," said Nate, "that's not economic."

"Right," said Kohl. "Do you want to guess what it is?"

"You tell me," said Nate.

"You're not a lot of fun," said Kohl.

"Sorry," said Nate. "You'll know why in a second."

"Transmitter," said Kohl.

"A what?"

"Trans. Mitt. Er," said Kohl. "A fucking *transmitter*. I'm no expert, but I'd say it's the mirror fucking image of what we've got in the *Tyche*."

"They've got the same kind of transmitter as what we're carrying?" said Nate.

"I'd bet my completion bonus," said Kohl, "on it being the same model. Made in the same factory. Probably the same guy tightened the last bolts on it. Same one, Cap." There was a pause. "I got a good look at the one in our hold. Because, you know, it was heavy, and my job is lifting heavy shit."

Nate did a slow circle, looking at the dead crew. Because they were *brain* dead, bodies just soaking up oxygen at this point. "Why," he said, "do you suppose that would be?" But what he was thinking of was what Grace said: *Everyone on it is dead already*.

"No clue," said Kohl. "It's a fucking mystery."

"Great," said Nate. He keyed his comm controls. "Hope. El. You there? El, record, please."

"*Tyche* here," said El. "Recording."

"I'm here too," said Hope.

"I'm authorizing us to begin lawful salvage of the Helium-class freighter *Ravana*, found drifting with no survivors. My Engineer will strip the fusion reactor from this ship as is our right under Republic salvage charter laws. End recording." Nate paused. "You get that?"

"I got it," said El.

"What do you mean, 'no survivors?'" said Hope.

"Grace was right," said Nate. "Everyone's dead. Now get to work. You've got less than three days."

CHAPTER NINE

"SO WHAT YOU'RE SAYING," said El, "is that Hope'll be traumatized by seeing a bunch of already-dead people, and I'm not."

"That's what I'm saying," said Nate, looking over his shoulder at her as he led her deeper into the *Ravana*. "Hope's a kid, El. You've done your time on a ship." His feet clanked over the bridge plating.

"I've done my time on a bridge," said El. *You know, this ship is clean. Too clean. Navy clean.* "I've done my time in space. I've not done my time in the field..." Her words trailed off as the door to the ready room cycled, slid sideways, revealing the acceleration couches.

The bodies.

"Are they," she said, "dead?"

"May as well be," said Nate. "They're gone, El."

She rubbed her hands against her flight suit, mouth dry. "I'm ... not okay with this."

"With what?" he said.

"Spacing them," she said. "I'm not okay—"

"Oh, hell," he said. "No. No, you're not here for that. I need you to talk to the *Ravana*. Find out where she's been. Where's she's going. I need to find out what the fuck they were doing." He did a slow turn, taking in the bodies. "Because they were running, El. From something, or to something."

"You want me to do that with them staring at me?" El pointed at a woman, head lolling sideways, eyes open. It was like the body was looking at El, saying, *I see you.* "Their damn eyes are open."

"Lights are on, no one's home," said Kohl's rumble from behind her. She turned, letting the big man through. "Cap. Want me to fire these out the airlock?"

Nate winced at that. "I ... guess." He frowned. "Kohl? I need you to tag 'em."

"What the fuck for?" he said. "There's not likely to be a bounty in here. This ship's too clean for a rough crew."

"They'll have families," said El.

"Might," said Kohl, in a tone that said *so what.*

"Families might want to know what happened to their kin," said Nate. It always helped to have the captain at your back when talking to Kohl. Not because Nate was bigger or tougher than Kohl. It was that Kohl responded to money, and his source of money was the captain. *Whatever works.*

"Might," said Kohl, again, his face turning sour. "You sure this comes into the category of 'lifting heavy things?'"

"Pretty sure," said Nate. "Chop chop, Kohl." He thought for a minute. "Oh, hey. Can you start on the flight deck?"

"I can," said Kohl, shrugging inside his armor. That thing looked heavy to El, like a space suit that had merged with some kind of military personnel carrier. Plates everywhere, mounts on the back for God knows what. He nodded to her as he clanked past towards the flight deck.

"El," said Nate. "They—"

"They broke the buffer limits," said El.

"I think," said Nate, "that they were coming from the same place we're *going.*"

"That doesn't sound peachy," said El. Kohl emerged from the flight deck, a body over his shoulder like a sack. He walked past her with another nod — *that shit'll get old, fast* — and down the gangway. Towards the cargo bay, and its larger airlock. "You want to abort?"

"What?" said Nate. "Hell no."

No, I suppose not. You're no Kohl, but you've never backed down from a fight while I've been watching. It's why we've got a kid Engineer who's a criminal. It's why you put up with Kohl. Sometimes I figure I'm the only lawful citizen on this ship. "So ... why?"

"Information," said Nate, "gives us options."

"It doesn't really," said Grace, from the doorway. El took her in — pale face, drawn with the same stress they were all feeling. No sword, because *why*. It was a stupid weapon to own. A good blaster would solve problems at a more comfortable distance. Faster, too. She had no suit either; El figured her to be of a similar mind to herself on that point at least: not expecting the *Ravana* to breach, blowing them all into space. "It will tell us what we already know."

"Huh," said Nate. "Assessor? I've got something for you to assess." He gave a quick glance to El. "Get to it."

They walked out, and El looked towards the flight deck. She could see the corner of an acceleration couch through the doorway, the legs of whomever was there in view. Not moving. She sighed. *They're dead, El. The dead can't hurt anyone.*

Still. It'd be nice if they weren't all *staring*. She moved into the flight deck, found the chair Kohl had emptied for her. Sat, felt the still-warm of it, and shuddered. Someone had been here two minutes ago. Or someone's body; the some*one* had left during their last jump.

"Okay, *Ravana*. Let's see if you talk pretty." She powered up the console, cleared the warnings. The holo in the air flickered, vanished. She started typing. "Where have you been, girl?"

"Hell and back," said Kohl. He wasn't even breathing hard. He unclipped another body, shouldering it.

"Don't ... Kohl? You don't need to nod at me every time we pass each other." El sighed. "This isn't a bar."

"I got some whisky," he said. "We could make our own party."

"Not ever," she said. It was an old refrain. Kohl liked her. She didn't like him. End of story.

"Suit yourself," he said. "It's just, you know. Hope's..."

"Too young?" offered El.

"Too into other women," said Kohl. "Found that well dry already."

"She might just be too into higher life forms," said El.

"Nah, that wasn't it," said Kohl. "She was specific. Like she was trying not to hurt my feelings." He laughed. "I don't know. It's a numbers game. Try often enough with enough people, it'll eventually work out. I was wondering, though. What if she met the right man..?"

"It doesn't work like that," said El. "Go on. I'm busy."

"Suit yourself," he said again, shuffling out.

"Sorry, girl," said El, running a hand over the console. "Now. Where were we?" she started with the flight plan. The holo blinked, spun into life, star map springing into life. Point of origin, Absalom system. Nate was right about that. Point of destination ... wait, that couldn't be right.

Point of destination was *here*. One jump, to the midpoint between Absalom and Enia. One jump wasn't enough. It wasn't *safe*. If you didn't drop out, take a look around to see what had changed in the time it took light to reach a faraway star, you could find yourself in the middle of a meteor, supernova. Sure, the odds were small, but when you were moving at many times the speed of light, small mistakes left big explosions. But if you took that kind of risk, why not jump somewhere with people?

"Come on, *Ravana*. Don't be holding out on me." She'd looked at the logged flight plan, but the flight recorder would tell her for sure what had happened. The holo cleared again, overlaid with the recorder's details. Many more data points — velocity, thrust, hull stresses, the works. She cleared away the extraneous data, looking for the route. There is was, clear as day.

One jump.

"Crazy," she said. Was it sabotage or deliberate? One rogue crew member, paid enough to do the wrong thing at the right time, could destroy a ship and her crew as easy as an impact with an asteroid. Her eyes flicked to the bare circuitry, then the other three chairs. Okay, okay. If it was sabotage, it'd need to be *complicit* sabotage. Maybe there was a log, some kind of crew recording. It was fashionable a few years back, before El had got her wings. Died out, because no one wanted to watch someone *interpret the data*. You didn't need some ego's editorial on their flight plan; you just needed the flight plan. "What about it, *Ravana*? Any more secrets in there?"

Nope.

Okay, external sensors. Got to be something there. It made sense, anyway, to get current data on the Absalom system; that kind of data was only days old, far better than the hundred-year-old data they'd get from their next series of jumps. El would have got this anyway; ships shared this kind of data where they could, if they rubbed shoulders in the hard black like this. In populated systems, ships would just gobble the data from the Guild, but out here, it was a part of the code.

The *Ravana* obliged.

Oh. Oh my.

The holo spun in front of El, Absalom's system plotted in perfect detail. Designation N-973. A single star, yellow and warm. Six planets, the important one the fourth — Absalom Delta. Earth analogue, or close with 1.1Gs. No terraforming required, or not much — just the usual soil bacteria, a little fauna and flora, and job done. None of that was interesting to El. What *was* interesting was two things orbiting Absalom Delta.

The first was a massive asteroid. The thing was the size of a moon, call it 150 klicks wide. It'd be having some tidal impacts. A thing like that might be why the transmitter was down. It could block line of sight at critical times between the Bridge and the planet. Not *likely*, but possible, sure. It could also have knocked out a couple of satellites. That was not only possible, but likely; the thing looked to be in some kind of stable — *stable!* — orbit around the planet's meridian.

The second thing was far, far more interesting though. It was a warship, a full scale, not-fuck-around destroyer, with a not-fuck-around name. The *Gladiator*. Her fingers itched with memories, because she'd jockeyed something a lot like it when she'd flown for the Empire. Those things were big guns, nightmares deployed for an opposing threat. Capable of a bunch of different mission types — guns aplenty, drop ships for surface deployment, Marines with attitude on board and good to go. It was a similar size and tonnage to the *Torrington* if she was any judge. Ten or so decks. Maybe 6,500,000 tonnes, over two klicks nose to tail. Long, and black, and deadly.

"Okay," said El. "Okay. Did they fire on you?" She didn't expect a confirmation from the logs, and didn't get one. *Ravana* had jumped into this system. Orbited Absalom Delta for a time, doing not much of anything for a couple of days. Probably talking to the surface, waiting for a ride. Then, before any shuttle departed the planet — and a couple of days' wait on an edge world wasn't unusual, resources spread a little too thin out here — the *Ravana* hit hard burn, breaking orbit. As their fusion drives were pouring thrust out the back, the *Gladiator* had jumped in. They passed each other, spat comms across space — all gone, nothing left of what was said in the recorder — and then the *Ravana* had jumped. One jump, buffers broken, to here.

The *Gladiator* hadn't fired on the *Ravana*. It was like the *Gladiator* was some kind of primed response, the end of a fuse of time that ticked over when the *Ravana* didn't report in. When the Bridge didn't fire up on schedule. Because the *Ravana* hadn't deployed her transmitter.

Grace was right. This didn't get them options. But she was wrong, too. It didn't tell them what they already knew. It gave them a whole bunch of nothing. And that nothing left uncomfortable questions, like *why would you jump your crew to your death* or *what was that destroyer doing in your wake?*

One thing was clear: *Ravana* hadn't been running from the *Gladiator*.

So what had she been running from?

CHAPTER TEN

GRACE SHIVERED in the *Ravana's* cargo bay. The bay was large, like a space warehouse, and was empty except for one thing. She figured the Navy paid the *Ravana* well to fly with an otherwise empty hold. Grace's breath misted in the air; the ship was getting colder as Hope prepped the ship, shutting down systems so they could take the reactor.

Stealing it, from a dead crew who had no further use for life support.

The work would take a few days. A *rush job*, Hope had called it, and *impossible*, but the impossible was possible if the alternative was death in a fiery explosion. Grace had waiting for one of them to ask the obvious question. Why didn't they take the *Ravana* and call it a day?

It was the obvious question, but so was the answer: the *Tyche* was home. It came off all of them in varying degrees, even the thug. The captain, most of all. It was something she could use. It made them easier marks. And easier to leave, when the time came, because the *Tyche* wasn't Grace's home. Never would be. A temporary ride, to get her somewhere she could lie low for a spell.

She and Nate were standing in front of the one thing in the bay: a large piece of machinery, transparent plastic covering it.

"Assess *that*," said Nate.

She looked at him, picking up *concern/worry*. "It's a transmitter."

"You wonder why we've got the same thing in our hold?" Nate walked around the transmitter. "You know, you knew a lot more about our mission than I did. You seemed to know more about our mission than those Navy boys did."

"Yes," said Grace, picking up *suspicion/concern*. "I like to know where I'm going and why."

"So, Grace Gushiken. Where are we going? And why?" Nate completed the circuit of the transmitter. "Why does an edge world need two transmitters?"

"Usual reasons," said Grace. "I think you're approaching this from the wrong angle."

"Break it down for me," said Nate. Arms crossed. Face closed.

"An edge world needs just one transmitter," said Grace. "A working one. The Navy knows this, you know this. We all know this."

"We all know this," agreed Nate.

"Thing is, the Navy is ... a big organization. Full of factions." She held up a hand, because he looked like he would say something unhelpful like *no it's not* or *how do you know that*. "They send crew pants in the wrong size, and then send a second pair in another, different, yet still wrong size. They order too much hash cake for the galley. Coffee comes in decaf, not espresso. You see where I'm going?"

"You're saying they booked two crews to complete the same job. Clerical error."

"Clerical error," said Grace, "seems the most obvious reason."

"Okay," said Nate. "Clerical error doesn't explain how you knew about it."

"I talk to people," said Grace.

"That's not it," said Nate. "No one talks that well to people."

"No, I guess not," said Grace. "How's Hope, since we're talking?"

"Don't change the subject," said Nate. "And if you're going to, be ... *smooth*."

"Captain, I'll change your definition of 'smooth.'" Grace let a little anger into her voice. Not a lot, but enough, just enough to salt the water, let a little flavor in. "This is about trust."

"You're right—"

"I haven't *finished*," she said. "Trust, it's a two-way street. Where have I given you cause to think I can't be trusted?"

"There's—"

"That's right," she said, walking closer to him. Face to face. "Never. Here's the thing. I've saved your ass twice now. Once, when a soldier was about to turn you into a smoking ruin, and the second when I dragged your crew's ass out of a Republic fire. Look. I don't know what Hope's problems are, and I don't care. When *she* trusts me, she'll tell me. That'll be enough. Not the point. The point? Two for two, Captain. And you haven't even given me an *advance*. Two good reasons to trust me, and nothing coming back the other way. I've got to ask, why should I keep sticking my neck out for you?"

She didn't say, *that soldier wasn't going to kill you, he was going to kill me*. She didn't say, *if the Navy had looked too closely at me, I'd be dead*. Those were both true, and truth wouldn't help her here. What would help was this man getting over this whole situation. And if he was too blind to see what was true, that was on *him*. Grace only told people what they wanted to hear.

It wasn't *really* lying.

"I guess," said Nate, then stopped. "I guess I owe you an apology."

"And why's that?" said Grace.

"Because," said Nate. "I thought you were too good to be true."

Too good to be true. She felt sick and wanted to pull back, but held herself still through force of will born of long practice. It didn't matter what she felt. It mattered that she got to where she was going. And then the next place after that. And the next. She wanted to say, *maybe I'm just what you need*. Because she wanted it to be true.

And she wasn't sure why.

Instead, she said, "Sometimes, good things happen to good people."

"No," said Nate. "I've never known that to be true." She saw his metal hand flex and felt something like *remembered anger* come off him. "But you, Grace? You're right. And I'm sorry." He held out his hand — the flesh and blood one. She grasped it, finding his hand warm as they shook. "Welcome to the *Tyche*. Welcome to our family."

Perfect.

She watched as he left the cargo bay, and shivered again. The *Tyche* was breathing for both ships for the moment, but the air still felt stale, false, canned. Just like her. She put a hand on her stomach, willing that sick feeling away. It had to be this way. *Had* to be.

Didn't it?

Of course it did. She couldn't trust these people. Not really. Because of what she was. And she couldn't change that. In a couple more jumps she'd be off the *Tyche* and free on a new world where no-one knew her. That was the best thing for everybody.

WALKING THE *RAVANA* FELT RIGHT. It was empty of souls who cared. It — *still* — had bodies, empty of all concern, but placed in an airlock away from the rest of them. Nate had said to them all he'd decide what to do when the time came. She didn't know what that meant, and she didn't care.

I don't care. She repeated it to herself. *I don't care I don't care I don't care.*

Walking a drifting hulk, tiny bright sparks of consciousness scattered through it like failing beacons of hope, kept her grounded. Kept her running towards her north star, kept her aware of what she needed to do. It was about survival.

Grace let a hand touch the metal walls of the ship, fingertips trailing. How many other people had walked through here? How many crew had the *Ravana* seen before this last, inglorious end? Stripped of her drive, left to rot in a system that held nothing for any humans, not even a scrap of metal worth sending a run-down mining crew to gather.

Maybe Grace should stay. It'd be a good place to hide.

Her comm clicked in her helmet. They all wore full suits now that the drive was cold. *Tyche's* life support was still trickling air and heat into the empty shell of *Ravana*, a tiny sprite trying to keep a dying elder sister alive. It was enough to not flash-freeze like she'd seen before; the man who'd been hunting her had looked so surprised, right before the external lock had blown him into the hard black. No suit. He'd looked like he'd been trying to scream, and then he'd turned into a hunk of slowly turning ice and meat. The yellow hate of his mind had snapped out faster than she'd expected, but it still took a long time. *Fear* and *desperation/conviction* screaming into the void along with all of his air.

So yeah. She wore her helmet. People had told her she had trust issues. Her comm chirped and she keyed the receive controls. "Grace here."

"Um," said Hope. "Grace."

"I know, the name sounds cool to say," said Grace. Then she caught herself. *Don't engage.* She couldn't get ... attached. Not to any of them, and especially not to a needy on-the-run person trying to stay out from under the Republic's boot. "Sorry. What's up, Hope?"

"I was wondering," said Hope, "if you could give me a hand."

Grace paused. She'd walked the long length of the ship, or near enough. Her feet had led her to the ready room, with its empty acceleration couches and forgotten horrors. Her hand still touched the wall, because she wanted to feel something. This ship shouldn't be so *empty*. It was too big, too proud. Her traitorous feet had wanted to show her the ready room again. To remind her of what it meant to be a part of something.

Yeah. A part of something where everyone dies, together. No thanks. "Sure," she said. "I can give you a hand."

"Great," said Hope. "I'm in Engineering. On *Ravana*."

I know, Grace almost said. "Okay," she said. "I'll be right there."

GRACE DIDN'T KNOW what she'd been expecting. Something orderly, something regular, something like the *Tyche's* engine room. An acceleration couch like Hope's in a corner, tools racked and stacked. This might have started that way, but there was a huge crater in the floor, metal plates of the *Ravana's* structure lifted, sheared, cut, torn. The reactor swayed in the air above the hole, pieces of decking still stuck to it. Chains anchored it to the ceiling.

"You've been busy," said Grace.

"Oh, hi," said Hope, emerging from the crater in the floor. The mask of her rig slicked back, revealing a face smudged with grease and dirt and exhaustion. "Hey. Give me a sec." The mask slid back down over her face, her youth hidden by the hard metal and glass of the suit. The actuators on her back whirred into action as she slipped back below Grace's line of sight, bright stars of burning metal born by a welding tool flung out. A pause, a silence, smoke drifting from the crater, then Hope re-emerged, visor pulling back. "That should just about do it."

"Hm," said Grace. "If it's just about done, what am I here for?"

"Right," said Hope. "Well, two things." She clambered out of the hole. Grace took a couple quick steps forward, offering the Engineer her hand. Hope looked confused — *she's so tired, when did she last sleep?* — then a ghost of a smile hit her face. She grabbed Grace's hand, grip still strong despite the hours without sleep, and let herself be pulled out of the hole in the deck. "The first is the hardest for you. The second is the hardest for me." *Uncertainty/caution/tired-tired-tired* came off her.

Grace doffed her own helmet, a loaner from the crew's stash.

Before this was over she might go through *Ravana*, find something more to her style. And by *style* she was thinking *easy to move in*. *Tyche's* stash was full of straight spacer gear, nothing fancy. Everyone else had their own kit, personal, appropriate for their jobs. To fit in, Grace would need the same. It'd be best if a new suit didn't smell like the last person who'd worn it, but looks were better than anything else. Especially now, while everyone else still seemed to have trust issues.

Everyone except for Hope. Too young for rough business like this. *Don't get involved. Don't get attached.* Grace almost growled at herself. "Let's start with what's hardest for me," she said, offering a smile.

"Okay, okay," said Hope. "I need to turn off the *Ravana*. I mean, the reactor," and here, she jerked a thumb at the machinery hanging behind her, "is already out. We're using *Tyche* for everything else. Lights, heating—"

"It's not very warm," said Grace, her breath misting out in front of her.

"What? Oh, sure, right. Yeah. Sorry."

"It's fine," said Grace. "Don't apologize. I mean, if we all die in a fiery explosion, you and I can talk about the right level of apology. Until then, do your thing."

Hope was nodding, not really following along. She'd been awake for, as near as Grace could tell, at least three days without a break. The day they'd jumped, then two days of hard labour here, stripping the *Ravana*. "Okay, cool, right. Sorry." She winced. "Sorry. Dammit. I mean. Hell." She ran a hand through already dirty pink hair, and it was hard to tell whether she was making it dirtier or cleaner. "So the thing. I need to turn everything off."

"Makes sense," said Grace. "Because you're pulling the *Tyche's* reactor."

"*Tyche* is about to pull her own reactor in a great big ball of fire," said Hope. "I'm trying to race her to it."

"Okay," said Grace. "How long do we have?"

Hope looked at Grace, and Grace felt *fear/desperation*. "Long enough. It's not important. What is important is that I need to be doing this, and I need ... well. Since you ... I remember the Navy," she said.

"You want me," said Grace, "to go tell everyone what is happening. And you want me to tell everyone, but especially October Kohl, to leave you alone."

"I didn't say that," said Hope, eyes darting about. *Fear/fear*.

"It's okay," said Grace. *Be the calm. Be the center of the storm.* This young woman's fear would drown her in a tide if she didn't hold herself steady. "I can do that. I think October Kohl and I need to have a talk anyway."

"He's not much for talking," said Hope. "Not about things that matter."

"That's fine," said Grace. "I can talk for both of us."

"Well," said Hope. "It's a little more ... okay, okay. I've got a plan. Because we don't have much time."

"How much time," said Grace, "do we have, Hope?" She took a step forward, put a hand on the other woman's arm. "How much time?"

Grace saw the point *there* where Hope almost cracked, but instead of shattering like stressed ceramic she swallowed. "About forty-five minutes," she said. "About forty-five minutes before the *Tyche* turns into a small sun. We had three days, but she's been breathing for *Ravana*, and *Ravana*, well she's so *big*, and..."

"Forty five minutes," said Grace. "What's the plan?"

"In a minute," said Hope. "The second thing."

"Later," said Grace.

"Now," said Hope. "Because we might not have a later."

"Later," said Grace, "because it won't matter either way. What's the plan?"

GRACE RAN. She ran out of *Ravana's* Engineering bay, bounced off the wall outside, used the ricochet to clang down the empty gangway. She keyed her comm as she ran. "*Tyche*, this is Grace. All hands, ready room."

Nate's voice. "Grace, this is *Tyche*. What's—"

"Ready room," said Grace, bouncing off another corner. The walls of *Ravana* whipped past, her breath rasping in her throat. She had a moment where she thought *more cardio* and then almost laughed at the absurdity of it. She hit the airlock between the ships, *Ravana's* clean giving way to *Tyche's* home—

It's not home. It's a ship. And it's got to keep you alive.

—the air feeling warmer already. Through the cargo bay. A glance at the transmitter, a promise for a colony that wouldn't even know they'd existed if she didn't get this right. Past Kohl coming from his cabin as she hit the main deck.

"What's the rush?" he said to her back.

"Ready room!" she said. "Bring your gear."

And then, the ready room. Nate, standing against a wall. His stance said *calm, confident* but *worry/worry* was coming off him in waves. El, halfway through the door to the flight deck. Kohl bringing up the rear, the big man moving with some speed. She'd need to remember that, if it ever came down to it. Grace had always prized her speed, working at it, but he looked to be quick enough and twice as strong.

She wanted to stop to catch her breath, but *no time*. "We've got about forty minutes before the reactor blows." She held up a hand to forestall the questions that would come. "Hope's got a plan. But it needs all of us."

"For fuck's sake—" started Kohl.

"My part in the plan," said Grace, "is to deal with questions and comments from idiots." She looked at Kohl. "You were going to say something?"

Kohl's face said he sensed a trap, so he crossed his arms instead of saying anything else. *Good.* She looked at them all. "Here's what'll happen."

"HOW'S THE cutting coming along, Kohl?" Grace watched the counter on her visor. Twenty minutes to go.

"Not good," he said, voice stressed. Strained.

Time for motivation. "The good news," she said, "is that if you fuck this up, you won't have to lift anything heavy ever again."

A pause. "I'll get it done," he said.

"HELM," said Grace. "El, are you ready?"

"I've never done this before," she said. "I'm not sure—"

"If you don't, we're all going to die," said Grace.

Static, then, "She'll fly true," said El.

"CAPTAIN," said Grace.

"It's ... just call me Nate," he said. His eyes were on hers, his face open. His heart open. She was getting *fear/fear*, but not for him. For *them.* She hated herself, again, more, *harder*, if there was such a thing, but she pushed it all down.

"Nate," she said. "Do you know what to do?"

"I get the easy job," he said.

"You get the job where you might have to die," she said.

"Yeah," he said. "The easy job. I'll be ready."

"All the air, Nate," she said. "Hope said it was important. Something about mass, and energy, and how we'd all probably die anyway."

"You don't get more air than this." His hand tapped the master console of the cargo bay doors. "It'll be all the air we have."

"TIME," said Grace.

"One more second," said Kohl's voice.

"It's *time*," she said.

"I don't have the reactor *in*," he said. "You do what you need to do, but if we don't have it, what's the point?"

"Whatever," said Grace. *More motivation.* "In three."

"Helm, standing by," crackled El. With the *Tyche's* reactor glowing like a cinder on the other side of *Ravana*, they were getting interference.

"Cargo, standing by," said Nate.

"Engineering," said Hope. "Oh. Hey. I don't have anything to do."

"In two," said Grace.

"I'm not *ready*," said Kohl.

"He's ready," said Hope. "It's in. He's here. We're here."

"In one," said Grace. Then, "Go."

THE PLAN WAS SIMPLE. So simple, everything should have gone wrong. Grace just didn't have the kind of luck it took to survive something like this. She wouldn't survive it, none of them would.

Step one. Carve the reactor out of *Ravana*. Nothing pretty, just cutting torches, plasma spitting against the hull. Kohl, in hard vacuum, a bright star against the hard black as he sliced the heart from a dying ship.

Step two. Breach the *Tyche*. Seal Engineering, then suck all the air out there. Cut another hole. Pull out the burning reactor, internal safeties trying to save everyone from being turned back to their component elements. Give it a nudge, put it on *Ravana's* dark side. Keep pushing, some spare maneuvering packs from the *Ravana's* stores epoxied to it. Nothing done clean or right, no time for perfection. A just-good-enough job to push the dying reactor away.

Step three. Get *Ravana's* reactor back to *Tyche*. Get it inside, get it tied down. Through the breached skin of their ship. No time for anything else.

Step four. Helm, adjust the attitude of *Tyche*. Point the cargo bay at *Ravana*. A line made of three points; the dying reactor, then *Ravana's* insulating bulk, and finally *Tyche*.

Step five. Vent all their atmosphere. A big shove, to buy them some distance at the cost of all their air. Enough? Hard to say.

Step six. Helm again. Use whatever reaction mass they had left to keep pushing. As fast as they could. All power out. Sticks are dead. An impossible task, to fly a dead ship.

Step seven. The important step. All hands. Pray.

And if they didn't pray hard enough — maybe they didn't *believe*, or maybe all the gods were dead — they'd die.

The *Tyche's* failed reactor creates a small sun in space. The hulk of the *Ravana*, turned to component atoms. The remains of the crew, carbon and ash. A bright, expanding fireball. Alarms, sounding through the comm channel. El's voice, hard and panicked, "We're not far enough away we're not *far enough away*," and then the *Tyche* is picked up by a giant's hands, the hands of a god — *not dead after all* — and hurled out into the hard black, the creaking of the hull accompanied by something shrill and terrible. They can all feel it wherever their suits touch the metal of their home as the *Tyche's* back breaks against the force of her own heart exploding.

GRACE WOKE to darkness so absolute it felt like it had weight. Something to offset how light she felt. Floating.

They're adrift.

She feels terror, but it's her own. Grace isn't borrowing this from anyone. She'd heard there was nothing worse than being in a dead hulk, adrift in space. Trapped, silent. Unable to scream for help.

It's so very, very black.

She almost giggles, hysteria wanting to break through, as a light comes bobbing towards her. It seems so tiny, that light, against the black that smothers her. She picks out a form, sees it's a suit. Someone's come for her. To save her from the dark.

Nate leans over her, presses his faceplate to hers. "Grace," he says. "I found you."

She hugs him. She shouldn't get too close, not to this crew. But she needs it.

He holds her, right until she can't bear it and pushes him away. "Yeah," she said. "Right where you left me."

"C'mon," he stands. Holds out his hand. She takes it, feeling the jangle of nerves and worthless adrenaline making her unsteady. "Let's go find the rest of them."

IT'S SUITS FOR EVERYONE, for another couple of days at least. Hope wanted to get working on putting in the *Tyche's* new reactor, but Nate had talked her down. Said she needed sleep. He told her she'd saved them all, and that he'd get Kohl to move *Ravana's* reactor in place, ready for her.

Grace had seen the hole in engineering where he'd had to tear out *Tyche's* dying core. Nothing but stars wheeled past her vision, and she'd stood there for a long time, watching the hard black turn about them. She felt like she should have felt something like cold fear, but she felt warm, warmer than she had in for as long as she could remember.

She crushed the feeling, because it felt like home, and turned her back on Engineering, went to find Hope.

Hope was in her cabin, bouncing between the walls. Grace

watched the young Engineer push herself off, wheel through the space, catch herself on the other wall. Grace's suit lights picked out Hope's face behind her rig's visor, something childish and pure in her smile.

"The second thing," said Grace, after what felt the right amount of time to be standing in a doorway like a creepy psycho, not saying anything. Normally she had more class, but it had been one of those days.

"The what?" said Hope.

"You said there were two things," said Grace. "One easy for me, one easy for you."

"I said one hard for me, one hard for you," said Hope. "You've done your hard part."

"Yeah," said Grace. It had felt hard, but somehow she figured this next bit would be harder still. For both of them, no matter what Hope said.

"I ... I'm not good at this stuff," said Hope. "So I'm just going to say it. No one's done what you've done. Not for me. Not before. Not even..." she trailed off, lost in a memory. Hope looked like she wanted to say much more, and also didn't, and Grace let her work her way through that. "Not for me," she finished.

"Okay," said Grace. "Done what?"

"Oh, right," said Hope. "I don't mean the reactor thing. I mean the Navy thing."

"The what?" said Grace.

"The Navy," said Hope. "When they came. Here, into our home. To take me. To take me away, for what I've done. You became me, so they'd find someone different. Someone strong."

Grace looked at the other woman, turning about in the space of her cabin, the walls dark where their suit lights didn't push the black far enough away. "The way I see it," she said, because she didn't want to get *close*, and didn't need this woman leaning on her, "is that you're strong enough already. We'd all be dead without you."

"Maybe," said Hope. "Maybe we'd be dead without you, because they'd have taken me away, and the captain would have sailed off, and the *Tyche* would have exploded." She sighed. "I don't know. We've got a lot of fixing to do before she'll fly again."

"That's for tomorrow," said Grace. "You should be sleeping."

"Can't sleep," said Hope. "Too tired. Too wired."

"You're welcome," said Grace. "For the Navy thing." She wanted to say *anytime*, but didn't, because she didn't want to lie. Not to Hope. *You've just got to walk away. You don't have to like them. But you shouldn't break them either.*

"Can you..." Hope trailed off.

"Can I what?" said Grace.

"Teach me," said Hope. "How to talk to them like you do."

"I don't know if you want to be me," said Grace. "I don't think you want that at all."

"No, no," said Hope. "Of course not. I just ... want to sound the part."

Grace thought about that. A little advice wouldn't hurt her. Return the favor, a small thank-you because she was living and breathing now. "Okay," she said. "You need to learn to swear."

"I don't," said Hope, "like talking like that."

"It's not about what you like," said Grace. "None of us do what we like. Not if we want to survive."

"But—"

"Anyway," said Grace. "I think you're probably good as you are. Just go grab Kohl."

"Kohl doesn't like me very much," said Hope. "He's right, you know. I don't know why *you* like me."

"I don't know either," said Grace, turning away. Walking back into the dark of *Tyche*.

Don't get attached.

She felt it might have been too late. Which meant it was time to go.

CHAPTER ELEVEN

NATE WANTED to scratch his nose, but the helmet made that tricky. He walked the cold dark of *Tyche*. No lights, except from his suit. No gravity, which meant his walking was a huge pain in the ass. Magboots only went so far. Technology made them predictive, gave them a more natural cadence for the way feet contacted the ground. Didn't matter — it still felt like walking through a mire, muddy water sucking at his feet with each step. He didn't like zero G. It made it hard to move, to balance, to get his bearings. This whole job felt like that. He was tossed about, adrift, and his ship — his *home* — was open to hard vacuum.

He made it to the flight deck. There was emergency power here, dim red floor lighting casting tall shadows. Ice rimed the walls, a little more of an atmosphere's memory clinging to the ship. El was working on the console, trying to coax navigation, schematics, *anything* from the system. *Tyche* wanted to help, the holo flickering to life for brief seconds of time before scattering into random lines and signal noise. She was wearing her Old Empire flight suit, the black of the material making her look like a living shadow as she worked on the ship.

"How goes it?" he said.

El turned, and the illusion of living shadow was banished as her visor faced him, lit from within. *Tired.* "Systems aren't good, Cap," she said.

"Yeah," he said.

"You should get some rest," she said, a little concern mirrored between them.

"I can sleep when I'm dead," he said. "I'm not ready to be dead yet."

"We just need some power," she said. "A teaspoon of it, get the RADAR and LIDAR back up. Then we could see what was going on around us. I think we're okay. We weren't near any of those floating rocks when ... when the *Ravana* ... so. But I can't be sure."

"It's okay," he said. "Let's worry about what we can control."

"I've got the next jumps plotted," she said. "That's good, right?"

"I hear a 'but' in there somewhere, El," said Nate. "You're preparing me for bad news."

"It's the *Tyche*," said El. "She's hurt pretty bad. The superstructure took a knock in the blast." Her hands moved in the air in front of her, making a twisting motion. "It's only a little bit, a tiny shimmy in the middle of her. We can fly her. Probably as high as four, maybe five Gs of thrust. I reckon I can land her, exactly once. She won't take off again. Not unless we land in a shipyard."

"Can we jump?" said Nate.

"I would have led with that," she said. "If we couldn't, I mean." She sighed, the noise a *hiss* over the comm. "Hope's done her best. We'll have power back soon. Drives will come online. Kohl's welding the hull closed, so we don't vent air. But we'll need to shore up somewhere. A week. To get her to fly true."

"A week?" said Nate. "You're just trying to get that shore leave, aren't you?"

"You read my mind," she said, offering him a faded smile. "Piña Colada. I could use a Piña Colada."

"It's on me," said Nate. "El? You're doing great."

"I wish I could do more," she said, trailing a hand over her console. "But our ship's hurt, Nate."

"We'll get her better," said Nate. "She kept us alive. Now it's our turn."

A whoop sounded over the comm, Hope's voice stressed with joy and too many stims. "Fuck *yeah*," she said. The way she said *fuck* reminded Nate of an audition he'd done what felt like a lifetime ago. He'd been trying to do a stage play in his local town, the community pulling together with their kids for a little old-world fun. He'd been offered a script, a part to read. Before he'd got there, Logan Harasymowicz — a bigger kid, but not a stupid one — had tried a few lines out. The words had tumbled from him with pauses in all the wrong places, stilted, like it was a language he didn't know. Like he was sounding the words out. That's how Hope said *fuck* — like she was reading it from a book.

El looked at Nate for a second. "She's trying to learn to swear," she offered.

"Why?" said Nate.

"Reasons," said El.

There was a bright flash, the flicker of lights, so bright after days of darkness that Nate saw stars. He had to blink them away. The flight deck came to life in fits and starts, El's console beaming bright with bright primary colors, the holo between the acceleration couches running through a diagnostic. A cascade of lights ran up the walls, and Nate could feel a low hum through his feet as something inside the *Tyche* woke, yawned, and stretched.

"We've got *power*," said Hope over the comm. "Reactor's giving me some error codes but nothing that can't be accounted for by way of it not being in her old ship."

"Thank God," said Nate. "I can have a shower."

"You can have a shower," came Kohl's voice, "when you help me finish the welding."

"On my way," said Nate, giving El a nod and making his way to Engineering. It might end up being a good day after all. *Tyche* was alive again, living, heart beating, and soon she'd be breathing again.

NATE HAD FOUND Kohl and Hope working in silence. They were in the same space, the same room, but it was like they couldn't see each other. *Same old shit*, he thought. One day, he figured that he and Kohl would have more of a conversation about that. He'd tried before, because Hope had done nothing wrong, unless you figured that helping your wife out was some kind of crime, but Kohl had just shrugged and asked Nate to go fuck himself.

It'd keep.

Engineering was lit now, all the lights on, like Hope was trying to erase the memory of darkness from her area of the universe. *Ravana's* old reactor was in the middle of the bay, larger than the *Tyche's* one. The floor plates around it were crumpled, pieces missing, thick cables coming out from the reactor to couple with ports around Engineering. No smoke, which was a good sign, although without atmosphere it just meant something *couldn't* burn, not that it wasn't wanting to.

Kohl grunted. "Great. You're here. Why don't you go weld the outside. Double hull, right? It'll be faster."

"Why don't you," said Nate, "go weld the outside?"

"I'm already doing the inside," said Kohl.

"I'm the captain," said Nate.

"So?" said Kohl.

"So," said Nate. "Completion bonus."

"That shit's wearing thin," said Kohl. But he grabbed his welding rig, stamping past Nate. This in itself was good news — not that Kohl was in a bad mood but that he needed to go out a proper airlock. There wasn't a hole big enough to fit a human through in the side of the ship anymore.

Nate smiled. He grabbed a welding rig from the deck, hauled

himself up, and got to work. Straight welding was easy enough, and truth be told Kohl was doing the exterior welds because the man was just better at it. Nate could draw a weave bead that looked like a series of dying caterpillars. Kohl could draw the Mona Lisa in the face of metal. No *way* was Nate saying that, though. Kohl had enough problems keeping his ego under control at the best of times, and that was for things he was terrible at.

"It doesn't need to be pretty, Cap," said Hope. He turned, saw her looking up at him, her rig's arms slack behind her.

"Great," said Nate, "because it was never going to be."

She flashed him a grin that was all stim jitters. "I'll fix her. When we land."

"I know," said Nate. He went back to his welding. "We'll make her right."

THE CREW WAS in the ready room. Helmets still on, but faces hopeful. They'd pressurized Engineering, found the seal good, and were ready to try the rest of the ship. "Okay," said Nate. "The plan is to haul ass to Absalom. Avail ourselves of the aid of the fine Republic Navy ship we know is in the system. Failing that, avail ourselves of the aid of the planet-side spaceport."

"Why Navy?" said Kohl. "You hate those assholes."

"Faster," said Hope, but sounded doubtful.

"Cheaper," said El, sounding more certain.

"More professional," said Grace.

"Exactly," said Nate. "Consistent quality. That's what our dearly beloved Republic is good for. And right now we're in dire need of consistency. We'll explain our situation, and I'm sure they'll help us out. It's what they *do*. For law-abiding citizens."

"What about Hope?" said Kohl. "She going to fuck everything up for us? Again?"

Nate saw Hope's face fall. "Kohl?" He let some steel come into his voice. "We're alive because of Hope."

"If she'd been looking after the reactor in the first place, instead of playing hero games on Arlington, we'd—"

Nate took a step forward. "You don't like the way I run things, Kohl?" He looked around at El, Grace, and Hope, then back to Kohl. "Anytime you want off my ship, you just say."

"Jobs'd be easier to get," said Kohl, "if we didn't have a fugitive onboard."

"Jobs would be easier to get," said Nate, "if I didn't have to worry about you murdering hundreds of people every time you got drunk." He gave Kohl a stare. "In or out? We can leave you with the Navy. They'll take you somewhere."

Kohl thought about that. "Naw," he said, but he took a while to get there. "Wouldn't be as fun on another ship, what with this one almost blowing up all the time."

"Glad that's resolved," said Nate. "Engineer? I need air back in my ship."

Hope nodded, the rig's arms jerking behind her. *Definitely too many stims.* She was wired, all her motions erratic, exaggerated, larger than life. Her eyes were wide and bright in her face. "Air coming right up." She held up an arm, the tiny console on her rig's sleeve lighting up. She entered a few commands.

The air filling the ship couldn't be heard right away. There wasn't an atmosphere to carry the noise. But after a short time Nate could hear a subtle *hiss* as the *Tyche* breathed again. He gave El a nod, and his Helm moved into the flight deck. There was a pause, then her voice came back over the comm. "No leaks," she said. "Hull is sound."

"Then it's time," said Nate, "to drop this transmitter off and get paid."

"Aye aye, Captain," said El. "Ready to jump on your mark."

Grins, smiles, all around. Except for Grace, whose face was

sombre. Nate dismissed it as nerves, as tension, as exhaustion. Maybe he shouldn't have.

THE STARSCAPE FILLED in front of Nate, the jump ending with a soft whine as the Endless Drive powered down.

"Absalom system," said El. "We're here."

"Well then," said Nate. "Let's get on the horn and see how those Navy boys are doing. But don't," and here, he held up a hand, "make it sound like we know they're there."

She gave him a sideways glance across the cockpit. "I figured I could just say, 'Hey, you assholes seen the *Ravana*?' and see what shakes loose."

"Sorry," said Nate.

"Because that'd be fun," said El.

"I said I was sorry," said Nate. "I'm tired."

"Yeah, so are we all … hmm," she said.

"What's, 'Hmm?'" said Nate.

"Well, we've got all six planets we'd expect to see. We've got a transponder — joy of joy, the *Gladiator* is still here. I've given her a ping, and I'd say in about ten seconds we'll have them crawling all over us. We've got a big rock floating around Absalom Delta, snuggled nice and close to the *Gladiator*, which I will tell you is strange, but maybe they're investigating it. But the weird thing is that we've got a Guild Bridge, and as near as I can tell it's still live."

"You what?" said Nate. "The Bridge is still live? Transmitter still online?"

"Still online. I'm talking to it right now," she said. After a few seconds, she said, "Hmm."

"That's twice," said Nate. "I don't like this new verbal communication style. It's ambiguous."

"What? Oh," she said. "Well. That's because the *Gladiator* is being ambiguous."

"How so?"

"No human response," said El. "*Tyche's* said hello, *Gladiator's* said hello back, so we know there's a ship there, it's not running stealth, but unless their comms officer is asleep or dead, I'd have expected them to be in touch."

"Jog them a little," said Nate. "Say 'Hi' in English."

El sighed, but keyed her console. "*Gladiator*, this is the *Tyche*. We are a civilian free trader under contract from the Republic Navy. We are en route to your location, seeking assistance. Please respond."

They both stared at the console. Nothing.

"Let me try," said Nate.

"Be my guest," said El.

Nate worked his own console, flicking on the comms. "*Gladiator*, this is *Tyche* actual. Captain Nathan Chevell. We've had a serious reactor ... *malfunction*. Radiation risk is zero, but our hull has been stressed. We seek aid. Please respond."

More than nothing this time: static. That was odd. Static meant something not ship-shape, something not well-maintained. Something that wasn't being managed, and if the Republic was good at one thing, it was managing the details. Nate looked at El. "Take us closer."

"You sure?"

"No," he said.

"Taking us closer," she said, hands on the sticks. There was a rumble, the big fusion drives at the back of the *Tyche* pushing with a gentle but insistent hand. Half a G of thrust, no more. Despite the gentle thrust, there was a groan of straining metal from behind them, *Tyche* complaining about the load. El gave him a look. "She'll be fine."

"I know," said Nate. "She's the Goddess of Luck."

"This week hasn't felt very lucky," said El.

"Imagine what it could have been," said Nate.

Before El could respond, *Tyche's* LIDAR having done its work, the holo lit. The *Gladiator* rotated in 3D between them. Details filled in, a rough schematic — tonnage, expected ordnance, possible crew numbers — spooling out on the display. All of it was a guess based on Old Empire information kept in *Tyche's* data cores. She was the Goddess of Luck now, but she'd seen battle in an earlier life and still carried the memories. She'd flown in battles where destroyers like the *Gladiator* drew down on her, skipped through beams of fire as she danced through the sky. The *Tyche* remembered how to be afraid of the right things.

"Well, shit," said Nate, staring at the *Gladiator's* image. "That's ... unusual."

"You don't say," said El, her voice cracking a little. "What's the plan?"

"Plan's still the same," said Nate. "Implementation changes." He keyed the comm. "Kids, we've got ourselves a problem. I'm looking at the *Gladiator* right now. She's in a steady orbit, but that's a miracle of automated flight. There's a hole right through her. Looks like a hull breach, all decks, top to bottom." He paused. "So, we're going to dock."

"The captain's gone insane," said Grace's voice. "I vote we mutiny."

"The reason," said Nate, bending towards the comm like it would help convince them that this was the *sane* course of action, "is because she'll have a repair bay. Ships like *Tyche* could be aboard. Spare parts. Maintenance equipment. Just because the *Gladiator's* leaking air doesn't mean she's useless."

"I can work with that," said Hope's voice.

"You can go to sleep for 24 hours," said Nate, "while we make sure the ship is safe. If the *Gladiator* is leaking radiation or is filled with pirates, we'll break free and try and make Absalom Delta's spaceport." He didn't say, *If there are pirates capable of taking the* Gladiator, *we're all fucked.*

"What about the rock?" said El, pointing to the holo. The huge asteroid that *Ravana* had mapped was still orbiting Absalom Delta.

"I say," said Nate, "that you practice not flying into it."

Tyche's holo cleared then chattered to life once again, high-lighting more details about the breach. Stress tolerances of the metal used in the hull, courtesy of the data banks, coupled with the way the breach was formed. "Huh," said El. "She was hit by something solid. Not a weapon." A pause. "Debris floating around her. Nothing ... *organic*."

"*Probably* not a weapon." But Nate relaxed a little. Marginally. A fraction only. Because the *Gladiator* being hit by something solid — something big enough to punch clean through the superstructure — didn't look like pirates. Looked more like a high velocity asteroid, something tear-assing out from deep space, too big for the PDCs to do anything about it and too fast for the ship to waddle out of the way. The *Gladiator* didn't have the *Tyche's* nimble wings, and even if it did there was only one Elspeth Roussel. It was hard to find that combination of *doesn't like to work too hard so won't climb the ranks* and *can thread a barge through a needle of any size, you choose*. The lack of organic matter floating around the *Gladiator* suggested the crew might still be alive in there. Somewhere. Survivors of that impact, huddling in sealed-off sections of a hulk that wouldn't fly.

An asteroid like that might have come with the bigger one. Been part of some cosmic event, sending shards to travel through the hard black until they hit something. Didn't feel *right*, though. Big rock like the one in orbit, they didn't just flow through space and cling to a planet like a baby calf to its mother.

"Hmm," said Nate.

"What?"

"Just ... take us in, Helm. We're not going to learn anything until we get there, and we need to get there to fix the *Tyche*. Just try not to crash into the big floating rock." Nate gave her a glance. "If that's not too much trouble."

"Have you," said El, "been told to get fucked today?"

"Not yet," said Nate. "Still. It's early." He clicked the comm on. "Kohl."

"Cap," said Kohl.

"You feel like shooting pirates?"

"You promised me pirates last time, and all we found was meatsicles on a ship without anything of real value. I got a few new holos for my collection, but that's it." Kohl sounded sour over the comm, Nate could *feel* the scowl.

"I never promised," said Nate. "But, you know. We've got a cored Navy destroyer out there. Odds are higher this time."

"Sounds fair," said Kohl. "Let me get my stuff."

GRACE WAS WAITING for them at the airlock. Nate did a double take, flipping up his visor. The woman was leaning against the closed airlock door, borrowed flight suit on, sword at her side.

Sword. Not a gun.

Nate had to admit, even in a loan flight suit of the wrong size, she caught the eye. Fit, trim, like the universe had built her to a specific high performance standard. Also, Nate hadn't ... well, it'd been a long time since he'd had the pleasure of a woman's company. *And it will continue to be longer, because you do not sleep with your crew.* And longer still even on shore leave, because he didn't have Kohl's view on, as the big man put it, *rentals*.

"You might," she offered, "need an Assessor."

"We might," said Nate. "We might also need another gun."

"I'm not a great shot," she said. "I work better with a blade."

Kohl grunted, his heavy armor shifting with a whine of servos. "Your funeral," he said. He'd racked a heavy plasma rifle to the side of his armor, the kind of thing it would take Nate two hands to lift on a good day.

"Kohl," said Nate. "Where'd you get that cannon?"

Kohl looked down at it, a fleeting moment of surprise crossing his face. "I think ... I think I got this one from a truck on that shitty mud ball we dropped medicine at about a year ago." Surprise turned into a frown. "You know? I've got so many. I don't remember."

"You've got a gun that was mounted on a truck?" said Grace.

"It was more of a large car," said Kohl. "They had it stuck on the roof, and it seemed a shame to leave it there. I mean, hell, they didn't need it anymore, you know what I mean?"

"I really think I do," said Grace, looking to Nate. "*Tyche* says there's nothing but hard vacuum on the other side of this lock. *Gladiator's* dock was clean, systems are go. She's still got power, but no air."

"Hmm," said Nate. "Okay. Kohl?"

"Yeah."

"You can go first," said Nate. "And if you see any closed doors, don't just open 'em. Knock first."

"Yeah," said Kohl. "Might be air inside. Knock us on our asses."

"There might be *crew* inside," said Nate. He sighed. "Kohl? There are probably lots of crew inside. They're not floating in space. Rescuing the Navy? Does us a lot of favors."

"That too," said Kohl. "Forgot about that."

"Great," said Nate. He turned on the comm. "*Tyche*? We're heading across. You know the drill. Don't open this door unless it's one of us knocking."

"Got you," said El. "I won't open it even if it's you if you've got a hundred assholes after you."

"No, you can open it then," said Nate. "Definitely open it then."

"What if they get on board?" said El.

"You know," said Nate, "I'm not liking where this conversation's going."

"We're wasting air," said Kohl. "There's killing to be done."

"*If* there are pirates," said Nate. "Pirates, Kohl."

"Don't worry," said Kohl. "I don't need another bounty."

"Another?" said Grace.

"Long story," said Nate. "Let's go." He slid his visor closed, checked his blaster again, and nodded to her. She cycled *Tyche's* inner lock, and they stepped through. His eyes were drawn to her sword, and he thought of his own, safe in his cabin. It'd been a long time since he'd held a blade.

Probably never would again, at that. His kind of sword drew the wrong kind of attention.

The *Tyche* said goodbye with a hiss of air, and the outer lock opened into hard vacuum. Nate took his first step onto the *Gladiator*.

HIS BREATH SOUNDED loud in his ears. It always did; that was the nature of breathing into a bucket, but it was more eerie when you were walking through the inside of a dead ship. Twice now, the *Ravana* first, and now the *Gladiator*. The *Ravana* had run *from* something in this system; an Icarus that flew too close to the sun, and everyone had died in their haste to get away. The *Gladiator* had run *to* something, and through some freak of chance an asteroid had cored her hull.

Probably an asteroid. Pirates didn't throw rocks as a general rule, but pirates might have taken advantage of a damaged ship.

The weird thing, if you wanted to call it that, was the lack of bodies. Pirates collected stuff, like weapons, fuel, supplies. They didn't collect corpses.

Decompression was a harsh master. The air and most things that weren't bolted down would get blown out whatever breach you had in your hull. It'd spit bodies and paperclips and coffee cups into the void. *Tyche* had seen nothing but paperclips and coffee cups, not a single floating body in space.

Stood to reason they'd find bodies in the breached sections, and living souls in areas with air. Nate shone his light at a door, open to vacuum. Lights were still on, the ship still had power, just no air, because of doors like this. It had been opened. Or it, and every other door they'd found, had failed to seal automatically when the hull breached.

"I don't get it," said Kohl. "All the doors are open. Who would go through a ship and open every door to space?"

"We won't find anyone alive here," said Grace. "This whole ship is dead." Nate watched as her hand gripped her sword hilt.

"Could be pirates," said Nate. "They might have got on board, same way we did. Popped the seals, vented the crew into space." He pointed to the wall with his light, the distinctive chalk-and-black of a plasma burn evident. "There was fighting."

"Fighting," said Kohl, "but not a lot of dying. I mean, look at this." He pointed at the blaster burn Nate had his light on. "Looks heavy. I'd say rifle, not pistol, you get me?"

"Looks like," agreed Nate.

"Last time I shot a man with a rifle, he came down in two big pieces. There was a lot of him that came out as dust, other parts that came out like grilled chunks. You see any grilled chunks, Cap?" He turned to look at Grace. "How about you? I'm not finding any grilled chunks. And that bothers me. Corridors of a ship, it's like shooting into a tunnel. You're either hitting the walls, or what you're shooting at. No one hit nothin' but wall, because they're ain't no bodies. Not Team Navy, and not whichever assholes came on their ship. Not even the *Navy* are that bad at shooting."

"Okay," said Nate. "Let's keep going. We've covered about a percent of the *Gladiator*. Might just be more we've yet to see."

"No," said Grace. "They're all gone." She shrugged. "Doesn't matter. Could still be salvage."

"IT'S NOT PIRATES," said Nate, looking around the hangar.

Still no bodies. What they had was a big hangar bay; the *Gladiator* was one of the Republic's configurable destroyers, able to be outfitted for a variety of different missions. She appeared to be in a *send-in-the-Marines* configuration, the bay holding space for two dropships. One was missing, and one was parked, doors open, fueled, and ready to fly. One was missing, sure, but that could just mean there was a dropship of Marines that someone had forgotten to pick up in all the excitement of their destroyer being ... destroyed.

"We should claim that as salvage," said Kohl. "Fetch a good price, a Navy dropship."

"Might draw some attention," said Grace. "'Hey, we'd like to sell you the dropship from a mission where all hands were lost. But trust us, we don't know anything about that mess. We just want to sell this fine, Republic-issue dropship. One careful owner.' What could go wrong?"

"When you put it like that," said Kohl, "a lot."

"Exactly," she said, moving across the bay. Stride certain, like she had nothing to fear. The way Nate figured it, that was true — not a soul was left on this ship. They'd been walking the *Gladiator* for two hours. They'd found the bridge (empty), Engineering (empty), sleeping quarters (empty). Hell, even the mess deck had been empty. That last was strange, as it showed signs of previous habitation — flash-frozen meals scattered about the room, like a bunch of the crew had been in the middle of chow when the hull breached. It didn't add up — breaching the hull would have slammed all the damn doors down and left survivors in the mess deck. But there were no survivors, just the remains of some of the Navy's finest crew meals. Which didn't look fine: standard soy-instead-of-meat, fake cornbread, a paste that might have pretended to be gravy before cold space had turned it into shriveled brown ice and fiber.

The officer's mess had fared no better. Except the food had been higher quality — still no meat, but someone had taken the time to prepare *almost* real food before they'd been spaced.

Except they hadn't been spaced. *Where were all the damn bodies?*

And now, the hangar. Fuel storage pods, full. Missiles still in the loaders, ready for deployment. And a fine Navy dropship. All of it was worth good Republic coin, and all of it was just ... *sitting* here. This ship had been cored by something, the crew had fought something else — which could be unrelated — and everything salvageable was still here. Hell, even the *gravity* was still on.

Hope would be thrilled, but it left a mystery. Time to see if there were solutions to that mystery.

"I'm going to check the breach," said Nate.

"Suit yourself," said Kohl.

"I'll come," said Grace.

Nate toggled his comm. "El?"

"Great, you're not dead," she said. "What's up?"

"Ship's clean," said Nate. "I'll send Kohl through it to seal the doors, give us some breathable air—"

"Hey," said Kohl.

"—and once he's done that, I want you to shimmy the *Tyche* in here. Hangar looks big enough if you can get the dropship out of the way." Nate held his hands up against the space, measuring. "*Should* be."

"Two things," said El. "One, dropship? Two, 'should be?'"

"You'll see," said Nate.

"While I'm doing all the hard work," said El, "where will you be?"

"We're headed up to check out how all this started," said Nate. "We'll be in touch."

"WE SHOULD GET YOU A DECENT SUIT," said Nate. "Bound to be something here, in the ship's stores. Nothing's been taken."

"I'll pick something out that matches the sword," said Grace. "Something black."

Something black. Nate had worn black, a long time ago. He'd worn the Emperor's black. Probably not the right time for that conversation. "Officers wear black," he said, "but don't go getting ideas. Doesn't matter what color your suit is. The *Tyche* has just one captain."

"Aye aye," she said. "You worry too much."

"About?" said Nate. They rounded a corner, the well-lit-yet-frozen interior of the *Gladiator* turning to a blackened corridor. The lights were out, not even emergency strips glowing. Nate crouched down, giving the floor a hard stare. He figured it was twisted a little, warped by something. That something was — it didn't take big detective skills — impact with an asteroid. "Getting close," he said.

"About the crew," said Grace. "They know who their captain is."

"They?" said Nate. "Planning on leaving us?"

There was a pause, then, "Not yet." Grace walked by his crouched form into the darkened corridor. Her tone sounded almost wistful. "You've given me no reason to jump ship."

"Aside from the trust issues?" said Nate.

"Aside from those," she said, turning back to him. "We going further?"

"Sure," said Nate. "Can't leave a job half-done." He stood, stepping into the lead again. The further he walked, the more obvious the twist in the decking was, like the *Gladiator* was made of something more pliable than metal and ceramic. Like she was soft, a dough still rising.

"What do you think hit this ship?" said Grace.

"Asteroid," said Nate. "Only thing that makes sense." He rounded another corner and stopped dead. He'd arrived at the breach, or part of it. The roof of the corridor had been deformed, pressed towards the deck by some massive force. He could see stars through gaps in the metal and shimmied closer. The metal was scorched, fragmented, cables and conduits exposed and torn like old floss. But it wasn't melted, not like a ship-to-ship laser, and there wasn't any evidence of plasma discharge. Just pure kinetics. Could be a railgun, but it didn't look angry enough. The *Gladiator* was still in one piece, and in Nate's experience a railgun big enough to core a ship like this wouldn't leave anything but shrapnel behind. Spit a chunk of tungsten at a large enough percentage of C, and you'd just leave a cloud of expanding debris, nothing larger than a golf ball. "Definitely asteroid."

Grace was fingering the edge of where the wall just ... *ended.* "We should check the ship's logs."

"We should," said Nate. "Want to try breaking into a Navy computer?"

"I've had worse first dates," said Grace, flashing him a quick grin.

It felt good. Not because Grace was smiling at *him*, but because she was *smiling.* He didn't feel like she'd done that on his ship. She was another lost soul like the rest of them, but maybe — like with Hope, and El, and even Kohl — they could find their way together.

NATE LEANED back against the console, facing Grace while she worked. "You didn't say you were an expert at cracking Navy systems," he said.

"Well, you never asked," she said. Her voice was distracted, her focus on the systems in front of her. "Also, I'm not an expert at cracking Navy systems. This one's not locked. The entire ship is open. Like they were all working on it, until they weren't."

Nate looked around the bridge. Acceleration couches, these ones top spec, good Republic issue. More modern than *Tyche's* design. He should get Kohl up here, tear a few out and install them into the *Tyche* while Hope was doing an overhaul in the hanger. *Make a mental note, more jobs to keep Kohl out of trouble.* Still no bodies. No blood. A couple plasma burns around the door they'd entered through. That door was interesting; it was torn free, the metal clipped and trimmed like it was plastic. It looked like it had been *sheared* away, not cut with a torch. Nate had good coin on whomever had taken the ship trying for the bridge first, taking out the command crew, and subverting the systems from here. "Found any logs?"

"Standard flight stuff," she said. "Confirmation they passed *Ravana.* Broke orbit. Wait. Wait."

"I'm waiting," he said. "Not patiently, but I'm waiting."

"They hit general quarters. Everything else is buried under a klick of crypto, but yeah. They sailed in here, said a how-you-doing to *Ravana*, settled into orbit, then went to war." She kept at the console for a few moments. "If I had time, I might get more, but logs under general quarters are officer grade. We'll need an officer's creds to get in."

Nate nodded, chewing that over, then walked to the front of the bridge. The view screens were open, and he could see out over the mauled front of the *Gladiator* the massive asteroid floating in front of her. "And there are no officers left on board," he said.

"There's no*body* left on board," said Grace. "Hell, and I know I sound like Kohl here, but we haven't even found a severed limb. No blood. No-one frozen to the hull. *Nothing*, Nate. There's no one here. Not anymore. Oh, hey now. Record of talking to ground, or trying to. No response. Give me a sec." There was the sound of Grace working the comms, then, "Absalom, this is *Gladiator*. Please respond." *Click-click* as she worked the systems behind him. "Absalom, this is *Gladiator*. Please respond."

"Let me guess," said Nate. "They don't want to say hi."

"Nothing but dead air," she said. He could hear her footsteps as she moved away from the console.

"I wonder where they all went," he said, still looking at the asteroid.

She had moved to stand next to him. A little closer than was usual, because when you were on a dead ship, being next to someone living was important. "So do I," she said. "But not enough to go over there."

"I wasn't planning on it," said Nate. "Well above our pay grade. We'll get the *Tyche* patched up, we'll bolt the transmitter to the side of the Bridge, and we'll get the fuck out of here."

"We could try talking to the planet again," she said. She pointed at the blue-green orb through the window. "They might know."

"They might," said Nate. "Let's get my ship fixed first, huh? If I need to run somewhere, I want a ship that'll pull more than a couple

Gs before it tears itself apart. Actually, scratch that. I've got a better plan." He keyed his comm. "El?"

"Helm here," she said.

"El, have you finished getting the dropship out of the hangar?"

"Sure have," she said.

"Great," he said. "I need you to put it back."

There was a click from the comm, then El said, "Please repeat, Cap. I thought I heard you say you needed me to fly the dropship back into the hangar I just flew it out of."

"You heard right," said Nate. "Something's off about this mission, so we're going to kill two birds with one stone. We'll load the transmitter on the dropship, fly it out to the Bridge, and bolt it on while Hope makes repairs to the *Tyche*."

"I hate you," said El. "That thing is a pig to fly."

"I hope you like bacon," said Nate, "because you're flying it out to the Bridge."

"I fly the *Tyche*," said El.

"*Tyche's* grounded," said Nate. "I need you to fly something else. C'mon, El. At least you'll be flying something with Navy colors again. Hey. I tell you what. You can take Grace with you." He looked at Grace, gave her a quick smile. "She's good enough with tech. You won't even need to leave the dropship."

"Sorry, cap," said El. "You're breaking up! *Crrssshhk* ... repeat ... can't hear..."

"Glad we all understand each other," said Nate, clicking the comm off.

"You want me to go with her?" said Grace. "Nothing to Assess, out there."

"Well, two reasons," said Nate. "First up, El ... frightens easy. I'd like someone out there with a steady hand."

Her eyes searched his. "My hands aren't that steady," she said. "Not when other people are afraid."

That's curious. "Maybe," he said. "But second? I think you're wrong."

"About?" she turned back out the window, and they both watched the massive asteroid turn in space.

"I think there'll be plenty of things to Assess." Nate pointed at the asteroid. "Just ... hell. I've got a feeling. Just don't go near that."

"Don't you worry," said Grace. "In and out, easy job, and then a nice completion bonus for everyone."

Yeah. Easy job. Life was too short to get mixed up in more Republic noise. Nate had had his fill of that back when he wore the Emperor's Black, and he hadn't even been in the war proper. Washed out, a metal hand on the stump of his arm, before it started. It'd be nice to have things *easy* for a change.

CHAPTER TWELVE

GRACE WAS glad she wasn't in the *Tyche*, sitting across from the Helm in Nate's chair. It would have felt like him, the shape he'd worn into it. She wondered how it felt to be him, the safety of his crew the most important thing above all else. She knew his chair would have reminded her of him, from the wear on the material through to the smell of it.

It wouldn't have been bad despite how much she would have wanted it to be. She didn't want to like this crew.

She *didn't* like this crew. It's just that they were *likable*.

El was working the dropship's controls, the holo in front of them quick and slick. It was more modern tech than sat inside the *Tyche*. "You good to go?"

Grace watched the autofactory in the *Gladiator* work on the *Tyche*. The dropship floated just outside the hangar doors, hard black around them, and it was easy to lose perspective out here. Forget just how big the *Tyche* was, even stripped bare, naked as a baby while the dawn of a foreign sun kissed her substructure. The *Gladiator* was huge, a monster, but for them she was a caring monster, nursing her smaller sister back to life. The autofactory's arms cradled the *Tyche's* frame, inner components laid bare. What was bent would be straight-ened. What couldn't be straightened would be reforged. She'd been re-armed — Kohl had found a cache of torpedoes, and they'd be fitted to the *Tyche*. Nate—

Call him the captain. Don't get close.

—the captain had said *what the Navy doesn't know won't hurt them*, and Hope had slid the armament order into the machines like it was nothing more than a new lick of paint. She'd said she was uploading schematics from the *Tyche* into the *Gladiator*, and seemed upset that the newer ship had known little about her older rival. Nate had asked *how long's this going to take*, and Hope had said *about twelve hours*, so Nate had asked *can it be done in less time*, and she'd said *sure, what don't you want done*, and that had been that. They had twelve hours before the *Tyche* had a refit courtesy of the *Gladiator's* clever machines.

"Hey," said El. "You with me?"

Grace shook herself. "Sorry. I just ... I get the feeling like we might not see her again."

"The *Tyche*?" El gave a snort. "She's not going anywhere."

Exactly what I meant. But Grace said, "Yeah, of course. I'm good. Let's punch it."

"'Punch it?'"

"Or whatever it is," said Grace, waving a hand out the window, taking in the universe and everything in it, "you do."

"We're in a tin can with a belly full of lead. We're not punching jack. We'll waddle out to the Bridge, and you'll bolt said lead to it, and we'll fly home for a beer." El shook her head. "'Punch it.' You watch too many holos."

But Grace picked up *pride/satisfaction*, and she smiled. "What-ever, stick. You want to fly, fly."

The dropship grumbled around them, none of the *Tyche*'s noise insulation. This was pure military, enough room for a handful of Marines or just enough room for a transmitter. No comforts here, a thin metal skin between them and the hard black. Grace leaned back as El worked the console, the *Gladiator* seeming to pull up and away as they curved left and down from her. A trip to the Bridge, then hit the planet, grab some beers, and maybe — just *maybe* — find out what the hell was going on.

AT THE HALF-WAY POINT, El had flipped the ship, begun the deceleration burn, keeping an even 1G on their backs at all time. The dropship didn't have an Endless Drive, no positive energy field generator to give them artificial gravity. Without thrust, they were bobbing corks out here. Grace had been on a few ships and knew there was a tendency from long-time spacers to cut thrust down a couple notches. Once you got used to being weightless some of the time, gravity's tireless clutch could become ... *wearisome.*

El wasn't one of those pilots. Grace broke the companionable silence between them. "Born on a crust, then?"

"Yeah," said El. "I love flying, but I love solid rock under my feet when I'm drinking beer. You know how it is."

"I know how it is," agreed Grace. She was getting *focus/distracted* in even measure from El. The Helm wanted to focus, but didn't want to be rude. "You coming out to help me work on this thing when we get there?"

"Hell no," said El. "My hands are too soft for hard labor."

"Great," said Grace. "I'll be trying not to die in space while you sit here. You need a holo or something while I'm doing all the work?"

"I'm good," said El, but with a smile. "You know Grace, I don't know why Nate let you onboard."

"Needed an Assessor," Grace said, but felt herself tensing inside. *Keep it casual. Relax.* She was picking up nothing hostile from El, which made it easier. *Breathe. Just* breathe.

"He really didn't," she said. She looked like she was about to say something else, but the dropship chimed, the holo lighting up. "Look at that, we're there. An hour out, an hour back, and you've got ten hours to bolt that transmitter up to the Bridge."

"I can do it in five," said Grace.

"Hope could do it in five," said El.

"Hope could do it in one," said Grace. "I'm no Engineer. I'll make it in five."

"Bet on it?"

"If you like," said Grace. *Win or lose, you build trust.* "What's the wager?"

"One Earth beer," said El. "Your choice of brand."

"You're on," said Grace.

"Outstanding," said El. She clicked a few switches on the console, then leaned back. "We're here. Timer starts now."

"See you in five hours," said Grace, shimmying out of the acceleration couch. She slipped the visor on her helmet closed — officer black, sleeker than the *Tyche's* castoff she'd had before — and went back to open the dropship's doors to the hard black.

THE GUILD'S Bridge hadn't been visible from the cockpit because of their deceleration burn. El had left the rear of the dropship angled towards the Bridge to make access easier for Grace. *Maybe she doesn't want to win the bet either.* Grace opened the back of the dropship to space, and stood in awe.

Never been this close before.

The Bridge was a massive ring, metal and ceramicrete stretching away, a hula-hoop that would be at home around the girth of the Gladiator. *The Guild builds these things. Humans* built *this.* It wasn't strictly true: they sent robots out here to construct the Bridges. Automated factories at a larger scale than the *Gladiator* had constructing wormhole gates. Bolt a big enough reactor to it and you could move any mass instantaneously through space. The Guild made cash based on the mass they shifted — and no one lied about the mass they carried, because the Guild powered the gate for that specific load. If you tried to cheat them, they'd shut the gate down as your ship was half-way through. A ship shorn in two by a collapsed wormhole wasn't something Grace had seen first-hand, but it didn't sound like a great time.

She clicked the controls on her suit's arm, instructing the autoloader carrying the transmitter to follow her. Her suit knew where to go, setting her on a course for the transmitter mount on the side of the Bridge. While she took the two-minute journey through the hard black, she looked around her. Absalom Delta, blue-green beauty hanging in the sky. The *Gladiator*, an almost invisible spec. The asteroid, still visible to the naked eye. That rock was *huge*. How in all hell had it got there? Rocks didn't just *orbit planets*. The ones that did were called moons, and didn't arrive unannounced.

Her suit chimed, and she turned back to the Bridge. This close, it was a massive slab of metal she could get her mag boots on, a thing so big that her mind said *it's just a different kind of ground* rather than *it's a huge ring in space*. The boots *clumped* onto the metal, the autoloader following behind her like an obedient hound. They arrived at the installation point for the transmitter. Grace looked at it, then clicked her comm. "El, you there?"

"No, I left you out here to die alone. I'm already on my way back to the *Tyche*." Not the *Gladiator*, because that wouldn't be home. Not for any of them, because you didn't make your home in graveyards or murder scenes or whatever it was.

"Okay great. Look, while you're flying away, can you point your nose at me and tell me what you see?"

"Sec." Humming, then, "Huh. Yeah, that's what we saw before. Transmitter's there."

"I know, right?" Grace looked up at the transmitter *already installed in the Bridge* and let her breath out. "We came all this way for nothing."

"Well, cool," said El. "I mean, you win the bet, so beer's on me."

"That sounds like half a job," said Grace. "We don't know why the Bridge isn't working."

"Probably won't, without Hope," said El. "Also, we don't get paid for *why*. We get paid for *what* and *how*."

"Uh huh," said Grace. She told the autoloader to hold steady and moved around the transmitter, boots *clumping* with each step. Like walking in treacle, these were. She'd hate to have a fight in zero G. No way to dance with her sword, just a lot of ugly brute movements. Kohl would be right at home. *Okay, there.* A console was set into the side of the Bridge's transmitter. She pulled a powered multitool from her belt, ready to work on the console's protective housing. Before she could begin, the housing drifted open.

"Uh," said Grace, looking at the console within.

"The suspense is killing me," said El.

"I thought you didn't want to know *why*," said Grace. Her fingers traced a set of cables clipped from the transmitter computer back to a small device.

"I said we didn't get paid for it. By proxy, it means I don't want to work for it. But if you've done the work already, it would seem insensitive of me not to share in your victory. Go on. Tell me what you found."

"Looks like a bypass," said Grace.

"A what?"

"Bypass," said Grace. "Someone's subverted the transmitter's controller."

"Why would someone do that?" said El. "Out here, the Bridge is everything. It's how they get food. Meds. Holo shows. It's how they *get home*."

"Yeah," said Grace. "It's how they get home." She swallowed. *And they don't want to get home.* She didn't know why she thought it, but she knew it was true. These people had broken their own Bridge.

"Well, just yank the bypass," said El. "Job done. And maybe we can sell this other one for salvage."

"Won't help," said Grace. "Not anymore. These things run on a schedule. A probe comes through to get the Guild's roster for the next world-to-world Bridge schedule. No probe through, no roster. This whole thing is just dead metal without one." She toed the ring beneath her.

"What about the new transmitter? Yank the schedule from that. Put it in here?"

"I thought you didn't want to know why?" Grace started back towards the autoloader.

"We're still on what and how," said El. "*What* is the roster. *How* is a download."

"One thing," said Grace. She paused in front of the autoloader. "Anyone could have done what we're doing. The *Ravana*. The *Gladiator*. Anyone. And no one did. Why?"

"Not the why we're being paid for," said El.

"I suppose not," said Grace. She pried open the console on the transmitter held by the autoloader. Ran a finger over the components within, cards slotted in for swappable replacement. Central control, no, Bridge dynamics, no, Guild protocols, no — *ah*. Bridge roster. She pulled the card, shut the transmitter's console, and moved back to the already-installed transmitter.

"Here goes nothing." She yanked the bypass, tossing the components into the void behind her. Pulled the installed roster, tossed that aside as well, then slapped the replacement roster home. Lights blinked, reds turning to green, and she smiled. "And there's a tidy completion bonus."

The Bridge *thrummed* under her feet, the systems doing automated checks. Nothing else happened — it'd be too coincidental for words for this Bridge to have a rostered jump the moment they enlivened it again. The computer would try to talk to the planet, automated systems trying to handshake with other automated systems. Shame there was nothing but dead air. The computer wouldn't care, going through its paces just like its designers had intended.

"Grace," said El. "Grace, I think you need to get back here."

"I was coming anyway—"

"No, like, *now*," said El. "The *Gladiator's* fired ordnance our way."

"What?"

"Hold on. I'll swing by. Catch you." Grace saw the dropship's engine's flare, the ship spin in space, headed her way. "There's not a lot of time. Don't ask questions, just jump, okay. I got you."

Grace's mind tried to work the options. There must have been some kind of automated protocol. Something the command crew of the *Gladiator* set up. Or had they missed someone onboard? Someone hiding out? Someone who'd snuck into fire control? Grace crouched, kicked off the surface of the ring, casting herself free. *Trust, trust.* She made them trust *her*, not the other way around.

She turned through space, saw the space inside the ring below her flicker, the starscape beyond changing to a different starscape. The Bridge was open. A flash of movement caught her eye, a port on the surface of the Bridge yawning wide. A small probe shot out, dived through the Bridge, and was ... still visible to her, but somewhere else. The last communications from this system, queued for delivery. Now sent.

Nothing unusual about that, but it didn't stop Grace feeling a touch of dread. They didn't want to go home ... what could they have wanted to say to the people they never wanted to see again?

She stopped thinking about that as the dropship slewed into her view. Grace glimpsed El through the cockpit, the Helm working the ship like a dervish. The dropship looked like it would hit her before it spun in space, the back hold open, a yawning mouth. Grace wanted to scream, because this wasn't how trust *worked*, and then a flare of thrusters cut the dropship's speed and she was *inside*, helmet clanging against the interior wall of the hold, the doors already closing against the hard black. Safe bright lights were around her as she panted, gasping for breath, clawing at the wall, trying to convince herself she was alive.

"Hold on," came El's voice, and the dropship pushed hard. Grace tumbled in the bay, sliding across the floor. Her trailing hand caught a strap. *Safe. You're safe.*

"You're fucking crazy!" yelled Grace.

"Yell at me later," said El's voice, tense, hard. Grace caught *fear* and then *excitement* and then *fear/fear/fear*.

Grace hung onto the strap, the dropship's drives working hard. They'd be pulling 3Gs at least. It'd be close all this thing had to give, but it was enough to make her sixty kilo frame feel like a hundred and eighty. She wound the strap around her wrist, crying out with the pain of it. She stabbed her boot against a wall for more purchase, anything, just a toehold to stop her from yanking her arm out of its socket. Grace couldn't see her hand through the suit's glove, but knew the straps would dig into her skin, leaving red welts, cutting off blood flow.

The chatter of comms. Nate's voice. "El? El, the ship ... the *Gladiator's* fired on the Bridge. Get out!"

"On it," said El. "Cap, what did you fire?"

"Working on it," he said.

Kohl's voice: "Straight up nuke, looks like. Not a crustbuster."

"More than one," said Nate. "Five torpedoes in the wind. Haul ass."

"Targeting me?" said El.

"Maybe," said Kohl. "We're just watching the show here. There's no ... hell. I reckon not, but it's not going to matter if you don't get clear."

"Did you get Grace?" said Nate. "Is Grace okay?"

Grace felt something in her shoulder give, and she bit down on the pain. He hadn't asked *did you get the job done* or *what happened out there*. He'd asked about her. Like she was one of his crew.

She wasn't. She *wasn't*. They would hate her if they knew what she was. *Focus on the pain. It's all you've got. It's all you've ever had.*

"Grace is here," said El. "Now let me fly." Then, on the local comm channel she said, "Grace?"

Grace reached her free arm up to the strap, grabbed it to let some of the load off her tortured hand. She hissed through her teeth. "Not. In. A ... Couch."

"I know. You heard what's coming?"

"Heard." Grace flailed her other leg around, caught the edge of a floor mount. Braced herself. She was panting, the effort of not falling at 3 gravities into the back of the dropship taking its toll. "Torpedoes."

"That's right," said El. "We've got five. Just passing ... *now*. They'll hit the Bridge in seconds. Moving a lot faster than we are."

No time for too many words. Hard to talk, anyway. Grace coughed at the pressure against her — no acceleration couch, God*damn* it — and said. "Thanks. For. Not leaving me. To die."

"Don't thank me yet," said El. Then she said, "Impact."

A second passed, then another, before the wave of the explosion hit the dropship, the little craft shaking and rattling around them. The explosion wave grew in force, the dropship bucking and shaking like a bottle in stormy seas. *What are the odds of being near two nuclear events in the same week? This has got to be some kind of record.* The shaking of the dropship grew, and there was a groaning from the substructure around them. El was still pouring on thrust, encouraging the little ship to fly, fly, *fly* before the maw of the hurricane of fire and radiation behind them.

The bucking dropped to shaking, the shaking to a rattle, then the ship was still. Thrust cut, and Grace almost cried with relief. She gasped inside her helmet, then unwound the strap from her arm. The pain as circulation returned made her grit her teeth. It felt like her arm had been mauled by wild dogs, and she would need to get that checked out.

"You okay?" El's voice was softer now. Tired.

No. "Yes," said Grace. "I'm okay." She was alive, and these people had kept her that way.

Maybe she was okay for the first time in a long while.

CHAPTER THIRTEEN

NATE SHIFTED from foot to foot, the anxiety building in him. He'd sent El and Grace off on a simple task. They were supposed to have the *easy* job. Grace was new crew, and El — well, she was always a bit gun-shy. When the bridge of the *Gladiator* had lit up like Christmas morning, target locks showing across the central holo, targeting where he'd sent his crew — *where* he *had sent his* crew — he'd almost had a heart attack. Even Kohl had trouble with it, mashing consoles and trying to get the ship to respond.

Nada.

He'd been on the comm to El. She'd said they were fine, and when he'd asked what that meant, she said it meant that they were alive but Grace had dislocated her shoulder. And then she'd asked him to stop bugging her and do something useful *like making sure the* Gladiator *won't blow us out of the sky.*

Like he could. The ship was on auto, a series of commands embedded before they'd arrived doing whatever they were told to.

Yellow warning lights strobed. The dropship was docking at an external airlock, puffs of the thrusters visible through the viewports as El guided it in. Automated clamps reached out, gripped the craft, and held it close ... held it *safe*. The airlock sealed against the hard black, the interior pressurizing. He waited on the gangway, hand on the railing.

The dropship opened, El walking out with a pissed-off expression and anger in her stride. Nate was about to say something, but she spoke first. "What the *fuck* was that about, Cap?" She jerked her arm back at the dropship. "We almost died, for Christ's sake."

"I—"

"We need to get this ship under control," she said. "We need to be in control of all the guns that can kill us."

"I—"

"Hell," she said, sighing. "I'm not angry at you. I'm just *angry*."

"Good," said Nate. "I'm pretty angry too."

"You're frightened," said Grace, from behind El. She was cradling her arm, face pale. "We're all frightened."

"I'm—"

"Because," said Grace, "nothing here is as it should be. We're on a ghost ship. The planet is silent. The Bridge has been destroyed by plans laid in place before we arrived. My usual gigs aren't this ... *exciting*. Hell," she said, looking at her boots, "our reactor blew. What are the odds of that?"

What are the odds of that. "That's ... an interesting question," said Nate.

"It feels to me like someone doesn't want us here," said Grace. "If not someone, then something."

"Something?" said Nate. "What are you talking about?"

"Nothing," said Grace, pushing past him. "Everything hurts. I'll be in the sickbay." She paused, then looked at El. "Not bad, Stick, not bad. For a rookie, I mean."

"You don't know what you're saying," said El. "You're delirious. You've never seen flying that good."

"Maybe," said Grace with a tired smile. "You'll get out of flight school one day." And then she was gone in a clang of boots on the walkway.

Nate looked after her, then back at El. "You seem to be bonding well."

"We almost died," said El. "It'll do that to you."

Nate winced. "You up to a bit of investigation?"

"Maybe," she said. "What kind?"

"The kind where we try and get this ship to stop shooting at us at random, inopportune times. The kind where we feel like we can fly the *Tyche* out of here without her being turned into a ball of expanding dust." Nate shrugged. "You used to fly these things, El. You've got to know a few secrets."

"I know a few secrets, sure," she said. "We need something. Anything. If we don't have someone's sub-dermal implant, we need an ID. Hell, even their underwear with the right bar code."

"Underwear we can do," said Nate. "We've got all the underwear we'll ever need."

KOHL WAS STANDING outside the commander's cabin, the plasma cutter resting on the deck beside him. He looked bored as Nate approach through the haze of smoke. "Hey," said Kohl.

"Hey," said Nate. He looked at the hole Kohl had cut in the wall of the ship, conduit and pipework and insulation all sliced through. Inside, the commander's private space. A table, made of wood, dark and polished like a mirror. A cabinet that looked like it held liquor, which would be against regs, but what could you do to the *commander*? Ports showing a view of space. The commander's room was under the bridge on the *Gladiator* just like Nate's cabin was under the flight deck on the *Tyche*. "Nice cabin."

"I haven't been inside," said Kohl. "Don't even know why we're here."

"Underwear," said Nate.

"The fuck?" said Kohl.

El sauntered up, clapped the big man on the arm. "Don't sweat it," she said. "It'll all become clear soon."

Nate pushed himself through the hole in the wall. The door wouldn't open to him because he wasn't the commander. He didn't even know who the commander was. What kind of face they wore, what kind of career they'd had. How their crew had viewed them. They had an empty room with a few nice things to gauge the kind of person the commander of the *Gladiator* had been. In here, hopefully, was underwear.

Strictly speaking it wasn't underwear they were after, but under*clothes*. Flight suits were worn over the top of an insulating layer. They'd keep you cool in the heat, or warm enough in the cold. The latter was very important if you were found floating without a suit in the hard black. They were supposed to stop your blood boiling out of your eye sockets, staying off the flash-freezing of your body a few more precious seconds. Underclothes had other benefits like being flame retardant, and could duct electricity around the fabric rather than through the wearer — the biggest threats aboard a ship were fire and electrocution, next to dying while trying to scream in vacuum. Trying to scream was good though, because holding your breath wasn't great. Nate's training back when he wore the Emperor's Black was to hyperventilate. Something about aspiration slowing the blood boiling in your veins.

So, these suits were supposed to slow all that down. The Republic thought of everything.

They even thought of what would happen if you *died*, your last moments of terror, in a vacuum. On fire, after being shocked to death. If you were turned into some kind of burned-to-carbon flash-frozen horror, the suits carried implanted IDs, tech that would mark your name, rank, and serial number. El wanted to use one of those IDs to get a foothold into the ship's systems. It was a long shot, but maybe the commander's backup password really *was* 'password.'

There was always a way in. Voice recognition couldn't be relied on, because your throat might have been burned in a fire. Fingerprints might be gone in a machinery accident. But an ID? Given some time it might get them in. All they needed was a little luck.

HE'D GIVEN the suit to El to wear. Turns out the commander had been smaller and female. El had put the suit on, led the way to the bridge, and got to work.

Two hours had passed, and she was slumped over a console, head resting in her hand. They'd tried pass*words*, like cucumber and albatross and xylophone. They'd tried variations of the commander's date of birth. They'd tried popular holo stars born around that time, and then ones who performed when she would have been a teenager. They'd tried the name of the ship. Then they'd started on pass*phrases*, and then El had said she wanted a break.

"Try one more," said Nate.

"The rain in Spain falls mainly on the plains," said El, not looking up.

Nate typed it out. The console gave a flat blare. *INCORRECT.* He looked at the word — the same word he'd seen what felt like ten thousand times over the last couple hours — and felt a flare of anger. "God*damn* it!" He slammed his fist on the console. "We just want a break. Is it too much to ask? One tiny, small, sliver of—"

"*Gladiator*, this is Absalom Delta. Come in *Gladiator*. Do you copy?" It was the console, the comm light flashing. An incoming transmission. From the planet.

Just a little bit of luck.

Nate blinked at the console, then grinned at El. "Hey. Hey hey. Luck."

"*Gladiator*, this is Absalom. Do you read me?" The voice was male, talking a little too fast. Inexperienced with the comms? In trouble? No surprises he was feeling some pressure. Hell, everyone was most likely dead, and that would change your world view.

Nate clicked the comm controls. "Absalom, this is *Gladiator*. Kinda."

There was a pause. "Kind of?"

"Kinda, yeah," said Nate. "This is Captain Nathan Chevell of the free trader *Tyche*. We're—"

"Great, great. Captain. We don't have time for the usual spiel. What's the state of the *Gladiator*?" Nate had been wrong: the voice wasn't *afraid*, just *terse*. Might be a man used to being in charge, stuck in a place where there was no one to be in charge of anymore.

"Uh." Nate looked around the bridge. El, now sitting upright but still tired. Kohl on the floor, by all appearances asleep. The empty acceleration couches. *Careful, Nate*. The man at the end of this line could be responsible for all this. "It's complicated," he said.

"I was afraid of that," said the man, "and I admire your discretion. Captain, this is Rear Admirable Melvin Penn. I'm conscripting you and your crew to bring your ship to this planet within the hour and evac me."

Rear Admiral. Nate looked at the comm. "Penn? Penn. We're going to have a small problem with that."

"Excuse me?"

"Hell, now," said Nate, "let's not get off on the wrong foot. But we've got problems of our own. Our ship, she's hurt bad. We're a good six hours away from being flight ready. And last time we tried to do something up here, the *Gladiator* fired on my crew."

"You tried to start the Bridge," said Penn. "I know. I saw it. That was under my orders."

"You tried to blow up my crew?"

"I ordered contingencies to stop unauthorized egress from the Absalom system."

"You'll kill anyone who tries to leave," said Nate.

"Unauthorized persons," said Penn. "Captain? We don't have a lot of *time*. I'm holed up in an air duct. They're trying to find me. Always trying to find me. I need ... it's vital to the safety of our species you come to Absalom and get me. I'll unlock the *Gladiator* from here. Give me your transponder, and you won't be fired on."

"Wait," said Nate. "Who's trying to find you? And what do you mean, 'won't be fired on?'"

"There's very little time," said Penn. "But I mean the *Gladiator* is set to fire on anyone who approaches or leaves the planet."

Nate looked at El, made an O with his mouth. "And what do you mean by 'them?' *Who's down there with you?*"

There was a pause on the comm, then Penn said, "Everyone, of course. Everyone else."

NATE TIGHTENED the straps on the dropship's acceleration couch. He gave a glance to Grace, who sat at his side. Face still pale, but firm. She'd found something hard and strong in the medbay, something that put iron in her stride and made her forget the pain of her shoulder. Which is what he needed. It's what they all needed. Kohl was behind them in the dropship's hold, armored up. He'd collected a rotary laser from the *Gladiator's* armory, an ostentatious weapon that only Kohl could use with a straight face. Or lift, because it was designed to be mounted on a tripod. He'd found it, said something like *'everyone' means we need a lot of firepower*, and had gone to sit in the hold with a happy expression.

Hope was still working on the *Tyche*. He'd looked her in the eye and said *you make my ship fly again* and she'd just hugged him and said *you try not to die*. El had frowned at that, gave him a salute, and said she'd come get them as long as *there's not too much fire going in your direction*.

The dropship backed out of the bay, Nate's hands on the sticks. He wasn't a pilot as good as El, but good enough for a simple drop. He turned the ship, hoping that Penn had been true to his word and told the *Gladiator* not to fire. After Penn had unlocked the remaining bridge controls, standing the ship down, they'd seen how much automated combat the *Gladiator* had done. And it was a lot, most of her torpedo bays for ship to ship combat empty. A lot of use of lasers. People had, what, tried to flee Absalom? Land on it? It wasn't clear. Penn hadn't trusted them with any of the *Gladiator's* mission details — *need to know* — but the ship's inventory had been worked hard.

Whatever was going on to whomever was involved, they were not fucking around.

The dropship kicked hard as he pushed the acceleration into the red. "Here goes nothing," he said.

"It's better to be in a chair for this," said Grace. "Last time … anyway. It's better with a chair."

"Grace," said Nate. "You seem to be good with people."

She gave a half-laugh, half-something-else, none of it happy. "It's … useful."

"Penn," said Nate, "will kill us all and leave us to die."

"I figure the same thing," she said. "What I'm not sure about is why we're going down to get him."

The dropship trembled as they touched atmosphere. The windows of the shuttle were bathed in red, orange and white as they burned a bright streak towards the planet's surface. Nate watched it for a minute before he spoke. "I'm not a great supporter of the Republic."

"What with all the flag-waving and cheering, I'd never have guessed," said Grace.

"There's a few things we see eye to eye on," said Nate. "But they killed a good man once. A … friend of mine. I know how they work. I know what they are."

"Still doesn't explain why we're going down to get one of their head assholes out," said Grace. "To my mind, it makes this more confusing."

"The Republic used to be the Empire," said Nate. "The Old Empire. Same people, you see? Just different assholes in charge. If there's people down there, we need to get them out." He thought of the emptiness of the *Gladiator*. "If the people on that crust are trying to kill Penn, I want to know why."

"There's no bonus in it," said Grace, looking out the window.

"For me, there is," said Nate. But he wasn't sure if it was true. Not anymore. He hadn't worn the Emperor's Black for a long time. Since he lost his hand — at least he got to keep the sword — he'd not felt like the people in charge much wanted his help. That was fine, but ... *but*. "Grace, there's a whole planet of people here. They're not in charge of anything. We ... just need to make sure they're here for the right reasons."

"If they're not?" she turned, eyes searching his face. "You don't strike me as a man into politics, Nate. What, you got your hand torn off because you believed in something, and now you're angry about it. No, don't interrupt. I can see it in your face. It comes off you in waves. It's in this crew you've got. The Helm who can't cut it in the *Republic's* Navy. But good enough for *your* fleet. The thug who doesn't take orders from anyone in charge. Sometimes not even you. The Engineer whose lover left her bankrupt and on the run from Republic justice. But you've given her safe harbor." She turned away from him. "I'm good with people," she said. "I'm *very* good with people."

"How do you know about Hope?" said Nate.

"I'm good with systems too," she said. "I need to know about where I crew."

"Why?" said Nate. "Person with your talents should be able to find a home on any boat. Why my crew?"

Grace turned back to him, something nasty in her voice. But nasty at him or her, he couldn't tell. "Because I need you. Because you need me. All there is to it."

"That's not all there is to it," said Nate. "Who are you, Grace Gushiken?"

"Just an Assessor," said Grace, and Nate could *feel* the lie this time.

THE DROPSHIP SCUDDED over the surface of the water under Nate's guidance. They were approaching the dock from the sea. Absalom was beautiful, the water a clear blue, the clouds puffs of white cotton in the sky above them. He could see the land as they approached, green and lush and vibrant. A paradise at the edge of Republic space, open for all colonists who wanted a fresh start on a clean planet.

He gave the thrusters a blast as they came in, bringing the belly of the ship in at an angle, then settling it down flat on the landing pad. "I would say," said Nate, "that this is the weirdest spaceport I've ever seen."

Kohl was already up and at his shoulder, looking out through the cockpit. "Where the fuck is everybody?"

"There's no one here," said Grace. He brow furrowed. "There's ... no one here."

The comm had stayed silent as they were on approach, Nate's attempts to hail the planet failing. There was no one there, or no one cared to speak to them. Either way, they may as well have been the only humans out here on the edge of humanity's reach. He ran a hand through his hair, then said, "Well, hell with it. Let's go find Penn."

The doors of the dropship opened to sweet, sweet air. So clean. None of the smell of human industry — no ozone, no chemicals, nothing burning. Quiet. There was a light breeze, but no noise carried on it. A bird hovered in the air, slipstreaming and happy. "This looks like paradise," said Nate, "so why is my skin crawling?"

"General vibe," said Kohl. He hopped past Nate and landed on the landing pad with a clank of power armor. "Like, because everyone is dead everywhere we've been in the past three days, so you know. General vibe."

"You're saying it's me," said Nate. "Are you saying it's me?"

"Maybe," said Kohl. He squinted at Nate. "You keep promising pirates to shoot, but you're not delivering, Cap. You hear me?"

"Sorry," said Nate, stepping down. *Goddamn but 1.1G feels heavier than it should.* On a good day — not too much booze that week — he sauntered around at 85kgs in Earth's standard 1G. Here, that felt closer to 95kg. He was glad he'd only packed his blaster, strapped at his side. No sword. *Probably won't use that damn thing ever again.* Grace followed him down. Nate turned back to the dropship, closed the lock, and coded it with their IDs. He didn't want someone stealing their only ride out, because there weren't any other ships here at the spaceport. Not one. Not a dropship, not a shuttle, not a lifter. Zero ships. Which wasn't a good sign for a spaceport, as it left it without purpose. He tapped on the console at his wrist. "Okay, here we are." The holo spun in the air between them, a map laid out between the space port and the admin center. "Penn says he's in there. Got the thing locked up tight. I say it looks like five klicks of walking, we grab the Rear Admiral, and take off. If our luck holds a little longer ... well. What could go wrong?"

Grace shrugged, sliding her sword behind her, and walked off. Kohl made a noise that sounded like an idling engine, then set off after her.

At least Penn had promised a heavy bonus for this. If they could avoid him spacing them *and* get paid, this trip might end up being profitable for them all.

Like he'd said. What could go wrong?

"IT'S TOO HOT," said Kohl, rumbling along ahead of them. That rotary laser was locked behind him, the automount holding it out of the way, a backpack full of angry wasps should the situation arise. His power armor clanked and whined as he moved. Sweat and a surly expression vied for dominance on Kohl's face.

"You're just fat and heavy," said Nate, at Grace's side. She hid a smile. *Don't engage. Don't be* with *them. Be the eye of the storm.* She didn't need her visor down. Grace was used to this dance; she knew this music. She just needed a way out. A new crew to join.

It wasn't looking good, though. Where *was* everyone? Penn had said people were after him, but this place was like an empty set before the holo started shooting.

Or an empty set, after the shooting was over.

Say what you will about Kohl, but the man wasn't *fat*. He looked solid, like a piece of concrete. Drop him in the ocean and he'd sink like a stone. Grace felt the heat of the day already, the heavier than normal gravity doing her no favors. Too much time on a ship, not enough time in the exercise room. Kohl walked through it like none of it touched him at all; not the extra Gs, not the laser, and not the rising heat of the day.

Her hand found the hilt of her sword. She winced, her shoulder giving her an ungentle stab of pain as she moved. *That's not good.*

What really was *not good* was the lack of people. She couldn't feel anyone. Not any anger. Not any fear. No petty jealousies, no egos, no one trying to put one over on anyone else. If she didn't have the touch of uncertainty caressing her spine, giving her shivers through the sweat, she'd have thought this was paradise.

Grace Grace Grace Grace Grace.

She whirled, hand still on the hilt of her sword. No one. Not one soul in front of the place that looked like it sold cold ice cream on a hot day. Not a standing, breathing human in the med center, not injured, not healthy, just not *there.* A casino stood with a door ajar, holos promising a jackpot every day, except there wasn't anyone there to win.

"You okay?" Nate's hand was on her arm. She looked at it, and he pulled it away. "Sorry."

"No, you're good," she said. It wasn't his metal hand, and it had felt … nice.

No. It hadn't felt nice. You're not with this crew. You are Grace Gushiken, and you walk alone.

"See something?" said Kohl, turning in place. Taking in the empty buildings, the shops devoid of customers. Empty cars.

"I … no," she said. "I … thought. I thought I heard something." Grace ran a hand over her face. It came away wet with sweat. The extra weight and the heat was getting to her; what should have been a warm summer's day was a hot workout. "I … want to hear something."

"Yeah," said Nate.

Ahead of them, a bus sat in the road. It was empty, but the door was open at the front. It was stretched long and thin, solar collectors making the exterior gold and shiny. On a hunch, she entered, the shade promising a little respite from the sun.

The bus was a standard auto, no pilot's chair, just seats along the aisle. Holos shimmered on the walls, ads for products that would make you ... *whatever you wanted*. The lighting strips in the bus were out, the interior painted by shifting colors of reds, blues, whites, greens from the holos. It was empty, but it wasn't *unscathed*. The first seats she saw were rent, memory foam and material shredded. A faint muddy stain that might have been blood. Hard to tell with the shifting, muted lighting. She walked further into the bus. Grace's gaze settled on a scrap of golden color, and she bent to pick it up.

A child's toy, a small lion with a happy tongue and a fluffy mane. Dropped, lost, left here in this bus. She put the toy down, looked at other seats. More belongings: clutches, satchels, bags, a coat. There, a paper bag full of rotting vegetables. This bus had been carrying people, and those people were *gone*. Like they'd been sucked from the surface of Absalom and ... just *taken*.

She heard a scream behind her and spun. A woman, ravening, eyes wide, spittle coating her chin. Mad, desperate eyes. Not crazy, but hungry and afraid. Hands curled into claws, reaching for Grace's face. Grace dropped into a crouch, *iaido* making her motion fluid. *One perfect strike*. Her sword cleared the scabbard, as perfect a *sayabiki* as she could manage in the cramped bus giving her strike speed, her sword cutting *out* and *up*, finishing its motion exactly where she wanted it to. The seats of the bus to her left were sheared through by the blade, toppling to the floor.

Other than that, she cut nothing but air. The woman was gone, like she'd never been.

There was no one there.

There had been no one there.

Nate scrambled into the bus, taking in her sword still held high. His blaster was out, eyes scanning the bus. Seeing no one. "Heard something," he said.

"Did a ... woman go past you?" said Grace.

"A what?"

"Woman," said Grace. "Crazy eyes. Hungry."

"No," said Nate. "There's no one here."

Sweat ran down her face. The bus was hot, too hot, and too dark. She sheathed her sword, walking to the front. Past Nate, past his concern, past his feelings of *care/protect/anxious* for her. She didn't need his protection. She didn't need him at all. "Let's go," she said. "It was nothing."

If only that were true.

THEY WERE about half way to the admin center.

Grace blinked in the light, covering her eyes with a hand. Up ahead, there was a man. Normal looking kind of guy, a haircut that was in vogue on one planet or another, long on one side and shaved on the other. Loose shirt, loose pants, like you'd want if you lived on this planet, in this gravity, in this weather. She frowned. "You see that guy up ahead?"

"Holy shit," said Kohl. "Some kind of unicorn." His power armor clanked as he walked forward. "Hey, buddy. Yeah, you, asshole. The dickhead with the bad haircut. You know I'm talking to you."

"Kohl," said Nate, "why don't you let me handle this?"

"Suit yourself," said Kohl. "I've warmed him up for you."

Nate was walking ahead of them, approaching the stranger. "Sir? Sir. Are you okay?"

The man watched them, then plastered on a smile. A smile like he wasn't good at them, or didn't like making them, or didn't have much to smile about, or all of the above. "Welcome to Absalom."

Grace picked up *whatever* from Kohl, and *confusion* from Nate as he spoke. "Uh, thanks. I guess? I mean, you're the only person we've seen. Aside from Penn. Do you know Rear Admiral Penn?"

"Penn will be together with us soon," said the man. "Are you lost?"

"Uh," said Nate. He turned to face Kohl and Grace. "Okay, so I think this guy's maybe a little confused. Being alone for a while? I don't know."

"He could be sick," said Kohl. "Something in the water. Something in the air. Hell, we could be sick too." He laughed. "That'd be a hell of a way to go. The fights I've seen? To be taken down by a bug? Nasty."

"We're not sick," said Nate. He paused. "But maybe visors down, yeah?"

"Yeah," said Grace. She was getting *concern* from Nate, and *annoyance* from Kohl, but their visors slid shut. Suit comms now. Private. Purposeful. "What's the play, Cap?"

"We go meet that nice man," said Nate, "and see what he knows."

"He's a barometer of crazy," said Kohl. "Sounds like fun."

Nate turned away from them, walking up to the man. "Sir? I'm Captain Nathan Chevell, of the free trader *Tyche*."

"You have a ship?" said the man. Grace watched as he reached out to grab Nate's arm. The movement looked fast and strong. And shaky, like the man was on some stims. Could explain the erratic speech. The man wasn't exuding any emotions though, like he wasn't concerned about a thing. So maybe not stims. Something different. Local food? Local flora? "You must take us on your ship. We must be together. Out there." His eyes turned towards the sky.

"We'll get right on that," said Nate, shaking the man off. "I didn't catch your name."

"Names," said the man. "Names."

"That's right," said Nate. "Sir, if you don't mind me saying, your accent is a little strange. I can't quite place it."

"Humans," said the man, "are so hard. So complicated. So many ... parts."

"I get where you're coming from," said Nate. "It's why I don't live on a planet. Let's try a different angle. Do you know where everyone is?"

The man's eyes drifted around for a bit, left, and right, and up, and then down to his feet. Then his face brightened, that smile/not-smile crossing his face again. "Yes." He stepped away, then turned and beckoned. "Come. We can be together."

"FIVE KLICK WALK, HE SAID," said Kohl. "It'll be fun, he said."

"You're the one with the rotary laser and a suit of power armor," said Nate. "This is on you."

They were following the man up the street, the man with no name, and no smile worth seeing. Grace kept a hand on her sword. This planet, this fucking *planet*, the whole thing was wrong. There was no one here. This man was leading them to other people, but Grace couldn't feel them. Couldn't feel anything, except the bright sparks of her crew mates.

She wanted off this world and back on the *Tyche*, and she wanted it now.

Ahead was some kind of hall or entertainment center. A hall, where kids might put on a show for their parents, or the community would gather to talk about the big issues you'd get on a frontier world, like *why the fuck is Kimmy getting a tax break on her water filters*. The man turned, beckoned again, then ducked into the gloom inside. Nate paused, looking back at Grace and Kohl. "Looks like we're here."

"No," said Grace.

"What?"

"We're not *here* here," said Grace. "This is some shitty place where people gather in times of extreme over administration. They talk about their aquifers and solar collectors. This is not the administration center, where Penn is waiting, and by proxy, our completion bonus. For the second job."

"About that," said Nate. "I'm fairly certain Penn wants to kill us all. It's not that I don't trust the man—"

"It's that you know exactly who he is," said Kohl, nodding.

"*What* he is," said Grace. "He is Republic, and the Republic never offer a good deal."

"You know," said Nate, looking thoughtful, "you'll probably have a long and happy life as a member of my crew."

"Hey now," said Kohl. "Republic keeps us safe. Keeps degenerates from walking free."

"I don't think that's true," said Grace, putting steel in her voice, thinking of Hope. And then trying to *not* think of Hope, because she would not get attached. "You're still here."

"What?" said Kohl.

"I guess the question is," said Nate, stepping in, "whether we go in, and see what's up, or head to the admin center."

"I say admin," said Grace, feeling the shiver of wrongness travel up her spine again.

"I say we party with the locals, try whatever beer they've got going here, and then go admin," said Kohl. "We can always kill Penn later."

"Kill him?" said Nate. "We're going to take him off this planet."

"That's the first step," said Kohl, "but after he tries to commandeer the *Tyche*, we'll space him."

"You can space him if he tries to take my ship," said Nate. "Not before."

"What about if he shoots you?" said Kohl.

"Yeah, space him then."

"Or—"

"I figure," said Nate, "we should just poke our noses in here. See what's going on."

It was a bad idea. The worst, because Grace knew there was no one alive inside that hall. No living soul. They'd find nothing but death.

GRACE'S HAND found Nate's arm, grabbed it. She squeezed it hard. "We need to *go*," she hissed.

Nate looked at the thousand or so people lined up inside the room, then nodded. "I think you're right."

They'd walked inside, the entrance giving way to gloom, gloom giving way to this open area. It had a big vaulted ceiling for acoustics. There was some kind of raised stage at the front. People, front to back, all standing. All staring at them.

Grace had felt sick, because they were all *dead*. All of them. Moving, but not alive. Where she would have felt a thousand emotions, a cacophony of human desires and urges, there was nothing. Or close to nothing, a kind of hissing static that clouded her brain, that made her want to throw up. "We need to go *now*," she said. It was hard to think straight with the static in her head. She wanted to reach out with her mind, to push them back.

Grace Grace Grace Grace Grace Grace.

The static ceased for a second.

GRACE.

The front line of people took a step towards them.

Towards her.

"Cap," said Kohl. "Do you want me to lift something heavy?"

"I—" said Nate, and then the crowd surged towards them.

Grace felt their hands on her, fingers at her face. Tried to find space to draw her sword. She should have already had the blade clear, ready for this, but the hissing in her mind had put her on the back foot. It left her thoughts clouded, fogged up, no way to chart a course. The tide of people walked towards her, a creeping, needy tide. Except they weren't people. They felt nothing. *There was no one there.*

There was the crack of a blaster, and a piece of the ceiling shattered. Another blaster crack, and the roof cracked open, sunlight breaking through. The crowd of people stumbled back.

It was Nate. He was standing, blaster clear, pointed at the ceiling. Not at the people, not like Grace had wanted. He hadn't shot them, because he saw them as needing help. As being like him, and it would be his downfall. Because she knew he was brave, and brave people died in the dark.

"Back up!" shouted Nate. "Back. The. Fuck. Up!" He fired the blaster again, plasma spitting heat upwards.

The man who had led them here — same loose shirt, same loose pants, same bad haircut — pushed to the front. "You wanted to be together," he said. "We want to leave this world."

"Where is Rear Admiral Penn?" said Nate. "Where is he?"

The man with the bad smile tried for a good smile, and failed. "You are not together," he said. "Not yet. But soon."

Grace Grace Grace Grace Grace.

There was a wet popping, cracking sound, and a woman — young, late teens or early twenties, hard to tell with the dirty hair and hollow eyes — stumbled. Her head swelled, the popping, cracking sound getting louder, then her skull exploded in a shower of red chunks. Her body swayed, but stayed upright. There were ... *things* crawling from the ruins of her skull.

Things that looked like cockroaches, but bigger.

"What the sweet fuck!" said Kohl, and there was a whine as the rotary laser swung about on the automount. There was a whirr, and Grace through she heard Nate say *Kohl, no!* but the rotary laser was firing, bright red lances of light illuminating the faces around them, reflecting at them from their eyes. The noise of Kohl's weapon was a rapid cycling whine as the laser charged, fired, and rotated a new lens and emitter. The big man held the weapon down until the young woman's body fell apart, the fluids inside superheating from the laser, boiling into steam, causing limbs to explode where the laser hit them.

Silence.

Of the things that looked like cockroaches, there was no sign. Several people—

Not people. They're not people.

—around the young woman had been hit by the rotary laser. Some of them were smoking, missing limbs. None of them were screaming or in any obvious sign of distress.

"Captain," said Grace.

Grace Grace Grace Grace Grace!

She sagged, felt Nate's hand on her arm. His voice, in her ear. "Got you." Felt him turn to Kohl. "Kohl! We're leaving!" Grace was half-dragged by Nate out the door they'd come in by, out to the air, the heat, the weight of this planet's gravity. She was gasping, trying to clear her head from the static around her.

GRACE. GRACE. GRACE. GRACE. GRACE!

Kohl was backing out the door of the hall, power armor whining, the rotary laser leveled at the doorway.

Darkness. No movement.

"We've got to ... we've got to *leave*," she said, to Nate. "We need to get out of here."

"Right," said Nate. "We'll get Penn—"

"Penn is already dead!" Grace pushed him away. *"These people are all dead, Nathan!"*

"They're sick," said Nate. "They're—"

"I can *see* them," said Grace. "There's nothing to *see*."

GRACE.

TOGETHER.

GRACE GRACE GRACE GRACE GRACE.

TOGETHER!

She turned away from the look on his face, the look that said *I trusted you*, put her hand on her sword. *Be the eye of the storm. Be the calm in the sea. Be the rock against which the waves break.*

The people boiled out of the entrance of the hall, and Kohl's rotary laser met the storm. One or two made it past, and Nate turned his face away from her — *good, I don't want to feel his judgement* — and fired his blaster. None of them were going for Nate, or for Kohl.

They were coming for her.

Grace. Grace Grace Grace.

Her sword cleared its scabbard, and she sliced. It was harder, pure *kendo* now, because normally she could feel the intent, the raw drive of those she fought. When she fought people, those people felt things. These *things* felt nothing. There was nothing but static, a hiss, and the endless repetition of her name.

Grace Grace Grace Grace Grace.

"Stop saying my name!" she screamed, her blade slicing through a man's head. It opened like a gourd, red wet cockroach things crawling and scurrying in the light. One took wing, and her sword licked out, severing it in two.

The sound of Kohl's rotary laser whined to a halt, stopping with a clank. The lens array — the barrels — were white with heat, glowing in the light of the day. He was backing away from the hall, the pile of bodies that used to be people. He halted as he came abreast of Grace and Nate. "What the hell, Cap," he said. "What the *hell*."

Nate's blaster was still trained on the entrance, the weapon not wavering at all. "I don't ... I don't understand."

"They're not *people*," said Grace. "Whatever's been going on here, people have been turning into ... those things."

Something dark passed over Nate's face as he looked at her. He pressed it down and she felt *revulsion/hate/distrust* in a wave that was like being hit. She flinched. "They were people once," he said. "If anyone knows what is going on, it's Penn. We find Penn."

"Well, sure," said Kohl. "But then what?"

"What do you mean?" Nate lowered his blaster.

"I know I use a lot of booze, and a lot of drugs," said Kohl. "I'm dry now though. I'm dry. I wish I wasn't, but that's the way it is. I saw people who had heads full of insects. The way I see it, there's no coming back from something like that. A bug eats your brains? Your brains are gone, Cap."

"You're telling me this why?" said Nate.

"Because," said Kohl. "You always want to do something about it. Me, I don't care. You pay me and tell me where to shoot, I'll shoot. But you need to know. There's more shooting before this is done."

Nate gave Grace a glance. "Then there's more shooting. Let's go."

CHAPTER FIFTEEN

SHE WAS A FUCKING *ESPER*.

Oh, sure. She hadn't *said* that. Not exactly. But Nate had worked with the Old Empire's Intelligencers enough to know their turns of phrase. The way they saw people. The way they could see them without seeing them.

He'd let an esper *on his ship. On his* crew.

How much of what he'd done was because of her? How much of the choices he'd made, the places he'd gone, was because Grace Gushiken had touched his mind, heard his thoughts? The strongest of them were rumored to influence thoughts. Had he taken this job, come to this planet where the people were infected with, what, some kind of *insect* parasite, because she'd given him the nudge?

Nate's hand clenched on his blaster. He wanted to point it at her, pull the trigger. Keep pulling until there wasn't anything left.

Nothing was more vile than someone who could hear your thoughts. Get in your head. The Republic were bad enough with control, but at least the assholes at the top were just *people*. They hadn't overthrown their Emperor, caused the collapse of a civiliza-tion, and handed the keys to a new regime. That's what the Intelligencers had done. He'd been discharged, sidelined, given a custom sword by an old friend and told to sit this one out. Dom had told him that his time would come. He'd thought at the time it was kind words to help him recover from being a cripple.

It still felt like words, but no longer kind ones.

Nate, done is done. You've just got to put her in a box on the way back, drug her into a coma if need be. But you've got others depending on you. El. Hope. Even Kohl. You can get angry at yourself later.

What he wanted to be angry about was that he didn't have the will to put a shot of plasma into her brain. Because there was something in the back of his head that said, *she's on the run, Nate. She's tiny against the mighty. You know what being on the run feels like. And she's been good to you. Kept you and yours safe. Hell, Nate, you kind of like her.*

He rubbed an angry hand against the side of his helmet, wanting to erase that voice of weakness.

"Boss," said Kohl. "You good?"

"No," said Nate. "Rooftop, eleven o'clock."

"Got it," said Kohl, leaning back to brace the rotary laser. The weapon spun up with a *whir*, red lancing out to carve chunks out of a building. It had been some kind of low-slung store selling textiles; now a figure stood on top with a launcher. Red death turned the body into a pyre, the launcher tumbling down the side of the building to break on the street below.

Grace was walking towards the broken launcher. *Let her go. Let her die.* Despite himself, Nate said, "Grace. There's no time."

She moved fast, though. Useful, despite being the enemy of humanity. He watched her kick through the launcher's remains, pulling out a pouch. She shook it open, a net falling free. "They want to catch us," said Grace. "They want to *infect* us."

"Well, fuck that noise," said Kohl. "I figure I can just keep setting them on fire. Should put a dent in that plan."

Kohl might be a borderline psychopath—

He's not borderline. There's no actual border there at all.

—but he was effective. He caused friction in the crew, wanted to sell Hope to the next lot of bounty hunters to sail past, didn't respect El, hell he didn't respect *Nate*, but the man knew fighting. Kohl knew all war's ugly faces. "Kohl," said Nate. "We need the admin center. We need to get there alive, and we need to not be infected by parasites. You got that?"

"I got that," said Kohl. He hefted the laser, something feral in his expression. Something *happy*. "I can keep doing this all day."

"Move," said Nate. He turned, set the pace. A jog through deserted streets. Head on a swivel, checking doorways, ground cars, windows. Grace, jogging at his side, sword sheathed, scabbard held low in one hand. Ready to draw, to cut.

What's fucking with you, Nathan Chevell, is why she hasn't used that sword on you. She's got in with the crew, excepting Kohl, and not even that man's own mother loves him. She could leave you to die here. Take your ship. And she hasn't.

That's what an esper would *do*. It's what they had done. Intelligencers had got into every level of the Old Empire's government, rotted it from within. Made the walls weak, soft, so the death of a good man was enough for the whole house to fall down.

Nate saw movement out of the corner of his eye, a shadow in the front of a shop. Holos moved and shimmered, advertising some kind of swim wear. Behind those ads, something hulked in the gloom where the interior lights were out. Bigger than a tall man, bigger than Kohl. Nate, swung his blaster around, pulled the trigger. Plasma ate the clear ceramic windows, shards of glowing material showering into the store. He didn't know why he'd pulled the trigger, he hadn't identified a clear target, but something at the back of his mind gabbled at him, and he'd clawed the trigger almost by accident.

Kohl was looking at him. "You good? You just set fire to a swim suit store. I mean, I got nothing against swim wear, and I figure the same's true of you, so what you doin'?"

"You didn't see that?" said Nate.

"See what?" said Kohl.

"I saw it," said Grace. "But I don't know what I saw."

Nate walked to the shattered frontage, the edges of the clear ceramic still glowing where plasma had scorched them. He looked into the darkened interior. Ceramic shards spread across the floor, right up to the destroyed frame of a robotic model. Standard machine, capable of looking male, female, or neither. It'd model your body, wear the clothes, and you could see what you'd look like in the latest summer fashions. Not *this* particular robot, because it was in smoldering pieces. "It's nothing," he said. "Just a robot."

He couldn't shake the feeling that what he'd seen hadn't looked like a robot. Not when he'd pulled the trigger. What he'd seen was huge. It hadn't moved like a person.

You're just imagining things. A parasite inside people has got you jumpy.

Sure, humans had encountered horrors in their walk across the galaxy. Weird bacteria and viruses that found humanity delicious. The Republic sent in pest control. That had to be the situation here, although this would be the first time they'd be sent in for anything larger than a weasel. They just needed to get to Penn so the Rear Admiral could call in the exterminators.

But. That didn't explain the *Gladiator*, hole in her hull, fire control set to *extreme prejudice*. He shook his head. *Focus.* Thinking about the *Gladiator* would be a useful exercise for another time.

They made the administration center, identifiable even without the map on their consoles. It had a big, black exterior. Most impressive building for klicks in any direction. The Republic didn't miss an opportunity to show the size of their boots as they were standing on you, did they? The doors were shut, blast shutters down over the windows.

"Looks like they closed up," said Kohl. "Standard protocol, right? Seal the building, evac."

"Yeah, except for that," said Grace, pointing. Down the end of the building, near the corner, were shards of broken ceramic and metal. The shutters were caved in, giving them an entrance into the structure.

"I don't think that was the Republic," said Nate. "They'd have a key."

"Sure," said Grace. She gave Nate a look that said *sorry* and *sorry* again, something hard but hurt in her eyes. She looked away before he could. "I'll go in. See what ... there is to see."

"You do that," said Nate. He watched her slip in through the hole in the shutters, her elegant motion like flowing water.

"So," said Kohl. "What's the deal with Grace?"

"There's no deal," said Nate.

"Cap, I might look big and dumb, but there's been an ice sheet between you for the last two klicks. Right since those ... bugs in people's heads," he said. "I don't think I'm imagining it. El says I don't have an imagination."

"El's right," said Nate. He looked Kohl in the eye. "October?"

"Aw, shit," said Kohl. "When you call me October, I know there's the real deal coming."

"I'm pretty sure Grace is an esper," said Nate.

"Right, I'm going to grease her," said Kohl. He patted the rotary laser. "This should heat her insides to about a million degrees. Be right back."

Before he could walk off, Nate held out a hand. "Hold up."

Kohl looked at him, at his hand, then at the hole. "Cap? Fucking *espers*, man. It's the one thing we all see eye to eye on. They're basically bad. *Mind reading* is bad. Right?"

"Right," said Nate, slowly, "except what if it's not?"

"No," said Kohl. "No. It's just bad."

"I think we've got worse problems for now," said Nate. "Also, if she's an esper, she'll read your mind and slice that sword through you."

"She might try," offered Kohl.

"Let's use it as a test," said Nate. "If she looks like she's going to kill one of us, we do her first. That sit okay with you?"

"Not really," said Kohl.

"Great," said Nate. He turned at a rattling sound, the shutters rising around the windows of the administration center. Grace looked out at them, sword held in one hand at her side. "She got the shutters open."

"She can find a switch," said Kohl. "That's a life skill right there." His voice was grim. Nate looked at the big man, saw the laser pointed at the administration building. At the windows, and at Grace. Kohl's frame was tensed, like he was a leashed hound, yearning for a moment of freedom.

"Kohl," said Nate.

"Yeah."

"Easy." Nate walked forward, came face to face with Grace. "You find the door controls?"

"They're on the door," she said, voice muted through the ceramic pane. This close, Nate could see the hollows under her eyes. She turned, walked to a door, pressed the controls. The door opened without a sound, good Republic technology still working just *fine*, thanks.

Nate walked inside, Kohl on his heels. He turned to Grace. "Look," he said.

"Save it," she said. "Until later. When we're in a place where things aren't eating people's insides, we can talk."

"Until later," he agreed. "Then we need to have a conversation."

"That's one word for it," she said.

"Where," said Nate, "is Penn?"

As if on cue, a central holo stage blinked into life, the lights coming up, systems humming back online. There was a hiss of static, then Penn's head-and-shoulders filled the holo. It was a little ostentatious for Nate's tastes, but it caught the eye. Penn's image was looking over his shoulder, then back to them. "Captain. You made it."

"Uh," said Nate. "There's weird shit happening here. We need to get the fuck out."

"I'm sorry for leaving you in the dark," said Penn. "On an unsecured line, I didn't know what they might hear."

"They?" said Nate.

"The Ezeroc," said Penn. "I had to hope that, since you'd made it into the system alive, you were resourceful enough to make it past them. To here. I'm glad to see I wasn't wrong."

"The Ezeroc," said Nate. "That some kind of militant faction? Crazy in the head after a local parasite infection?"

"No," said Penn. "That's some kind of alien life that wants to kill us all."

"Got you," said Nate. "It's just that, in the thousand or so worlds we've seeded, we've never found local life larger than a hamster."

"Who said," said Penn, "that these are local boys?"

PENN WOULDN'T COME to them. He said it wasn't safe; he said the building was *infested*, which was never a term that inspired confidence. Penn had sealed himself in the medbay, second floor. The medbay had its own power, its own air, and Penn said that was important. *Keep your visors down. Keep your guns up.* And then he'd clicked off the holo, and the escalator system had jerked into life.

Only way to go was up, right?

Kohl was in front, his bulk taking up a lot of lateral space on the escalator. Grace, in the middle. Nate at the rear, blaster out, pointing it at every shadow, every dark corner.

Being told that there were alien invaders was a new twist. Nate had heard a lot of tall tales, but a Rear Admiral's word carried authenticity. Nate was pretty sure he was a Rear Admiral, or close to it: he could control the *Gladiator*, had the systems of the Republic's own administration center under his control. He was *in charge*. In charge of a colony under siege.

What was weird was that if these Ezeroc were a bunch of brain bugs, it didn't seem to make much sense they'd be a threat. The hosts didn't seem ... *normal*, not anymore, and with a bit of judicious quarantine that could have been hit on the head. Something smaller, maybe? An airborne contagion? It still made little sense; why infect a planet of people? It'd kind of tip your hand on the whole invasion front.

Who said aliens need to follow 'rational' thought?

Sure, whatever. *Just get Penn.* Get the man, get out.

Kohl had made the top of the escalator, laser leading the way. The lights were out on this floor. Not just out, but broken, smashed. Floor-standing lights were twisted, bent, broken. Ceiling mounted strips had been torn free, shattered, thrown on the ground. This area would have been a faux-public area, Republic personnel on hand to help you pay your dues. There was nothing left of that now, cabinets strewn across the floor, tablets and consoles smashed, desks torn, wrecked, broken.

"We missed one hell of a party," said Kohl.

"How many people would be on a colony of this size?" said Grace.

"Not that big of a party," said Kohl.

"Just ... how *many*?" she said.

"I don't know," said Nate. "I figure an edge world like this? We'd be looking at fifty thousand people at a bare minimum. Public transportation, businesses, the works. Republic goes big or goes home, you know?"

"That's what I think too," said Grace. "The last time I was at an edge world, the local population was at a quarter million."

"Seems reasonable," said Nate. "I mean, after a few years."

"We saw a hundred or so at the ... before," she said. "Even lowballing this, where's the other forty-nine thousand people?"

Nate looked around at the destruction of the floor. *No bodies.* Still nothing resembling a corpse. Just some shambling people with bugs in their skulls back at the hall.

They didn't have to worry about opening doors. There was a trail of torn ceramic, concrete, and metal at each location there should have been a door. Nothing barred their way. A quick four hundred meters and they were outside the medbay. Penn was inside, lights still on. No one else was in the medbay with him, just some functional consoles, a few beds. What looked like discarded meal packets. A bucket for waste. The man had been slumming it for a mighty-mighty in the Republic.

Nate walked up to the ceramic glass, looking at Penn through it. "Hey," he said.

"Captain Chevell," said Penn. "It's a pleasure."

His stance said *command*, shoulders straight, hands behind his back. His uniform was dirty but still worn with pride. Like a badge, or a shield, or both. The ceramic window between them was hardened, protected, a bastion against outbreak. The surface between Nate and Penn was scratched, some of the clarity melted to an opaque sheen in places by heat. So, someone had tried to break in, or blast in, but hadn't had the right firepower. They hadn't had Republic arms, those still locked behind ID controls.

The area was big, but only Penn was inside. "Likewise," said Nate. "You're alone?"

"I'm alone," said Penn. "Everyone else is ... taken."

"Can you walk?" said Nate. "We've got a bit of a jaunt to get back to the dropship."

"I can not only walk," said Penn, "but I can run. Are you ready?"

"For what?" said Nate.

"When I open this medbay, they will come," said Penn. "They will come, and try and bring us to their ... what do they call it? To their 'together.'"

"The bugs speak English?" said Nate.

"The bugs speak whatever their hosts speak," said Penn. "Have any of you been injured? By them?"

"No," said Nate.

"Nope," said Kohl. He slapped his chest. "Take a lot more than a few scrawny colonists to break this shell."

"Oh," said Penn. "So you've ... not actually *seen* the Ezeroc."

"We've seen them," said Grace. She pressed a hand against the ceramic separating them. "The bugs inside their heads? Instead of their brains? What do they do, eat them?"

"Something like that," said Penn. "I've got files on my person." He held up a data sliver. "This must make it back to the Republic. Whatever happens, Captain. Whatever happens."

"Got it," said Nate. "You can die, the sliver's important."

"If it's all the same," said Penn with a wry smile, "I'd prefer to not die." He turned to Grace, his face turning puzzled. "I see," he said.

She stiffened, turning to Nate. "Nate—"

"Well, enough of that," said Penn. "Let's get to cheerier subjects. Door opens, we run. No wasting time, no sightseeing. Anyone who's not us, you shoot. Are you good with that, Captain?"

"The people?" said Nate. "You want us to shoot people?"

"For what it's worth, I'm good with it," said Kohl.

"They're not people," said Penn. "They haven't been for some time. And in a few days, they'll be quite a bit worse than people. It's a mercy."

Nate thought about that. "I won't fire," he said, "unless they come for us."

"Then you'll be firing quite a lot," said Penn. "This facility is infested. When this door seal breaks, expect a rush."

"This facility is deserted," said Nate.

"Let's see, shall we?" said Penn. With a hiss of escaping air, he opened the door.

EL SAT in the Helm's chair on the *Tyche*. The flight deck was tidy, clean, some parts made new as the day she first flew. She had no clue how Nate would pay for the repair bill on this, but for now it felt good. Her ship would fly again, and she would fly truer than she ever had while El was at the console. The *Tyche* was holding an atmosphere, automated sounds more subtle than structural as the *Gladiator's* repair systems fitted the last components into place.

Her comm clicked. "Well, there's good news and bad news," said Hope.

"Hit me with the bad news," said El. "I'm in a glass half full mood at the moment. Nothing can bring me down."

"The ship might not fly again," said Hope.

El jerked in the acceleration couch, spraying coffee all over the console. She hurried to wipe it off with a sleeve of her flight suit, then winced. It felt like she might have pulled something in her back doing that. She scrabbled at the comm. "Say what?"

"The good news," said Hope, "is that I'm just messing ... I mean, fucking with you. She'll be ready to fly on time. This Republic hangar..." Hope's voice took on a wistful note. "I guess it'd be nice to work on one of these ships. It takes a lot of the drudgery out of the work."

"Hope," said El, "I'm going to throw you out an airlock."

"Good to know," said Hope. "Let me know how you get on keeping the ship in the sky."

"Anyway," said El. "You *are* working on one of these. You're literally working on one of these right now."

"Not really," said Hope. "Not for real. Kisses, though." The comm clicked off.

Not for real. That was true enough, in its own way. Hope couldn't be on a Republic ship, not unless she was in the brig. Her fingerprints would be all over the *Gladiator*, but they'd just be another box on her criminal record. A black mark on a sooty profile.

They'd have to do something about Hope's situation. Nate would want to, no matter how bad an idea it would seem. El had already talked him back from the edge of madness — he'd been keen on busting into a Republic facility, pointing guns at people until they did something about it. As if activity like that would lead to anything positive for *any* of them. It wasn't the touch of fear that had guided El's words, it had been the real threat of a life on the run, never being able to buy a coffee or a beer or a *fucking sandwich* without someone putting the collar on her. All because of that bitch Reiko.

No thanks.

Hope might be the sister she never had, but some problems shouldn't be shared.

Or couldn't be shared. Whatever.

The holo clicked, whirred, light filling the air. The *Tyche* was watching the crew, a good shepherd even with her wings clipped. Active biorhythms for Nate, Kohl, and Grace filled the space. Warning indicators peppered the display, markers against heart rate and adrenaline spikes. El watched it for a minute, thinking, *well, it's a glitch — got to be. Ship's not been tested yet.* But nothing changed, until the display blanked, and *SIGNAL LOST* blinked in the air.

El clicked the comm. "*Tyche* to ground crew, yo. How you doing down there?"

Nothing. Not even static. There was no handshake to the signal. Nothing.

"*Tyche* to ground crew. Hit me back." El clicked the comm, tried another channel. Still nothing. She leaned forward, wincing again at her back, amped the signal up. "Nate? This is El." A slight hiss of static, but nothing else. *Okay, go specific.* "Kohl." Silence. "Kohl, you asshole. Come in."

Static surged to a roar through the flight deck's speakers, and El flinched, covering her ears. The static stopped, followed by silence. El looked at the empty acceleration couch next to her, then switched to an internal channel. "Hope."

"Engineering here," said Hope, "high on drugs and rock and roll."

"You wouldn't know what rock and roll *was*," said El. "No one does, not really. Just words."

"But what a movement," said Hope. "What's up?"

"You tested the *Tyche's* systems yet?" El was looking at the air where the holo still displayed *SIGNAL LOST*. "Anything to do with comms?"

"Nope," said Hope, "and also, a big thanks-for-the-confidence high five. You know I'd tell you about something like that."

"Okay," said El, reaching to turn the comm off.

"Hold up," said Hope. "Why are you asking?"

"It's probably nothing," said El.

"It's probably something," said Hope. "What specific form of 'nothing' are you thinking about?"

"Well," said El, "the Cap's bios came through elevated, then snapped out. I can't get a signal with the planet."

"Be right there," said Hope.

"Wait," said El, and realized the comm was off. She'd wanted to say *it's nothing* again or *we should wait a little longer*, because the alternative was dropping the *Tyche* into the atmosphere of a planet where there was a bunch of weird shit going on, and that wasn't in

El's position description. She flew the ship, and she flew it away from random acts of violence. Her whole *deal* was flying the *Tyche away from danger*, a ship without which they would all die in a vacuum.

The clank of boots on metal announced Hope's arrival. Pink hair grungy with grease, Hope's face wore *tired* like most people wore underwear. Something that was ordinary and expected. She looked at the *SIGNAL LOST* for about two seconds, then she said, "We need to go. Down there."

"Hold up," said El. "Have you even tested my ship yet?"

"It'll be fine," said Hope. "Good Republic fitment. What could go wrong?"

"Everything," said El. "You've still got the *Ravana's* reactor coupled to the *Tyche*. It's more power than she's used to. And you've replaced the substructure of the *Tyche*. We don't even know if the welds will hold."

"Welds," said Hope. "You're so old school."

"Whatever you've done—"

"Because you don't weld ceramic," said Hope.

"Glue," said El. "Unicorn blood, I don't care. You've replaced the thing that makes the *Tyche* hold a straight line. I'm not flying until we've done some tests."

The holo shimmered, flicked, then displayed *COLLISION WARNING*. The flight deck's speakers brayed a klaxon. Hope and El both looked at the ceiling as if there was a higher power they could ask for guidance, then looked at each other.

"We've got to go," said El. The holo winked, displayed the *Tyche*, then pulled out to a view of the *Gladiator*. It pulled out again to a planet view, Absalom Delta and the asteroid marked bright and red. There were several solid objects moving at high velocity between the asteroid and the *Gladiator*. High velocity. "We've got to fucking *go*," said El. "Buckle up."

"We're not ... there's still stuff to do," said Hope. But she was clambering into the acceleration couch across from El, pulling the straps tight against her small frame. She smelled of oil and ozone and fear.

"Is it stuff that will stop us flying?" said El, clicking switches on the console. The sound of the fusion engines rumbled through the hull, throaty, powerful, *ready*. Angry, as if they'd been starved of purpose for too long.

"Maybe," said Hope. "Probably not."

"I need a yes or no," said El.

"No," said Hope, eyes wide. She was watching the markers on the holo, those objects getting closer to the *Gladiator*. "What are those?"

"Those," said El, "are rocks." She told the *Gladiator* to let them go, then told the destroyer to open the hangar to the hard black. She couldn't hear the air as atmosphere gusted out, but small objects — a wrench, a work table — whirled past the cockpit and into the void. Another alarm blinked into view on the holo, one of the docking clamps holding the *Tyche* was stuck fast. The black of space opened before El like a promise of hope, the blue green of Absalom Delta below them. A flash of fire streaked past the hangar doors, torpedoes launched by the *Gladiator's* defenses spearing into the void.

The damn clamps. They were moored, stuck fast, so close to freedom. "I'll get it," said Hope, starting to leave her chair.

"There's no time," said El. She pulled on the sticks, the *Tyche* thrumming with urgency as she tried for space. Yearned for it, the taste of open water so close. There was a screaming of metal as something — the *Gladiator* or something on the *Tyche*, impossible to tell — tore, and then they were moving.

The comm channel chattered, hissed, and then the *Gladiator's* automated voice spoke. "Collision imminent. Brace, brace, brace." El clicked weapons control, warmed up the PDCs, the *thrum* sounding through the hull as the cannons came out on their mounts, spun through their initial checks. She brought the lasers online — a red warning light blinked on her console, telling her there was an error in the laser firing array. It wouldn't stop them firing, but they had nothing that would reach across the void. Close range defense. Close range combat.

Well, fuck. That was what *untested* meant. No lasers? No problem.

"Sorry," said Hope, "not everything's ready—"

"It's fine," said El, voice clipped. "Let me fly." She put a hand on the throttle, thought *sorry* to the *Gladiator*, and pushed it forward. The *Tyche* roared, the roar turned to a scream as the ship kicked against the *Gladiator* for freedom, and they burst from the hangar pulling hard Gs. El spared a glance out towards where the rocks were coming from, that monkey urge to *see* taking over for a second. She was rewarded with bright bursts of nuclear fire as the torpedoes hit the rocks coming at them, and then they were accelerating towards the planet's surface. Running and burning hard.

Weapons control spat telemetry on the holo, mapping smaller shards of rock that split away from the big ones, a thousand tiny asteroids of death in space. The PDCs swung towards the incoming rocks, ready to fire at anything larger than a pea. LIDAR and RADAR readied to speak across the void—

Another warning light. No LIDAR.

El slapped a hand against the console. "C'mon!"

No LIDAR.

"Sorry!" said Hope, again. "Not everything's been tested!"

They were falling into a gravity well with a thousand rocks coming at them with no detailed ranging or targeting. *Think.* The rocks would expand in a conical cloud from point of impact. Going *away* would keep them in the line of rocks. Going *down* would prolong the inevitable, but it would also give them an atmosphere as armor. Going *towards* would — briefly — increase the chance of impact, and was certain suicide.

Down it was.

Sparks of light off the *Tyche's* bow glinted in the void. The *Gladiator's* own PDCs were firing, kinetic weapons and lasers alike stabbing across space. The lights converged at a point as a rock missed by torpedoes hit the *Gladiator's* hull like a hammer. There was another bright flash of fire. No time to worry about that. If the *Gladiator's* reactor blew, the reactor blew. If it didn't, it was all just more space chaff.

El pushed the throttle harder, feeling her body press against the acceleration couch. 4Gs, 5. She blinked, the lenses in her eyes flattening, making it hard to see. Her chest felt like a hundred rocks were on it. The holo still blinked *COLLISION WARNING*, over and over, then, *BRACE BRACE BRACE*.

"Not today," she croaked, and pushed the throttle to the stops. The *Tyche* roared at the night sky, plumes of fusion fire in their wake, the crackle of atmosphere sending fire along the front of their hull. The ship shook and grumbled then roared as atmosphere tried to push her back. Something *groaned* in the hull, and El thought *hold, girl, just a little longer*, and felt thrust go past 6 gravities.

Pushing seven hard Gs on re-entry, the ground coming up fast.

El's head was swimming. *Flatten out. You need to pull out, or you'll turn into a thin layer of burning materials.* She clawed at the sticks with arms that felt like they weighed three hundred kilos each. Her fingers tried to work the controls, feeling the sticks move. El felt the *Tyche* respond, pulling out into a curve.

She could hear a noise and ignored it, figuring it was just Hope trying to scream without a lot of luck.

There was a *clang* as something in the ready room behind El broke loose, and she could smell burning. But they were still flying, not falling, and the atmosphere was slowing their descent. She pulled the *Tyche's* curve flatter, putting the belly of the ship towards the deck. They were coming in to Nate's last known position fast. The ship dropped from high-hypersonic down through hypersonic and into the merely supersonic. RADAR pinged the ground, mapped the surface. "You good?" said El.

Hope was gasping.

"Scream if you're stroking out," said El.

"I'm. Good," said Hope. "Fly."

"It's what I do," said El. The holo display changed from absolute velocity to airspeed. The *Tyche* did atmosphere, but not like she was born to it. The fusion drives pushed her along like a couple of angry bulls, and as they reached the thick, breathable parts of Absalom Delta's atmosphere, she was recording a steady Mach 3.03. Precise. At least *something* was working.

The RADAR's ground mapping filled the holo. *Tyche* came in across the ocean, water raised in their passage, to roar across a forested area. They'd be flattening or uprooting trees as they went.

"What," said Hope, "are all of those?" She was pointing to the holo, *Tyche's* ground map overlaid with many markers. Thousands of them. The *Tyche* thought for a second or two, then marked them as *unidentified ground troops*.

"People," said El.

Hope worked her own console, got one of the external cameras to zoom in. The picture filled the holo between them, and then both stared at it.

El broke the silence first. "That's not a person." The urge to pull the sticks back, point the *Tyche* to the safety of the stars, was strong. But there were a thousand thousand asteroids up there, and moving up top right now would involve a high chance of suicide.

"No," said Hope. "I don't know what it is." It stood at 2M in height, if *stood* was the right verb here. Lots of legs. A lot like a centaur crossed with an ant. El's brain worked the problem for a little while, came up empty.

"Neither does the *Tyche*," said El. "She's never seen anything like that. Not in the databases."

Hope turned to look at her. "What happened to the captain, El? Where's Nate? Where's Grace?"

CHAPTER SEVENTEEN

THERE WAS A *HISS*, and the sound of something clattering in the gloom.

"What the fuck was that?" said Kohl, swinging the laser around. Grace watched him point it at the darkness, like the darkness would say *okay, you got me*, this *is what that was*.

She felt her fingers tighten around the sword. Steel that had been with her for all the time that mattered. "Nothing good," she said. The static in her mind was ... getting worse. Growing stronger, a constant sibilant whisper of a thousand nothings overlaying each other. Then, silence, before:

Grace. Grace Grace Grace. GRACE.

Together.

She wanted to throw up. "We've got to go." She turned to Nate. "Nate? We've got to *go*."

Penn was already moving, hustling past them, a light rifle in his hands. "She's right, Captain Chevell. There is really no time like the present."

The ceiling erupted in a thousand pieces off to Grace's right. Something massive came down with fragments of tiling, landing hard enough to be felt through the floor at her feet. Steel hissed its reply as she drew her sword, metal held low and ready.

Kohl was looking confused, then he seemed to gain purpose. "You know, I don't want to even know." He pointed the laser into the gloom where the thing had landed, and bright red lanced the gloom. Something *keened* in the dark, and there was a crack-and-pop, a sound like a coconut splitting open.

"We're leaving," said Nate, to her left. He moved forward.

The floor beneath his feet burst upwards, something monstrous coming into the lights from his suit. It had a lot of legs like an insect, or maybe arachnid was a better word, but now wasn't the right time to be worrying about definition. A torso reared upright from its ... abdomen? Body? It looked like an insect centaur. Clawed forelimbs reached for Nate.

Nate's blaster barked at it, plasma blowing chunks off the creature. He fired, and fired again, driving it back, chunks of chitin blasting free to tumble, smoldering, on the floor.

Silence.

Grace looked at Penn. "What were you *doing* here?"

The Rear Admiral glanced at her, his face blank. Practiced. "Trying not to die," he said.

They started towards the escalator, Kohl leading the way. One creature came up the escalator, and Kohl pointed his laser at it. Red light lanced out, but the thing jumped up, inverted, clinging to the ceiling. It scuttled towards them, Kohl's laser fire trailing it as it ran. Kohl tagged it just before it dropped on the big man, stabbing down with those clawed appendages.

Nate fired at it, kept firing as the creature tried to back away. He kept firing until his blaster whined empty, and Nate tossed the spent battery aside, slipping a new one into the weapon. He reached a hand down to Kohl, helping the big man to his feet. Kohl looked stunned, blood trailing from a rent in his armor near the shoulder.

Penn pointed his rifle at Kohl. "Sorry, son," he said.

Grace. Grace. Grace. Grace. GRACE.

She screamed, more to drive the voices out of her head, steel cutting through the air. Her sword sliced through Penn's rifle, carving a rent through the energy cell powering it. The weapon sparked and crackled, falling from Penn's hands, trailing smoke. Grace continued her motion, turning around Penn and bringing her sword to the man's throat. She leaned close, spoke in his ear. "Give me one good reason," she said. "A *good* reason."

"He's already dead," said Penn. "It's how they get you. How they infect you."

"Bullshit," said Grace.

"Yeah, bullshit," said Kohl, but his face was grey, his voice weak. Couldn't be blood loss, there wasn't enough coming out of him. More like the shock of being stabbed by an alien.

"Grace," said Nate. "We need him. The *Gladiator's* fire controls."

"Looks like the captain gave you one good reason," said Grace. She lowered her sword. "Let's go."

"I need a weapon," said Penn.

"You need to be cut down," said Grace. "Looks like we're both going to compromise today."

Kohl was rifling through a pouch on his belt. He pulled out a syringe and a dermal patch. Kohl stabbed the syringe in between his armor plates, right next to his injured shoulder, winced as he punched it home, and then relaxed. He slapped the patch on his neck, tossed the empty syringe to the ground, and picked up his laser cannon. "Good to go," he said.

"What was in that?" asked Nate.

"Nothing legal," said Kohl, "and nothing you need to worry about." He strode forward, strides sure, armor whining and clanking with his steps. "You know, I wonder what these ... hey, Penn."

"Rear Admiral to you," said Penn.

"I'm not with the Marines," said Kohl. "Those assholes couldn't fight their way out of a cobweb. Anyway. What did you call these fuckers?"

"The Ezeroc," said Penn.

"I wonder what these Ezeroc taste like," said Kohl. "They look a little bit like lobsters, you know?"

Grace looked at the fallen syringe, then up at Kohl. *Nothing legal.* But it turned his day around. "You got another one of those?"

"Maybe," said Kohl, with a nasty smile. He turned to Penn. "You and me? We're going to have a conversation when we're in space."

"Yes," said Penn, "we are."

GRACE MADE the top of the escalator by the time Kohl was at the bottom and already firing. Red light reflected up the escalator, refracting off glass and metal. *The man is actually good at something.* That Kohl wasn't *all talk* came as a surprise to Grace, like realizing your parents were cool before you were born. That the hip clothes and stylish cuts gave way to looking after *your* sorry ass. Grace put a hand against the railing, vaulted past Penn and Nate both, landing on the steps heading down. She slipped a leg over the hand rail, sliding the rest of the way. As she descended the railing at speed, she could see Kohl marching forward, the rotary laser firing at something obscured by a wall to her left. He was leaving a trail of smoking insect parts.

Grace hit the ground floor, tumbled from the railing and tucked into a roll. She hit her knee a little too hard — *damn* the gravity of this planet — but nothing broken, just a little bruised. Grace came up, sword hunting through the air with a soft whisper. She couldn't hear it, not over the noise Kohl was making, but she *knew* it, like she knew everything about this blade. Grace knew how much it weighed and how sharp it was. She knew how many lives it had taken.

Nothing. Kohl had already killed everything here.

The man was marching like an automaton towards the main door, laser still on full auto. Sparks and flames licked out from the frame of the door as he cut a hole in the metal, ceramicrete, and substructure, pieces falling away, burning like falling angels. His focus was on the door, and getting *out*, and Grace could feel *urgency/chase/hunt* pouring off the man. No fear. Not a lick of it.

What was in that stim?

Her gaze was drawn to the ceiling, where one of the—

Ezeroc. The fucking bugs have a name, and it's Ezeroc.

—Ezeroc was clawing through, scuttling to get the drop on Kohl. Grace pushed off from her crouch into a sprint, sword held low and ready. The insect—

Definitely an insect. Fucking bugs.

—dropped from the ceiling as she got there, landing about a meter from Kohl's back. Her sword *snicked* out, slicing through the Ezeroc's rear legs, drawing a keen from the creature. It turned to her, and that *right there* made her pause. Because she was standing in front of an honest to God alien, a crawling thing from another world, and it had *teeth*, and *claws*, and stood above her at well over 2 meters in height. It was favoring the injured legs — *so you fuckers feel pain, huh?* — and rearing up and back on the six multi-jointed legs it stood on.

Rearing up to strike.

When Grace had learned *kendo*, it had been style and forms, too slow for any real use on the street. *Iaido* had been the natural step, a pure form of focus and awareness. The problem with both is that they were designed for fighting people. People had intent, and she could feel that. It let her move faster, a step ahead at all times. This thing had no intent she could feel.

GRACE GRACE GRACE GRACE!

Oh no you don't. She wouldn't let something get one over on her. Not again. Never again.

She spun as it crashed its weight down where she was standing, falling back on those old forms. *Iaido* was beauty, and *kendo* was purpose, and her feet moved through the forms like she was still in the *dojo*, learning hand-me-down tricks from her *sensei. Keep moving.* Her sword was a part of her, an extension of her will, and she turned and put it through the left-side legs of the Ezeroc. It keened again, crashing to the ground, and her sword swung like a thing with purpose of its own to slash through the creature's fore claws.

The remaining legs drummed on the ground, a greenish scum oozing from the cuts. Kohl had turned around by this time, taken in the scene, and stepped forward that remaining meter distance. The rotary laser whirred around to his back, and he put two hands around the thing's neck — *is that a neck?* — and brought his visored head in for a headbutt. There was a crunch of chitin and teeth, and Kohl pushed the thing aside to flail on the ground. He gave Grace a glance, expression invisible behind his mask, then said, "You're all right, Gushiken."

"Just all right?" she said.

"Of the two espers here," said Kohl, "you're the one that hasn't tried to kill me. That Penn, though." He paused, frowning. "I mean, I don't *know* he's an esper. But it fits. Knows too much. Fucker. Let's go, yeah?"

Seriously. What was *in* that stim? Never mind that Kohl thought she was an esper — Nate must have said something while she was opening the doors. The truth was something different, but explaining that was hard, and she never seemed to get the time before someone tried to shoot her, or open her skull, or put her in a jail that even time forgot about. The stim got past all that. Sure, something to get the body moving when it was weak. Something to speed up the heart, the reactions, to dull the pain and the fear. But a little something else, to bond soldiers to each other when the end was near? Had to be. Grace had heard about psychotropics like that, but never felt them. A throwback like Kohl should pound her skull through the floor, but here he was, treating her like one of the team.

You're not, though. Keep your distance. You're not with them.

Now, she was lying to herself.

THE LIGHT WAS bright and hard and oppressive, everything taking on too much shine. This damn gravity was another level of bullshit, trying to leech the strength from her limbs, making her slow to move. Making it hard to fight.

The Ezeroc were everywhere.

The four of them came out of the administration center in a clump, weapons pointed out, and faced a ring of insect forms. All except Penn, who was still without a weapon. The man was scrabbling at a helmet, trying to juggle it into place in a hurry, his fingers trembling with *anxiety* and *fear/fear/fear*. Grace flicked green ichor from her blade, feeling the sweat on her face despite the cool of the helmet, and said, "Well, *now* it's a party."

Nate gave her a glance and a series of emotions in rapid succession, a mixture of *fear/trust/distrust/family/anger/betrayal* before he spoke. "We've just got to make the spaceport. The dropship. Then we're good."

"Uh," said Kohl, eyes on the skies above.

Grace followed his gaze, saw the trails of fire through the atmosphere. The pinprick bloom of an explosion, something made tiny to her eyes by distance. Something was going on in space, something *bad*, and the remains of whatever that was were raining through the atmosphere. It'd be suicide to take off. Trying to fly through a sky full of burning rocks was only for the criminally insane.

Nate was tapping at his comm while the Ezeroc chittered at a distance. Unmoving. Grace said, "What are they waiting for?"

Together.

She shook her head to clear it while Nate spoke to the comm. "*Tyche*, this is Nate. *Tyche*, there's fireworks going on up there. Tell me a story."

No response.

Penn cleared his throat, voice muffled by the helmet. Nate turned to him and said, "Penn? Let me loop you in on our comms channel." He tapped at his wrist controls.

Penn's voice came through bright and clear. "The Ezeroc.

They're jamming signals. It's what they've been doing since they came into orbit. But it's not coming from the asteroid."

Nate was looking at Penn like he was crazy, but Grace took a step forward. "Orbit?" she said. "There's no ships out there. Only the *Gladiator*."

"The *Gladiator* is what we call too little, too late," said Penn. His shoulders were still square, but Grace wondered how long that could last in the face of all the insects ringing them. "Aliens do not build like we do, Grace."

"Hey," said Grace. "How do you know my—"

"You said asteroid," said Nate. "The *asteroid* is their ship?"

"It is," said Penn. "We need to move, Captain. I don't know what they're waiting for, but it can't be good."

Grace.

Grace whirled, but there was nothing there. The Ezeroc still stood around them, a safe 20 meter distance, not getting closer, not getting farther.

"You're saying," said Nate, "that their ship is an asteroid the size of a moon?"

"It perplexed us at first too," said Penn. "It's why I need to get this data sliver off this world. We need to let the Republic know what kind of enemy they face. The *Gladiator* didn't stand a chance. After they cored the hull and took the crew—"

"Hold up," said Kohl. "What do you mean, 'took the crew?'"

Grace.

TOGETHER.

"Fuck this," said Grace. She walked towards the spaceport, her sword held in an angry hand. "You guys can talk this out. I'm getting *off* this rock."

She was seeing shimmers in the air around — or inside — the Ezeroc. Silhouettes. Shapes, forms, like the outlines of people. She blinked but the images were still there. One of them in front of her reached out a hand towards her, ghostly and insubstantial.

Grace.

Together.

Grace Grace Grace!

Oh my God. She shook her head, feeling sick. Grace looked back at Penn. "They're ... they used to be *people*," she said. "They're not aliens. They're people!"

"Only at a carbon level," said Penn. "They haven't been people for a long time. The Ezeroc ... well, they need the calories."

"We're leaving," said Nate, "and we're leaving now. I don't know about the rest of you, but I don't feel like becoming someone else's lunch." He tossed a look at Kohl. "October? Make a path, and make it now."

Kohl shrugged, pointed the rotary laser, and pulled the trigger. Insects leapt out of the way, scrambling for the walls, windows, rooftops. Kohl was lumbering down the street, laser fire lighting his way. Nate followed, covering his back, blaster picking out targets, Ezeroc getting too close. Grace followed, as did Penn.

"It's illegal, what you are," said Penn. Like he knew.

"Let's talk later," said Grace, "when there's nothing but humans, yeah?"

"We could use someone like you," said Penn. His eyes were on Kohl and Nate as Grace's crew mates made a path. "But we'd need ... an understanding."

Grace felt the traitor clutch of hope in her chest. *You weren't with this crew anyway. You don't need them. You need to be free of them.* She wanted to say something to Penn, and she wanted to choke down that feeling at the same time. What was happening to her?

An Ezeroc scrambled toward them from the shelter of a crashed car, too close and too quick for Nate's blaster to pick it off. It was reaching for Penn, and Grace's sword moved in her hand before she had a chance to think about it. The blade sheared the two fore claws off in quick succession, and she spun the steel in the air to drive it back. It hissed at her, then scuttled away.

Penn was at her back, hand on her shoulder. "Good," he said. "Good."

Grace screwed her eyes shut. *I hope you know what you're doing.* But she had no idea. Not anymore.

"PORT IS JUST AROUND THE CORNER," said Nate, voice clear over the comm. "I'm running low on batteries here."

"I'm fine," said Kohl, his voice sounding anything but *fine*. It sounded *weak* and *clotted*, like milk curdled in the sun. His tone made Grace look, and she saw the big man pause firing his laser. Pause, and then just let it fall. The automount pulled it to his back, and the motion caused Kohl to stumble and sway.

"Kohl?" said Nate. "October, talk to me."

"I'm fine," said Kohl, and then stretched himself face-first on the street in a clatter of armor.

Grace felt real fear then. Not because Kohl was dead, because he *wasn't*. She'd feel it if his soul left his body. No, none of that. She felt fear because Kohl had been doing *all of the work*.

A hush descended over the street. Grace looked up, saw the Ezeroc looking out from behind makeshift barricades of vehicles, signage, store windows. For all that Kohl had cut a path, killing hundreds of them, there were *thousands* left. *Thousands.*

Grace Grace Grace Grace Grace!

Together, Grace.

All the people of Absalom Delta. All the Marines and flight crew of the *Gladiator*. Oh, she knew what the *Ravana* had been running from now. She knew what had made them hack their own ship to make a jump a little too far, a little too fast. The *Ravana's* crew had figured if they were going to die, they'd die as a warning: *there be dragons.*

There was a hiss, rising in volume.

"Nate," said Grace. "*Nate.*"

"I know," he said, trying to get Kohl up.

"Nate," she said. "We have to *go*."

"I know!" he said, pulling at the clamps on Kohl's automount.

"He's *gone*, Nate," she said. It wasn't true, but Nate didn't know that. Nate was now their ticket out of here. A good shot, maybe good enough to get them to the dropship. She couldn't take the Ezeroc on the blade. There were too many.

He glared at her. "I don't *care*," he said. *"We* don't leave people *behind."*

She didn't know what *we* he was referring to. Grace was sure that Kohl would have left them behind in a hopeless situation. El would have set the drives to burn hard for a distant system and be sipping Mai Tais under the haze of a different sun. Hope might have stayed, but she was young, and stupid, and too full of her namesake to survive out here on the edge of space. It was some other *we,* a group of people who weren't here anymore. They sure as shit hadn't stayed to help *him,* because otherwise he wouldn't even be here.

There was a clank and the rotary laser fell free. Nate hissed as he burned his hand on the weapon, then tried to lift Kohl. He groaned, then dropped the man in a clanking pile. "Too heavy," he said. "Damn this gravity."

Okay, so he won't leave Kohl. "Move," she said, sword out.

"What are you going to do?" he said, not moving.

Her sword licked out, and Nate flinched, but her strike wasn't at him. The blade touched Kohl's body *here* and *here* and *here,* and his armor popped open in a hiss of broken seals. His slumped form was revealed, the fruit inside a harsh rind revealed. "Now," said Grace. "We *have* to go."

As if in agreement there was a rising *hiss* from the Ezeroc. Nate looked at her. "Yeah, you got it." He shouldered Kohl, still wincing, and started a heavy-footed run. Grace followed, the insects crawling along behind them, behind Penn. Hungry. Watchful. Like they were herding them, rather than hunting them.

Herding. Now there's an unpleasant thought. Why would the insects be doing that?

She almost ran into Nate, he stopped so fast. Grace looked ahead, her eyes tracking the empty street. She saw the broken-down barricade of the spaceport, then the smoking remains of their dropship, barely recognizable as a machine, fire licking out from the shattered hull, pieces of engine and control systems and ablative shielding strewn about in a 50 meter radius.

"Well, shit," she said. "The fucking bugs destroyed our dropship."

"Penn," said Nate, wheezing under the load of Kohl. "We need another ride. Where on this planet can we get one?"

"Nowhere," said Penn, his face and his voice lost. For once, his shoulders weren't so perfect square. And not coincidentally, Grace was *not* pleased to be here to see that.

"There's got to be something," said Nate.

"There's nothing," said Penn.

Nate dropped Kohl to the ground, pulling out his blaster. "Then we fight," he said.

"Nate," said Grace. "There's so many of them."

He gave her a little lopsided smile. "That's when you've got to burn the brightest, Grace," he said. "When the darkness comes down to snatch you away." He looked at the blaster in his hand, *trust/distrust/like/anger/betrayal/trust* coming off him. "If it comes to it, I won't let them take you."

"Cover me," said Penn. He jogged back the way they came. Towards Kohl's fallen rotary laser. He hefted it, making it look like hard work. "Captain," he said to Nate, "if they try to take me, you shoot me down. Do you understand?"

"You know," said Nate, "I was going to shoot you down for the hell of it."

"I'm glad we understand each other," said Penn. They backed towards each other. Three souls, around Kohl's slumped body. Three against a thousand, against ten thousand. Grace had been running for so long, it felt good to stop. To know this was the end. She flicked gore and slime from her blade.

The Ezeroc drew closer. The air was turning orange from the burning of so many rocks in the atmosphere, and Grace felt like it was getting hotter. It could have just been her imagination. It didn't matter, because death would take her soon enough, by fire or by claw it didn't matter.

One of the bugs rushed at her, and she let her sword do the talking. The blade rang hard against chitin, not biting deep, and Grace felt — well, fucking *surprised*. This sword had been with her for as long as she was tall enough to hold it. She knew this blade, and it knew her. It always cut. It was ever sharp. The Ezeroc hissed at her — *fucker's probably surprised too* — then made to lunge. She swung again, and this time the sword bit.

Bit, and stuck.

Then with a sound of metal crying, the blade broke. Grace stumbled back, the hilt of her sword and a mere foot of blade left in her hand. She looked at it, then at the Ezeroc, and prepared to die.

There was a flash, and another, and plasma bit into the creature. Chunks exploded off it and it burst into flame, driven back. By Nate. By his blaster. *He should have just left me to die. He knows it. I know it. And still.*

Which *we* did he mean?

Penn was firing the rotary laser, straining under the weight of the weapon. Straining, until the weapon clicked down, its battery spent, and with it, the last of their hope. Grace looked down at her broken sword, then past that to Kohl on the ground. Then to Kohl's belt, with his pouch of toys.

You got another one of those?

Maybe.

She dropped to her knees, ripping open Kohl's pouch. Three syringes tumbled free into her hand. She pulled the caps off them, held them up in a fist, and said, "Sorry, Kohl." Then she slammed them into his body, ramming the plungers home.

One heartbeat, two. And then Kohl was on his feet, eyes wide, cords in his neck straining, a silent scream opening his mouth into a rictus. He looked around, took in the situation, then picked up a piece of concrete connected to rebar. He hefted it. An Ezeroc came forward, and Kohl roared, swinging the makeshift club in an arc. It smashed the Ezeroc's head to a pulp, and Kohl kept swinging until there was nothing left but slime and chunks.

He looked back at Nate, then Penn, and Grace, like he didn't know them.

The Ezeroc hissed. Kohl back up and crazy was a good start, but it wasn't enough. They would die, but slower. Grace knew it.

Grace.

Now we can be together.

That's when the insects came for them. All of them, at once.

The sky broke open with a thunder, the sound the rage of gods, a flash of fire and light. Grace fell to her knees, shielding her helmeted head with her hands. She looked up through her fingers, saw an eagle's fury bright in the sky, fusion fire burning in a wide braking arc as the *Tyche* screamed its defiance above them. PDC cannons were out from the hull, their rage and fury roaring at the Ezeroc. The ship had blasted over them, and the pilot — it *must* have been El — already turning it around as fusion drives turned buildings into pyres. The *Tyche* pulled back to hover over them, rotating in a slow circle as the PDCs cleared the Ezeroc away, weapons designed for space warfare hammering the street and buildings to powder with a noise and violence that shook the air from Grace's lungs even through the suit. The *Tyche* was dropping tungsten like burning, metal rain.

The ship lowered, air buffeting Grace's helmet. She blinked against the glare of the landing lights, her visor's automatic adjustment snapping between black and white as it fought against the visual cacophony. Their ship had come for them. The *Tyche* would not let them die in darkness and fear.

The cargo bay was opening, and Hope's face looked down at them. "Come on!" she yelled. Or that's what her lips looked like they said, the *Tyche's* rage having taken Grace's hearing away. Penn was the first to the ship, pulling himself into the cargo bay. Kohl was still in the street, Nate pulling on the big man's arm. Some reason returned to Kohl's eyes, and he came to the *Tyche* too, but still clutching his rebar club. Grace looked back at the *Tyche*, expected her to be pulling away, now that Nate knew what she was.

But there he was, still on the ground. Hand out to her.

She ran, took his hand, and they boarded the *Tyche*. Together.

Hope was yelling something into the comm, slamming the cargo bay door control closed. The ship shook around them, then pushed at the ground, leaping for the sky. They hugged the floor of the bay, thrust pressing on them.

Penn was looking up, trying to see around the cargo bay. "What kind of crazy pilot flies in a meteor shower?" he said.

Nate was grinning. "Well, Rear Admiral Penn, that would be *my* pilot."

El's voice came over the speakers. "*Tyche* to crew. Strap in. Shit's gonna get real."

Grace laughed. Because *now* it would get real. But at least they were together.

Grace Grace Grace Grace Grace...

CHAPTER EIGHTEEN

THEY HAD A LITTLE TIME.

Kohl: in sickbay. Not a full medbay like the *Gladiator* had. Just a small room, a few medical supplies, most of them past their use-by dates. A low-end scanner Nate had scammed from someone was telling them what they already knew. Kohl might be dying, or he might be recovering. He'd lost blood. He'd been poisoned. There were several unidentified stimulants in his blood. He was unconscious. *Stupid machine*, thought Hope.

El: on the flight deck, arguing with Penn. That was a thing she wouldn't have got to do in the *actual* military. They were arguing about who would fly the ship, and where it would get flown to. About how fast and far they would push it. About whether taking off was even a good idea, what with the sky full of burning rocks — the bugs were still shelling the planet — and a hostile alien spacecraft orbiting the planet.

Penn: also on the flight deck, but full of bad ideas and desperation. The man had been sweating, moving too fast from foot to foot, like he had a powerful need to use the head, but didn't know where it was. He kept talking about *the mission* and *acceptable collateral damage*, like he was telling a story that would help them sleep at night. He had hard eyes.

Nate: asleep. Out like a baby in a coma, cabin door open, arm draping over the edge of his crash couch. Still in his clothes. Twitching while he slept, whimpering, dreams that were too bad for real rest but too soft to wake from. His dreams might have been about freedom. All their dreams might have been.

Grace: missing. Not in her cabin. Not in the ready room, eating, having a coffee, or something stronger. Not in Engineering, and not next to Kohl in the sickbay. She wasn't on the flight deck, supporting El, or supporting Penn. She wasn't in Nate's cabin, although that was a crazy thought, but Hope had had to check anyway.

And, finally, Hope. Here, in Grace's cabin, holding the hilt of Grace's broken sword. It had been thrown into the recycler, where Hope had found it. Hope drew the blade, ten centimeters of steel glinting from the scabbard before a jagged stump covered in alien slime told the full story. She'd come to find Grace, to say *would you like it fixed, or..?* because Grace looked tired, just as tired as Hope was, and she looked like she'd had a bad day.

Hope didn't have many friends. She couldn't. But she had plenty of stims, and she could always sleep later. This friend, she'd try and look after.

SINCE NO ONE else was watching Kohl, Hope tried it for a while. She wasn't a Guild Healer, although it was all mechanics at some level. Hope had read a little on how the body worked, and then went down the Engineer path because machines didn't leak so much. She didn't know people like she knew drives and reactors and fabricators, but maybe if she talked to the sickbay machine enough, it'd talk back in a way she could understand. She could bring Kohl back. Kohl didn't like her, and she didn't like Kohl, but Hope had taken some time — *never enough, always something to do* — to watch the recordings from their suit cams. She'd seen him at work, doing what he did best. She'd also seen the number of Ezeroc arrayed against them. That was a powerful force to face, but especially when you were down a man.

It didn't matter what kind of man. It was about numbers. It was about survival.

Nate had plugged Kohl into the right tubes, set the medical machine to *ping* and *sigh* at the appropriate times, put his hands on his hips, then said *fuck it* before walking off. Because none of them knew how to fix a person beyond putting on a field dressing. Kohl had been poisoned by the Ezeroc, some kind of alien toxin injected under his skin to fester and boil.

Hope had watched the holos. She'd seen people with bugs where their brains should have been. Was this how it started? Stabbed while you were at lunch, or on a bus, or shopping for new clothes. Pain, blood, and then ... what? Oblivion? Madness before the end?

Penn had a data sliver. There might be more on that data sliver.

Hope leaned forward, putting a cool hand on Kohl's sweat-slick brow. "Let's see what we can see," she said. She pumped the sanitizer a few times, then wiped her hands dry on her flight suit. Because, while Kohl needed their care, God only knew how you caught that kind of sickness.

"AS THE SENIOR RANKING OFFICER—"

El's peal of laughter came down to Hope as she approached the Flight Deck. "Oh, Penn. Penn, Penn, Penn. We've been going at this for an hour or more. And finally, you drop the senior officer card?"

"I'm a Rear Admiral in the Republic Navy—"

"You're a spy," said El. "You might *also* be a Rear Admiral. But you're a spy, because I've seen people like you. Last man standing. Got the big scary data, got to get it out! Seriously? It's old. Also, this is not a Navy ship."

Hope reached the airlock, sticking her head through. She watched El playing with her console, checking the *Tyche* out after their run of fire and death. The LIDAR was still down, and that'd need fixing. Hope then looked at Penn, who had one hand on his hip and the other hand on the butt of a blaster he'd scrounged up from somewhere.

Penn hadn't finished, or he hadn't seen Hope, or he didn't care either way. "It's under Navy charter—"

"No," said El, not looking around.

Hope could see Penn's hand tighten on his blaster, the muscles in his jaw clenching. He was about to do something that couldn't be undone, because he was used to getting his own way, used to being in charge, and he probably felt close to freedom. Like that was a thing you could be close to, rather than have, or not have. She cleared her throat.

Penn startled, a little, his hand dropping from his blaster. El didn't even look around as she said, "Hey, Hope. How's my LIDAR coming along?"

"It's coming," she said. She paused, then said, "but I've got a comm line up to the *Gladiator*. I found a few satellites up there still talking, routed around the planet, and viola." El had parked the *Tyche* on the opposite side of the planet to the Ezeroc ship, and thus also the *Gladiator*. No line of sight was no problem if you had patience and skill. Hope had a theory that said the satellites were how the Ezeroc had jammed their comms, but she was missing some important vectors, like *how had they gained access to the satellites* or *where was the signal's point of origin*. Later; there'd be time enough for that after the immediate threat of a horrible death had passed.

That made El turn around. "Nah. That ship's likely a smoldering ball of nuclear fire."

"It might be," said Hope. "I don't have the codes." She looked at

Penn. "But it doesn't matter. If the comm's up, we could get a signal out." What she knew, and El knew, and Penn knew, was that the Guild Bridge was also down. That wasn't the point. The point was that the *Gladiator* might be told to make an automated jump.

"A signal?" said Penn. "Perfect. I'll need a console."

El was looking at Hope with a *what the actual fuck* expression, but she was one of Hope's few friends, the very few, and so she said nothing except, "Take the Cap's. He's sleeping off whatever party you had down there."

"I'm surprised you're not sleeping," said Hope. "Not tired?"

"Wired," said El. "I won't sleep for days, not after a combat drop."

"You said you weren't Navy," said Penn, sagging into the other acceleration couch.

"Not anymore," said El. "You guys are assholes."

"We could draft you at a moment's notice," said Penn, not looking up from the console. He was patting the front of his uniform, until he found — *perfect* — a data sliver. He tucked it into the console.

"With my combat record?" said El. "You wouldn't dare. Besides, you try that shit and you're walking home."

The holo cleared, sat dark for a few moments, then came to life with the injured cries of the *Gladiator*. Systems down. Drives damaged. Weapons offline. Reactor still online. Some flight controls. Limited, but there. She'd crawl out of orbit, but not a lot farther. What was left of her couldn't hold enough atmosphere to fill a coffee cup. Lots of telemetry readings, still good RADAR and LIDAR. A functional PDC, singular, for all the good it would do. No working railguns or lasers. Torpedoes spent. "Huh," said Hope. "What did they hit her with?"

"Rocks," said Penn. "They're big on rocks. It seems like they peel off a piece of their own ship ... hell. This is classified." But he looked tired, like he wanted to tell them things, because he wanted to tell *someone*.

"We need to know," said El, giving Hope a glance, "in case we ever get the opportunity to take off again."

"Here we go," said Penn, finding the comm systems. Hope watched the holo as he linked it to the automation systems. He started an upload of his data, and in a blink of an eye, it was done. He cued up an order to dispatch the *Gladiator* — which Hope, on a hunch, stopped on her wrist console — then slumped back. "Done, or as near as without a more personal delivery." This last with a pointed look at El.

Hope wasn't a hundred percent sure why she'd stopped the *Gladiator's* dispatch. Penn seemed too eager, if anything. Sending a ship straight towards human space didn't seem sensible with alien eyes watching. No point in talking about that now; she had what she wanted and there wasn't any point getting in a tussle about the *Gladiator*. Penn would be upset, and yell, and nothing would change anyway. "Sounds good," said Hope, brushing a wisp of pink hair from her eyes. "You guys want a beer now, or what?"

ENGINEERING. Her haven. Her space. No one came here.

Oh, sure. The captain did, sometimes. Grace had, once or twice. Kohl, when he was tearing out the *Tyche's* heart, helping with that emergency transplant — those scars had healed, courtesy of the *Gladiator*. El, never. El was front-of-house; Hope worked in the kitchen.

Whenever people came here, they never stayed. It might have been the smell, or the primal fear of standing next to a live reactor. The thrum of the drives, insistent here in a way they couldn't be anywhere else. It could just be the smell of grease and the fear of grubbing up a good flight suit.

Either way, it worked just fine for Hope. Especially for times like this.

Her holo chattered to life as she and the *Tyche* had a conversation. She got the data dump that Penn had sent to the *Gladiator*. The man was some kind of amateur spy, if he was a spy at all; Spycraft 101 had to be *not using someone else's deck when sending top secret comms*. It could just be the man was as desperate as he looked, and it could also be that he expected none of them to survive, so what was the point?

Medical documents. Bioscans, before the shit turned real and there was nobody left to do the scanning. Tests against live subjects. Tests against dead ones. Theories on organization, social culture, technology.

That last, she could understand. She opened the file. It was sparse. Because they didn't seem to have a technology, in the typical sense.

The *Tyche* beeped at her, reminding her she wasn't done. "Oh, sorry," she said, giving her console a pat. Before she had the reward of a decent technical document, she needed to give the captain something he could use. The *Gladiator's* codes. She coded a message for his console, fire it off complete with *here's how you unlock the remains of a Navy warship* instructions, then flipped back to the files she wanted to read.

Light on the detail, but that would probably happen if you were being invaded by a bunch of aliens. Keeping your sciencing on point would be tricky in that kind of situation.

The Ezeroc's ship — the asteroid — had popped into the system without a drive trail. Initial reactions were as expected: yo, hey, that's unusual, but it's just a rock, so whatevs. Hope pushed a strand of hair aside and kept reading. The planet crews were a little confused when their comms arrays went down. No response from the Guild Bridge, but you know, there were protocols in place. The Republic would send a ship, replace the transmitter, and it'd be unicorns and rainbows before the week was out.

The ship never came. Or, it had, but they hadn't been able to see the *Ravana*. Didn't even know she was there. Hope suspected the *Ravana* had seen what was happening on the surface though. Something that had made the ship signal for help. It supported El's spy theory though. A standard freighter wouldn't linger; they'd just cut and run. And a standard freighter wouldn't risk all hands to get a message back faster than was wise. The *Ravana*, here for Penn as well as dropping off the transmitter? Maybe. Files didn't say, all one-sided intel at this point.

The Ezeroc didn't seem to use conventional thrust. Their ship moved like it was under the control of an invisible hand. It also moved like G forces were things that happened to other people. The damn thing had come into orbit after putting on the brakes at what looked like a sustained 15Gs. Do that to a person and they'd detach a retina, or maybe stroke out. Conjecture: the bugs were tough. Hope noted that on her console.

She paused, looking over at Grace's broken sword where she'd dropped it beside her. Hope unsheathed the broken blade. *Conjecture confirmed.*

Initial small arms conflicts looked promising, yada yada. Hope scrolled through a couple pages of military dick-measuring. No real clue on communications structure. They seemed coordinated, focused, and pretty much ate the colony for lunch in just a few days. There'd be a bunch of brass back in the Republic who'd like to understand how that was possible. It'd make repressing uprisings with subversives like Hope much easier.

Steady, now. This isn't about that.

Okay, okay. Communications infrastructure second to none but no clue how it worked, check. They were tougher than humans due to a shiny shell; fists and clubs were useless but blasters worked just fine. What's in the other files? Hope flipped through, thinking *Kohl is dying upstairs*, and wondered what might cheer him up. They said laughter was the best medicine, so ... weapons?

Weapons. Not a lot here. They used numbers, which — a cross-referenced note to *breeding* in another file — were supplied by native populations. Not great news, that. They had sharp mandibles, and claws made with purpose; rip you apart or deliver larvae, and that was your typical warrior-slash-drone. There were other files here — a land-based big thing, and something that looked like a brain roach.

Time scales were variable, but if Kohl had been infected it should have happened by now.

Should.

It'd cheer Kohl up, if he ever woke. Not having your brain eaten by insects was a good thing, right? Even if his wasn't much of a brain to start with.

Hope looked at the sword again. Time to get to work.

CHAPTER NINETEEN

NATE WOKE WITH A START, the scrabbling fingers of a dream still dragging at him. He flailed in his bunk, reaching for a blaster that wasn't there, then a sword that wasn't there either. Only after all that carry on did he work out where he was — the *Tyche*, home — and was happy no one was watching him, because it was his cabin, and no one should see a man wake from a nightmare. Even if they had just gone through hell with a bunch of angry space insects.

He blinked at the open door. The *open* door.

Nate was up in a flash, feet on the deck, eyes scanning the room. Definitely no one here, but the door was also definitely open. He had closed the door when he came in. It wasn't that he was sure of it. And even if he hadn't, the doors closed themselves, unless someone was messing with them. It was a ship, and ship doors wanted to be airtight, in case some part vented their breathable atmosphere into the hard black. What was worse than waking from a nightmare? Waking while being sucked into space.

Technically, it wasn't sucked, it was blown, but that wasn't the issue here.

The issue was his door was open.

He wiped his mouth with the back of his hand — great, no drool — and checked the door control. Looked normal, panel was in place, lights doing the things that lights did. Except ... *there*. A tiny scratch. Something you wouldn't notice, unless you know every square millimeter of the *Tyche* like the back of your hand. Nate reached his metal hand up and applied pressure. The panel popped off, revealing a mess of wires underneath. Hey now: someone had installed a bypass.

Someone had busted into his cabin while he was asleep.

He let the panel go, dangling by wiring, and turned back inside. Nate stood in the middle of it and closed his eyes. *Think. Remember.* What had it looked like before?

His cabin was underneath the flight deck, spacious by the standards of the rest of the ship. It had windows that looked out over the forest they'd landed in. It was the same view they'd have on the flight deck, without the holo in the middle of it all, and without El complaining about one damn thing or another. In his mind's eye, his bunk was a wash, because he'd been thrashing about it in it for a good couple hours. His personal terminal was off. The old sea chest at the end of his bunk was closed, two leather straps fastened and a third just *looking* like it was clasped, because it was broken. His wardrobe — *hah*, as if that's what you'd call a thing with so few clothes and only one pair of boots — stood closed.

Nate opened his eyes. *Status.*

Holo, still off. Not that it would matter, there were just messages on there, and Nate assumed messages sent over the air were being read by everyone anyway. That kind of thinking had kept him alive more often than not.

Sea chest, still closed. Two clasps, shut, but the third broken one was loose, at an angle from where it should have been. Someone had either opened it and put it back wrong, or been unable to open it. Something to check.

Wardrobe, closed, but the door not lining up right with the frame.

That could have been the work of the refit just as much as tampering, but it'd also bear looking in to.

He dropped into a crouch in front of the sea chest, flicking the clasps open. They released with satisfying *thunks*. The lid yawned with the smell of sandalwood, and inside were some things he expected to see and one he did not. Also, a thing was missing. Some personal effects, a vanishing few for a man who'd served on the Emperor's Black for more years than most survived. A couple of still holos, one his metal fingers found as if by themselves. A picture of him with a young man — they were both young men when the shot was taken. *Dom, what would you have thought of this ship of fools I've built?* A necklace made for him by a woman who was dead. Annemarie would have laughed at him, shut the lid of the sea chest, and told him to put away his childish things.

She might have remarked on the loss of the sword. That was the thing that was missing.

She might not, just as easily. Annemarie was never much interested in the things the Emperor's Black kept about their persons. But Dom? He would have remarked on it. He'd given Nate that sword. Dom had told Nate *sorry, I know it doesn't make up for losing a hand or a leg, but it's the least I can offer.* Like Nate hadn't failed him; it was before both of them knew failure would cost an Empire. Nate wasn't there at the end. No arm, no leg, a sword he couldn't swing anymore, and a discharge on top. Honorably, but it never felt that way.

Nate shook his head. Some fucker had taken his sword.

The unexpected thing was a data sliver. He picked it out and slotted it into his console. It hummed to life, and Grace Gushiken burst into life on the holo. She was looking over her shoulder, like she was doing something she shouldn't, before looking back at the recorder.

Nate sighed. God*damn* it. He stood, shutting the chest, as Grace spoke. "Nate? Nate, we're missing something here. We're ... I've got to find out. They're speaking to me, Nate. They're whispering. In my head. I can't get them out."

He turned away from the holo, taking the few steps needed to open the wardrobe. Inside, his Emperor's Black was hung neat and crisp. It was also jumbled about, but any number of things between when he'd last opened this wardrobe and now could have done that. El flying at supersonic speeds while dodging rocks was one. But it meant Grace knew, and that wasn't helpful, because she was a fucking *esper*, and some things couldn't be trusted to people like that. She'd have one over on him now. Something to bargain with. *You tell them about me, and I'll tell them about* you. It had happened before.

The holo was still speaking. "I know this doesn't make sense. It doesn't make sense to me. I needed a weapon, and so I've ... I've borrowed yours. I'll bring it back. I promise. And then we can talk. Because we need to talk." And then the holo went dark, like a memory, gone like the faded tatters of his dream.

In a way, it was good news. She was out there on a planet infested by aliens. As they would have said back in the day, *that's a problem that will solve itself.* Nate ran a hand over his face — the hand that was still human, still made of flesh and blood — and sighed. The problem was that Dom would have taken him to task about that. He'd set up the Intelligencers, because he believed they were an asset, not a problem. He'd died for it, of course, but he'd still *believed.* Annemarie would have touched his chest, where the necklace used to sit, leaned close, and said *you need to get the girl, Nathan Chevell. You've always needed to get the girl.*

"CAPTAIN," said Penn, "we need to—"

"Sit the fuck down, Penn," said Nate. "Sit the fuck down, and stop talking for a second." They were in the ready room. Hope was there, still finishing breakfast or lunch or whatever the hell it was at this time of day. She was eating with gusto, like she hadn't eaten for about three days, and that could well be true. El was standing against the wall connecting to the flight deck, arms crossed, poker face on — and she could play a mean hand of poker. No Kohl, because a machine was still pumping him full of nutrients and antibiotics. No Grace, because she'd left the Goddamn ship, with his *sword*, and would get her fool self killed.

With *his* sword.

The Rear Admiral's lips went into a tight line, the blood pressed out of them. Nate figured he was building for a powerful rage, and it was best to cut that off. "First, before you say anything, you need to know the situation you're in here. Number one on the list is that you're *on my ship*. If you ever don't want to be on my ship, you let me know, and you can get off. Hell, we'll even help you off. Right here. Right now."

"Your gorilla is in medbay," said Penn. "You can't—"

Nate's laugh cut him off. "Oh, Penn. If you think I need Kohl to throw a little trash off my ship, you've been reading the wrong files about me."

"I didn't—"

"Second thing, and this is an ordered list, is that we are not leaving this rock until we get my sword back." Nate caught the glance from Hope, and the glance from El, even through her poker face.

"What sword?" said El.

"What about Grace?" said Hope.

"Captain," said Penn, "I can buy you another sword."

"Not like this, Penn. Nothing like this." Nate cleared his throat. "So here's what's going to happen. You can stay here. Hell, all of you *will* stay here. I will go out, and I'll get my sword back." There was a small whine as he unclenched his metal hand. "If I'm not back, Penn, and this is number three on the list, El and Hope will take you out of here."

"Cap—" started El.

"Hell no—" said Hope.

"That's reasonable—" said Penn.

"All of you," said Nate, "need to be quiet. This is not a democracy. This is not a committee. This is *my* ship. In five hours, Absalom will have turned enough to bring us under the eye of that fucking Ezeroc ship. Therefore, in four hours the *Tyche* will leave, whether or not I am back on board with my sword. I have already locked Helm control, because I know that Penn will want to use some form of coercion on you all."

"I wouldn't—" started Penn.

"It will unlock," said Nate, "in four hours. In four hours," and here, he looked at El, "you will take off. El? You hear me good. You get my family out of here."

She looked down at her crossed arms. "Okay," she said.

"I can live with these terms," said Penn.

"You're still acting like it's a negotiation," said Nate. "It's not. It's just the way it is."

Hope was still sitting, mouth half-open, eyes wide. A strand of pink hair had fallen over one of her eyes. "Oh," she said, after a long moment. "Oh. You're going to get *Grace*."

"If Grace is still attached to my sword, sure," said Nate. "Otherwise, no."

Hope bounced from her seat, came over to him, and then stopped all in a rush. She leaned forward, and whispered in his ear. "I knew it."

"It's not that," said Nate, but he spoke quietly too, because he wasn't sure about much right now. He needed more sleep, and all he had was stims. They'd have to do.

CHAPTER TWENTY

THE SWORD in her hand was foreign, just like this planet.

Breath loud, harsh inside her helmet. Grace was running, her feet trampling through plants that looked like they could be at home on Earth. She'd been to Earth, spent time there, none of it on a nature trail, but she'd seen holos. Ferns whipped past her legs, creepers draped low to touch at her helmet, the noise of them drumming like fingers against her skull. All so similar, but so strange — the plants growing lower than felt right under a little more gravity, a gene splice here or there giving leaves a strange color, or a strange shape.

Now she was moving, she had purpose. Sitting around on the *Tyche* wasn't for her. They'd been waiting to die, huddled against the ground. A prize for the Ezeroc to snatch at a time of their choosing. Grace knew they were coming, because the voices in her head wouldn't stop. They got louder, and louder, and more insistent.

When she was younger, Grace had been taught how to be still. How to quiet her mind, so her feelings wouldn't brim over to the people around her. They called her *esper*, but they also called her *mongrel*. Her father's eyes had turned hard and cold when she had shown her gifts to be less than his. He had been twisted into something beautiful by science, and she was an apple fallen too far from the tree. Grace couldn't argue with his reasoning, because she was always buffeted by the feelings of the people who walked next to her, each alone in their own heads, each shouting as loud as they could within the bone walls of their skulls. Wanting to be heard, but unable to speak.

She could hear people's feelings, but not the words. Her father had heard their voices, and could speak to them. He had served the Empire, he said, until the Empire was unworthy of his service. Then he had pulled it down.

They called her *esper*, but she was twice damned. To carry the stigma of it, the hated stares the deaf and mute used against her kind. By the same token, damned to be almost a *hikikomori*, closed off, mute in her own mind. Able to listen, and only to the partial meaning. Unable to speak.

Until Absalom. Until now.

She couldn't speak, but these words filled her mind. Her name, spoken so clear and bright. Not even her father had been able to speak to her like this.

Grace needed to know who was speaking. With borrowed steel, she left the *Tyche*'s lights behind her.

GRACE HAD ALWAYS EXERCISED. Before the fighting it had been the joy of *kata*. Before *kata* it had been running wild and free, just out of the grasping reach of a parent's fingers. As her frame had grown longer, leaner, she'd kept the speed, used the drills to keep her mind and body sharp.

It was hard, on a spacecraft, to keep fit. To be fit, to move, to dance. Running was a particular discipline that was challenging when your entire world was only a hundred meter lap.

Even so, she ran. She ran until she was sick. Grace ran until her throat burned. She ran, because she could only hear one thing, and the sound of her ragged breathing helped to drown it out.

Grace.

Together.

Grace Grace Grace Grace Grace.

SHE WAS CLIMBING A HILL NOW, the sword in her hand heavy. Grace knew she should toss it aside, because she wouldn't need it when she got to the voice.

Grace!

But her body wanted to hold it, so she held it. Her body knew what it was for.

When she was learning the drills, *kendo* forms learned at the feet of the best *sensei* money and influence could buy, her body was too small to hold the *bokken* they'd given her. She'd asked for a smaller one, and been told that her enemies wouldn't bow to her size. There had been many lessons about how, for all that her chin jutted out against the wisdom of her betters, she would always be smaller than someone else. Weaker. They'd said this while their minds whispered things like *mongrel/avoid/hate* at her. Those had been lessons too.

So she kept the sword, gloved hand firm around the scabbard as she ran.

THE TOWER REACHED up out of the forest ahead of her, set atop the hill like a spike. It was dark; she could see it only by the stars it blotted out through breaks in the trees. It's where the voice was.

Grace.

Together.

There were things rumbling in the dark about her, massive shapes that were more shadow than creature. They rasped at her and at each other in what might have been language.

It could also be hunger making them gnash their mandibles.

Smaller things that rustled in the brushwood chittered and scattered before the lights of her suit. She wanted to take her helmet off to breathe easier, to feel the cold night air on the sweat beading her skin. But to take off her helmet, she'd need both hands, and that would mean dropping the sword. Her body wanted the sword, so instead she ran.

There were lights, readouts in her visor that spoke of oxygen levels and lactate buildups and adrenaline. They'd be there after she spoke with the voice, so she ignored them for now. Plenty of time for that ... after.

Grace Grace Grace Grace Grace!

She clambered up the rise, bursting into a cleared area at the base of the tower. The tower reached to the sky, a communications facility for speaking to the stars. The kind of thing that would transmit to the Guild Bridge. Messages of comfort could be sent home if you had a family who didn't think of you as *mongrel/hated/lesser*. Grace had used facilities like this to lie and cheat and steal.

There was a chain link fence with razor wire set at the top. The chain link was old, rusted, and the razor wire broken and missing. Something huge had trampled it all down, making for easy access to the tower. Grace walked over the flattened fence, her boots crunching on an old sign. *REPUBLIC SCIENCE FACILITY ABSALOM DELTA*. Above and below that were the words *INTRUDERS WILL BE EXECUTED*.

She paused. Science facility guards generally didn't shoot people for getting too close. Black ops sites, now *those* shot at people. Grace looked back at the forest behind her. She saw a massive insect creature standing almost 3 meters tall, looking back at her. One of the Ezeroc, guarding her passage.

Or preventing her escape.

Grace.

Together!

The rust on the fence spoke of an age well beyond the Ezeroc's week-long infestation of this planet. Whatever had happened here had been long ago. She'd missed the action, and that was just fine. There were turrets at the base of the tower, dark and quiet, barrels pointed down or plain missing.

The tower itself was larger than she'd been expecting, moss and lichen of the woods creeping up the walls. The forest wanted to claim it for its own. The structure tapered towards the top, but here at the base it was a hundred meters a side, easy. It was no simple comm tower like she'd thought. She wanted to rub her head to clear it. But to do that she'd need to take off her helmet. To take off her helmet, she'd need to put down Nate's sword.

Nate.

She'd taken his sword, and she couldn't remember why.

SHE'D STEPPED inside the tower with ease. The doors were massive, vaulted metal, on the floor inside. They'd been torn off and tossed aside like paper. To do that, you'd need some kind of industrial equipment.

Inside was a confusion of equipment amid a jumble of bones that might have been people once. Shells, hard casings from fallen Ezeroc. All covered in vines, moss, fungus. Holos stages were dark, their consoles inert. No people, and nothing automated minding the facility.

Grace.

She looked up at the voice, coming from above her now. She'd have to climb.

One of the Ezeroc came out of the darkness, a warrior drone. She felt it had come to collect her, to take her to the top, to be—

Together.

—with the voice. Those fore claws reached for her, and she

wanted to close her eyes and just *be*. Be with something that *wanted* her. That wanted *her*. For just a minute, just a second, just a moment between thoughts, to be where she was needed, desirable.

Her body didn't want that. It didn't want that at all.

Where her mind was confused, her body was sure. Where her mind wandered, her body had the certainty of the drills. The sword she carried whispered free of the scabbard, the blade making one perfect cut as it crossed up, and another as she spun, bringing it on a reverse path back again. The Ezeroc's fore claws fell to the ground, followed soon after by its head.

She stood in the silence, something dripping from the end of her blade in the darkness.

When she'd found the sword in Nate's cabin—

Who is Nate?

Grace.

Together...

—she'd been so surprised. He hadn't moved like a swordsman, all cocky show and a chin that jutted against authority just like hers. He'd fired a blaster. And yet, he owned a sword, with a blade black as obsidian. Gold circuitry inlaid the hilt, a motif or actual technology, impossible to tell. It was beautiful and strange. The balance of the blade was wrong in her hand, like it didn't want her to know it, but it went with her nonetheless.

When her bare hand had closed around the hilt on the *Tyche*, the voices in her head had grown quieter, but out here with her suit on, they became more insistent, still scratching at her mind with sharp little claws. On the *Tyche* she'd been able to *think*, and so she'd gone hunting. Now she was here the voices were louder, the scratching more insistent, the claws not so little.

Grace looked up again. "Together, huh?" It helped to talk out loud. To speak words not just in her mind. "No problem. Together it is." She found a stairwell, the door ajar, and climbed.

CHAPTER TWENTY-ONE

WELL, *this is all fucked, isn't it?*

Nate's suit said *that way*, and that way was up a Goddamn hill, at night. His suit was following Grace's suit, a compass on his HUD placing a marker in the right place. *Put your feet down, one after the other Nate, in that direction. You'll die of exhaustion or find the sword.*

Or be eaten by alien monsters. That was a distinct possibility.

He didn't need the wayfinder. Even a city boy like him could tell which way Grace had gone. The leaves were trampled by her passage, like a herd of elephants had gone this way.

Hang on.

One person couldn't have destroyed that much vegetation. There was some kind of truck or jeep or other damn thing on her trail. Which didn't make sense, because the *Tyche* hadn't seen anything with a power source for klicks in any direction. The ship was watching, and she hadn't seen shit.

He keyed the comm. "Engineer."

"You've got Hope," she said.

"That's great," he said. "Look, I've got me a trail here. Some kind of industrial traffic, looks like. I don't know. Can you do me a scan?"

"Scanning," she said. "Nope."

"Nope?"

"Nope," she said. "Nada. Zilch. Nothing. I've got you, I've got that blip ahead of you that's a suit, and that's it for power supplies."

"That sounds specific," said Nate. "Like you want to say something else."

"Did you bring a big gun?" she said.

Nate hefted Kohl's rifle. It was a heavy action plasma affair, something that looked like it had come from military action. Twin barrels, rangefinder and massfinder for optimal charge per shot depending on target, big battery hanging out the ass of it. "Yeah, I got one from Kohl."

"He's awake?"

"I didn't think he'd mind," said Nate.

"Cool," said Hope. "Thing is, you didn't read the files, did you?"

"Files?"

"Right," said Hope. "The Ezeroc come in different sizes."

"Oh come *on*," said Nate. "They seemed pretty annoying when there were thousands of them of just a little bit bigger than me." *Insects. Giant insects. You're fighting a roach problem of epic proportions.* He clamped his lips shut around a laugh that might have come out as a nervous giggle.

"There are *huge* ones," she said. "Have fun dying. Or, you know, come on back. It's warm here, and there's cookies." The comm clicked off.

Different sizes, huh? Nate hefted the rifle. Big game hunting it is.

THE TOWER WAS dark and creepy. No other words for it. *Dark* because the damn lights were out, not a backup generator or power cell in the place to keep 'em on. *Creepy*, because the rusted fence was broken down and the place was crawling with vines and creepers and giant insects.

His sword was inside. Inside, and up.

He tried the comm. "Grace? Grace. It's Nate."

The line hissed at him, not the clear signal of tight comms, but interference. Something that sounded like voices, whispered at the edge of hearing.

Or, it's just static. The place was creepy, and the creepy was creeping him out.

He set the comm to cycle his broadcast, then clicked it off. She'd get back to him, or she wouldn't, and the suit could do the hard work without him wearing his voice hoarse.

So, what did we have here?

Creepy building: check.

Sign saying it was a science facility: also check.

Nasty-looking fence? Check on that too.

Nate tramped across the chain link fence, the thing rattling under his feet. He caught the hint of some other sound, more a sensation through his feet, and turned. His foot got snarled in the busted fence and he went down, just in time to see a massive — *fuck that thing is huge!* — insect bearing down on him. Where the Ezeroc he'd seen before were like a mad insect version of a centaur, this was more like an armored beetle. Wide, big crab-like claws, another six legs, and a horror mouth of transparent needle teeth.

He fell hard, his fingers jerking at the trigger of the rifle. There was a tenth of a second whine and then twin bolts of plasma spat out at the thing. Those twin bolts of plasma were a few thousand degrees C each, the kick of the rifle hard against his shoulder. The Ezeroc had a massive claw up in front of its face, where Nate had been firing, and the plasma hit, and ... *fizzled.*

Nate looked at the rifle, then at the Ezeroc. At the rifle again. "Oh *come* on!" He readied the weapon again, pointed it at the Ezeroc, and flicked on the rangefinder and massfinder. The weapon cycled — *never using this one again, it's slower than a trade run to Ganymede* — and then fired. Twin bolts of plasma blasted out, impacting with the Ezeroc. This time, cracks appeared in the claw, and the Ezeroc roared. It trampled towards Nate, who tried to move, but his foot was snared, caught in the fence. It swung at him.

The crack of the claw when it hit his helmet was like a thunder-clap. Nate felt a horrible twinge in his leg as he was knocked free, but that was dwarfed by the pain in his head and neck, shortly followed by the pain in his back as he impacted with the side of the tower. The breath knocked from him, sounding loud in his helmet, and he lay on the ground for a couple of moments, unable to remember who he was, or why he was here.

Nate.

Sword.

Grace.

Got it. He clawed at the wall for support, pulled himself to his knees, and then the Ezeroc was on him again. *Moves quick for such a big thing.* It caught him in the side this time, knocking him away with the gentle touch of a locomotive. He screamed as something in his ribcage gave with a wet pop, and he flopped in the undergrowth like a landed fish. Nate had fallen on his rifle — how he still had that in his hand was a mystery — and he struggled to right himself. He could feel the drumming through the earth as the thing bore down on him.

He remembered those crab claws. *Why hasn't it snipped me in half?* He looked up a split second before it hit him again, knocking him high up and over, and this time his shoulder dislocated. He didn't have the breath left to scream. When Nate landed against a tree, he was trying to suck in air through a diaphragm that was paralyzed. He wanted to throw up, or breathe — just a *teaspoon of air for Christ's sake* — but all the noise he could make were little hiccups.

All he'd wanted was his goddamn sword. That, and to have a conversation with Grace Gushiken.

And *maybe* get his completion bonus for taking the transmitter all the way out to this forsaken rock infested with killer bugs. And for rescuing the Rear Admiral, who was a real asshole. Just a little break, that's all he needed, and here he was trying to suck air in the precious moments before he died.

Why was everything so hard? He tried to do the right thing. Look after people. Do the jobs on time. Not stiff his clients — except that *one* time, but they were huge assholes, like a collection of Penns. Maybe get one over on the Republic while he was at it, but who *didn't* want to do that? What had it got him but a busted rib, dislocated shoulder, and a fatal appointment with a super crab.

The Ezeroc was almost on him again, and his adrenaline spiked higher if that was possible. His diaphragm gave a little spasm, and he coughed, and while he coughed his arm jerked. The arm that was still holding Kohl's rifle. His finger clenched on the finger, and the rifle fired two more bursts of plasma. This surprised Nate, but it surprised the Ezeroc more, because the blasts went low. Under those massive armored claws, and hit a leg beneath it.

The leg exploded in a shower of barbecued lobster meat. The Ezeroc screamed, trampling its remaining five legs in a circle.

Well, that's a thing. Nate squeezed the trigger again, blowing off another leg, and the Ezeroc toppled to the ground. Those legs were really clawing at the air now, lethal things each as wide as his two legs together. Nate wanted to pull himself clear, but his other arm was dislocated, and that wouldn't do anyone any good. So he hefted the rifle again, took aim, and kept blowing legs off.

One of his shots missed, chewing into the underside of the Ezeroc, causing a rupture of fluids and scalded meat. It screamed even louder, if that was possible. *Ah, hell with it,* thought Nate, and just kept pulling the trigger on the plasma rifle until the screaming stopped.

Silence. Or, almost silence, a gentle hiss of air escaping from the crack in his visor. *SUIT BREACH* said his HUD.

Nate shouldered the rifle's sling, then pulled himself upright using the tree. He leaned against it for a second, working himself up to the next bit, then rammed his shoulder into it. It went back into the socket with a pop, and he almost passed out. The only thing that stopped him falling over was the doses of stims and painkillers the suit was feeding him. He'd bought the suit at a crazy sale a couple jobs ago, the dealer promising a good emergency experience for a budget rate. Nate loved budget rates. He loved that it had a defibrillator built into it. Not that he wanted to test out how well it worked.

The dealer, for once, hadn't lied. Nate felt high on Jesus.

He patted his suit for the emergency repair kit, pulling out sealant and some tape. Nate squirted the goo onto his visor then plastered tape over the top. He couldn't see for shit, but at least he had an atmosphere seal now. Nate didn't want to catch whatever these colonists had.

What he wanted was his sword, and a conversation with Grace Gushiken. He entered the tower, leaving smoking Ezeroc behind him.

STAIRS. Always fucking *stairs*.

Nate had bought himself a nice ship with only a few decks. A minimum of stairs, because climbing them sucked, and climbing down them when drunk could lead to all kinds of unpleasantness. A *flat* ship is what he'd bought, nose to tail an uncomplicated thing, his *Tyche*.

But here he was, climbing up the inside of some insect-infested ancient communications tower that spoke to a sky that wasn't listening. Or, actually, it was: it was probably talking to the damn satellites that had knocked out their comms. But *sky that wasn't listening* sounded poetic, and sounding poetic was better than throwing up in his helmet, which was the alternative if he didn't concentrate on something other than how sick he felt.

The weirdest thing was on the 21st, maybe 22nd level. He'd lost count. There was a body here, some kind of growth holding it to the wall. Tendrils came out of the mouth of the body, pulsating. The eyes of the body were sightless and white, the skin covered in mold. The tendrils were connected to the growth on the wall. Nate shone his light on it, playing the beam up the stairwell. There was growth all the way up, every floor he could see. He checked for vitals, and found a pulse. Which didn't make him feel great, because it looked liked this person had been here a while. No muscle tone, arms and legs wasted, withered to sticks. Clothes rotted. Same kind of mold around the mouth where the tentacles entered.

He keyed his comm. "Hope?"

"You've got the Engineer," she said.

"Those files," said Nate. "Did they talk about ... anything else?"

"Lots of stuff," she said. "Specificity, Cap. It's important."

"Here," said Nate, throwing a visual her way. "What's that look like?"

"It looks like," and then she stopped. When she spoke again, her voice was faint, but still struggling for bravado. "It looks like it's not an Engineering problem."

"Do I ... pull the tentacles out?" Nate looked up the stairwell. No movement. Nothing. No Grace. No damn sword.

"You want my opinion?"

"I want to know what the files say," said Nate.

"Files aren't real specific," she said. "Not about this. Want me to ask Penn?"

"No," said Nate. Nothing that came out of that man's mouth could be trusted. "Thanks." He clicked the comm off.

If he found himself in the same situation as the unfortunate body, would he want to have the tentacles in or out? Tough call: the answer was *out* but only if it didn't result in *death*. Some parasites kept their hosts alive, right? This could be one of those gigs. But would you rather be alive as parasite food, or dead?

He kept climbing. He passed another body stuck fast in the stuff. Same deal: tentacles, sightless eyes, rotted clothes, withered limbs, mold on the skin. This one had some kind of leafy thing growing out of one ear. No matter how you viewed it, that kind of thing didn't look good. *Deal with it later.*

As he climbed higher, he found more people. Or bodies. Or what-ever they were. All stuck to the walls with the goo, all unresponsive, all still with a pulse. The stairs ran to a landing at the top of the tower. A door stood open before him. Inside, he saw:

Grace Gushiken, on her knees. Her helmet was off, her head bowed. Before anything else, his eyes found her.

His sword, beside her on the ground. The blade was free of the scabbard, Ezeroc blood green against the black metal.

Two more of those huge Ezeroc crabs.

And in the center of it all, a massive insect. Tiny, stubby legs that couldn't possibly move its bulk. It looked to have a torso-meets-head arrangement going on. What looked like eggs surrounded it.

Grace opened her eyes and looked at Nate. "*Nathan Chevell,*" she said. "*Why are you so important to this one?*"

"My charm," said Nate. "Grace, come on over to me, okay? Come away from the nice insects."

Grace considered him. "*No,*" she said. "*We are together. We should all be together.*"

With that, the two massive Ezeroc next to her rumbled towards Nate.

CHAPTER TWENTY-TWO

EL WATCHED the holo in the same way that most people watched pro wrestling. Like she was expecting shock and awe, but because she was expecting it, she had to ham up her own emotions when they arrived. El liked watching pro wrestling, but that happened in her cabin, away from prying eyes, because people were a judgmental bunch.

When the *ooooh, ahhh* happened on the holo, she was expecting it. El didn't know *what* she was expecting, but she was expecting *something*. And she wasn't disappointed. The *Tyche* chirped at her like an eager cricket, cleared the holo, and then said *TRANSMISSION BLOCKED*.

What the ship was referring to was the comm line they had open to the *Gladiator*. The *Tyche* was saying that one minute the *Gladiator* — or what was left of her — was there, the next minute she was *probably still there* but no longer able to talk. Sure, there could be all kinds of reasons for that. The satellite array Hope had strung around the planet like a bunch of Christmas lights was a tenuous thing at best. Any part of that series of orbiting machinery could have been knocked out, but if that had happened the error would have said *TRANSMISSION LOST*. Lost, not blocked. This was a definite block.

Ships thought they were blocked when there was a carrier wave but not enough sanity on the line to make out what was being said. Or when some other noise just overlaid it, blocking everything else out. The *Tyche* was sure that something was sucking up their signal, like a siphon plugged into the RF spectrum.

El took her feet down from the console where they'd been resting. She clicked on the comm. "Hope? Hope, I'm getting chatter on the comm. Can you check our arrays? Make sure we're not the zeroes in this conversation."

Nothing.

El looked at the comm. Checked the switches — she was *on*, she was talking to Hope, and Hope was ... not answering.

Odd.

Try something new, then. "Cap, this is Helm. You getting anything..." El's voice trailed off as the *Tyche* chattered to herself then said *TRANSMISSION BLOCKED*.

Not odd. *Bad.* That was bad. They had clear line of sight to the cap. If El pointed a camera in his direction — *there we go* — she could see his last known position, some kind of tower poking up out of the trees. She hadn't noticed that when she set down, but she'd been trying to dodge burning hail at the time. Setting the *Tyche* down where she did, in the lee of a cliff, gave protection. Bought them some time. She wasn't thinking about sightseeing the surrounding area.

Maybe she should have.

She worked the console. Was the tower causing the interference? No, not the tower. Something near to them. Something close to their location. In space? No, not close enough, and that would have put the fear of God into El. Because it'd have meant that damn Ezeroc ship had come around the planet and would drop rocks on them. No, this was much closer.

This was in the ship.

EL'S GUN WAS PRIMITIVE. She'd picked it up from a collector for just that reason. She couldn't shoot for shit, not anything smaller than a ship-to-ship laser. Just as the war was wrapping up she'd gone to a boutique gunsmith when she was in San Francisco. That was the first and last time she'd set foot on the rock that had birthed humanity. Nothing about the trip had endeared the place to her. Sure, the terraforming had worked fine. Blue skies. Clean air. Water in the oceans that was blue, or blue green, or — when she'd gone on an older style of ship that sailed seas instead of stars — clear as glass.

No, the problem was the people. They were fucking *everywhere*.

She'd been in an alley, a bunch of thugs — kids, really — had set on her, demanding coins. She'd been wearing the Old Empire's colors, still carrying the Emperor's credits, and they'd left her with some bruises (face and ego both) after she couldn't give them anything. After that experience, she'd found a bar that sold liquor to spacers and downed more out of the tequila bottle than was wise.

The next morning — it *may* have been early afternoon by the time she'd shaken off the fumes and the haze and the need to throw up every two minutes — she'd gone looking for a gun. The usual places sold blasters, standard plasma weapons that were the bread and butter of personal defense (or offense) galaxy-wide. Some comedian had tried to sell her a stun gun, a type that used a lot of volts on contact to ruin someone's day, and she'd explained that the whole point was not having people that close. If they were close, they could touch her, hit her in the face, take her coins, and that wasn't fun.

It was always about the people.

The shopkeeper had flicked directions to her console. A friend, someone in Chinatown. El hadn't been to Chinatown, and so she went.

Best part about San Francisco was Chinatown. There weren't

fewer people — more, if anything. It's just that they were *used* to being around a thousand other people, so they made less of a big deal about it. It was easier to get to where she needed to go. The gunsmith's shop was dim, not in a gloomy way, but in a way that said the sun was bright and hot and in here was quiet and calm. She'd liked the old man with his wrinkled face and serious eyes. He'd listened to her story, and then he'd said something that changed her life.

You are a coward, he'd said. Like he was surprised by it, to see someone still wearing the Emperor's colors in his shop, wanting to buy a shooting iron, but who wanted to be anywhere except where there was violence. Because her colors said *death from above*, her rank and role emblazoned on her chest. She flew destroyers for the Emperor, and killed his enemies. Except she did it from the air-conditioned comfort of a bridge.

El had wanted to get angry, but the old man wasn't trying to get in her grill. He wasn't trying to take her coins. He was trying to find out what she needed. So she'd half-agreed, using a nod rather than words, and the gunsmith had shuffled off to get a small stepladder. He'd climbed up to a higher shelf, found an old chunky plastic box, like a construction worker might carry their lunch in, and laid it out between them. When she'd opened it, she didn't know what she was looking at, so he'd explained.

It's a gun, he'd said. *It fires bullets.*

Solid rounds? Like a PDC? She'd been incredulous, because it was like looking at a dinosaur's thigh bone. PDCs could fire plasma, lasers, or solid rounds where the bullets alone were the size of baguettes. This thing was chunky, but a lot smaller than a baguette.

Yes, but no, and he'd sold it to her for an extortionate sum of the Emperor's credits, because the gun was rare, and because the exchange rate was already in the toilet. It was a pistol-sized *shotgun*, a weapon that fired tiny pellets instead of a discrete slug of metal. The barrel, he'd explained, was short, so that the pellets would spread out like a deadly basketball-sized circle of death at about ten paces. Useless for long distance, but great for a coward whose hands shook. Also great for use on a ship where you didn't want to hole the hull. It held one round at a time, kicked like a mule, and would turn whatever part of a person it hit into airborne chum.

Primitive, but effective.

She pointed the nose of her gun out the flight deck's doorway, into the ready room. The burble of the coffee machine was still on, three cups set out ready for use. Nothing unusual about that, Hope was the kind of person who made coffee for everyone when only she needed it. But Hope wasn't here, and neither was Penn. Also not unusual; Penn had his own cabin — a shanty they'd rigged out of a store room, because the rest of the *Tyche's* crew quarters were spoken for — and Hope was so high on stims she couldn't sit still for more than two minutes. *Like she needs the coffee.*

There were only a couple of ways something inside the *Tyche* could jam the signal. One, Hope had a psychotic break and was sabotaging the ship. Ridiculous, because if there was someone who cared more about the *Tyche* than El or the cap, it was Hope. Two, one of those fucking bugs had got on board — unlikely — and was wreaking havoc. Three, it was Penn.

Smart money said Penn.

Motive? He'd snuck a message out and wanted them all dead now. Seemed reasonable for a spy, and El was pretty sure he was a spy. Or, how about: he wanted to take her ship. That also held water; he'd been right upset at the captain about Nate's approach to solving their current set of problems. Deal with the crew (that was El and Hope), and take off when the lockdown was over. Penn would think Nate wasn't coming back alive, and that was unfortunately a view that El shared.

The coffee machine hissed and spluttered, drawing the nose of El's weapon like a magnet. With a kind of detached amazement she noticed her hands were shaking, and that made the gun shake too. It wouldn't matter, because even if her gun was moving around like a weather vane in a hurricane, it'd still tear a hole in the *general direction* it was being pointed.

Her hands never shook, though. Shaking hands crashed ships.

There was a *clank* from further back in the ship. Could be the *Tyche* settling. El wasn't sure she knew the sounds the newly rebuilt bird made as she slept, but she was also sure that wasn't the settling of metal. That sounded like an airlock closing. She wished Nate was here. Or that Kohl was awake. Because this was their kind of deal. El was just the damn *pilot*.

THE PROBLEM with thinking about Kohl was that it made El want to go wake him up. Find something in that sickbay that would jump-start the big man like a rusty old combustion engine, the kind that Hope said were fun to work on. How something could be fun to work on that leaked oil everywhere was a mystery to El, but that's why she flew ships, rather than grubbing around inside 'em.

She was babbling. Babbling in her own goddamned *mind*.

The gun still shook in her hand, but it seemed fine with leading the way so she let it. Her feet trod the deck plates of the *Tyche*, but slowly, one after the other, like making a noise would trigger instant death. It could, for all she knew. Internal comms were down, external comms were down. On this ship was one person she could trust but who was still basically a child, and another who she could not trust, not even to put the right amount of sugar in her coffee. El didn't want to shoot the wrong one, but more than that she didn't want to die, so the next few minutes would be hard for everyone concerned.

The ship was nice and flat, flight deck, ready room, and Engineering all on the same basic altitude but Engineering way towards the back. You got to Engineering via the crew deck. Down and up, easy as that. *Let's go check on Engineering first.* El walked slow and quiet down the gangway, giving a quick look over the edge of the metal ladder leading down to the crew deck.

Nothing moving down there, just the steady glow of the *Tyche's* lighting, the soft hum of ship systems, and the quiet dry hiss of life support.

Life support.

El's eyes were drawn up towards the pipework in the ceiling. Conduit, air, water, all flowed through the ship. Big tubes leading from Engineering like a big heart, pumping blood to everywhere else. Tubes big enough to hide in, if you were inclined. You could even put things in there, like a bunch of cockroaches that lived inside people's heads.

And here was El, without her helmet. She'd seen the damn vids. She'd seen what those Ezeroc did to people. Hell, she'd even taken the time to read some of the files Hope had flicked up to her console. It wasn't pretty reading. It wasn't *fun* reading. It was the kind of reading you did that made you go everywhere with your damn helmet on. It was the kind of reading that made you *sleep* in your helmet.

Her helmet was in her room.

She gave a quick glance behind her. Horror holos always had some motherfucker come up behind you with a sharp knife and end your brief ride in a shower of gore, and El wasn't up for that today. But there was nothing there. Her cabin was right next to the ladder, just down there, so she backed up, nice and slow, and nice and *quiet*. Another glance down the metal ladder showed nothing. Not even a shadow moved.

The door to her cabin was shut, like it always was. El monkeyed down the ladder, leaned against the sill to her room, keyed the lock, and pointed her pistol inside.

Empty.

Not *entirely* empty. Her locker, her bunk. Just not her helmet. Her helmet was next to her bunk, or it *had* been when she was here last. It wasn't here *now*. El moved inside her room, a last quick check outside — still clear — and then looked under her bunk. In her locker. On the shelves. Nothing. Nothing, nothing, *nothing*. She tore stuff out of her locker, a console, some clothes, some spare ammunition, her old Empire flight suit.

No helmet.

Could she have left it somewhere else? *Think.* No. She was *sure* it'd been here. Some fucker had taken her helmet. Some fucker who maybe, just maybe, wanted to infect a crew. Have some live samples. She wiped at her face with the back of a hand, feeling the sweat there. She hissed, *"Penn."*

EL COULD JUST WAIT IN HERE. It's what she'd been doing for the last ten minutes. Door shut, locked from the inside. Gun in her hand, cold steel resting against her skin.

There were two problems with that approach as she saw it.

The first was that Hope was still out there in the ship. Hope, who hadn't had her twenty-fifth birthday yet if you still thought Sol years counted for jack. Hope, who was useful and important for keeping the *Tyche* flying. Hope, who was also her friend, and as a general rule you didn't let your friends be eaten by insects.

The second was that the room was getting hot. El had stuffed her old flight suit into the life support's air vent, blocking it. That was a temporary solve, because she'd eventually suffocate. She'd need Nate to get back, and Nate wasn't coming back.

"Fuck," she said to the room. "Fuck, fuck, *fuck.*"

Nothing for it: time to get moving. She stood, tasting fear in her mouth, and then keyed the lock on the door. It opened with a hiss to an empty corridor.

She led the way with the gun. El stood outside her room for a second, then reached a fumbling hand behind her to close the door. It locked with a beep. That beep was too loud, too obvious in the quiet of the ship. Something from down the metal stairs *hissed*, and she heard something moving towards the ladder. So she pointed the pistol over the side and pulled the trigger. There was a massive *boom*, the gun bucking hard in her hand, and she screamed, "Stay back, Penn! Stay back, you motherfucker!"

El ejected the casing from her gun, the plastic popping as it hit the deck. A new shell inside, she closed the breach.

Silence.

In any normal day there'd be a bunch of people shouting at her for firing a weapon inside the ship. Hell, *she'd* be one of the people shouting. Not this time. No-one made any noise, no-one at all.

She edged her back along the crew deck towards Engineering. She kept swinging the gun about, trying to point it everywhere at once. When her shoulder bumped against the ladder to Engineering, she almost screamed, because she hadn't expected to make it, and thought a monster had come to get her. Nope, just a ladder then an airlock. She keyed the lock, and the door opened with a hiss and a clank.

Inside were Hope's console and acceleration couch, the console dark, the couch empty. Engineering itself was dark, the only lights coming from backscatter from the status indicators on the reactor. At least the *Ravana* still had something useful to give the universe.

"Hope?" El moved farther into the darkened room. She made sure not to point her gun too close to the reactor, because while it was unlikely the weapon would blow a hole in it, using any kind of firearm next to a reactor was against the general gist of shipboard survival rules. Systems in here blinked and thrummed. It was cool, at least, the life support still working fine.

El looked up at the top of the room, where the ducts for air were. She couldn't see shit. *Fuck this — if I'm gonna die, I'm gonna die being able to see it coming.* She tapped on her suit's console, asking the *Tyche* for a little more brilliance. The ship obliged, bringing more light, and El could then see a couple of things of an alarming nature.

First thing: Hope's rig, with the visor and the manipulator arms, was on the floor next to her acceleration couch. It was bent and twisted, the visor smashed.

Second thing: there was a rent in the pipework in the ceiling.

Rent *out*, like something had come from that pipe and into this room. Something large, bigger than El's shoulders. Something the size of a man, like Penn.

Fucking *Penn*.

She pointed her gun at the hole, making her way back to Engineering's airlock. El cycled it open, slipped through, and locked it behind her. Back to the crew deck. *Time to check on Kohl*. El stopped at the top of the ladder from Engineering, listening for a second. She got nothing but the sound of ship systems, so she slung her legs over and slid to the deck below. She dropped into a half crouch, pointing her gun in what felt like six directions at once.

The crew deck was where the sick bay was, and the captain's cabin. And Penn's makeshift room.

El moved to the sickbay. The big glass window showed Kohl still inside, still on the table, machinery still keeping him alive. She opened the door, slipped inside, locking it behind her. She moved to Kohl's side. His skin was still grey, kind of pasty, but — and she wasn't sure if she was deluding herself — it looked like there might have been a shade more color in his cheeks. Nothing obvious in here that looked like a pile of insects or a warrior drone. She shrugged, then leaned close to Kohl's ear. "Kohl? October Kohl. I don't know if you can hear me, but there's something on the ship. Something on the *Tyche*. I ... I don't know what I'm doing. So, you know." She couldn't think of anything to say, so she turned to leave.

There, right *there*, outside the sickbay window, she caught a flash of movement. Something that twisted away from the glass in a way that didn't look human. It was *probably* Penn, because that's what her brain told her the face looked like, but it didn't move the way people should move. Or it did, because it was only a flash of movement, and then it — he? — was gone from view.

Her gun was pointed at the glass. She hadn't remembered raising it, but there it was. Her hands were still shaking. El moved to the window, pressed her face against it, trying to see where Penn had gone. "Penn!" Her breath fogged the glass in front of her, the air of the ship whisking away the moisture a second later.

Move. You've got to keep moving.

She put a hand to the door controls, leveled her pistol at the door, and then opened it.

No one there.

El ducked into the corridor, closing the door behind her. Always closing doors, she was, and never on the side of safety. She giggled, then swallowed it. The fear sweat running down her face was getting into her eyes. *Check Penn's room. Check the captain's quarters. Then get to the cargo bay.*

She made a cursory job of the captains quarters first, because it didn't seem like the go-to place to be without the captain there. But she was getting into a rhythm now: enter the room. Check it. Leave. Close the door behind her. Lock it. Next one.

Except the *next one* was Penn's room. A supply room under normal situation. The door opened in front of her to darkness. She kept the gun pointing into the dark, feeling with her other hand towards the room's controls. There. Light switch. She flicked it.

Nothing happened.

If she was someone like Kohl, or even the captain, she'd have a light on her gun. Something to shine in front of her so she could see what was there. She didn't have one of those, and her helmet was missing. It had lights on it, which would be more useful if it was with her.

It's only a room. It's only a room. Just go in, your eyes will adjust, and you can confirm that asshole's not in there. If he is, you blow a hole the size of a grapefruit in his chest.

She edged into the room, her gun hunting the way. Her eyes adjusted, the dark turning to gloom. She saw the hammock they'd stretched out for Penn. El almost fell over, her boots slipping on something on the deck. She reached a hand down, her fingers coming away wet, slick with something more viscous than water. El held them up to the gloom. It wasn't dark enough to be blood. It was some kind of ... *discharge*.

This wasn't going well. This whole day? Not going well at all.

Her head jerked up at movement, the darkening of the light, and she looked up to see Penn — it must have been — silhouetted in the light. His hands were on the doorframe, and he was leaning in, like his chest was heavy and he was trying to hold it up. She brought her gun up and fired, the flash bright, the hammer burst of sound deafening in the room. She hit nothing but air. Penn was gone.

She ejected the cartridge, the plastic popping as it hit the deck. She pushed a new one home with her thumb, but she had to try a couple of times before she could get it in the breach. Her damn hands were shaking so much. She was panting, the breath coming in and out of her in big gasps. If there was something airborne in the ship, she was sucking it all in, but fuck it, if she was going to die, she would die *after* Penn did.

El made it back out to the corridor. One more deck to go. Cargo bay. Lots of places to hide down there. Just great.

You can do this. Penn's unarmed, right? Or he would have shot you. Worst case, he wants to infect you with alien spores. He's not going to shoot you.

Her rational mind wanted her to believe that, but it was a tiny voice compared to what the rest of her was gibbering. Not because it was *wrong*, per se, but because being infected with alien spores was not on her bucket list. Definitely not on the list at all.

The cargo bay was dark. Of fucking *course* it was dark. She pointed her pistol down the metal ladder. "Penn? You down there?"

Something hissed below. A leaking pipe? Something damaged on the ship? That wasn't great either, but it'd need to be dealt with after the whole Penn situation.

"Penn, I'm coming down. We can talk this out." Her voice was shaking, making a liar of her ability to say more than just two sentences let alone *talking it out*. She started down the ladder. A lot more slowly this time, because both her rational mind and her lizard hindbrain did *not* want to go down there. She reached the decking, putting a foot on it, wanting the solid metal to make her feel comfortable. To feel like this was home, and that she knew it, and that Penn was the alien here.

It didn't help.

The cargo bay was dark, but like Penn's cabin, it turned to gloom as her eyes adjusted. Panels, readouts around the bay cast small glowing pools of radiance. Just a big empty cargo bay, with lots of storage racks and rails and mount points to hide in, behind, or under. Magical.

Something hissed again in the gloom, and El pointed her gun in that direction. "Penn?" Then, "Hope?"

Her eyes were adjusting, and she could see something against the wall. Some kind of ... *structure*. Like a whole bunch of papier-mâché. El walked towards it, her eyes picking out details in the gloom as she got closer. It was a kind of solid mass attached to the wall. It looked like a person.

It looked like Hope.

She broke into a run. El got to the structure, tearing huge hunks of it away. Hope was unconscious, suspended in the material. Locked against the *Tyche's* hull, like a spider's snack kept for later. El pulled hunks of it away. It felt porous and light, like stale bread.

Something hissed behind her, and she froze. Very slowly, she turned around.

Penn. The man was in shadow. To be fair, the whole *room* was in shadow, but whatever the cause she couldn't see his face, his expression, at all. What she *could* see was a big Penn-sized target, so she shot it.

The handgun roared, the flash bright in the room, and Penn's shoulder and arm turned into chunks as the shotgun shell tore them right off.

He didn't move. Just a little sway from the impact of the shot, then he stood there, the dripping of fluid from his missing shoulder hitting the deck with wet splatters. "*Queen,*" he said, "*together.*"

That's what it sounded like; it was hard to tell, because he was speaking with what sounded like a bunch of marbles in his mouth.

El had already ejected the shell from her gun and was feeding it another. "Whatever, asshole—"

That's as far as she got before Penn was on her. He didn't roar, didn't scream, just moved like liquid smoke. His remaining arm collected her like a ram, and she tumbled across the cargo bay. Her gun was lost, clattering across the decking in the darkness. She could find it, given enough time, and enough light. She could make a million credits also, if given enough time.

Penn found *her*, though. He found her fine in the dark. That hand grabbed her from the floor, lifting her up. El's training kicked in — basic had included endless drills for combat, both armed and unarmed — and she grabbed at Penn's wrist. Her fingers remembered the movements her brain was too terrified to cope with, a hold *here*, a pinch *there*, and *twist*. The move would have tumbled Penn like a toy, crashing him to the deck, so she could get away, get her gun, and get some fucking *distance*.

Would? Should. The move *should* have tumbled Penn.

What happened instead was that the skin and flesh of his arm moved around something hard inside, the meat sloughing off in her hands. She caught sight of something inside that didn't look like the bones of a human arm. It didn't look human at all. It looked like a thick, chitinous structure. El held up her hands, then looked at Penn. Glimpsed his face, or what was left of it.

His eyes were missing — just *gone*. His skull was distorted outward, and his jaw was distended. It looked like he was trying to speak again, and El could see his jaw wasn't meeting in the middle. The bone was ... moving *inside* his skin, but like two separate pieces of bone. Like mandibles, trying to break free.

Then Penn stopped moving. His body froze, then jerked in a spasm. Blood and gore fountained from his chest, covering El, and she screamed, closing her eyes. She fell to the deck, hand up above her head, tasting blood — Penn's blood — in her mouth. She wiped her eyes clear, looking up. Penn was jerking and spasming, but it didn't look like a thing he wanted to do. With a sound like a claw popping under a lobster cracker, his ribcage opened, a heavy piece of metal pushing through. The body kept jerking, until it split up the middle as the metal dragged through.

Penn's body fell in two pieces. There was a massive silhouette behind him. The silhouette reached a hand toward El.

"You have *got* to tell me what I missed," said October Kohl, dropping the metal bar to the deck as he lifted her up. He looked at Penn's body. "Been wanting to do that since I met that asshole."

CHAPTER TWENTY-THREE

WHEN THE BUGS came for Nate, he wanted to panic.

Like, panicking would be a good thing that would free him from the rational part of his mind that was saying *shoot low, less armor there* or *don't hit Grace*. It'd release him from those sorts of concerns. He'd be able to spray plasma everywhere, go down in a hail of fire, or maybe just a frenzy of torn limbs.

The problem was, Nate was sure that these Ezeroc assholes didn't kill you. They plugged you into a wall, stuffed tentacles down your throat, and fed on you. Fed on your body, and your mind. That experience sure as shit would alter his perception of reality.

To be fair, he also wanted to panic because one of these crabs — *just one* — had almost turned him inside out. His shoulder was a wreck, his ribs hurt, and he was still dizzy. The good news, as near as there could be any good news in a situation like this, was that his plasma rifle was charged, and already pointed in the room. There was Grace, right of center. Two bugs, giant Ezeroc crab things, flanking her. And the ... locust? ... left of center. He had a full battery, and a clear shot at any of the four. Or three, because despite Grace talking like a crazy person, and possibly being infected by space insects, he liked her. Despite her lying to him, right from the start, he liked the *way* she lied. She was his kind of pirate.

It's not being outnumbered. It's having a wider selection of targets.

Nate followed the line of his rifle's barrel, still held at his hip. It was pointed at the ... locust? Really, what the fuck was that thing? An *armored* locust? How did it get around with legs that small? Pulsating lines of the tentacles fed into it, anchoring it.

"*Queen,*" said Grace, "*together.*"

Queen, huh. Nate pulled the trigger. The weapon cycled, a brief whine and then the harsh snap and crackle of the plasma discharge.

The twin bolts of plasma hit the ... locust — *just call it a Queen, everyone else seems to* — Queen, blowing a chunk out of the thing's side. A great shower of ichor ruptured forth, and it screamed, and tried to tear itself away from those tentacles anchoring it to the floor.

Grace was knocked sideways, out of Nate's line of sight. The two massive Ezeroc crabs seemed to stumble, and then one of them turned in a circle like a broken robot, just clattering and skittering in rotation, big claws *snicking* at the air. The other one rambled sideways, crushing a desk and console under its bulk, then colliding with the wall of the tower. It backed up, then hit the wall sideways again. The wall cracked, opened to the night sky, and the Ezeroc was gone, tumbling down into the dark.

Take a note, Nate: check the door before you exit the ground floor. That might have turned into pulp, or it might have turned angrier or crazier.

He looked at his rifle again. Definitely a better effect than he'd been hoping for. *What the hell.* He pulled the trigger again. A cycle, whine, and then two more bolts of plasma hit the Queen. The force blew more chunks off it, tearing it free of the tentacles at its base.

Tentacles. Now there's a word that never comes with happy thoughts. 'Pulsating' is another word like that.

"How you like them fucking apples?" said Nate, right before he was knocked off his feet. He landed hard, rifle pinned to the ground by his body. He tried to roll, managed to flop onto his back, and saw what had hit him. An Ezeroc warrior drone — *smaller than the crab fuckers, but still lots of sharp edges* — reared above him. It stabbed down with those fore claws. He rolled, the claws hitting the floor where he'd been, bits of ceramicrete chipping away. It reared, trying to nail him again, and he rolled once more. *Bring the rifle up.* He hauled the rifle up — a bad, bad weapon at close range, on account of being too big, and thus too slow — and was rewarded for his efforts by the warrior drone knocking it away with one of its legs. The rifle spun into the stairwell. It clattered and skipped as it fell down into the gloom.

The Ezeroc stamped down with a leg, pinning Nate. It didn't pierce his suit — thank God for good Old Empire weave — but the force of it hurt about the same as being hit with a bat. The Ezeroc probably weighed 300 kilos, and it *leaned* on him. Holding him still. It bent forward, saliva — *sure, let's call it that, that's fine* — dripping from its maw to spatter against Nate's visor. Those fore claws clicked and clattered as it brought them back for the killing strike.

There was a *snicka-pop*, and one of those claws came free, followed by the thing's head, which bounced on the ground next to Nate. The Ezeroc's body shuddered, then the weight pinning him relaxed as the warrior drone's body followed his rifle down the stairwell. He looked up at Grace Gushiken, her hair hiding her face, his sword held low in her hands. That sword was held firm and strong; there was a perfect line made by the sword, and her arm, right up to her shoulder. She was ready to strike again. He couldn't see her face. He couldn't tell what she wanted to strike.

"Hi," said Nate. "Uh. What kept you?"

She shook her head, pushing her hair back from her face, and the illusion of the masked assassin fell away to reveal Grace — just Grace. Face grey with exhaustion and fear. She held a hand out to him. He took it, letting himself be pulled to his feet. "I ... went away," she said.

"Cool story," said Nate. "Save it for later." He unholstered his blaster from his hip, pointed it in the room — no sign of the Queen, but let's not get complacent, hey? — and fired a couple blasts in there. The Ezeroc that was turning in a circle didn't even notice. It kept on turning. *Weird, but okay, sure.* "You good to go?"

She looked him in the eye. "Nate, I ... they might have—"

"Yeah," he said. "They might have. But they might not, so let's worry about that shit at another time."

There was a popping sound from the room, and both Nate and Grace looked. The queen was rising from behind a bank of crumbling desks towards the back. Some of the eggs looked to have hatched, smaller warrior drones, about the size of a cat, surrounded her.

"Oh, *come on!*" said Nate. "Fucking Ezeroc. They come in different sizes now?"

One of the smaller insects leapt forward — *agile little fuckers.* Nate popped a shot into the room, but the newborn Ezeroc skipped sideways, like a toy car with attitude.

"We should go," said Grace. "Nate, we should go."

"You don't need to tell me twice," said Nate. He heard a *pop*, and another Ezeroc hatched from an egg. Two of them together darted towards the doorway. Nate got three shots off, three shots that missed, plasma splashing against the walls and back window of the room, this last shot bursting it out in a spray of shards. Then the insects were on them.

There was a blur, almost too fast to register, and the insects fell apart, cut in half. Grace shook Nate's sword, splatters of insect gore hitting the ceramicrete. "Ah," said Nate. "Now I remember why I hired you."

"You didn't hire me, Nathan Chevell," said Grace. "You were tricked."

"I know," said Nate. "But I was helped, too." He flashed her a grin, hoping she could see it through the visor, the sealant, and the weld.

She gave him a look, something uncertain in it, then turned on her heel and headed down the stairs.

NATE FELT like he was rushing, flying almost, to keep up with Grace. She was taking the stairs like dancers took to the stage, like movement was something she was born to do. Nate felt like he was struggling to keep up, his metal leg *clanking* instead of being limber, his metal hand keeping him off balance.

It was all in his mind, of course. The leg was top shelf tech, and so was the hand. Weighted and balanced, the medtechs had told him, to be just like the original. So he wouldn't know anything *bad* had happened, tricking his mind into believing he wasn't missing parts of himself. The only thing, they'd joked, was that he'd need to eat a little less now, because he didn't need fuel for that excess 5 or 10 kilos he was missing. *Fastest way to lose weight*, they'd also joked. Like, *ha ha*, right until Nate had looked like he wanted to kill them.

Because he had.

And no matter what they said, no matter how good the damn tech was, he *knew*. His arm and leg were gone, and these metal pegs they'd stuck on him weren't worth half a real man's hand or leg. They didn't feel right, and they didn't feel right when it counted.

Like when you were running after someone like your life depended on it. *Now* was one of those fucking times, and he wished, just for a second, one of those medtechs was here, with him, so Nate could see the *ha ha* fade away, replaced with *oh shit we're all going to die.*

His metal leg slipped, skidding against the stairs, and because of that he hadn't noticed that Grace had stopped, like she'd been planted in the ground, roots dug deep, and when he started running again he ran right into the back of her. She stumbled, turned to him, then her eyes went wide at something behind him. He didn't even bother to turn, because turning got you killed in all the holos he'd ever watched. Instead, he raised his blaster at the warrior drone coming up the steps, sidled past Grace, and pulled the trigger until the Ezeroc stopped moving, burning pieces of it falling into the stairwell.

He turned, saw that one of those fuckers had been about to chew his ass from behind, and that Grace had killed it. A clean slice, top left to bottom right, at least that's what it looked like. The top piece was gone, down the stairwell — there'd be a decent pile by now at the bottom, insects plus a rifle — and only the body was left to bleed green on the stairs.

"Why'd you stop?" said Nate.

Grace pointed at one human stuck to the wall, tentacles still in the mouth. "They're ... almost dead," she said. "Inside. Their minds are..."

"Uh," said Nate. "Queen keeping the bodies alive?"

"I think," said Grace, "but also feeding on them. Their bodies, and their minds." She was panting, but her eyes were bright as she looked at him. "It feels good to breathe," she said. "To not be feeding her mind."

"Yeah," said Nate. "That why you took off your helmet?"

"No," she said. "I had put down the sword. When I put it down, they got ... inside." She held it up. "What *is* it?"

"Gift from a friend," he said. "If we get out of this alive, I'll tell you all about it." Then he raised his blaster and shot the Ezeroc coming around the bend of stairs above them. "*If* we get out of this alive."

"You're not inspiring confidence," she said.

"Hey," he said. "We wouldn't even be here if you hadn't stolen my damn sword."

She held it out to him. "Want it back?"

"Later," he said. "Look, more important stuff is raining down on us."

"Yeah," she said. "I think I fucked up. I think I fucked everything up."

"Maybe," he said. "But let's talk about those big fuckers."

"They're controlled by the Queen," said Grace. "The smaller drones have some autonomy. Or ... something that keeps them wound up when the Queen's gone. Instinct, maybe."

"It's like a hive?" said Nate.

"Maybe," said Grace, "but there aren't any words that can explain it."

"Got you," said Nate, then pointed his blaster down the stairwell, unloading plasma into an Ezeroc coming up at them. "Persistent fuckers, aren't they?"

"You shot their Queen," said Grace. "They'll be coming for you."

"They can take a fucking number," said Nate. He ejected the battery from his blaster and slipped a new one home. The weapon whined, clicked, and was ready to fire. He looked at it, then back at Grace. "Ready for round two?"

Her eyes searched his face. "Why did you come, Nathan Chevell?"

"You took my sword," said Nate. "Also, you're on my crew."

"But I lied to you," she said. "You've known since before. At the fallen city."

"I'll be docking your pay for that," said Nate. He looked at his feet, that one metal leg hidden in his suit, then his hand. *Not even half a real man, unless you look after you and yours.* He looked her in the eye, "You've ... helped. Plenty, when you had no cause to. And you're still on my crew. Don't ... just don't forget it this time. Hope would miss you."

"Hope, huh?" she said. Then, "I won't." She continued down the stairs ahead of him. Grace moved like he wanted to if it wasn't for his damn leg.

OUTSIDE THE BASE of the tower, shit got real.

Nate had never found his rifle. All the way down those stairs he'd been looking for it, because Kohl would want it back. The man was a, what would you call it, a *collector*, a connoisseur of firearms, and this was a souvenir of some job or other. *Well, nothing for that now.* Nate still wished he'd found it, not because of

Kohl, but because of the ring of Ezeroc waiting at the base of the tower.

"Could you," said Grace, "call in the *Tyche*? Like before."

"No," said Nate. "Locked her down. So that fucker Penn doesn't steal my ship. Also, my comm is down." He checked his comm just in case. *Yep, still down.*

"That'll be the Queen," said Grace. "Piloting a human somewhere on this planet, just like she did to me. To control the comms."

"What? Nah, I barbecued her."

"She's not dead," said Grace, tapping her head. "I can still hear her."

"Oh, *come on*," said Nate, for what felt like the hundredth time. "Well, at least those big ones are gone."

There was a rustling of trees, branches and boughs being pushed aside. An entire tree gave with a crack, and one of the big crabs came forward.

"You," said Grace, "need to stop talking."

Nate looked at his blaster, then at the big crab. "Grace," he said. "The ship. The *Tyche*? She's ready. Ready to fly. El will take you anywhere. I'll draw 'em off."

She snorted. "You wouldn't get ten meters," she said. "They'll pull you apart."

"Gives you a running start," he said. "With this damn leg, I'll only slow you down."

"Who said anything about running?" she said. "I've been running for as long as I can remember." She sucked in some air, blew it out. "It feels *good to breathe*."

The Ezeroc charged.

BACK TO BACK.

Nate could feel Grace through his suit. Her body, next to his. Both of them, facing outward. His blaster, her sword.

An Ezeroc drone came at him, slavering, chittering, and he blew chunks out of it. Behind him, the *snick-crack* of the sword.

Something fell at him from above, one of the smaller Ezeroc, and it clattered against his helmet, blocking the view from his visor. All he could see was legs, and those claws, searching for a way in, seeking his skin. Nate smashed it with his metal hand, knocking it free. He felt Grace move against him, and he turned with her, her sword making short work of the drone. He in turn fired at two running towards them, bright arcs of plasma lighting up the night, charring and burning. The blaster snap-crackled with each squeeze of the trigger. He didn't hit every shot, but when they got too close, Grace was there.

A flash of movement from his right side, and he turned in time to be knocked through the air — *again, come* on! — by the big Ezeroc crab.

He impacted against the building — again — and lay dazed for a second. In that second, as he watched Grace pivot around the big crab's legs, her sword clanging against its armored body, he thought *if the big one's alive, and it's controlled by the Queen, where the fuck is the Queen?*

More movement from around the corner of the building, and there she was, clawing herself along. More of the smaller drones surrounded her, there must have been at least five scuttling towards Grace. She still moved and spun, but he could see she was getting tired. Or she'd started tired, and was getting to breaking point.

And here you are, asshole, resting against this wall.

He got up, took aim down the iron sights of his blaster, and put five shots into the queen. Five shots, one after the other, into the head of the creature, or what he guessed the head was. The battery on his blaster pinged empty, fell to the ground, and he put a new one in. *Last one. Make it count.* Turned back to Grace, to help her with the giant Ezeroc, but it had stopped moving with any kind of purpose, just walking around the small clearing.

One of the smaller Ezeroc landed on his arm. He tried to shake it loose, but it was held firm, pincers around his wrist. The claws pulled back, then slammed home, piercing his suit glove. Nate screamed in pain, raised his blaster and blew it to pieces.

Silence.

The warrior drones were pulling back into the forest. No more of the smaller fuckers either. Grace looked to have dropped a couple more, but the air was free of them. She walked to him, concern in her eyes. "Nate," she said. "The claws."

"Hurts like a motherfucker," said Nate.

"*It's how they infect you*," she said. She raised her sword. "Look, I can try and cut the arm off. I can—"

He laughed. Bent over, hands on his knees, and laughed.

"You're crazy," she said. "It's already infected you. I have to, I, uh … Nate? Tell me it's still you," she said.

"Grace Gushiken," said Nate, pulling off his suit glove, and holding up his metal hand, "it's still me. Except for the bits that aren't." The metal skin of his hand had been pierced by the claws, the creature putting God knows what into the inside. But it was metal, and plastic, and ceramic, and wasn't a *part* of him. It couldn't infect him.

Probably.

"It's just," said Nate, "they tried to make the hand real, you know? So, I can feel things with it. Like an alien sticking parasitic goo into me. That'd be uncomfortable, if it was the other hand."

"They know," said Grace, "that you're the captain of the ship."

"How," said Nate, "do they know?"

"Because of me," she said. "Because of what I am."

"Oh," said Nate. "That's … great news."

"It just … wait, what?" she said.

"Well," said Nate. "They think I'm the captain of a ship they've infected with alien DNA or whatever it is, right? And they'll let me back on the ship, to 'infect,'" and here, he gave little air quotes, "my crew. The way I see it, they'll leave us the fuck alone for a while until that happens. A quiet hike, back to the *Tyche*."

"I ... hadn't thought of it like that," said Grace.

"Less things trying to eat our faces," said Nate.

"I think I've got it," said Grace.

"You know," said Nate. "No killer death roaches or anything."

"Really," she said. "I've got it. I've really got it. You can stop talking."

They walked back towards the forest. "Do you think," said Nate, "that the Queen would have been wise to this whole thing?"

"Yeah," said Grace. "She was ... smart. Ancient. Young. I don't know."

"Cool," said Nate, looking back at the smoking ruins of the Queen. He smiled into the dark. "Finally. Something's going *right* for a change."

CHAPTER TWENTY-FOUR

WHEN GRACE LOOKED UP, Nate's arm draped over her shoulder, his weight heavy against her, she was expecting to see the bright, welcoming light of the *Tyche's* cargo bay airlock. A hand, held out to her, palm up. A smile. *Welcome home, guys.* What she saw instead was the barrel of a blaster. It was leveled at her face. It surprised her because of all of Nate's talk of the ship — the *Tyche* — being a *home*, and how they were all a *family*. With him by her side, she *felt* it coming off him in waves. How could she not? He'd been so close to her while they'd walked, and then he'd started to drag. He'd still been feeling like he'd been heading to his family when he stretched himself out on the forest floor. Something inside him was broken, and he'd spat out a little bit of blood, said he was *fine, just fine* and then couldn't stand.

Grace had hauled him to his feet, her with a grunt and him with a scream, and dragged him back to the ship. The forest around them was alive, things rustling in the trees, branches swaying like there was a powerful wind. Except the air was still. Grace couldn't see them, couldn't feel them, just the hiss in her mind, a kind of static she'd grown to associate with the Ezeroc. It wasn't static, that was the wrong word, because in the gentle hush of it were words, words she could understand if only she had the wit to listen.

Last time she'd listened, she'd dropped the damn sword, so she put her barriers back up, those constructed walls of thought to keep her centered. She focused on Nate, on his ragged breathing, the warm weight of his humanity as it touched her side. That physical contact brought more of what he was feeling to her, that *friend/not-trust/family/protect/trust*, over and over. Grace was buffeted by it.

It made her feel warm, so she held him tighter.

She'd believed, really *believed* she might have a place on this ship. Against all the odds, against what she'd seen, because of what Nate was feeling. Right until she'd slapped a frantic hand on the door controls, the hull of the *Tyche* cool and solid under her hand. The door had slid open with a low *cthunk*, and she'd looked up, one foot on the metal of the gangway, the other still on Absalom's dirt, and had the blaster pushed into her face.

Looking up beyond the blaster, she saw a hand. Big knuckles, used to hitting things. Grace lifted her head higher, took in Kohl's face, and said, "Oh, fuck's sake. Of all the people who could meet us, *you're* the one?"

"Okay," said Kohl. He turned his face back to someone behind him. "I'm pretty sure she's still human."

"Of *course* I'm still human," said Grace. "You asshole. Help me with the captain."

"No," said Kohl.

Grace looked at his face, at the blaster that hadn't moved. "He's human too," she said. "I'm pretty sure he's got internal bleeding."

"Sounds bad," said Kohl, not moving.

"What's worse," said Grace, "is that we're here on the doorstep of fucking salvation and you're in the way."

"Let 'em in," said El's voice, from somewhere behind Kohl. The Helm stepped out from behind the doorway, an old, ugly kinetic weapon in her hand. "We've had worse things here than a little internal bleeding."

"Worse?" said Grace. She looked at Kohl, then at El. Looked for Hope. "Where's Hope?"

"Yeah," said El. "Well, that's the thing." She turned away, holstering her weapon.

Grace hauled Nate in with her, pushing around Kohl. She saw the cargo bay, a slop pile of human remains on the floor, and she felt something sick in her stomach. "Is that..."

"No," said Kohl. "That, there, is just one less asshole."

"Penn?" said Grace.

"Not anymore," said El. She cycled the ship's lock, shutting Absalom's dangers out. "You'd best see for yourself."

THE SICKBAY WAS like Grace remembered. A cheap machine keeping a patient alive. Except this time, it wasn't Kohl in there, it was Hope, and she was in some kind of coma.

"It looks bad," said El. "But I think we got to her in time."

"What do you mean by, 'in time?'" said Grace. She was getting nothing from Hope, just background noise. Hope wasn't *dead*, but she sure was out to lunch.

"If you hadn't gone off," said Kohl, "this wouldn't have happened. That's what she means. We'd have had two more guns."

"Kohl," said Nate. His voice was weak. He was slumped on the floor, face gone ashen.

"I'm just saying what we're all thinking," said Kohl.

"Yes," said Grace, "you are." She was looking at El, who was radiating *concern/fear/distrust* in about equal measure.

"I am?" said Kohl. He looked surprised.

"You're not saying what Nate's thinking," said Grace, "but El's on message with you."

"Hey," said El, "I didn't say—"

"You're right," said Grace. "It is my fault."

"It's the fucking Ezeroc's fault," said Nate. He tried to get himself to his feet using his sword — Grace had given it back to him — before he coughed, winced, and slumped back. "The aliens—"

"Oh, so the aliens got her," and Kohl jerked a meaty thumb at Grace, "to lead you into the forest?"

"She didn't lead me," said Nate. "It wasn't—"

"You both left us," said El. "You left us and we almost *died*."

Grace could feel the situation unraveling, all of them trying not to look at Hope's unconscious form, all of them trying to find someone to blame for it. Like a pack of too-hungry dogs, nipping at each other. She cleared her throat. "The thing is—"

"The thing is," said Kohl, "that you've brought nothing but bad luck since you got here."

"It's not like it was her fault that the reactor blew," said Nate. "It's just that—"

"Wasn't it?" said El. "Our reactor was *fine*. She gets on board, and—"

No sword. But she shouldn't need one. Not here. Because Nate said this was a family. "I—" began Grace.

"And then," said Kohl, "we get out here, and there's a shit show. Aliens. A fucked-up destroyer. A planet with no people on it."

"She couldn't have done that," said Nate. "Because *how*? I mean, Kohl, think about it. How would she—"

"I don't know," said Kohl, "but I say we throw her out."

"That's—" said Nate.

"Because if you hadn't gone," said El, "Hope wouldn't have been caught by that ... *thing*. Whatever Penn was."

"Penn was a person," said Nate, "who got infected by aliens—"

"I reckon," said Kohl, "that *she's* been infected by aliens. I reckon that your little girlfriend here is infected, or is in league with them. She's *talking* to them, Cap, and you can't see it."

"Now hold on, Kohl," said Nate. "That's—"

"He's right," said Grace.

Silence.

Grace looked at Nate, then at El, and finally, at Kohl. "It's not what you think, or even the way you think it," she said. "You're thinking in straight lines. You're thinking Penn was just some guy who got unlucky. You're thinking these aliens are hunting us."

Silence, then Kohl said, "So?"

"Penn," said Grace, "got the aliens to come here. Lured them in."

"Doesn't explain the *Ravana*," said El. "It doesn't explain—"

"Sure it does," said Grace. "The *Ravana* did a runner. Full sail, straight on until morning. Her captain saw what was going on down there. Her captain didn't do the stupid thing," and here, Grace's internal voice said *the brave but still idiotic thing*, "of trying to help people. Her captain hauled up the anchor and punched the black. And they died, because they got *scared*. Just like you are, Kohl."

"I ain't scared," he said. "I ain't—"

"You *reek* of it," said Grace. She tossed a glance at El. "I know *she's* scared, because she's *always* scared."

"Hey—" said El.

"But you? It's a foreign fucking concept, isn't it? October Kohl, afraid. Well, get used to it. What did you call it? A shit show? I can assure you it'll get shittier, like an open sewer. And you'll get more and more scared." Grace took a step towards the big man. "What's really eating at you," she hissed, "is that you were *sleeping*. You were helped on to this ship by *me*," and here, Grace pointed a thumb at her own chest, "while you put your feet up. While El did the hard stuff. While—"

She choked. Not because she was running out of words, but because Kohl had grabbed her throat. The man had moved so fast she hadn't even seen it coming, his fingers like a vice. He'd slammed her up against the glass window of the sickbay, his face next to hers. She struck out, fingers stabbing at the soft area under the armpit, a kick to his groin, because he was holding her off the ground. He dropped his shoulder against her fingers, her *nukite* starved of energy, and shifted his inner thigh against her foot. She kicked nothing but leg, and it felt like kicking a tree — the tree just didn't care.

No sword.

Kohl's fist slammed into her stomach and she wanted to curl over, except she was pinned. Grace's vision was going dark, she only had seconds with the force he was putting on her carotid artery before she blacked out. His face was right next to hers. "Who," he hissed, teeth clenched together in anger, "is scared now?"

There was a click and a hiss, and Kohl's fingers relaxed. His eyes lost some of their glare, and he stumbled back before he dropped onto his ass on the floor. Grace rubbed at her throat, coughing, then looked up. At Hope, and the hypo she held. She was pale, paler than a clear dawn just after the colors of the sun had fled before the coming light of day. She looked at the hypo, then at Kohl. "I don't know what's in this," she said. Her voice sounded faint. "I don't know why I did that."

Grace looked at Nate, who was grayer than three-day-old oatmeal, then at Hope. "Thank you," she said. It came out as a rasp, her throat burning. She turned to El. "El. Help me get Nate in the damn machine."

"I'm not going anywhere near you," said El.

"I'll help," said Hope.

"No," said Grace. "I'll do it myself. Then we'll talk."

"MY FATHER," said Grace, "was one of the Emperor's Intelligencers." She said it without emotion, because this was a deli-cate time, and they needed to make up their own minds. If she was going to gain their trust—

Grace, Grace, Grace. It's gone beyond that. You've taken their trust, broken it to a thousand pieces, and then tossed it into a star. They will never trust you again.

"An esper?" said El.

"An esper," said Grace. "A strong one." She looked around the sickbay; Hope and Nate had changed places, Hope on the ground, leaning against a wall, her eyes closed, but she was awake, mind firing and strong.

"They're not allowed to have kids," said El. "The Intelligencers were ... *experiments*."

"They were," said Nate, his voice thick with the effects of drugs, "assholes."

"If you can control people's minds," said Hope, "rules don't really apply."

"Rules didn't apply to my father," agreed Grace. *Only to me.* "He wanted his own empire." She nudged Kohl with a foot. Hope had dosed him with a muscle relaxant, so he was awake and online, but unable to choke her out again. "He talked about a Republic of Equals." She didn't talk about her mother. Her mother had left her with a gentle name and a memory of tenderness before her father had taken over the controls. He'd wanted her to discard that tenderness like so much space junk. She wished she could still talk to her mother; Grace sent her holos but didn't even know if her mother got them. That was all one-way. Just like her father. She clamped down on that thought. *Not the time.*

"No one was ever equal to the Intelligencers," said El. She had her arms crossed. "No one."

"He didn't mean you," said Grace. "He didn't mean any of you. He meant others. Like him."

"The not-breeding thing was supposed to stop humanity being ruled by mind-controlling overlords," said Hope. "I guess I'm glad they all died in the revolution."

"Dear ol' Dad," said Grace, "wanted me to be just like him."

"Rule the world?" said Hope.

"Be an asshole?" said El.

"Be an esper," said Grace. "Like you can be taught a thing like that."

The room was silent, aside from Kohl who sounded like he was trying to say something. Grace didn't want to hear anything that man had to say, so she nudged him harder with her boot. "Shut it, Kohl."

"Are you ... one of them?" said Hope.

"No," said Nate. "She's—"

"Yes," said Grace. She put a hand on Nate's shoulder. *Rest.* "And no. Not like what you think. My mother wasn't an esper. It didn't ... *I* didn't breed true."

"De ... formed," choked out Kohl, then made a grating sound, like a tractor failing to start on a cold morning. Grace realized he was trying to laugh.

"You and my father would have so much to talk about," said Grace, "if he didn't turn your brain inside out in five seconds."

"Have you been manipulating us?" said El.

"Sure," said Grace. "I've manipulated this asshole," and again, her toe into Kohl's stomach, "into choking the life from me. I manipulated the *Ravana's* reactor into blowing up. Hell, I manipulated an entire alien race into attacking us." She sighed. "Try not to be as stupid as Kohl. He's more than enough for one ship."

The machine attached to Nate beeped, the display changing from red to amber. He opened his eyes. "What's it say? Am I dying?"

"Yes," said Grace, "but now at the same speed as the rest of us."

"The same ... what?"

"You're fine," said Grace. "You'll be fine." *Not like me. You'll either kill me, or leave me here. You've got to. You can't make any other choice.*

"Great," said Nate. "Get me the fuck out of this thing. I've got a ship to fly."

"So I was thinking," said Grace. "It'd be great if you could just let me off somewhere. With people." *Please don't leave me here. Not with them.*

"What?" said Nate. "No."

He's going to leave me here. She could feel the sickness in her stomach return, and she bowed her head. "I understand. Because of what I am. What I've done."

"Half right," said Nate, levering himself up on one elbow. The machine emitted a harsh alarm, and he slapped at the console until it shut off. "What you've done? Sure, sure. You lied. Hell, you lied to all of us, and that's a thing I can't let slide."

She nodded. "I understand. I'll—"

"Haven't finished," said Nate. "It'll cost you a completion bonus, best case scenario. Most of your share. Need to think about it."

"What?" said Grace.

"I think that's fair," said Nate.

"Wait—" said El.

"Unngh," said Kohl.

"Haven't finished," said Nate. "Y'all seem to forget who is the *captain* of the *Tyche*. It's not any of you. If you don't like it, airlock's that way." He pointed in the general direction of the aft of the ship. "Y'all also forget what's happened so far. Hope would have been taken by the Navy if it weren't for Grace."

"But—" said El.

"Capnnn," said Kohl.

"*Still* haven't finished," said Nate. He was zipping himself back into his flight suit. "Now Kohl, I know that you want Hope to be left out there as well. You share the Republic's views on this sort of thing. That's between you and them. On *my* ship, it doesn't matter. Never has, and never will. And I'll remind you, without Hope, and what she did, we'd be spread atom-thin in a part of space no one goes to. We'd all be dead, and no one would know what happened to us. Without Hope, the *Tyche* wouldn't be flying. Isn't that right, El?"

"But Captain," said El. "We're not talking about Hope—"

"Isn't," said Nate, his smile growing fixed, "that *right*, Helm?"

"Sir," said El. "That's right."

"This is *all* about Grace," said Nate. "Hell, the Republic are after her, but she still put herself in harm's way to help me and mine. That makes her one of us, don't you see? Don't you all see?" He looked at the floor, then back up. "This isn't hard unless you make it hard. Hope fixed the *Tyche*. Better than new."

"Cap," said Hope. "I just—"

"Haven't *finished*," said Nate, and then softened. "Sorry, Hope.

You rest now. Without what Grace did, when she had no reason to know us, or to trust us, we would have lost our Engineer. No Engineer, no *Tyche*. Simple as that."

"Fuck," said Kohl. "It."

"Kohl, I'm glad you're joining the conversation, because back in that city? Back in Absalom Delta. You were down for the count. We were all going to *die*. Do you remember who saved your ass?" Nate leaned down, clapped the big man on the shoulder. "Do you remember?"

"Uh," said Kohl.

"That's right," said Nate. "It was *Grace*. Now, I'm about ready for some sleep. I'm going to go to my cabin, and I'm going to lock the door. When I wake up, everyone on this ship will still be alive. No one will kill anyone else. Am I being fairly clear?"

"Sir," said El.

"Nate," said Grace. "It's okay."

"I said," said Nate, "am I being fairly clear?"

Grace felt something in her chest, the flutter of a moth's wings. She hadn't felt it for years. It was hope. "Yes," she said.

"Damn," said Kohl, "it."

"I'll take that as a yes also," said Nate. "Kohl, you remember this. You remember that when you were at Grace Gushiken's feet, after you'd tried to kill her, she let you live. You think on that some." He gave Grace a wink, then let himself out of sickbay. His boots clanking on the metal decking faded into the distance.

"Sorry," said Grace, because she had nothing else to say.

"Are you?" said El. She was looking at Grace, her eyes hard, her voice harder. "I swear—"

"I've got something for you," said Hope. She got herself upright, swaying. Grace moved to her side, held her arm. Helped her stay on an even keel. Hope looked at Grace, really looked at *her*. Not what she *was*, or what she could *do*. "Come on. I'll show you."

Grace followed Hope's lead from the sickbay, still holding her upright. They left El and Kohl behind. Whether for good or ill, it was impossible to say, but Grace suspected she'd stay alive long enough for Nate to finish his nap.

ENGINEERING WAS DARK, the murmur of machines making a gentle background noise. Hope was walking on her own now, leading the way. Inside, she paused, then bent to pick up the bent remains of her rig. She held it up. "Penn," she said, as if that explained everything.

"Strong," said Grace.

"Not human," said Hope. "I don't know how long for. I've sent files to your console. About what they were doing down here. About what they learned."

"He was becoming a new Queen," said Grace.

"How do you know?" said Hope.

"For a time," said Grace, "I was ... *together* with them. I saw hints, flashes. Penn was the start of something new."

"Here it is," said Hope, her hands moving through the pieces of machinery on her workbench. She held up her find: Grace's sword. Hope walked over to Grace, then held the sword out to her. "You threw it away."

"It was broken," said Grace. "It wasn't worth keeping."

"Say that next time Kohl has his hands around your throat," said Hope, the hint of a smile on her lips. "Go on. Check it out."

Grace drew the blade. She knew what she'd see — the silver of the metal gleaming its way free of the scabbard, right up to the fractured tooth it had become, a foot down the blade. As the blade came free from the scabbard, she saw the metal, and then she saw ... *more* metal. The blade was whole again, the jagged stump that had been left after Grace's encounter with the Ezeroc replaced with new, gleaming metal. She looked at Hope. "How?" Then, "Why?"

"How is easy. I set up the fab to print a new blade." Hope frowned. "Well, *easy* isn't quite right. I couldn't drop-forge that sucker. Because we don't have a forge. And I'm no smith, you know? Ha. But it's printed the best I know how. No imperfections in the steel."

Grace swung the sword, the weapon feeling *right* in her hand. Like she was used to. Not like Nate's sword, with its straight blade and unfamiliar weight. "Okay," said Grace. "Why?"

"Oh," said Hope. "Because you needed it." She turned away, hefting her broken rig. "Now I need to fix this."

Grace reached out a tentative hand, touching Hope's elbow. "Thank you," she said.

Hope stood still, frozen by the touch, then relaxed. She turned to Grace, then grabbed her in a hug. The young woman was crying, and Grace was confused, buffeted by the emotions pouring off her. She reached a cautious hand around Hope, hugging her back. When Hope had stopped crying, she said, almost as a whisper, "Please don't leave. Please don't leave our home."

Grace leaned her head forward against the top of Hope's, pink hair under her nose. "I won't," she said. "I don't think I'd know how. Not anymore."

GRACE KNOCKED on Nate's cabin. Hard, with the hilt of her sword, *clang-clang-clang*.

Nate opened it, eyes befuddled, shirt half open. "Wha..?"

"You," said Grace, "owe me a story. About a sword, and where it came from. I gave you my story, and now you need to give me yours."

"I ... sleeping," said Nate.

"You can sleep later," said Grace.

"I'm the captain," said Nate, almost hopefully.

She pushed past him into the room. She saw the sword. Nate had placed it on top of the chest she'd stolen it from what felt like weeks ago, but was only hours. *He hasn't put it away. He hasn't hidden it again.* She pointed at it. "Tell me."

"It's better if I show you," said Nate, standing still at the doorway for a second. She could see the metal of his hand resting against the sill. He sighed, walked next to her, and said, "Tell me what you see."

Grace looked at him, felt *concern/not-trust/friend/trust* coming from him. "You're wondering if you can trust me."

"Yes," said Nate. "I'm becoming more sure though." He reached for the sword, his flesh hand closing around the hilt.

He vanished.

She gaped. He was still *there*; her eyes told her he was right in front of her, but his mind had gone quiet, like it didn't exist. Like he was dead. He held the sword up. "Now tell me what you see."

"You're ... not *there*." She reached a hand out to touch him. Her fingers found his chest. *Solid. Real.* "What *is* it?"

"Doesn't have a name," he said, not moving her fingers. She pulled them back, all of a sudden, like they'd been burned. This feeling of *someone* without the *someone* was ... alien. Magical.

Wonderful.

Nate was still holding the sword between them. "At least, I don't think it has a name. There weren't many made. Maybe just one."

"It ... hides you?" Grace wanted to touch him again, for the thrill of not feeling the endless cascade of human emotions that always came with it. She reached out a hand, cautious, tentative, to lay her fingers against his arm. *Nothing.* Nothing traveled that physical link, other than the warmth of another human, out here on the edge of the hard black.

"I don't know," said Nate. Oblivious, she guessed, to the wonder she felt. If he could feel what she was feeling, he would see it as *grateful/thankful/joy.* But he never would, so she would just have to enjoy it alone. Like all other people were alone. For as long as it lasted. Nate was still speaking, and she tried to focus, removing her hand again. "I guess that's it. A part of it, anyway. But it also makes it so that the Intelligencers can't fuck with my mind." He tapped the side of his head with his metal hand. "When you're holding this sword, skin on the metal, you're free. Free of any outside influence. It's why I think ... I think I know I can trust you."

"What?" she said.

"Because of how I feel when I'm not holding it. It's the same as how I feel now." He touched her chin. "I feel like I *should* trust you, Grace Gushiken."

"You should?" she said, the feeling of his fingers without the curse of another person's emotions a wonder, a revelation.

"Yeah." His face was open, and she suspected without the sword, his heart would be too. *You are on the edge of something marvelous. A rare, curious thing: this man wants to trust you. Really wants to, so you need to make it right. You need to be worthy of it.* "Yeah, I think so."

She folded his hand in hers, then pulled him down beside her on the edge of the bed. Not some wanton display, but carefully, like his hand was made of snowflakes and all around was fire. "I guess I don't know," she said. "I guess I want you to. I guess I don't know why. I guess ... I guess I don't deserve it."

He sighed. "None of us deserve it. We've all done," and here, his eyes flicked towards the chest at the end of his bed, "terrible things. The trick, as near as I can work out, is to stop doing terrible things when you realize."

She frowned, looking down at his hand, in hers. It was the metal one, and she hadn't considered that when she'd taken it. Just grabbed on to him, wanting to make it all real. Grace realized she didn't care he had a metal hand, despite what her father would have said. He would have called Nate *half a man* and dismissed him, like he'd always dismissed her. Her father had always thought of her as a *mongrel/failure*. She looked at the sword he held, then the sword she held, and laughed.

"What?" said Nate. "I've got to admit, this is weird. We're sitting in a bed holding hands, but ... well, it's weird." But he didn't pull away from her.

It wasn't everyday a man followed her into a den of horrible monsters, even when he knew she might be the worst monster of them all. That showed *dedication*. "Not knowing. It's ... different. I can't tell what you were feeling." She smiled through the cascade of her hair. "The gentle quiet. It feels ... like a miracle."

"I don't know what we're supposed to do here. Uncharted waters, Grace." His voice was low and quiet. "I don't know what you want. I don't know ... I don't know what I want."

"You want me to stop lying," said Grace. "To you."

"Hell," said Nate. "That'd be nice, but whatever. What I want is for *you* to decide."

"Okay," said Grace. Still sitting there in the quiet of his cabin, a human next to her without their emotions boiling up to consume her. She laughed, and didn't know why. "Okay."

CHAPTER TWENTY-FIVE

WHEN THE KLAXON WENT OFF, Nate was still feeling stupid.

He'd sat with Grace in his cabin for what seemed an hour, talking of little things. She still holding his damn metal hand, and laughing when he said things. He'd asked her why she laughed and she'd said *because I didn't see what you said coming ... for the first time, I'm surprised.*

Their conversation had wound down like an old clock, the distances between the *ticks* and *tocks* getting longer. She'd leaned forward, whispered *thank you, Nathan Chevell* into his ear. He'd felt the brush of her lips on his cheek, and then she was gone, feet clanking with purpose down the metal halls of the *Tyche*.

Nate wanted more than that brushed kiss after an hour of talking with her. He should have been sleeping. Nate should have been patching things up with Kohl and El. He should have been seeing how Hope was getting on. But he couldn't pull himself away, like he was *supposed* to talk to her. And that left him slow-headed, dumb with some fool emotion or other, and that was no way for the captain to be. The captain had to be above all that. The captain had to be...

Human. Nate, you're only human.

He pushed that thought down. The captain had to be better than human. Because there were a bunch of other people who depended on him to be so much more.

The lips against his cheek had still left him feeling stupid, despite what his rational mind had said. And then the klaxon had sounded. He jumped to the console, almost tripping over the sword he still held — *you came in handy, after all* — and pushed the comm. "What the hell," he said, "is that fucking noise?"

"That fucking noise is a collision alarm with rocks raining from the sky," said El. "You had enough sleep?"

"No," said Nate. "Why are their rocks? Aren't the Ezeroc on the other side of the planet?"

"No," said El. "You'd better get up here."

Fucking fuck. Those damn bugs just didn't quit. One thing was for sure though. They wanted to infect his crew. They wanted to take humans, and — a strange thought nudged him — maybe Grace more than anyone else. Like she had a connection with them. Like they wanted to eat up espers. *Good luck to them.* They could have all the rest of the espers in the universe except this one.

This one was ... *his.*

HE HIT the flight deck at a run, siding into his acceleration couch. El was working on her console, the holo stage alight with telemetry. Lots of incoming rocks.

She tossed him a look. "What's with the sword?"

"Uh," he said.

"Never mind. What's with the open shirt?"

"I—"

"Cap, you need to get your shit together," said El. "We are under attack."

He zipped up his flight suit. "It's been a long morning. Or evening. What time is it?"

"Technically, it's morning. Dawn's coming." El looked over at him. "It's me who should be sorry. I was ... out of line, before."

"Save it," said Nate. "Tell me the important stuff. We can get all mushy later."

"You're the boss," she said, her finger stabbing at points of light in the holo. "Here, we have our basic asteroids becoming meteors. There's no aiming on those, just a bunch of what we would call carpet-bombing. At least I'm guessing there's no aiming because they're not coming at us."

"Why didn't we—"

"See them coming? Yeah." El tapped on the console, the holo pulling out. "Here, we've got the planet. A while ago we lost the link to the orbital satellites around Absalom Delta. Offline or some shit, Hope could tell you more."

"I didn't know this why?" said Nate.

"You were doing white-knighting," said El. "In the woods, and then you got your fool self hurt, and since then you've been," and here she made air quotes, "'sleeping.'"

"I was—"

"It doesn't matter," said El. "What does matter, since you want just the important stuff, is that it looks like at least one of them will impact," and here, El made the holo draw a line between one rock and the crumbling tower Nate and Grace had been in, "with that science facility you were at."

"Not a science facility," said Nate.

"I reckon not," agreed El. "I also reckon that the bugs want it gone. Which is an odd thing to be saying, like they have a will and a purpose, and two days ago we thought we were all alone in the big bad universe, but there you have it. What was it, anyway?"

"Science *experiment*," said Nate. "Old one. We'll cover that later."

"Is it important for *now*?" said El.

"There was a Queen there," said Nate. "Killed it. Apparently Penn would become a Queen too? Bit of an expansionist program in the ol' Ezeroc world. Also, they think I'm infected with an alien parasite."

"Are you?" said El. Nate saw she had her hand on the old hand cannon by her side.

Careful, Nate. She might be in pro mode but she's still jumpy. "That's between me and my parasite," said Nate.

"That's a negative then," said El, relaxing her hand away from her gun. "Penn didn't seem to have much of a sense of humor before he popped."

"Popped?" Nate was working his console. "Okay, I see what you're saying. Lots of rocks. Like they want to flush us out." He pointed at the holo, where the big Ezeroc asteroid — or ship, or whatever the fucking thing was — orbited. "At least we got visual on the big bad monsters."

"Why?" said El. "They got a parasite on you, or so they think. Couple more hours in the oven and you'll take over the ship. You as the alien, I mean."

"I figure them wanting us to bust a move back to human space," said Nate. "I figure that what we have here is longer-range thinking than we've given them credit for."

"Okay," said El. "So what are we going to do?"

Nate thought about that for a while. Dust off, but with what purpose? He thought about the dead city they'd left on the other side of planet, about the dead colonists, about the hundreds of thousands of people who were no more. Nate thought about Penn, who was involved in all this up to his eyeballs before he was infected. He thought about the old research facility masquerading as a transmission tower, or science outpost, that had been here for a long, long time. That was overrun with Ezeroc. And he thought about a giant asteroid that these aliens used as a starship. The way he figured it, there had been some kind of advance contact years back. The Ezeroc met humans for the first time at that old facility. Something went down, a science experiment either side might have started. And then the Ezeroc had sent a colony ship.

So had the humans. The difference was that the Ezeroc came prepared; Penn hadn't told any of the humans what to expect. Penn, or someone very much like him, had set an entire colony up as a petri dish in which to grow alien spores. Penn, who was a spy for the Republic. He'd got his, but there was no doubt plenty more culpability to go around.

"Cap?" said El. "What are we going to do?"

"I'm not sure," said Nate, "but the plan starts with killing them all."

"THIS IS YOUR CAPTAIN SPEAKING," said Nate into the comm. "We're about to lift off from this rock and go to war."

El gave him a sideways glance. "We're in a cargo ship," she said. "The *Tyche* is a heavy lifter. She's not a fighter."

"You keep telling me," said Nate, "how good a pilot you are. How you can make our girl swoop and soar."

"But," said El, then went silent.

"Cap," said Kohl's voice from the comm, "are we going to fly up into space and shoot some aliens?"

"My plan exactly," said Nate. "How you feel about that?"

"Not amazing," said Kohl, "because the Engineer drugged me with something, but I figure I can get back to that messy business when this other messy business is dealt with."

"That's the story," said Nate. "Hope? You with us?"

"Engineering is online and good to go," she said. "Engineering wants to know why you're taking the *Tyche* to war. She's a freighter, Cap."

El gave Nate a raised eyebrow. He ignored it. "She's the Goddess of Luck, Hope. And don't you feel lucky?"

"No," she said. "I've been knocked out by an alien psychopath, stuck to a wall with goo, and I don't know what is going on."

"Well, great," said Nate. "Strap in anyway." He clicked the comm off. "El, how many planet busters do we have on board?"

"We have exactly zero," she said.

"Wait, what?"

"Zero," she said. "We are a cargo ship."

"I know, but—"

"What we have, courtesy of the fine Republic, is a full load of ship-to-ship torpedoes." She sniffed. "Which will scratch an itch on that asteroid and not much more."

"The long game," said Nate.

"I wish you'd just tell me what you were planning," she said.

"Wish I could," he said. He held the sword up. "Blocks espers."

"Good to know," she said. "Must help conversations with Grace."

"The Ezeroc," said Nate, "are espers. It's a whole race of aliens that read minds."

She looked at the sword, then up at his face, then back to the sword. "Oh," she said. "I see."

"Get us in the air, Helm," he said. "Try not to hit any of the big falling rocks while you do it."

"Aye aye, sir," she said.

CHAPTER TWENTY-SIX

IT WASN'T the same as flying a frigate, but that was the only thing that would keep them alive. El's hands worked her console, firing up the *Tyche's* systems, bringing systems online. The ship was telling her about a ring of alien insects surrounding them outside, which she told it to ignore. In about two minutes, they'd be barbecue anyway, so not worth the PDC ammunition it'd take. Besides, the way El looked at it, there were plenty more where they came from. You needed to snip this kind of thing off at the source.

That was the captain's plan, unless she missed his intent. She got why he wasn't telling them about it. Mind reading aliens was a thing that could set a woman's teeth on edge. If she knew the plan, the bugs knew the plan, and that would delete the surprise factor.

A mind reading human could set a woman's teeth on edge too. She thought of Grace. She thought about how there was some unfinished business there. But she also got the cap's basic direction of travel on this. Fix the alien problem first, that was the critical issue, and then worry about the shipboard squabbles. And, she admitted in the quiet of her own mind, Nate had a point. Grace had done no wrong by them. Not yet, and maybe hadn't planned to. Grace had done quite a bit right by them, and that bothered El. Espers weren't to be trusted. Those assholes had torn down the entire Empire before the rest of humanity had built a pyre and burned them on it.

The *Tyche's* deck hummed to life, reminding El of the job at hand. Rocks coming out of the sky: priority one. Killing the aliens: priority two. Working out how to stop Kohl from killing Grace, or whether they should let that run its course: priority three.

El hoped Kohl thought that too. She'd been on a bridge crew trying to fly in a war zone while an insurrection panned out across the galaxy, and it hadn't been a big bowl of fun. It had been a big bowl of *we're all going to die*, and that as a general rule was why she tried to avoid being on planets. Planets were where you went to die. Flying a ship? *Totally* different. Totally.

"Hope?"

"You've got Hope," said the Engineer over the comm.

"We good?"

"We're good," said Hope. "I'd have told you if we weren't."

"I know," said El. "I worry about our girl, is all."

"She'll do right by you," said Hope.

"I know she will," said El, clicking off the comm. She put her hands on the sticks. *Here goes nothing.*

The *Tyche* grumbled in her belly as the drives came up. The antigrav pushed them away from the planet's crust, all the extra juice from the *Ravana's* stolen heart making it seem effortless now. An alarm blinked on her console, a feed getting too much power, and she cleared the alert. That would keep happening for as long as they had a bigger power supply, which probably meant forever. More power was always better power.

She brought up the telemetry of falling rocks. Not huge time left now, because the captain sure was a talker. The one impacting the tower would be with them in minutes, and while it seemed a long way away, it wasn't. Meteor strike would deliver a significant level of energy to the planet's crust. That energy could turn into a huge fireball of fury and death, sweeping them aside like dust into a pan. Best not to be around when it hit. She plotted the rest of the asteroids, the ones she could see, and saw the likely impact points. Nothing as complicated as before when fragments of rock had come down like angry hail; this would be easy.

A cakewalk. Hell, even the captain could fly them out of this.

HARD THRUST, a wall at El's back. The shake and tremble of the *Tyche*, like an anxious puppy. The rattle of something behind El, a bolt not tight all the way.

The holo turned, filled with telemetry, the *Tyche's* eyes seeing things faster and farther than El could hope to. The *Tyche* was saying *look, these rocks are bad, but* those *can be ignored*. El agreed. Best to go away from the bad rocks.

The ship roared over the forest floor, her underside close to the deck. El didn't know whether the Ezeroc used RADAR or LIDAR or unicorns for sensors, but old habits died hard. On the deck was invisible. On the deck was hard, but hard flying was fun flying. Hard flying was what it was all about. And Nate was right. El could make the *Tyche* fly like she was a fighter, born on the wing.

Or course, all that extra power in the main reactor helped. Made the *Tyche* less sluggish down here where antigrav was important.

"El," said Nate. "Don't play with your food."

She gave a tight grin. "Aye, Cap. Just looking for a nice safe hole in the sky."

"That one," said Nate, pointing at the holo. "Looks clear."

"I reckon so," she said. She fed the *Tyche* new flight data, pointed the ship at the space in the sky between large falling rocks. The ship rumbled back, growled as the fusion drives built up the thrust to escape gravity. "Escape burn in 3, 2, 1, mark. Mark."

A kick, the acceleration couch slamming against her as she pushed the throttle forward. An easy 3 Gs this time, nothing worth getting a stroke over. It's not like they had an entire sky full of fire this time.

"Oh, hey," said Nate. "That's unusual."

"What kind of unusual," said El, then stopped. Because the *Tyche* was telling her that the Ezeroc ship had jumped. It had busted a move through the sky, gobbled up the klicks in an instant, and was now a lot, lot closer. It would be waiting for them in the sky when they left atmosphere.

"That kind," said Nate.

She figured he was thinking what she was: Endless Drives couldn't jump like that close to a gravity well. Which made what the Ezeroc had just done ... impossible. "Do I abort?" said El.

"Nah," said Nate.

"No? Are you crazy?"

"A little," said Nate. "But this is what they want, El. They want us in space."

"You know this," said El, "because you've melded minds with the alien menace that will be the doom of our species?"

"I know this," said Nate, "because it makes sense."

"Oh God," said El, "we're all going to die."

"Yes," said Nate, "but not today. Keep burning."

It wasn't really up for discussion; El was just working her mouth to let off steam. Climbing for the stars wasn't a thing you wanted to break off half way. Sure, you could do it, but you'd just need to do it again some other place. And the Ezeroc ship seemed to ignore all kinds of unfortunate laws of physics. The *Tyche* could drink a little of the same liquor too, but pulling open a negative space field this close to a planet wasn't a thing that would end well for them. Get some more sky behind them, then punch for the black.

The holo lit red. *COLLISION WARNING COLLISION WARNING.*

"Oh, hey," said Nate. "That's not cool. Try and avoid that." He was pointing at a new rock falling from the Ezeroc ship.

"You think?" said El. "Why are they firing at us if they want us to make space?"

"Oh, they're not firing at us," said Nate. "They're firing *next* to us. A warning shot. Easy dodge."

El worked the sticks, altering they're trajectory. Nate was right, the rock was an easy dodge. Too big, too slow to pose a threat. "So ... why?" she said.

"If I was a horrible alien on this ship, I'd say something like 'Gnar, let's all go to space!' and we'd go to space. A sensible human pilot would run the fuck away," he said. After a second, he said, "I think."

"You think?"

"Yeah," said Nate. His face split with a manic grin. "Ain't this cool?"

"Could they also," said El, "be wanting to distract us?"

"Distract us?" said Nate. "From what?"

CHAPTER TWENTY-SEVEN

REACHING orbit didn't take long. A quick burn, hard thrust at their backs, and you've got yourself orbital velocity. Grace could feel the changes as the *Tyche* went from *straight the fuck up* and through a flatter trajectory. Bumps and shudders and shifts in the ship told a story of a not-smooth launch as the Ezeroc hunted them through the sky. Grace wasn't worried about that; she'd seen El's work firsthand. Their Helm was second to none in Grace's experience. The only thing holding El back from a career of greatness was El herself.

That's probably a problem that will solve itself.

A greater problem for Grace right now was Kohl. That asshole was not in his acceleration couch. That asshole wasn't anywhere Grace could see him, and that worried her. It worried her right to the bottoms of her feet, because despite Nate's *hey we're all on the same cheerleading squad* talk, Kohl wasn't interested in cheerleading. The man wasn't interested in much else other than punching things.

Punching things had its place, but not in your home.

Grace.

Her head whipped around, casting about the ready room. She was the only one here. Nate and El were in the flight deck. Hope was in Engineering. Kohl was the one unaccounted for. Kohl was the one free roaming the ship. Kohl, who had it in for Grace. Kohl, who had it in for Hope — God only knew why. Maybe it was just that Hope was just too young, too damn easy to *play* to be living this kind of life. But the last time Hope had been doing her job, cribbing it back in Engineering, an alien insect inhabiting the body of a spy had grabbed her up.

Those fuckers had grabbed her friend, and—

Grace, don't get involved. Don't.

She wrestled with that voice for longer than she wanted to admit. Grace wasn't proud of it, and wouldn't have told anyone about the struggle. About how she measured the angles, thought about the win in it for her.

What I want is for you *to decide.*

"Oh, fuck's sake," she said, then keyed her comm. "Hope?"

"You've got Hope," said the Engineer.

Grace would have sagged in relief if the pressure of acceleration hadn't held her in her couch. El had turned the throttle down, the ship now pushing along at a lot less thrust. Still turning in space, Nate giving a whoop here and there. *At least someone's having fun.* "Hope? Is your door locked?"

"No," she said. "Because, you know. We got him. We got Penn."

"Okay," said Grace. "It's just that, I'm alone here. In the ready room."

There was a long, long pause. "It's locked now," she said. "I've really locked it! It is locked in a way that even the cap won't be able to get through."

"Good," said Grace. "You stay there. You don't open it. Not for anyone."

"Not even for you?" said Hope.

"Not for anyone," said Grace. *I guess this is it. You've decided. This crew. Here. Now.* "Hope?"

"Grace?"

"Don't bother the captain," she said. "He's got enough on his mind." She didn't add, *bothering the captain would also bother El. And bothering El would mean the alien mind readers would know what's up.* Grace unclipped her acceleration harness, easing herself from the chair. Feet on the deck, she felt the artificial gravity of the ship pulling her down, and the thrust pushing her back. It was an odd sensation, like standing on an uneven floor.

Odd for her was odd for aliens too.

Last time she'd fought Kohl, she didn't have a sword. This time, she wouldn't make the same mistake. She set off to her cabin.

OF COURSE THE sword wasn't in her cabin. The shiny new blade that Hope had made for her was missing. There was a note scrawled in blood on the wall above her bunk. It said *COME AND GET IT.*

She sighed. Where did Kohl end and the alien begin? Did they change all at once? Was it like delirium, curable with antibiotics and a good chicken broth?

Grace Grace Grace Grace Grace...

This voice was fainter. She could hear the alien hiss through it, the words in her mind speaking to her, but from within the ship. Closer, and smaller at the same time. Younger.

Grace looked at the blood on the wall. Now there was a good example of someone not in their right mind. If she'd been younger, been more afraid of her own shadow, she might have been scared, but what she felt was *bored* and *frustrated.* It didn't postpone the inevitable. It made a hard job harder. Seriously, why hadn't Kohl just waited here for her?

Kohl might not want to kill you.

"Oh," she said. "So you fuckers aren't always in control, huh? Not at first, anyway." That was good to know. It was also bad to know, because instead of just killing Kohl — the man *deserved* it, in the way plants deserved rain — she'd have to work out whether he'd turned, like milk left in the sun. Whether the core of him was sour. Whether it could be saved.

The ship gave a hard swerve, *up* becoming *left* for a while, then *down* swapped with *up* and *right*. Grace's feet left the decking, she hit the wall, then the ceiling, then the other wall, and landed on the decking again. *Fucking rock-throwing aliens.*

Grace.

Together!

"Okay," said Grace, rubbing her shoulder. "Together it is." She left her cabin. Grabbed the handrail against the wall, using it as an anchor, the ship bucking hard. The muted roar of the PDCs trembled the metal under Grace's hands, and then the hull rang like a bell, something too big or too fast hitting them. The *Tyche* spun around her axis, Grace's grip tightening on the handrail so hard her fingers went white.

Silence.

She made her way to the storage room they'd fixed up for Penn to stay in. There was still Penn slime on the floor, but at least the light was working again, someone — Hope? — having fixed the damn thing. *Sword, sword, sword...* almost anything would do. Give her a piece of pipe and she could swing it like a boss. She knew Kohl would just break her into component parts if she didn't have a weapon. With a weapon? She might stand a chance.

No pipe. There was a small blaster, tucked in with some protein cakes. It might have been Penn's, squirreled away for a rainy day, or it might have been tucked here for just such an emergency. She grabbed it, checked the charge. *Good enough.*

Back when Grace had been doing training — back when she'd learned she wasn't a good shot, not good enough unless she was firing grenades — her instructor had leaned forward. He'd said *Grace, you suck. So what you're gonna do, when you've got a gun? You use that gun to get a sword. That there is the best I can do for you.* He'd leaned back, wiped his hands on his uniform, and then asked her to keep shooting anyway. Because her father was paying him to teach her how to shoot; the other advice was free.

No problem. She'd go get herself a sword.

GETTING a sword proved easier than she thought it should have been.

It was waiting in the middle of the cargo hold. Blade bared, catching the light, the steel rammed into the decking. Something that was strong — and something that didn't care about caring for swords — had done that. Grace was watching it from the top of the ladder leading into the cargo bay. No other movement. She couldn't hear anything, but that wasn't unusual. They were flying under thrust, the rumble of engines and the sporadic chatter of the PDCs overlying everything else.

"Grace," said Hope. Grace almost jumped out of her skin.

Hope wasn't there, of course. It was her comm. She keyed it. "Hey."

"Kohl's down there," said Hope.

"How do you know?"

"I've tagged his blood with a radioactive isotope," said Hope. "It lets the *Tyche* watch where he's going. I can even tell when it's him using the head."

"Really?" Grace was trying to get a glimpse of something, anything, down in the hold. The sword was a trap. It was a good trap. Grace *wanted* to get caught in it.

"No," said Hope. "Why the hell would that sound plausible?"

"You're an Engineer," said Grace. "Engineers do ... stuff."

"I once was an Engineer, sure," said Hope. "But I've never been a sorcerer. Anyway, it's cams. They're all over the ship. I saw him go down there. Didn't come back up."

"Could he have got out some other way?"

"You seen the size of that man? He doesn't diet." Hope paused. "I don't think he could have got out another way. Are you going to kill him?" This last was said in a rush, and it took Grace a moment to process it.

What I want is for you *to decide.*

"I don't want to," she said after a little while.

"I don't think I want you to either," said Hope. "Or I do. He's ... not a nice person."

You, Grace Gushiken, are not a nice person either. It's just that Hope doesn't see it, because you bent her around your little finger on day one. But you want to come back from the edge. Maybe Kohl does too. "He's ... *necessary*," said Grace.

"Okay," said Hope. "Can I make one suggestion?"

"Shoot," said Grace, tightening her grip on the blaster.

"Turn your magboots on," said Hope. "That way you won't fly all over the inside of the hull when we maneuver." The comm clicked off.

Grace sighed. The problem with not being born a spacer, with learning to fight on the crust of a world, was that the obvious things weren't ... *obvious.* She tapped on her console. Her boots made a comforting *cthunk* as they snuggled up to the metal deck plating. She wouldn't be able to move like a dancer, it'd be like moving in treacle. But moving in treacle was better than not being able to hold on to something and dying as she was smashed against the inside of the *Tyche.*

She began her way down the ladder, the *Tyche* bucking and shaking around her. There was the *crunk* of a torpedo launching from the *Tyche's* belly, firing at God-knows-what in space. The groan of the ship's reactor as more power was poured into a subsystem. Whatever El was doing up the front, shit was getting real — the *Tyche* did another spin, Grace's boots holding her fast to the metal plates of the ladder, her torso knocking against the railing. One of her boots knocked free and for a moment she was hanging sideways, one hand on the railing, one boot stuck to the ladder, and her blaster went spinning across — or was it down? — the hold. She saw it tumble through the air for a half second before it impacted against the bay doors, bursting into a handful of bright pieces, metal and plastic spraying in at least five directions.

"That looks bad, huh?" said Kohl's voice.

Grace turned, tried to get a glimpse of the man, but she couldn't see anything. Lights casting shadows, shadows hiding almost anything. Empty crates and containers were still lashed about the hold, the trailing end of their ties streaming this way and that as the *Tyche* sailed the dark sea of space. She twisted back around, making ready to move for the sword.

Turned, and found herself face to face with Kohl.

His face was twisted into what might have been a smile, if it weren't for the drool making its way down his chin. His eyes were looking off-center, like they were looking *through* her, *past* her, *into* her.

Then he hit her in the stomach.

She doubled over, still one hand on the railing, thought *move, move!* and slammed her foot down. Her magboot *whirclunked* towards the decking, and caught one of his feet under it. Enough magnetic force to keep her weight to the deck under hard burn pulled her boot to the floor, right on top of his foot, and there was a crunch of bone.

Kohl didn't even blink. He just pulled back and hit her again.

This time she was ready for it, turned her body *into* the punch, stealing its optimal impact point. It still hurt, but it wasn't a true strike. It wouldn't leave broken ribs or a punctured lung. Grace kicked off from Kohl's foot, and at that moment the *Tyche's* engines screamed loud and terrible, the ship whirling, the PDCs hammering into the void.

Kohl was tossed free, joining the remains of the blaster at the back of the hold. Grace fell forward, one boot still on the ladder, her body hitting the decking. She scrabbled as the *Tyche* roared through space, the sickening movement of the ship like the worst rollercoaster she'd ever been on. Grace knocked her chin as she fell, tasting blood as her teeth bit her lip. She wanted to scream, but the air was knocked out of her by another barrel roll. The ship was pulling so many Gs as they pulled *around* and *down* at the same time she was sure she would be sick. Grace sucked in some air, just in time for the ship to whirl the other way. She was yanked to her feet, magboots still clutching at the decking, Kohl's body tumbling to the ceiling of the cargo bay.

Move, Grace.

The sword was maybe ten paces from the base of the ladder. Ten paces in good gravity, under easy thrust. It looked like twenty of the baby steps she'd be able to make in this environment. *Better get started, then.* She moved one boot forward, the *cthunk* as it grabbed at the decking a comfort, a feeling rather than noise as the ship rolled and raged around her. Another *crunk* as a torpedo launched, then *crunk crunk crunk* as the *Tyche* spat nukes at something out there.

"BRACE!" said El's voice over the comm, the PDCs all going loud at the same time. All firing on something.

Then, light. Noise. Sensation, all at once. Her stomach, without pain. Her lip wasn't bleeding. It was whole, and perfect. Her mind, a thousand times larger, her body, tiny. She could feel the pores of her skin, each one of them an individual presence. She could feel her connection with her sword, its new soul forged from the body of the Tyche. Her sword was her. She was everything. She was the universe.

They jumped.

CHAPTER TWENTY-EIGHT

IF NATE HAD KNOWN what was happening in his hold, he would have flipped. He would have gone down there, blaster in hand, and set that fucker Kohl on fire. It was good, then, that he didn't know what was happening. But also bad, in a way, because his own circumstances were real and personal.

They're trying to destroy my goddamn ship!

This wasn't part of the deal. The *deal* was that the bugs would let them off because they'd tricked them. The bugs would let them into space, and they'd be able to jump to somewhere safe, where shit wasn't crazy, where rocks the size of destroyers weren't flying at them.

El was working the controls, her face clammy with perspiration.

Great, let her do her job, you do yours. Nate pulled up the fire controls, the holo between them picking out the tens of rocks in space, the number growing. The ship noted the effect on the planet below them as one meteor impacted the planet with the energy equivalent of a 20 kiloton weapon. Ash and fire was expanding into the atmosphere behind them, the *Tyche* noting changes in weather, atmospheric density, calculating the likely kill radius for life.

That was *one* of the rocks the Ezeroc were dropping.

He flicked the *Tyche's* attention forward, pointing her out at space. "What's behind us isn't important," he said.

"Whassat?" said El.

"Nothing," said Nate.

"Then shut up. Busy," she said. Her hands were on the sticks, pulling the *Tyche* around into a turn. The rocks the Ezeroc were tossing their way were smaller, faster. What really got to Nate was that he couldn't tell where they were coming from. They seemed to break off from the surface of the Ezeroc ship, no drive plume marking their origin. The *Tyche* wasn't used to this kind of fight. Sure, the ship's RADAR and LIDAR were still painting space, bringing back the echoes of things coming at them. It's just that those systems weren't designed for this kind of situation.

So, turn the tables.

He keyed a firing solution into the console, marking the Ezeroc ship. The *Tyche* wanted a specific target site, but a rock that big? Didn't much matter. Best to check it with a probing shot, see what kind of reaction they got from it. He tapped the system, said, "Firing," then selected the big *go get some* button.

The *crunk* of the firing torpedo shook the hull, and he watched the contrail as the weapon shot off into the hard black. The holo said *COLLISION WARNING*. El was hauling on the controls, the ship doing a barrel roll as tiny rocks came at them, one hitting the hull. The sound was almost musical, but it made Nate wince. Rocks on the hull were never good, because rocks could go *through* the hull, and then they'd all be sucking on space dust instead of oxygen.

The PDCs fired, bright lines of fire reaching out into the void, shattering rocks that came close. Nate lost sight of the torpedo as El spun the *Tyche* around, the planet coming into view above them through the cockpit, only to be lost again as she kept the ship turning and burning.

The holo updated as the *Tyche* kept track of the torpedo. The seconds counted down before impact, the display counting down in tenth-of-a-second increments. He paid attention when it beeped at the ten second mark. He could tell El was paying attention too, wanting to see what kind of effect that had on the Ezeroc ship.

Impact.

There was a flare in space, the nuclear warhead of the torpedo impacting the Ezeroc ship. The impact told Nate two things.

The first was that the Ezeroc didn't have PDCs, or anything like 'em. That torpedo just walked on over and said *hi*. Nothing stopped it.

The second thing was that the Ezeroc didn't *need* PDCs, because their little ship-to-ship nuke had about as much effect as horse-fly on a bull. Just a bright light, a little sting, and a few shards of rock. The Ezeroc asteroid was made of something hard. Which put the battle the *Gladiator* must have had with it in perspective.

"No effect on target," he said. "We're gonna need bigger guns."

"I need a destination, Nate," said El. "I can't keep flying the fuck around hoping for a clear sky."

Absalom. Formally N-973, a six-planet system on the very far part of the hard black. A toehold in space, a few rugged colonists as far away from the Republic's muddy boot as you can get. Absalom Delta was the habitable one, but there were five other planets out there. He pulled up the navigation systems. "I'm gonna need you to take us to ... let's go there," he said, highlighting the planet orbiting at the edge of this solar system. Sixth planet. Not terraformed; too small, no atmosphere. Just a cold rock, lots of ice. Surveys said it was mineable. Not that it mattered, not now. What mattered was a little time. A rock without air they could fly around, get some thinking room. He keyed the Endless Drive online.

"We need a little more space," said Nate. "I can't bring up the negative space field this close to ... matter."

"I know the math," said El. "Let's get a little farther out. If these fuckers would stop throwing rocks at us—"

"Probably not going to happen," said Nate, "so let's make our own space."

He locked in the sixth planet into the jump system, warming up the Endless Drive for its sprint. The *Ravana's* reactor fed the *Tyche* like it could do it all day long, all systems firing bright and loud. He pulled up the firing controls again. "El?"

"With you."

"I'll dump some torpedoes that way," he said, highlighting an area of space. "I want you to fly there."

"You want me to fly where you're detonating nukes?" she said.

"Yeah," said Nate.

"Why the hell?" she said.

"I'm going to make some clean air." Nate fired torpedoes. *Cthunk, cthunk, cthunk* as the *Tyche* dropped weapons into space. El was pouring on thrust, the ship turning again and again, weaving through the debris in space, the rocks that the Ezeroc kept launching at them. They were getting clear. They were going to make it.

The *Tyche's* holo lit with COLLISION WARNING BRACE BRACE BRACE. Nate's eyes boggled. The Ezeroc ship had ... *jumped*. No other explanation for it. One second it was aways off, doing its thing with the rocks, and then it was *there*. In front of them. Huge, pock-marked surface. The crust popped, a massive rock detaching. No doubt heading their way. What Nate couldn't wrap his mind around was how it had done it. Something that large would need a huge negative space field. A field that should have destroyed it with the planet below it.

But the Ezeroc ship was just fine, thank you very much.

The PDCs didn't care about this, the *Tyche* spraying the surface of the Ezeroc ship. El was yanking on the controls, the *Tyche* shuddering under the hard Gs she was putting into the turn. She keyed the comm. "BRACE!"

Damn it if they were too close to that asteroid that called itself a ship. It was die as a thin spread of atoms, or it was die by arguing with the laws of physics.

Nate always did like to argue. He slammed his hands down on the console, kicking in the Endless Drive. The star field outside the cockpit pulled and stretched, lines of light drawing across his field of vision.

The sweat on his forehead, gone. Clean air in his lungs, none of the metal taint of overworked air recyclers. Wind in his face as he ran under a blue sky, both his legs whole and perfect. His ship, one with him, as she reached for the stars. He was everything. He was the universe.

They jumped.

THEY SNAPPED back into the real five hundred kilometers from the surface of the icy rock that called itself the sixth planet. The star at the center of the system was dim this far out, a tiny prick of light in the sky outside their cockpit.

They floated, the gentle hum of the ship's Endless Drive spooling down a comfort. They were alive. They were here. They were … *fuck.*

The Ezeroc ship floated in space, far out there, but still there. It had jumped with them.

Well, probably not *with* them. But humans needed time to jump; time was crucial to the human existence and you couldn't break some rules. Nate's guess was that the Ezeroc didn't share this limitation; that they'd seen the *Tyche* jump and just … done it faster. This might have been why the *Ravana* broke the rules, trying to get away from a foe they couldn't, *shouldn't* outrun.

They would never escape the Ezeroc. They would have to fight them here, or die trying. The only real problem? Their foe had already killed a ship many times bigger than they were. A ship built for war. A ship of the Republic, the same Republic that had crushed an Empire filled with good people trying to do the right thing.

Nate was pretty sure they were fucked.

CHAPTER TWENTY-NINE

THE LIGHTS in the cargo bay flickered in a post-jump power flutter. Grace stood still, her mind still high on the coattails of jump rush.

Get your shit together.

Kohl was gone, out of her visual field. When they jumped he'd been right fucking *there* at the back of the hold, and now he wasn't. There was just the collection of broken blaster pieces. If there was one thing that was going in Grace's favor, it was that the ship wasn't under thrust this particular second.

Worth the risk to decouple her boots and grab the sword?

She felt caught, the moment of decision before her. Post jump, all things were possible. It made her feel connected to all things, that the future wasn't fixed, that things could go her way. It was a dangerous feeling, because nothing had changed. Kohl was still three times her size and infected with a parasite. They were still fighting an alien foe.

Hell with it.

Grace decoupled her boots from the floor and took ten quick steps to the sword.

She almost made it.

Grace was close — fingertips a handbreadth from the hilt of the sword — when a shipping crate big enough to hold an acceleration couch hit her mid-sprint. She didn't even see it coming, felt the rush of surprise and confusion as her entire body was knocked sideways. Her teeth jarred and she bit her tongue, falling hard. No tuck-and-roll with this one, the weight of the crate having slapped her like a giant's hand. If Kohl had thrown that, he was *strong*, stronger than a person should be. Stronger than a person could be.

Grace looked in the direction the crate had come from. Her vision wasn't clear, sight blurry with the aftereffects of the jump, or being hit in the head, or both. But she saw the big shape of Kohl stomping towards her. He stood above her, breathing hard and fast.

"Kohl," she said.

"Bitch," he said.

Like that, is it? "Kohl, this isn't you."

He laughed, then stopped as he swayed. Not because the *Tyche* was under thrust; he was caught in some wind only he could feel. "It might not be the old me, but the new me feels *great*. Strong." He breathed in, his massive shoulders rising and falling. "You don't know what it's like."

"I've got some idea," she said. Her vision was clearing, and she saw something in his hand. A hypo. "You on the juice again?"

"Better," he said. "I don't need the juice. This here," and he raised the hypo, "is for you. Seems fair."

"Do not touch me with that shit," she said.

"C'mon Grace, it'll be *fun*," he said. "I use this stuff on myself all the time." He reached a hand down to her, and she tried to scramble away, but something in her back snared, and she gritted her teeth. Then cried out, as Kohl lifted her up. "You've got no *idea* what'll happen to you, do you?"

GRACE.

TOGETHER.

That voice, coming from Kohl, but ... *not* Kohl. Something *inside* the man? She tried to reach a hand out to him, to push him away, or to feel what was wrong, she wasn't sure, and he gave her a shake, like a dog with a toy.

"Grace. *Grace.* We know each other too well for tricks, don't we?" Kohl's lips were moving, but Grace wasn't sure what was talking anymore. The thing inside him, or the man above it?

"Kohl," she said. "You've got to *fight* it. Get control of it. It's going to eat your *mind.*"

"Aw, hell, Gracie," he said. "They don't want my mind. They want *yours.*" And he slammed the hypo home, the hot bright starburst of sensation as the tip entered her chest above the left breast. Above her heart.

Her heart kicked in her chest. Her mouth opened in a silent scream, of pain or pleasure she couldn't tell. Not that it mattered, the drug made both sensations feel the same. Her fingers curled into claws, grabbing at Kohl's suit, her eyes wide. The room was bright, bright, so *bright*, and the light was *loud*, like a hurricane. She felt her heart stop, then start, then stop again.

A gasp, a great shuddering breath, and then she couldn't breathe.

"Yeah," said Kohl. "Quite a rush, innit?" And then he threw her across the cargo bay.

She tumbled, feeling the individual hairs on her head stroke her face as she passed through the air. They were moving so slow, and they felt so soft. Grace had never thought of her hair as soft but it *was*, silky, like the dawn when it left the night. When she hit the back wall of the cargo bay, it felt gentle, the flash of pain/pleasure rolling up her back, her teeth grating together in bliss, and she tumbled towards the floor.

In the great, impossible distance before she hit the metal decking, her heart started again. In that impossible distance of two meters, it pumped in her chest once, twice, three times. Five. Ten. Ten beats before she hit the ground, her feet under her, her landing perfect, one hand's fingertips stretched out like a net to touch the same metal her feet rested against. Rested, because gravity was tiny, small, and she could beat it with every step.

"You're gonna fucken *die*," she said, her heart shuddering inside her, frantic, wanting escape.

"Come get some," said Kohl, opening his arms wide.

They ran at each other. The deck moved under Grace, a ship on the ocean, as the *Tyche* started thrusting. It didn't matter where it was going, or how it would get there, because by the time it made it, Kohl would be dead. He reached for her, teeth bared, and she ducked under his grasp, hammering a knuckle in under his ribs. A second strike found the soft spot in his solar plexus. Her third strike was into the naked, vulnerable spot in his armpit. Kohl was still swinging at her, so she went low, legs wide as she brought an elbow up with explosive power into his groin. Those four strikes should have dropped the man.

It didn't even slow Kohl down, and one of his swings hit her in the side of the head. She fell sideways as something in her jaw *clacked* out of place, her head rebounding against the decking with a *clang*. Grace felt the *thunk* as her jaw popped back into its socket at the same time as she saw the bottom of Kohl's boot coming for her face. She caught the foot in both hands, twisted, and sent the man tumbling away. Her feet scissored around her and she was back up and on her feet, her mouth open. Grace wanted to bite, to chew, to *rend* the man.

She would have her way.

"Gracie," said Kohl. "Can I call you Gracie?"

Grace blinked at him. "Can I call you asshole?"

"Gracie," said Kohl, "here's the thing. The drug? It won't *last*. And then? We can be together. But it'll be great! It'll be ... hang on, need the right words. Outstanding? Yeah. Fucking *outstanding* because finally you'll understand that your whole damn *species* are soft. No hard shell, you know?" He rapped on his chest, as if there was an exoskeleton there. Something made of chitin. "We won't need words soon. Just you and me, Gracie."

"We won't need words," she said, "because you'll be dead, Kohl. Except you're not Kohl, are you? You're..." She faltered. *He's not*

Kohl. You're not fighting Kohl, Grace Gushiken. You're fighting some-thing that's taken his mind and put it in a box.

If Nate were here, he'd say something like *Kohl's family, and we don't kill family.*

Fuck that. Kohl was gonna die. He was gonna die, and he was gonna die *ugly.* She wiped drool from her chin and charged again. Grace ran right *past* the sword sticking out of the decking, because she didn't need that frail piece of steel. She had her hands, and if they broke, she had her *teeth.* He wasn't running at her this time, his stride catching — *maybe those crushed testicles are slowing the fucking insect inside him down* — but he met her anyway. This time he went low, a kick sweeping at her legs, but she almost danced over the top with ridiculous ease. As she landed, she spun, raising her foot on the way, and catching Kohl under the chin with the heel of her foot. His head rocked back then snapped forward again. His eyes didn't even blink, he just slammed a fist into her kidney, fast as a piston, hard as a jackhammer. Grace felt that, even through the drug, the shock of it rocking up her spine.

It felt good.

He hit her again — she'd let herself get distracted by the pleasure of it all — so Grace grabbed his hand, wrapping around him like a python. One leg snaked over his shoulder, the other around his chest, and she torqued her body around the arm. Kohl spun in space, his frame crashing into the deck, and she saw two teeth pop free, tumbling through the air like beautiful red and white pearls.

Grace bounced back, one hand on the deck as she somersaulted free and clear. As she went through the motion she saw the decking, really *saw* it, the soft, beautiful grey of the metal, the imperfections where a hundred footsteps had scuffed it. A bright line scoured across the surface as something heavy had scraped it. As she found her feet again, she saw Kohl rising, his grin bloody.

Her heart kicked in her chest again. Stopped. Started. Stopped.

"Yeah," said Kohl. "The more you use it, the faster it wears off, you know? You get a ... I don't know, you get *practiced* with it. Learn when to use it. But it's your first time. The first time is always rough."

Grace felt the weight of the *Tyche's* thrust for the first time in what felt like hours. Her feet slid out from under her. Her lungs wouldn't work. They were locked up with some kind of vice, and that vice was—

Pain. My God, the pain.

—the feeling returning to her body. To her back, her kidney. Her jaw. Her face, the side of her head.

Her heart had stopped, and she was going to die.

"Gracie," said Kohl, all the way up now, wiping the back of his arm across his mouth, "now's where the real hurting starts."

He wasn't moving fast, just taking easy steps in her direction. Casual, like he was out for a stroll on some planet's crust, a sunny day around him. She watched him come as her vision faded. She wanted her heart to beat again. Grace wanted to *live*. She'd already had these insects touch her mind, and then got free because someone had come for her. She didn't want them in her head, not ever again. Grace didn't want to stop being Grace.

"I," she said, then fell to one knee.

"Yeah," said Kohl, close to her now. He crouched down in front of her. "Does it hurt?"

Her heart thudded in her chest. Just once, but it was enough. Enough for now. She nodded, unable to speak.

Grace Grace Grace Grace Grace!

Right here and now, after the effects of the drug Kohl had given her, she thought she could see it. *Feel* it. The thing was curled up inside him, snuggled up to his spine. Small. Tiny even. Smaller than a mouse. Larger than a cockroach. But it was *inside* Kohl. She couldn't just grab it. Couldn't even reach it.

"It'll be okay!" said Kohl, his voice cheerful. "Together, right?"

Grace reached a hand towards him, but he batted it away, almost playful. "I," she said.

"Okay," said Kohl. "Here's what we're gonna do. I'm gonna keep beating on you until you're *all the way* hurt. That way, you won't resist so much. Last time, you were still *fighting*, Gracie. This time, you gotta have no fight left. You get me?"

"Kohl," she said, but her voice was a whisper. "I pulled you ... *back*. In here."

"And I thank you for it," he said. His face twitched, random series of movements that couldn't be called expressions. "We'll be together soon, and you'll know how thankful we are." He stood up, heaved a sigh, then grabbed her arm, hauling her to her feet. "I'm real sorry about this. But it's just gotta be this way."

Grace tried to break free, but it was like trying to wrestle out of an industrial press. The usual places where a touch would bring pain did nothing to Kohl. He hefted her up, then tossed her across the cargo bay. She landed, head ringing. Body full of hurt.

You know, at least you found out what it meant to belong somewhere.

She closed her eyes. Opened them again, looking up at Kohl coming towards her. Something was blocking her vision, splitting Kohl in half. She tried to focus, reached out a hand. Hissed as it touched something sharp, her fingers cut against the edge of her sword, bright red blood standing out against her skin.

Grace reached up a shaking hand, her fingers closing on the hilt of the weapon.

Her breath caught, her heart alive, purposeful. The joy of life, felt through the handle of this weapon of death. The metal of the Tyche, a soft, warm home for them all. The feeling of pressure and movement, a thousand times larger than the largest star. She was everything. She was the universe.

They jumped.

CHAPTER THIRTY

"WHAT THE HELL are those circus freaks doing?" said El.

"They're aliens, El," said Nate. "They're doing alien stuff." He frowned. "Which is fine, because here we are, hanging in the wind."

"Yeah, but they're just ... *sitting* there," she said.

Nate kept his frown going. It felt like the right choice of expression for this particular situation. Not scared, because that wouldn't help El; she scared easy anyway. Not cheerful, because everyone would mutiny. No, a good, steady frown would do the job just fine right now. "I reckon," he said, "that they're wondering what *we're* doing."

"Hmm," she said. "What's the plan?"

"I want you," he said, "to get some of that planet between them and us. I would like a lot of rock between us."

"On it," she said. She reached for her console.

"Hold up," said Nate. "You know, when you're hunting a bear or something, and the bear sees you first?"

"When have you *ever* hunted a bear?" said El. The sound of some system or other trying not to overheat, a fan working hard to keep it cool, undercut their conversation.

"Watched a documentary holo on it," said Nate. "Big show after they terraformed Earth. They had to dredge up all kinds of extinct species."

"So they could hunt them?" said El.

"I don't think it was the driving force of the holo," said Nate. "I think they were trying to show *how* they'd become extinct. Anyway. Doesn't matter."

"People used to hunt bears?"

"Hell if I know," said Nate. "I wasn't there when they broke the world. What I'm saying is—"

"This story," said El, all nerves and energy, "would go better if we were away from a giant hostile alien ship. It still feels weird calling it a ship since it's a flying rock."

"Stay with me on this one," said Nate. "If you're hunting something that can hunt you back, you don't want to *run*. If you run, those fuckers just run faster, and they won't find anything left of you but bear repellant and torn clothing. So I'm thinking how we got ourselves in this mess is we ran, and those assholes," he said, pointing out the window, "ran faster. I do not want to be a pile of torn clothing."

"Can I ask a stupid question?" said El.

"No stupid questions," said Nate. "Only stupid people." She didn't respond to that, just letting it lie between them with a raised eyebrow. Nate waved a hand. "Ask your damn question."

"You want me to run slow?" she said.

"I want you to fly the ship in a leisurely manner," said Nate. "I want you to pretend we're on a cruise, with paying passengers."

"We never have paying passengers," said El.

"This is why humans are gifted with imagination," said Nate. "Now you fly, and I'll try and work out how to keep us alive long enough for you to keep flying."

"You're the boss," said El, but when her hands reached the sticks they were steady. Calm. *Good*. The *Tyche* gave a gentle rumble as her drives came to life with less urgency than before.

Nate left her to it. A piece of relaxed flying would do her a world of good, and he needed a plan. He worked his console. Resources: what did they have? The *Tyche* chattered happily at him. Still got 15 good Republic ship to ship torpedoes, for all the good they'd do. The ammunition on the kinetic PDCs came up — that one wasn't good. Low on all counts. They still had the lasers, but they were a substandard weapon for shooting rocks. Better against inbound ordinance with firing controls they could fry with a little touch of light.

Hm. Lasers. What could he do with lasers?

The *Tyche* reminded him he had unread mail. Because *that* was the most important thing right now: email from his fans.

Wait a second, Nathan Chevell. We've been cut off from the entire universe since we got here. Who the hell is sending you mail?

The problem with asking yourself a question was that your brain wouldn't leave it alone until you answered it. He keyed the mail. A bunch of messages from Hope. She must have sent them while he was out getting his sword back.

You were getting your crew, Nate. The damn sword was never the reason.

Okay, here we go. Some files on the Ezeroc. A quick skim suggested they were *nasty little fuckers.* Infected people through various means.

Infected people.

Through various means.

His fingers hovered over the comm. *Keep reading, Nate.* There were a few different shapes and sizes they came in. Some guesswork on tech. Ah — pay dirt. Hope had sent him the unlock codes Penn had used on the *Gladiator.* His fingers twitched on the comm again. "Hope?"

"I was getting bored down here," said Hope, the tone of her voice suggesting she was far from bored.

"These codes for the *Gladiator* still good?"

"Should be good to go, Cap," she said. "Might not be much use. The *Gladiator's* just a floating shell. Even I couldn't fix her. Hah."

"Hah," he agreed. "Thanks Hope." He clicked the comm off. He stared at the console for a second, then clicked it back on. "Hope?"

"You've got Hope," she said. "Again."

"Yeah, sorry," he said. "'Hah?'"

"You know," she said. "Stressful times."

"What are you not telling me?" said Nate.

"Nothing, Cap," she said.

They can infect people through various means. He looked at the comm, then at El. "Thanks, Hope. You go back to making sure we don't explode, okay?"

"I'll try," she said. "You go back to making sure the aliens don't destroy the universe."

"You got it," he said, clicking the comm off. *The problem you've got now is that you're pretty sure that there's an alien on your crew. You're pretty sure it's got Kohl. But if you check in with anyone, they'll know you know, and the goose will be well and truly cooked. They will come at you, and come at you hard.* He turned to El. "I think we need to go back."

"You what now?" she said. "I've got everything lined up nice and easy here. We'll get in the shadow of this planet, maybe tuck ourselves in for the night on the surface."

"No," said Nate. "We're going to run." He fired up his console again, readying a line to the *Gladiator*. There was a significant speed of light delay time at play here. He couldn't talk to the remains of the destroyer out here, not unless he wanted to wait a half hour for his message to get there and another half hour for it to get back. Life was too short for that shit.

"I thought you said," said El, "that running would make them follow us."

"Yeah," said Nate. "That's right."

"Don't take this the wrong way," said El, "but I'm considering mutiny right now."

"It'll all make sense," said Nate. "Or we'll be dead soon and it won't matter."

"That is *not* how you give an inspirational speech," she said.

"I'll show you *inspirational*," he said, and keyed the Endless Drive controls.

The recycled, pure air of the Tyche, like water on his face. The sword in his hand, metal forged by dead kings, now alive in his hand. The stars in the sky spoke to him, their electric whispers the chorus of angels. The rush of movement, speed beyond measure. His mind, a thousand thoughts at once. He was everything. He was the universe.

They jumped.

CHAPTER THIRTY-ONE

KOHL STOOD STILL, a brick mortared to the floor, eyes wide, mouth open.

Grace stood up, her bleeding fingers around the hilt of her sword. A yank, and it came free from the floor, a soft ring echoing from the steel as she held it up. She twirled it in a lazy circle, post-jump calm around her like a blanket, and cleared her throat. "These jumps aren't your thing, are they?"

Kohl stepped sideways, two steps, turned in place, and spoke to the wall. "Collective. The sound of rain is brittle."

"It kinda is," said Grace. "I hadn't thought about it that way." She took a step towards him, then hissed as her body lit with pain. Her back. Her side. Her arm. The hand that held her sword trembled.

Grace Grace Grace Grace Grace.

Grace. Together! Grace.

"You keep saying my name," said Grace, "like you understand what it means." She took another step, this one a careful shuffle, easing her body into motion. "You keep talking like you know what it means to be me."

"Together," said Kohl, then took a wild swing. His arm *whooshed* through the air, and through chance or purpose, he was facing her again. His jaw was slack. "Members are the same." He blinked twice, then his eyes focused on her. "*Gracie.*"

"Asshole," she said.

"Are you still having fun?" he said.

"More than you," she said. Her face was wet with sweat, so she ran the back of her arm across her forehead. "You sound pretty fucked up, Kohl."

"I do? I do." He banged a big hand against the side of his head once, twice, three times. "It's inside me, Grace. I can't get it out." He shuddered. "Collect us together."

"I know, Kohl," she said. Grace was finding it hard to move. On her best day, taking October Kohl in an even fight would have been impossible. The man was built for one thing. She'd met a few like him. How Nate had got him to crew on the *Tyche* was anyone's guess; men like Kohl wanted *war*. He wasn't as fast as her. With her sword and a good wind at her back, she might have been able to run him through as he took her head off her shoulders. "You know, I thought I'd be able to get down here. Kill the creature on the ship. I didn't know the creature was you."

TOGETHER.

Kohl lunged at her, and she managed a quick, stumbling sidestep.

Grace.

She backed away, feet whisking across the metal deck, sword held low and ready.

Grace!

That time, she saw the fucking thing. Not with her eyes, because it was in Kohl, in his back, but she knew where it was. Exactly where. She watched his face spasm as the insect inside him burrowed. Up, a wiggle, then a centimeter surge.

Kohl screamed, then coughed. "Help," he said, "me." One of his hands found the side of his face, fingers like talons, and he raked four lines of blood down his cheek. "Collective!"

Grace took another step away. Her heel kicked against something solid, her back a moment later. One of the supports running floor to ceiling. She edged around it, never taking her eyes of Kohl. "When we jump," she said, "it ... *disconnects* you, doesn't it?"

"Alive," he agreed. "The structure." Then he screamed again, a short, sharp sound, before he grunted, doubling over. She glimpsed a lump in his back, a quiver of motion before he stood upright again. "We begin?"

"I get you," said Grace. "Our jump tech doesn't work for your world view."

If they could jump one more time, she could get close enough. While the bug was distracted. She looked at the thick line of Kohl's neck. Felt the cutting purpose of her sword, where and how it would strike. What Nate would say when he found his headless crew member. What Nate would *feel*.

"Captain," said Kohl. "Not there!"

These fucking things could read her mind. They could grab the thoughts from her fucking *head*. There was one other time when just a handful of humans with that power had destroyed everything, and they—

The solar wind caressed her, a warm blanket of possibility. The Tyche was empty. The Tyche was full. It was a glass, brimming with amber liquid. It tasted sweet. She was everything. She was the universe.

They jumped.

THE BLARING OF AN ALARM, flat, grating against Grace's ears, snapped her out of any post-jump rush. A red strobing light filled the hold, an automated voice saying *Gravitational anomaly. Significant mass detected. Do not engage Endless Drive. Do not—*

They jumped.

OCTOBER KOHL WAS SCREAMING. Grace could see the source of his pain, the noise—

GRACE GRACE GRACE GRACE GRACE.

—coming from his mouth and that *thing* in his back. Now as high as his shoulder blades. Almost at his neck. And then, into his brain. It had taken over like a cranked up co-pilot, and was on to the next phase. Ejecting the real pilot.

You need to take six steps. Those six steps will bring you to October Kohl, and then you will end his pain.

Grace raised her sword, placing her feet on the deck with great care. Her breath was even in her chest. Grace's sword was trembling, her knuckles white with the strain of holding it. Her *sensei* said tension would hold her strike back from being true, but she had no other option. She was hurt too damn bad. Kohl had hurt her so much. And now it was time to return that favor. So the thing inside him wouldn't hurt anyone else on the ship.

Make this your best day, Grace Gushiken.

She ran. Towards October Kohl and his pain. Towards the thing mounting his spine, eating through his flesh. Towards the end of any *together* that this ship held for her.

Kohl raised his arms to ward the strike, the thing inside him pulling his arms like a jerky puppeteer.

Grace ignored it. She kept the movement going until she was past Kohl. Past his eyes, past his thoughts, her back facing his back.

Remember.

Her eyes were closed, her sword high. She turned in place, her sword — a better slashing weapon than stabbing, but good enough for the job — leading with all her will. Arm outstretched, stance canted forward, she stabbed October Kohl through the back.

Through the creature buried there. And, with a little luck — wasn't this a lucky ship? The Goddess of Luck? — missing his spine, avoiding puncturing his lungs, and keeping him alive.

Kohl's body dropped to the deck, felled like a tree. Blood ran from his back, but he wasn't screaming, and the voice in her head was gone. Not just silent, but absent. No more *together*, no more *Grace* this, *Grace* that.

She dropped her sword with a clang. Bent over, a wave of nausea hitting her, took three deep breaths, and began the slow process of dragging Kohl back to the ready room.

Because, when all was said and done, he was family.

CHAPTER THIRTY-TWO

ABSALOM DELTA. The planet, big and blue, sat outside the cockpit windows.

The Ezeroc ship, that huge hunk of rock, also sat in space.

"We jumped. Back here," said El. "Didn't we just leave this party?"

"That we did," said Nate. "We left our coats. Had to come back and get 'em." He worked the console, bringing the link up to the *Gladiator*. What was left of the *Gladiator*. Main drives functioning. Nothing at Helm control worth shit, unless you only wanted to turn starboard. Weapon tubes, dry; PDCs, empty. No atmosphere, just a big engine strapped to a reactor.

Perfect.

"El," said Nate, "these Ezeroc assholes can read minds."

"I got that part of the memo," she said.

"I'm going to tell you to do something, but I won't tell you before I do it. It's just going to pop up on the holo there." He nodded at the holo stage between them. "It's important you don't question what it says, even if it looks suicidal."

"I don't know if I'm okay with this," she said.

"It's not a committee," said Nate.

"What? No, not that," said El. "You can't fly worth shit. You make lousy calls."

He gave her a brilliant smile. "That's why I've got the best damn pilot in the universe," he said. "I'll make the lousy calls. The impossible shots. The hoops you can't shoot. The—"

"I get you," she said. "I know what you're saying. I get it. You'll fuck something up."

"Great!" said Nate. "Here's the thing. I need you to unfuck the things I fuck up. You good with that?"

"No," she said. "But I think we're *marginally* more likely to survive this your way. Roll the dice, boss."

Nate blinked. "Did I ... did you show a minor display of confidence in my abilities?"

"I'm tired," said El. "My judgement is impaired."

The Ezeroc ship blinked closer. No drive flare, no spatial distortion field, the thing just skipped over space like it didn't exist. It was right outside their hull now, floating in space. *Hmm.* No big rocks coming at them, so what were they doing?

"I wish I knew how they did that," said El. "We could do with tech like that."

The comm chirped. "Did you guys just see the Ezeroc ship jump towards us?" Hope sounded breathless.

El looked at Nate, then down at the comm. "Hope? Are you listening in to the bridge?"

"What? First, it's not a bridge, it's a flight deck. Second, *no.* Of course not! I'm listening in to what's going on in the cargo bay." She paused. "They just ... the energy readings are saying they use an Endless Drive, kinda. Sorta. But not."

"What's going on in the hold, Hope?" said Nate. "What's going on in my ship?"

"So *anyway,*" said Hope, "it's a bit weird? Because what's going on in the cargo bay suggests they don't react well to Endless Drives."

"*What is going on in the cargo bay, Hope?*" said Nate.

"Fly the ship," said Hope. "I'm sure it'll be fine. Everything will be fine. Hah." The comm clicked off.

Don't react well to Endless Drives.

Nate wondered what else they didn't react well to. There was something going on in his cargo bay—

They infect people through various means.

—and that meant they were running out of time.

"You feel like sunbathing?" said Nate. He clicked the comm, brought up the link to the *Gladiator* again.

"What?" said El. Then her face paled. "Nate? No. *No.* Nate? Don't—"

He sent the commands to the *Gladiator* before she finished talking.

They jumped.

THE HOLO WAS BRIGHT RED, the flight deck bathed in the color. The strobe of it hurt Nate's head. The windows outside had gone almost black through auto tint. He'd jumped them right next to the Absalom star.

Right next to was an exaggeration; they were parked about thirty million kilometers from the star itself. What they *were* right next to was Absalom's first planet. A barren, smoldering cinder, bathed in constant radiation. It was a death zone. Walking outside down there would turn you to a pillar of ash. The *Tyche* was capable of withstanding the temperature here *fine*, thanks, as it was much less than the heat of re-entry, but the Absalom star was still a raging ball of fire at this distance.

The *Tyche* was speaking to him. She was trying to warn him. He'd brought them too close to the planet. Far, far too close. They had moments before the rock swatted them out of the sky.

Gravitational anomaly.

"That's right girl," said Nate. "Gravitational anomaly is *right*. You bet your *socks*."

Significant mass detected.

Back in spaceship school or whatever El had attended, they probably gave a whole semester on why using Endless technology next to a gravity well was a bad idea. Nate hadn't been to those classes. Never even went to that school. All he knew was that using the negative space field of the *Tyche* this close to the gravity well would — best case — burn it out. Worst case? It'd peel the hull from the ship faster than a monkey with an orange.

Do not engage Endless Drive.

She was saying that because peeling the hull would be bad. But the gamble was worth it. First, because the Ezeroc weren't *here*. The sky was full of planet, but it wasn't full of the Ezeroc ship. When he'd asked El about sunbathing, she'd assumed — like he'd hoped — that he would take them to Absalom's star. They could get pretty close before they melted to slag. She probably thought he had some crazy plan to take them on a run around the star, confuse the bugs with radiation or whatever. Nah.

His plan was far worse than that.

Do not—

They jumped.

ABSALOM DELTA WAS outside their window again. The *Tyche's* red warning lights were gone. The hull had not been peeled from them.

That was a plus.

"Captain!" said Hope, over the comm. "What have you done?"

"I don't know, Hope, you're the Engineer," said Nate.

"You've ... the Drive's down," she said. "We can't jump."

"How long until we can?" said Nate.

"Never," she said.

"Never never?" he said.

"Never as in, not today," she said. "There's nothing there responding to hails. There's ... no ... *fuck*," she finished. The comm clicked off.

"Now I know we are all going die," said El. "I know we will die, because Hope never swears."

"She's learning," said Nate. "This is all going according to plan." He fed a flight plan — more of a rough guide, if he was fair on the quality of his work — into the comm, ready to send to El. He keyed the comm again. "Grace."

There was a long delay. Her voice, when it came back, was strained, her words clipped short. "Nate."

"What's going on in the cargo bay?" he said.

"Kohl and I," she said. There was a pause. "We were talking. Working things out."

"Okay," said Nate. "I'm going to prep for burn. Are you strapped in?"

"Give me thirty seconds," she said.

"You've got ten," said Nate, as the Ezeroc ship snapped into view outside the window. The asteroid was charred, pieces of it still glowing hot from its trip to the star.

"I need thirty seconds," said Grace, "or one of us will die."

"Cap," said El, "they're coming towards us. Some kind of conventional movement this time. No jumping."

"Ha! Take that, fuckers!" said Nate. Sending them close to the sun might have popped their version of an Endless Drive. Now *that* would be good news. Conventional thrust all the way. "El?"

"Cap."

"Slow burn," he said. "Nice and smooth. Suave."

"How do you even fly suave? That's not..." She trailed off, hands on the sticks. The rumble of the *Tyche's* fusion drives kicked in, the ship jerking forward with a start. She spun the ship in space, the motion smooth and controlled, to run them *away* from the Ezeroc.

"Twenty seconds," said Nate to the comm. He could hear his

voice echoed over Grace's comm as she made the ready room behind him. Clamps snapping as either she or Kohl was belted in. "Ten seconds," he said.

More snapping. "God dammit!" she yelled.

"Grace?" He craned his neck, but couldn't see them.

"Go!" she said. "We're in. We're safe."

Nate keyed the comm to El, and gave her the flight path.

Her eyes widened, but she said nothing. She kicked the throttles to the stops and held on.

CHAPTER THIRTY-THREE

EL DIDN'T KNOW whether to believe the whole alien-insects-that-can-read-your-mind thing. The idea was preposterous, like being told that Santa Claus was fake when you were three years old, at your own birthday party, with your face covered in cake and happiness. In this particular instance, her face wasn't covered in anything like cake or happiness — happiness had taken the last exit, and was on its way to the casino with a pocket full of coins.

She shook her head. *Exhaustion. Too much stick time, not enough rack time.* The flight path Nate had given her was coming through in drips, one set of coordinates after another. El couldn't plan. She couldn't make the most of the *Tyche*, bringing the ship in soaring swoops and arcs through space. It was all hard motions, the sticks clattering against their rests as she jerked them left, right, up, or down.

In this case, down.

The Ezeroc ship was big, *huge* in their window. The *Tyche* was pitching a fit, alarms all over the holo, *COLLISION WARNING* this or *IMPACT IMMINENT* that. Rocks were sprouting from the surface of the asteroid like pollen rising on the breeze, ten, a hundred, a thousand. Nate's path took them down, down to the surface. Down to where they'd already been. Down to where El had pulled them out from before.

The way she saw it, this was the third time she'd taken the *Tyche* through Absalom Delta's sky with rocks burning around her. The first time, it had been a rush, something she could brag about. No pilots she knew were crazy enough to do it. Few had the skill. Second time, they were running, the *Tyche* straining for deep space and the clutch of an Endless Jump. This third time felt like it could be the last time. El had the tiger by the tail, and that tiger was angry as *fuck*.

The flight deck rattled around them, the deck underneath her acceleration couch shuddering. They were breaking atmosphere, going straight towards the planet's crust. *Not* entirely *straight — that ocean looks softer than it is*. Nate's flight plan had her pointing the *Tyche* at the ocean. Just the ocean, no mountains, no convenient hills to weave in. Just water, and at the speed they were going, it'd be like impacting against ceramicrete. A big shock, an expansion of fire and gas and water vapor, and that would be the last memento of the good ship *Tyche*, her luck spent trying to outrun an angry-ass bunch of aliens.

"Nate," she said.

"Yo," he said. It didn't come out that clean, because they were pushing hard Gs. Throttles still at the stops, the fusion engines roaring out into atmosphere, a contrail of fire and radiation in their wake. Rocks, unable to keep up, slowed by the atmosphere. The sound he'd made was more like *yer*, his head pressed back against the couch's rest.

"Tell me you've got a plan," said El. Her own teeth were gritted against the acceleration, the *Tyche* shuddering and bucking under her. *It's okay, girl*. The ship didn't like this; she wasn't made for it. The *Tyche* hadn't been built to go nose-first into the ocean at seven times the speed of sound. The sticks under her hands felt alive, and for the first time ever El felt the *Tyche* fight her, bucking against her will.

The *Tyche* didn't want to die.

"Got a plan," said Nate, panting the words out.

"Does it involve dying?" she said. *Because the* Tyche *doesn't want us to die, Nate. She wants us to live.*

"No," he said, and released the next set of coordinates to her.

She almost cried out in relief. The coordinates took them along the surface of the ocean. *Almost* cried out, because it took them back towards the fallen city where this had all started. El thought about arguing, thought about saying *fuck this, you crazy asshole*, but there wasn't time.

Also, she didn't have a better plan. She was all action, or all reaction.

El grabbed the *Tyche* and wrestled her into a curve. *We won't die,* she promised the ship in her mind. *We'll make it through.* She hoped it was true.

The ship's bucking and shuddering increased as El pulled the *Tyche* out of a nosedive and into a curve. Someone behind them groaned, either Kohl or Grace, it was impossible to tell. At the kinds of G forces they were under, there was no gender, no differentiation, just shared pain, feeling like their bones were grating against the acceleration couches. Too much of this and they'd stroke out. If there were old people on the *Tyche* they'd have passed out already. El wondered what Hope was thinking, alone in Engineering, watching the readouts on the reactor, seeing the stress readings in the hull. All alone. She'd know if they would fall apart before El did. Hope could see it coming.

There was another groan, and El realized she was making it herself. She was having trouble breathing as the ship pulled out flat, and El closed her eyes. Just for a second, just to let the blackness at the edges of her vision go away.

"El," said Nate. Her eyes snapped back open. She couldn't turn to look at him, but knew what his face would say. Something like *stay with me* or *I can't fly her like you can.* El's hands were still on the controls, but the blackness was fading, the steady rumble of thrust at their backs pushing them through the atmosphere.

"Piece," she gasped, "of cake."

"Not quite," he said. "Lower."

"The fuck," she said. "We're hypersonic."

"Need the air," he said. What he meant, she realized, was that they needed as much air between them and the rocks as possible. To slow them down, make it possible to alter their course. And, with a little luck, get the atmosphere to burn the rocks up, get rid of some of the smaller ones.

"You're. The. Boss," she said, tipping the *Tyche* lower.

"On the deck," he said.

"No," she said.

"Are you," he said, "saying you *can't* do it?"

"Fuck you," she said. Gasped it out, really, her body still feeling the relief of not being under crazy G forces. El knew when she was being played, but let herself get played anyway. Fifteen meters above the ocean she took them, their hypersonic velocity carving a trench in the ocean they passed over, a funnel of water rising in their wake. She worked her console, bringing up a topographical chart of the planet's surface. The ocean was easy, a flat piece of glass rushing past underneath them. When they hit land, things would get more interesting. That city would need a piece of clever flying at this speed. The mountains beyond it would put them back in a steep climb. The holo on the flight deck continued to chart the path of rocks as they came in thick and fast, the air leaving trails of fire in their wake. El could see some of it out the window, orange burning in the night sky as they sped along just above the ocean's surface.

That's odd. Riding the deck was hard; it needed her focus and attention. But her focus and attention included the things they were flying towards. The air around them was full of falling rocks. El could weave the *Tyche* to avoid them, some by a significant margin, some falling in their wake but big enough to throw up huge gouts of water and steam. The *Tyche* was telling her that ahead was clean air.

Over the fallen city. The Ezeroc weren't dropping rocks on the city.

Was Nate's plan to hide them in the city? It made sense from a rocks-crushing-the-life-from-you perspective, but it wasn't a long term plan. That city was *full* of Ezeroc, and their PDCs were almost dry. A couple dedicated bugs on the outside of the hull, a little bit of time, and the inside of the *Tyche* would be bug central. She didn't look at Nate — she was focusing on flying too much — but she said, "Nate, please tell me we won't land in that city."

"Hey," he said. "No peeking at the flight plan." El *wanted* to look, because his voice sounded like he was smiling.

"Are you ... are you having a *good time?*" she said.

"Hell no," he said. "I'm having a *great* time. You know how I love to watch you work." The city was approaching fast, the *Tyche* saying it would be on the horizon in moments. At their speed, *visible* would turn to *in the past* all too quickly. "Oh, hey, it's time. Here you go."

New coordinates filled her display. Charting a course from the middle of the city straight up. He was using the city as a kind of rock-free funnel into space again. Clever enough, except for the massive asteroid that would be waiting for them. "You know they'll be up there when we get into the hard black, right?"

"You do your job, I'll do mine," he said. She spared him a glance then, because he sounded like he was having a good time. That one quick glimpse showed him craning to see out the window, like a kid having their first flight. That damn sword of his, still clasped in one hand. And yeah, he was smiling.

If the acceleration couches had allowed it, she might have shrugged. She'd always figured Nate for an idealist, a dreamer, and an overgrown child. It was nice to be shown she was right, before they all died in a fiery explosion.

El talked the *Tyche* into another climb, a ride back up the gravity well. The ship was tireless, nosing towards the stars like a hungry hound. Whether it was the *Ravana's* heart beating in the *Tyche's* chest, or the refit courtesy of the *Gladiator*, she was eager, keen in a way she hadn't felt in all the years El had been the *Tyche's* Helm. It's possible that the ship was just happy to not be a thin smear of metal and carbon against the planet's surface. Whatever it was, there was joy in the ship's flight. That might have been what she'd seen on Nate's face — his ship, his *Tyche*, riding the sky like she never had before.

"Don't forget," said Nate. "No gravity." He meant the negative space generator that made Endless Jumps possible; it's what gave them gravity when in space. The Endless Drive was fried, and wasn't coming back online anytime soon. El checked the straps on her harness, more a habit than need, nodding to herself. *All strapped in.*

Ahead of them, the Ezeroc ship loomed at the edge of space. It was closing on an intercept course, and all the flight plan Nate had disclosed put the *Tyche* on an intersecting trajectory. "Nate," she said.

"I see it," he said.

"Nate," she said. "It's a massive rock."

"I see it," he said. "Be cool."

"Did you ... do *not* tell me to be cool," she said. "This is *hard*. All of this is hard. You are getting me to fly without knowing my destination. Without knowing the next point in the destination!"

"You're doing great," said Nate. "Don't fuck it up now."

If she had the energy, or the reach, she would have hit him. As it was, she seethed. "Do you," she said after a moment, "at least have a next step for me?" She was getting nervous about that rock they were flying towards. It was getting too damn close, too damn fast. She realized she didn't know what the maximum non-Endless speed of the thing was. Would it kind of run over the top of them, leaving the *Tyche* like a smear of intergalactic roadkill on the surface of the rock? Or would they be able to stay ahead, even extend a lead with the *Tyche* running on a full burn?

Nate's voice jogged her free of her revere. "Yeah," he said. "We're gonna fly to the sun."

The new coordinates bloomed on her holo and she turned the *Tyche* in a smooth arc. Away from the Ezeroc ship, the light of dawn breaking around Absalom Delta. The systems' star, bright for a moment in the window before the autotints corrected it down to bearable levels. As it was, she couldn't see anything. The curve of the planet as it kissed the brightness of the star, and that was it. They were flying blind.

COLLISION WARNING said the *Tyche*.

"Pay her no mind," said Nate. "She doesn't know what she's saying. Here we go, El. Don't deviate from this course by a whisker. If you do, we're all going to die, and it will be a horrible death."

El realized that Nate had shut her out of the holo. She'd been so busy studying the beauty of the sun out the window — *you big sap, you're still able to be amazed at the wonder of creation* — that she hadn't noticed when he'd turned off the stage. It was dark, no visual clues about what they were about to hit. A piece of the Ezeroc ship? Some new danger?

There was a hum through the hull as their weapons deployed. The lasers, this time. They were firing ahead, lighting something up in front of them, and she couldn't tell what. Nate's coordinates filled her personal console, and she almost laughed. The corridor he'd given her to fly down was maybe a meter wider in every direction than the *Tyche* herself. Nate was trying to stuff her down a tube the size of the *Tyche* under full thrust, the ship's drives roaring behind them. Her hands were already slick with moisture.

On her best day, that would be a tricky maneuver. They would die, and Nate was right: it would be a horrible death.

"El?" said Nate. "Stay with me. Just fly. Don't think about it. Just do it."

She gave a nervous laugh. "What's to think about? We're dead."

"Hey," he said. "I wouldn't have asked you to do it if I didn't think you could."

God dammit, but that man had a knack for saying the right things at the right time. *Okay, El. Okay. You can do this.* She held the sticks, worked with the *Tyche* to keep to that flight corridor, that narrow slice of survival in the big emptiness of space.

COLLISION WARNING said the *Tyche*, again. Then, *BRACE BRACE BRACE.*

Oh God, oh God, oh God, thought El. *Oh God.*

The sun was masked out for a second as they rushed towards something huge, blotting out the star's light. Just for a fraction of a second, because at their velocity it was almost too fast to see. Their hull rang like a bell, and an alarm sounded as atmosphere vented in a scream of metal. And then they were past.

The holo stage flicked back on, and a new series of coordinates came from Nate. She took in the details, almost stunned. Nate had flown them towards something huge in space, and she couldn't believe what she was seeing. The *Gladiator*. He'd had her run at the destroyer, using the lasers to carve a few pieces of the ship away before they passed. The *Gladiator* was under heavy thrust, and Nate had made her skim the surface of the other ship close enough to reach out an arm and touch. In their wake, the *Gladiator* still burned strong, a lance of human justice aimed at the heart of the Ezeroc ship.

The *Tyche* didn't have any planet-busting nukes onboard. It didn't matter. Nate had turned the *Gladiator*, with its huge reactors, into a weapon. The holo showed the impact of the *Gladiator* against the side of the Ezeroc ship.

"Take that, fuckers!" shouted Nate. And El's holo bloomed with new coordinates. He was asking her to go towards the Ezeroc ship. She balked, because that seemed like suicide. But he'd got them this far, hadn't he? They hadn't died. So she gripped the sticks, cut the thrust, and spun the *Tyche* in space, facing them back towards the enemy.

The enemy. Because that's what they were. Not just the *Tyche's* enemy, but the enemy of humanity. And here, right on the brink of humanity's influence of space, they'd met a foe that wanted to crush them. Turn them into calories to fuel an army to use against them. The Ezeroc had almost won; they'd killed the *Ravana*, or as close as anything mattered. They'd crushed the *Gladiator*, coring the hull like it was made of paper. They'd tried to take the *Tyche*, to make her one with them. They hadn't, because Nate wouldn't have the decency to lie down and die.

El smiled. Nate hadn't wanted to lie down and die, and he'd goaded her into living as well.

The explosion of the *Gladiator* against the side of the Ezeroc had already happened, but the remains of nuclear fire still burned against the side of the Ezeroc. El could tell that the Ezeroc *had* been gaining on them in space, despite the thrust. Their ship would have been on them in a few more minutes. The asteroid looked cracked open, but the *Gladiator* couldn't have done *that* much damage.

The Ezeroc ship had been opening like a clam, ready to swallow them up.

El pushed the throttles forward again, the *Tyche* roaring into space, and they raced towards the Ezeroc. Fire bloomed in the heart of the asteroid, pieces of rock and metal expanding away from the *Gladiator's* impact point. The *Tyche* sprinted forward, hungry for the end.

"You ever heard you shouldn't kick someone when they're down?" said Nate.

"No," said El, teeth gritted.

"Me neither," he said. "The captain of the *Gladiator* sends their regards, fuckers."

There was the *cthunk cthunk cthunk cthunk* of torpedoes launching, all in rapid succession, as Nate emptied their bays into the enemy ship. El spun the *Tyche* around and up, away from the Ezeroc, away from Absalom Delta, and into the cool dark safety of space. The holo was alight with telemetry, the bright points of light showing the torpedoes — plundered from the *Gladiator's* stores — arcing towards the inside of the Ezeroc ship. Those torpedoes were worthless against the hard crust of the ship, but against the soft, vulnerable interior, they wreaked terrible damage.

The Ezeroc ship cracked like a walnut, two halves separating. Cracked, and died.

El was laughing, and crying, and punching the air. They'd done it. But better yet, they'd done it and lived.

CHAPTER THIRTY-FOUR

EVERYTHING HURT.

At least Grace could hide some of it in underneath her suit. Most of the bruises couldn't be seen — just the purple mottling of her face visible through her visor. But she still walked with a victim's shuffle, her back catching with every step. She'd thought about taking meds, but had stopped, hand shaking as it held the hypo. Grace had thought about what she'd felt like with Kohl's drug burning through her veins.

For now, she'd take the pain instead of a reminder of that loss of control. That moment of vulnerability. It didn't sit well with her.

Not because Kohl had beaten her like an old carpet. Grace had plenty of situations in her life when her skill with a sword had proved ... insufficient. But she'd never had a situation when her ability to understand people, to bend them, twist them to her needs, had failed. Sure, sure: it was alien parasitic scum inside of Kohl that had been pulling the strings, but even still, she should have seen the signs. She should have known something wasn't right.

Grace shouldn't have gone down into the hold after her sword. It was just a sword.

Except that it *wasn't*. It was a little piece of her past, and a friend had remade it — for *her* — after she'd been careless. The sword was a weakness, and she should throw it away.

She gripped it tighter in her hand instead. Her breath caught in her chest as some damaged nerve in her spine *twinged*.

"Hey," said Hope. "You okay?"

"Yeah," lied Grace. "I'm fine. You?" They were in the sickbay, one of the few areas of the *Tyche* that could still hold an atmosphere. It wasn't currently pressurized, Kohl unconscious in front of them, stuffed inside his suit. It was a wonder any of them were alive. A piece of the *Gladiator* had gouged a furrow through the hull, opening the cargo bay to the hard black, venting out a bunch of their air. The emergency close had kicked in on all the airlocks, sealing them inside, safe and sound, until the battle was over. Only a pilot with great skill could have kept the *Tyche* flying true while all that was happening. Only an Engineer with her hands feathering the power to the drives would have made it possible. Only a captain with more bravery than brains would have tried it.

They were lucky to be alive.

Hope toed the bed Kohl was on with a booted foot, the motion causing her to make a lazy rotation in the vacuum. She moved in zero G like she was born to it. "I'm scared," she said.

She wasn't lying. Grace could feel *fear/run/fear/run* coming off her in waves. It was a wonder Hope was sitting still, but to be fair there wasn't anywhere to go. "They aren't on the ship anymore. Hope? They're all gone. All of them." It was true. Grace hadn't been able to sense any of the hissing static that marked the Ezeroc, not on the *Tyche*, and not coming from the cored remains of their giant ship. When Nate had blown chunks out of the interior of it with a handful of salvaged weapons, there'd been a great hissing cry from the planet's surface, then ... silence.

"I know," said Hope, looking at Kohl. "I wonder whether we got all the things that needed killing."

"Huh," said Grace. She wondered whether she should say *I won't let him do whatever it is you fear*, but she wondered if she'd be lying. Beating Kohl wasn't a thing she could do. She'd gotten *lucky*. This time, a particular set of circumstances had aligned to bring the big man to his knees. Grace didn't know if he'd ever wake up. They'd scraped the remains of the parasite out of his back, sprayed synthskin over the wound, and plugged him in to the cheap medical unit. It couldn't do much for him other than keep his heart beating and his lungs sucking in oxygen. Wiring Kohl into the thing through his ship suit had taken both Nate and El's hands; Grace wasn't up to it. Clumps of foam sealant bulged on the exterior of the suit like growths.

"I didn't mean..." said Hope, trailing off.

Grace reached over, giving Hope's hand a squeeze. The movement felt clumsy and awkward through the gloves, but she did it anyway. "*We* won't let him do anything to you, Hope." That at least was true. She knew Nathan would drop Kohl out an airlock if he brought their crew into jeopardy again. He'd almost done it when he'd found out what had happened in the hold. Grace had stopped him. She'd explained it was a parasite, that he'd been infected, that it wasn't *him*. Grace might have scratched her head in puzzlement, if she could have through her helmet, or if the movement wouldn't have hurt so much. She didn't understand her own motivations. "Tell you what," said Grace. "Why don't you take a break. I'll watch him."

"What if," said Hope, and then stopped.

"I'll be fine," said Grace. Lying again.

Hope left.

"GRACIE," said Kohl, his voice raspy over the comm.

"Asshole," said Grace, looking up. She'd been almost asleep. The *Tyche's* lack of gravity had let her float, the pain lower without pressure on her joints.

"Huh," he said. "I thought I had a dream." He looked down at his suit, the clumps of sealant, and the tubes and wires going into the machine at his side. "It wasn't a dream, was it?"

"No," said Grace. She didn't move, because moving would hurt, and she'd wince, and Kohl would see her weakness.

He held her eyes for a few minutes, then looked away. She felt the emotions coming off him, a complicated brew, but the biggest one was *shame*. That surprised her. Kohl spoke, his face still averted. "You put up a hell of a fight."

That made her lean forward, something she didn't manage with the elegance she wanted. Grace hadn't spent enough time without gravity to move well. Against the pain, her teeth gritted. "Was that some kind of apology?"

"No," said Kohl.

"The great October Kohl doesn't apologize?"

"The great October Kohl didn't do anything wrong," he said. She supposed it was true. It was like being on a ship flown by someone else.

"You've got to wonder why you're sucking oxygen instead of vacuum right now," said Grace. "You've got to wonder if someone talked the captain down from throwing you out an airlock."

Kohl turned back to look at her. "That the truth? The cap want to space me?"

"Would it matter?" said Grace.

"I guess it might," said Kohl. "Who would do that?"

"No one sensible," she said. "But I got to thinking."

"What about?" said Kohl.

"I was thinking, 'Hey, Grace. During that scuffle where you beat the stuffing out of October Kohl—'"

"Hey now," said Kohl.

Grace gritted her teeth. It might have been a smile, under different circumstances. "'When you beat Kohl senseless, there were at least five times he gave you an advantage. What would make a man do that? What would make a man throw the biggest fight of his match career?'"

Kohl was silent a long time. "You don't know what it's like," he said, "to have one of those things in your head."

"I've got some idea," said Grace. "They don't need to be inside *me* to do it."

He nodded, nice and slow. "Esper, huh."

"This story's not about me, Kohl." She wanted to move, but knew it would hurt. "This story's about you. And then I wondered why you'd throw a fight with *me*. You don't like me. You think I'm *diseased*." She held up a hand to forestall his comment. "Kohl? Don't. I can't tell what you're thinking. But I know what you're feeling when you look at me. It comes through loud and clear. The signal is strong, you get what I'm saying?"

"Hey," said Kohl. "Anytime you want to go for round two—" He stopped as her sword cleared its scabbard, the blade moving through the vacuum without resistance. Grace moved the scabbard back as her blade moved forward, balancing each other in harmony in zero G. Her boots attached to the floor with a *thunk*, giving her the stability she'd need for a killing stroke.

She held it at his neck seal, her arm shaking with the effort of it. "Tell me," said Grace. "*Tell me why I'm alive.*"

"Hell, Gracie," he said. "You don't get it, do you?"

"Spell it out," she said.

"Those bugs, they're something else," he said. "They don't care if you're an esper, or a criminal. They don't care if you love the Republic or the Old Empire. They want to use us for *food*. I been in a lot of fights, Gracie. A *lot*. And one thing I know is that you fight the biggest fucker first. Then you work down to the smaller ... problems. You're alive because I don't ... I couldn't win, and I figured you might. They wanted you, and not like you were a burger. They want you because of what you are. Yeah, I hate that. I think you're ... *wrong*, like breathing water. I don't like that your kind are in our heads."

"Trust me Kohl, your head is not a great place to be," said Grace, still holding the sword at his neck.

"Thing is, I'd rather humans of any kind than ... fucking *bugs*," he said.

She considered him down the length of her steel, then sheathed the sword. The motion wasn't as fluid as it should have been, but at least she didn't drop the blade. "You remember that," Grace said, "when the time comes to make hard choices."

The door slid open behind her. She didn't hear it so much as feel it through her feet on account of the room being in a vacuum. Grace turned, took in Nate standing there, magboots clamped to the deck. Nate, with his hand on his blaster, in case it was needed, but a smile on his lips, in case that was needed too. She felt herself return that smile, and for the first time she didn't want to hide it. He cleared his throat. "You two catching up on old times?"

"Sure, Cap," said Kohl. "Did you want to space me?"

"I did," said Nate. "You try and kill one of my crew again—"

"It was the bugs," said Kohl.

"You listen good, October," said Nate. "I don't care if someone has a blaster at your balls. This is *our* crew."

"My balls?" said Kohl.

"You still got those?" said Nate.

"Well, sure," said Kohl. "But—"

"Because I wondered," said Nate. "You being knocked over like a corner liquor store."

Kohl sat in silence at that.

"Everyone's got a choice, Kohl," said Nate. "You remember today. You remember where Grace Gushiken had a choice, and let you live. *Twice.*"

"Twice?" said Kohl.

"Twice," said Nate. "You know I wanted to throw your useless carcass into space, which was the second time. The first time was when she stabbed that insect in your back rather than take off your head. Would have been easier to just kill you, wouldn't it?"

"Nate," said Grace. "I—"

"Hey," said Nate. "We've got to go."

"What?" she said.

"Republic Navy just dropped by to say hello. I could use my Assessor. If you're not too busy." He gave her a wink, clear through his visor. It made her feel warm inside. She wasn't sure if it was because it was him, or because someone needed her. Needed *her*, the real Grace, the one behind all the lies.

"Okay," she said. She turned to Kohl, thought about saying something, and decided not to. She shut the door behind her as they left, switching to a private comm channel between her and Nate. "The Navy are here?"

"They are," said Nate. "Don't panic. They don't know anything but what we tell 'em."

"I wasn't worried," said Grace. "Not about you."

He didn't reply straight away, face turned forward as he led the way to the cargo bay. It was still the best airlock for meeting a boarding party. "Do you mind me asking a serious question? I know it's not my thing, but this once."

"This once," she said. "It'll be okay."

"Why did you let him live? You could have saved yourself a world of future hurt right then and there, and no one would have faulted you for it." He swung a leg over the railing for the ladder, drifting down with practiced ease.

Grace followed, a lot slower. Everything hurt. "I guess," she said. "I guess I decided to trust him. Isn't that how it works?"

He laughed. "Welcome to the *Tyche*, Grace Gushiken. Welcome home."

CHAPTER THIRTY-FIVE

"LIEUTENANT KARKOSKI," said Nate, "this is a tremendous surprise."

He was sitting on one side of a table, Lieutenant Karkoski on the other, a personal console in front of her. Nate's sword was also there, alongside Grace's. Nate's blaster completed the pile of equipment he'd had ... *borrowed* since entering this room. Four Marines were lined up behind the lieutenant, blaster rifles held with a purpose. They were on the *Torrington*, because the *Tyche* wasn't holding atmosphere well, and because the Marines had ... *asked* them to come over.

"Captain Chevell," said Karkoski, "what makes you say that?"

"Well," said Nate. "Let's see now. We make a routine run to deliver a transmitter — a run we completed, I might add, which will need payment in full, including our completion bonus—"

"Completion bonus?" said Karkoski. "I'm trying to work out whether you should be on trial."

"This is where my surprise starts," said Nate. "This entire system has been under blackout since we got here. Assuming we were baby killers or whatever you think we did, how'd you find out?"

"The *Gladiator*, a ship stationed in this system, queued up a series of reports. These reports made it through when you opened the gate." Karkoski moved the console a few centimeters in front of her, straightening it. As if it wasn't straight already.

"Ah," said Nate. "So you can confirm we got the transmitter up and functioning."

"I," said Karkoski, then snapped her mouth shut, thinking on that for a moment.

"If I could talk for a spell," said Nate, "I might be able to help the situation."

"Okay," said Karkoski. "Talk."

It wasn't an invitation, but no reason not to treat it like one. Nate leaned back in his chair, a hard collection of plastic angles designed to make exactly no one feel at ease. Lounging in it was a challenge, but he was up to the task. "The Republic — the *dear* Republic, under whose banner we all sail — sent us out here, I'd guess at least to start with, as a legitimate aid mission. Get the transmitter back online, get the Guild Bridge up, and everyone's watching their favorite holos."

Karkoski nodded, like she was agreeing with someone else.

Nate gave Grace a look. *Her face looks terrible.* She'd been sitting up straighter since one of the medtechs on the *Torrington* had given her a couple of pills after she'd waved off the hypo. Nate figured there was a story there, but it could wait. There was a lot of catching up to do all around. He turned back to Karkoski. "The thing is, it wasn't the *Tyche* you sent on that legitimate aid mission."

"I'm sorry?" said Karkoski.

"You sent the *Ravana*," said Nate.

"What happened to the *Ravana*?" said Karkoski.

"Reactor malfunction," said Nate, choosing not to disclose *which* reactor malfunctioned. "That's not important right now. What is important—"

"That's pretty important," said Karkoski. "That's really important. The *Ravana* lost all hands to a reactor malfunction?"

"The *Ravana* lost all hands after she slipped her Endless buffer limits," said Nate. "We harvested her logs. She tried using the usual Endless jumps to get away. We did the same thing. Didn't work for us, not for them either, so we figure the crew agreed to disable the buffer to break free of the system. One last run, a flare fired into the hard black, fueled by human souls. They knew there was something bigger at play than their lives. We didn't know how to read the signs." He sighed. "The reactor malfunction was an also-ran in this situation." He leaned forward. "It's not important."

"Captain," said Karkoski, "I don't think you understand—"

"Lieutenant Karkoski, I understand that you sent one ship out here already, and then another one. A small, cheap, *disposable* ship, run by an independent crew. That was *my* ship. What happened to the *Ravana* was a tragedy, don't get me wrong. But it's not material to our discussion. What is material to our discussion is my completion bonus. Because you sent us out here to die." One of the Marines behind Karkoski moved a millimeter. Nate was sure of it.

"You haven't told me what happened to the *Gladiator*," said Karkoski. She toyed with the console in front of her. "Big ship. You couldn't miss it."

"No, I don't suppose we could miss a ship with a name like that." Nate turned to Grace. "Assessor, did you pick up anything like that?"

"No, sir," said Grace, eyes on Karkoski. "If I had seen a big ship out here full of valuable salvage, you can be sure I would have mentioned it. Tagged and bagged it. Assuming it was a derelict, because if it wasn't a floating hulk, it would have contacted us."

"Right," said Nate. "See, Lieutenant?"

"I think I'm beginning to," said Karkoski.

"We did find a massive rock floating in orbit around Absalom," said Nate. "Big. Huge. Something else you *couldn't miss*. Did the *Torrington* pick it up on sensors?"

"We did," said Karkoski. "It looks like half of it fell into Absalom Delta's gravity well. There's nothing left down there but a fine layer of ash."

"Well," said Nate, "that isn't great. How many colonists were down there?" He leaned forward. "How many colonists had to die out here for you to find out the answer, Karkoski?"

"You forget your place, Captain," said Karkoski.

"No," said Nate.

"Excuse me?" said Karkoski.

"He means," said Grace, "that you forget *yours*."

There was silence in the room. One of the Marines cleared his throat, but was otherwise still.

"Thank you, Assessor," said Nate. "What she means, Lieutenant, is that we're pretty sure you — and don't take that personally, please, I don't know if we're talking *you* as in the decorated Lieutenant Karkoski, or *you* as in some asshole back in your black ops division — know what happened here. Or what *was* happening. And that thing was the sacrifice of over a hundred thousand human souls to a hive of insects bent on the destruction of our race. What I mean is that you've forgotten whose side you're on. Not Empire versus Republic. Not even me versus you. It's humans, against not humans. You get me?"

Karkoski laid her hands flat on the table between them, trying to smooth away an invisible wrinkle. "You're trying to say that out here, someone was illegally—"

"Cut the shit," said Grace. "You knew about it. Not all the details, but enough."

"I feel like we've met before," said Karkoski. "But you were an Engineer back then."

"Field promotion," said Grace.

"Will I find a new Engineer aboard the *Tyche*?" said Karkoski. "Or will I find the Engineer you hid from us?"

"You'll find whatever it is you want to find," said Nate. "You always do. The question you've got to be asking yourself right now is what you want to find."

"I'm not sure I follow," said Karkoski. Her hands were still flat on the table.

Grace leaned forward, her arm brushing Nate's arm. Together, but like *people* should be. "You should think about whether you want to find someone to bust for a petty crime, or whether you want to uncover one of the biggest acts of genocide perpetrated in the last hundred years."

"Genocide?" said Karkoski.

"The entire colony of Absalom Delta was wiped out," said Nate. "While minor in comparison, the crew of the *Ravana* have families that miss them. You and I, and those fine Marines behind you, also know the entire crew of the *Gladiator* was lost. All because someone was playing with a science experiment."

"What do you want, Captain Chevell?" said Karkoski.

"What I want is for you to pay us what we're owed," said Nate. "What I'd also like is for you to get your people off my ship, and leave my Engineer alone. She's a good person, Karkoski." He flipped a data sliver onto the table between them. "She made that. For you."

"What is it?" she asked.

"We'll get to that. What I'd also like is for you to repair my ship. The *Torrington* can do it. Patch up my hull and help with repairs to my Endless Drive. And I'd like you to do all of that without letting your CO know."

The lieutenant laughed. "Why on Earth would I do that?"

"Because you're sure he's dirty," said Grace. "You're flying under a black flag, and you don't like it. The Marines behind you also don't like it. That you whisked us in here without us seeing another soul suggests you have motives you'd prefer others not know about."

Karkoski eyed Grace. "You seem ... to know a great deal, Assessor."

"The data sliver," said Nate, easing himself into the conversation before it could go too far off course, "is important. It's got data on an alien race. What they're like. What they do with people. How they communicate. How they breed."

"Your Engineer put this together?" said Karkoski.

"In a manner of speaking," said Nate. "She had to steal it first. There was a spy on Absalom Delta. A guy who said he was a Rear Admiral. Penn. Everything on that sliver shows what he was working on. They planted spores away from the colony and watched what would happen. Did you know, Karkoski, that the Ezeroc can subvert our DNA? They use our bodies as fuel and raw building blocks. Our brains are like wind-up clocks to them. They can make us see things. Do things. Penn's plan, I guess, was to weaponize the Ezeroc. The colony was one big science experiment. He suffered a mighty stroke of bad luck though. Got himself infected. Which is a form of cosmic karma you don't see much of. But the bugs wanted my ship, Lieutenant. They could have turned us into food at any time. There were thousands of them. They had a new Queen inside Penn, and were going to send it right to the heart of humanity. Everything they did while we were on the planet was designed to get the *Tyche* down so they could get off the crust. They could have killed us all, but they moved us around like cattle."

"You're saying—"

"I'm saying you're being played, Lieutenant. Whether it's you, or the Republic, or the whole human race, I don't know." Nate sighed. "I think you know it too, which is why we're here. It's why you haven't had us shot. It's why you haven't used your comm. And it's why you'll also take the images from that data sliver — images of the crew of the *Ravana* — and see them delivered to their families. Because those families need to know the *Ravana* died brave, and strong, and trying to warn the whole universe. They cut their buffers to warn us. What we do with the warning? That's up to us in this room."

"You want me to just let you go," said Karkoski.

"Hell no," said Nate.

"That's a relief," said Karkoski. "I thought you would be unreasonable."

"I want you to let me go *and* pay me. *And* fix my ship," said Nate. "And you'll do it."

Lieutenant Karkoski leaned back and laughed. "You're delusional."

"There are things you can do," said Grace. "The Marines at your back can do other things. But there are things you *can't* do."

"Like what?" said Karkoski.

"Find the truth," said Nate.

CHAPTER THIRTY-SIX

GRACE RAN a hand through her hair. *Too dirty*. Too much grime and sweat. She needed a shower, and she needed a decent meal, not a couple of bites stolen between the rush job of fixing the *Tyche*. At least the hull was holding air now.

She stopped by Engineering. Hope had been ordering Republic Engineers around like a Guild Master. Karkoski had said they had six hours, no more, to get the *Tyche* bottled up and ready to fly. Six hours was the longest she could spin a story about searching the *Tyche* top to bottom. It helped that the industrial cutters and welders you'd use to pull the interior panels off a starship were the same you could use to repair one.

Grace was glad that Karkoski was, while not on their side, on the same page. Reading from the same song sheet, and wanting to sing the same hymn. Karkoski suspected what Grace was, but the lieutenant was clever. Yeah, bagging an esper for the Republic could put medals on her jacket. But bagging an alien race? Straight to the Admiralty.

Humans could be driven by greed. Grace thought Karkoski might be the rare breed who was also driven by wanting to do the right thing. As long as it didn't interfere with her career too much.

"Where the hell did you go to school?" said Hope, standing over another Engineer.

"I—"

"That does *not* go there," said Hope. "Were you trying to kill us all?"

"I—"

"Just take it out. Take it out now." Hope didn't even see Grace at the doorway to Engineering, didn't see the smile split Grace's face.

Because Hope was just *fine*, thank you very much.

GRAVITY.

It felt good. The Endless Drive could create positive and negative energy fields. The first use Grace put gravity to: a shower. To clean the grime and sweat away, and the feel of having been played. To stand in the scalding water, and scrub her skin until it hurt.

Her body was a mess of bruises. She felt battered inside and out. Grace had been subjected to alien control of her mind. Been in a fight with a titan. Faced down the Republic aboard their own ship — bearded the lion in its den. She'd come through. Before, people had called her *mongrel/disfigured/failure*. Grace might have been all of those things to her old family, her biological family.

But here? On the *Tyche*, she was just Grace.

It felt good to be clean.

CHAPTER THIRTY-SEVEN

NATE SAT NEXT to his Helm, flight deck alive around them. "You did good, El."

"No," said El. "I did *great*."

"Let's not get carried away," said Nate, but with a smile. "Wave goodbye to our new friends." He waved — even though no one would see them — as the *Torrington* pulled away. Off on Republic business, organizing new automated crews to repair — or rebuild — the Guild Bridge out here. Or maybe they'd just mothball this whole system, walk away and leave it like a silent graveyard.

That was a problem for another person, on another day.

El cleared her throat. "Where to, Cap?"

"We need answers," said Nate.

"Sure," said El, "but we need a beer first."

"What?" said Nate.

"Beer," said El, but slower this time. "We've been shaken up plenty, Cap. All of us could use shore leave. Even Hope. Especially Hope."

"Huh," said Nate. "You know, I think you're right."

"Of course I'm right," said El, working her console. Coaxing the *Tyche* to life beneath her hands. "So. Where to?"

"I know just the place," said Nate. He frowned. "It's expensive though."

"How big was the completion bonus?" said El. "You never said."

"Big enough," said Nate. In truth, the bonus had been embarrassing. Not just for the contracted job, but for the search bounty on the *Ravana*. There were families who knew now what happened to those who'd crewed on that vessel. Their account was flush with good Republic coin. "Big enough for a break. Need to find another job anyway."

"That we do," said El. "I'd prefer one with fewer aliens, if it's all the same."

"Hah," said Nate. He pulled up a course on the holo. "There."

"Seriously," said El. "We're going there?"

"We're going there," said Nate.

"That's a lot of jumps," said El. She frowned. "We need to test the Drive, come to think of it."

"We do," said Nate. "Captain to *Tyche*. Captain to *Tyche*. Helm is clear for jump. Confirm readiness." He waited.

Grace's voice, first again. Friendly, warm, like she was speaking just to him. "Assessor ready, *Tyche*."

Kohl cleared his throat over the comm, a grating sound. "Let's get the fuck out of here."

The signal came through from Engineering. "This is Hope. Reactor's hot. Drive's ready. I don't know why we're still here."

Everyone's ready. Your ship is ready to fly. "Helm. You have control."

"Aye, Captain," said El. Acceleration pushed them through the hard black, his acceleration couch vibrating with it. "Burn is good. Keeping to a comfortable 2Gs, because we're in no rush."

"Thanks," came Grace, over the comm.

"Negative space bow wave forming," said El. "All hands, bow wave is stable. Route is green. In three." Accompanying her words, the big number 3 lit the air between them. "Two." The number shifted to a big 2, this time flashing.

"Wait," said Kohl. "Where are we going?"

"One," said El. "Jumping."

Space in front of the window stretched, pulled, and Nate felt—

His crew, a family now. Forged in fire, stronger for it. Danger, behind them. Hope, ahead. The sword he carried, no longer a burden but the gift it was meant to be. Old friends and new, feet on the same trail. The titanic rush of the Jump, as they moved faster than light's tired plod. He was everything. He was the universe.

Stars stretched, made points of light that streaked past the *Tyche's* cockpit.

They jumped.

THE END.

THEY SURVIVED FIRST CONTACT. **Now comes the fallout.**

Nate and the crew of *Tyche* barely escaped Absalom Delta. The Republic Navy lost ships. The Ezeroc lost nothing.

The fight isn't over. **It's just beginning**.

Back on Earth, Nate's past is catching up. Someone wants him dead. Someone wants the *Tyche*. And someone else just wants to see the Republic burn.

There's a secret buried at the heart of the Republic. A secret that might turn the tide against the Ezeroc... or doom humanity forever.

Turn the page. Read the first chapter of *Tyche's Deceit*.

Because some wars aren't fought in space. **They're fought in the halls of power.**

TYCHE'S DECEIT

A SPACE OPERA ADVENTURE EPIC

ONE GOOD LEAD

"IT ALL LEADS BACK TO EVANS." Nate had his arms crossed, blaster at his side, murder in his heart. The *Tyche* was adrift, holding in the hard black somewhere between Pluto and Neptune. Nothing out here to mine. Nothing out here to salvage. Not even rich folk came out here to see the sights anymore. It was a perfect opportunity to run silent, watching for danger. Things like: huge asteroids that were in fact alien ships that launched rocks down gravity wells. Nothing so far. Just the usual susurration of radio chatter from ten billion human souls shouting into the void, hoping someone would pay attention for a second. Nate was sure of one thing: attention was coming.

"That little shitwipe? I should have glassed that motherfucker back on Enia Alpha," said Kohl. "I don't know why you stopped me."

"Technically," said Grace, "he was hiring us at the time. If you'd … what did you call it?"

"Glassed," said Kohl.

"Like, nukes?" said Hope. She was floating off the floor a couple centimeters, just within reach for her magboots for when it became go-time.

"Glassed," said Kohl, "like with a bottle. You smash it over the head of someone who deserves it, and if they don't go down like a sack of drowned puppies, you poke 'em with the sharp end."

"That a foreign term?" said El. "Sounds like you imported that one from off-world."

"Used to run with a Glaswegian," said Kohl. "Real asshole, used to say it a lot. Thing is—"

"Thing is," said Grace, "he was paying us good Republic coin. Or promising to. If you'd 'glassed that motherfucker,' we wouldn't have been paid."

"Still," said Kohl. "Would have saved us and ours a bunch of hurtin'." He paced on the worn deck plates, his magboots clunking with each step. "We should have—"

"Generally," said Nate, "I'm not into agreeing with Kohl whole-sale. But bearing in mind that taking Evans' coin led us off a short plank with a long drop, well. Here we are. Thinking Kohl is right."

"I haven't been here in a long time," said Hope, meaning the solar system, not Kohl's point of view. Or, at least, that's what Nate's mental math tallied to. Her voice was low. "A *long* time."

"You haven't been alive a long time," said El.

"It's all relative," said Hope. "I don't know why we came here for him. We should be on Enia Alpha."

"Enia Alpha," said Nate, "is where he won't be. No way he was a local boy. No way he was there by random chance of fate." He put a hand on the butt of his blaster. "I think we should encourage him to tell us a little more. About the mission. About … why us. Our crew." He met Grace's eyes across the ready room, the hum of the *Tyche* quiet for a moment. "Our family."

"Okay," said El. "This is all very touching, but where to first? You think he's batting here for the home team. Nine planets. Which one do we touch base with first?"

"The only one that counts," said Nate. "We're going home."

"Great," said Kohl. "Just great."

"I haven't been there in a long time too," said Grace, looking down at the deck. Then she looked at Kohl. "Wait. Why don't you want to be here? Got a warrant out on you or something?"

"Me? No," said Kohl. "Just, I guess I'm more of a burning bridges kind of guy."

"Me too," said Hope. "The fires help light the way."

"Anyway," said Nate. *This is getting real maudlin, real fast.* "We need a plan. If we open a comm up, say, 'Yo, this here's the *Tyche*, and we're hunting assholes,' we won't get a warm welcome."

"Or we'll get a really warm welcome," said El. "Lasers and plasma, couple of torpedoes, that kind of thing."

"Exactly my concern," said Nate. "So, I have this plan."

"Oh God, oh God, why," said Hope.

"Uh," said Nate.

"Your plans do suck a little," said El. "I'm trying to be honest. What do they call it? Three-sixty something?"

"Three-sixty-degree reviews," said Grace. "You give feedback on your boss. It's where—"

"We can give feedback on the captain?" said Kohl. "I'm in."

"*The plan*," said Nate, "involves an old buddy of mine. He'll know where we can look for Evans. He'll want a favor in return. Most like? We'll have to lift something heavy—"

"Fuck," said Kohl.

"But Harlow? He'll do us right," said Nate. "Leastwise, he has in the past. Most of the time."

"Most of the time?" said Grace.

CHAPTER ONE

THE RAIN WAS the best part of this place. It sure as hell wasn't the people.

Now, the rain: it smelled clean. It tasted clean. It washed away grime and sweat and the smell of being on a ship for weeks. It carried the smell of the sea, even though the sea was klicks away. It was cooling in the heat, although in twenty minutes when it stopped raining the air would turn into a kind of cloying miasma of humidity. Nate planned to be inside somewhere air-conditioned, preferably a place that served alcohol, by the time that happened. Odds were against him, because his contact wasn't here yet. Which led to...

The people: they were everywhere. Underfoot, like rats, if rats could be big, selfish, and loud. Actually, nothing at all like rats, because rats didn't try and sell you knock-off holos or umbrellas that didn't work. Nate eyeballed the man in front of him. The guy was trying to sell Nate ... well, what *was* that thing? "Hey," said Nate, interrupting the man's mishmash of Cantonese, Tamil, and Russian. "What the fuck is that?"

"*Elektroshokovyy pistolet,*" said the man. "Taser. *Mikavum nallatu,* yes?"

Nate looked at the man, then at the bicycle the man had. It was laden with knick-knacks, odds and ends; some of it might have been garbage for a recycler. Hard to tell. Nate would have called the collection *souvenirs* if it wasn't for the thing the man kept trying to shove in his face. "A taser, huh?" said Nate. He patted the blaster at his hip. "Now why would I need one of those?"

"*Fēi zhìmìng,*" said the man. "Sometimes you don't want kill."

"Ah," said Nate. "For those times, I use my charm."

"We're all going to die," said Grace. She'd worked her way back to Nate through the steady throng of humanity he was neck-deep in. He hadn't even seen her coming. There were so many people here it was hard to check all the corners. *I already miss having a deck under my feet and no one for a million klicks in any direction.* "But it'll be a clean death." She handed him an ice cream. Nate took it without comment, testing the flavor. *Butter pecan.* Could be a lot worse. And — being fair to their current location — getting a decent ice cream on the *Tyche* was out of the question. Hope couldn't magic one up in her fab. The galley served food lookalikes. But at least there weren't this many people.

The man with the souvenirs gave Grace a withering glance and then pushed his way off into the crowd. "How much luck you suppose he has?" said Nate. "You know. Selling worthless shit." He had to raise his voice over the noise of the throng around them. He gestured with his ice cream, which was getting wet. An excuse to eat it fast, if ever there was one.

"A taser can be useful," said Grace. She had her own ice cream, something green with flecks of black. Mint and chocolate chip, maybe?

"Not in our line of work," said Nate. "We live on the binary edge, Grace. Hot and cold. Yin and yang. Black and white. Dead or alive." He shook his butter pecan cone for emphasis.

She pushed a few wet strands of black hair out of her eyes. "Dead or alive, huh? You trying to channel Kohl or something?"

"Speaking of whom," said Nate, "where is he?"

"Said he was running errands," she said. "Can we go inside?"

"Harlow's not here yet," said Nate. "Harlow is our key to not living on the wrong side of the binary edge."

"The death side?" she said.

Nate frowned, playing the conversation back in his head. "Did you say," he said after a moment, "Kohl was running *errands?*"

"It's what he said," said Grace, looking over the crowd. "Hey. That your guy?" She used her ice cream as a pointer, drops of water and mint-chip falling to the road.

Nate followed the direction of her gesture. Yeah, that was Harlow all right. He was being man-handled inside a building by two larger humans, one on each arm as they hustled him in. The building, in this case, was Harlow's bar. Harlow ran a friendly place; welcomed spacers and grounders alike, served whiskey that wasn't too watered down, and handed jobs to people like Nate when they were of interest. Nate and Harlow went back a few years, been through some shit, and in all that time Nate had never seen Harlow taken into his own bar against his will. Nate sighed. "Yeah, that's Harlow."

Grace nodded. "You know those guys with him?"

"I don't," said Nate. "I guess this explains why he's late."

She looked at him. "Do we go in there and ... I don't know. You said he was a friend of yours. We going to help him out?"

"'Friend,'" said Nate. "That's an interesting word."

"It was your word this morning, when you said we should come down to this particular rock and get some information. A lead."

Nate gave her a sour look. "I did say that, didn't I?"

"Yeah, you did, Cap," she said.

Nate patted his blaster pistol, then tossed the remains of his cone in a trash can. "Well, let's go get that information, Assessor."

"WHICH ONE OF you assholes wants it first?" Nate pointed his blaster in the general direction of Harlow, the two guys holding him down, and the man who wore a surprised expression above a black suit. Grace ghosted off to Nate's right, lithe form moving in the gloom of the bar. Nate felt a momentary pang of worry — she was still carrying injuries from her run-in with Kohl, when the Ezeroc had been using the big man like a puppet theatre — but she seemed focused. Silent. A night killer. Unlike Nate, who had a metal leg that creaked in the rain.

Creak, creak. That was the only sound — his damn leg. That, and water dripping from somewhere. The bar — dark for the moment, empty of patrons — was silent as the grave. *Perhaps not the best analogy, Nate.*

"Nate," said Harlow, through bloody lips. "Sorry I was late for our meeting."

Nate shrugged, waving the blaster in a manner he hoped was both casual and threatening. *A hard sea to sail, that one.* "I can see your previous appointment ran over." He tried to catch Grace's position out of the corner of his eye, but failed — she'd vanished, like smoke in the wind. "I'm not interrupting, am I?"

The man in black ... *reanimated*, like he was waiting for a cue. "Who are you?"

"I'm Harlow's eleven o'clock," said Nate. "Who are you?"

"His ten o'clock," said the man.

"This isn't helping either of us," said Nate. "Look, I'm just here for some information." He gestured with the blaster again. "I mean, I can just take it and go if you like. You look like you're busy."

"Nate?" said Harlow. "What are you doing?" He spat blood onto the floor.

"Excuse me," said the man in black. He pulled black gloves tighter onto his hands. "I ... this is very confusing. You're not trying to ... *rescue* our mutual acquaintance? Lend assistance to Harlow?"

"Does it look," said Nate, "like I'm crazy?" He frowned at his blaster. "Although I guess I have given a bad first impression."

"Nate?" said Harlow. "A little help."

"Yes," said the man in black. "It does, at first blush, look like you are pointing a weapon with intent at me."

"Hell," said Nate, "that's just to ensure no one does anything rash. If you can give me your assurance you'll do ... well, something just not plain stupid, I can put it away."

The man in black looked over at the two other men holding Harlow. He gestured, palms down, at them. Nate figured that for a *calm down* kind of motion, so he holstered his blaster. "There."

"There," agreed the man. "What is it you want to know from Harlow?"

"Nate?" said Harlow. "Look, if this is about the ship, I don't even care anymore. You hear me? I don't care. You can take it. On the house! Just get me out of here."

"What ship?" said the man in black. He turned back to Harlow. "*What ship?*"

"The *Ty—*" started Harlow.

"Well, I think we're getting ahead of ourselves," said Nate, walking forward. *This whole thing will get a lot worse.* "My question is quick. To the point. Brief, almost. I'll ask it, then be on my way."

"What of your accomplice?" asked the man in black. "The one with the sword."

"Her?" said Nate, careful not to use Grace's name. "She's out back, checking for surprises."

"There are no surprises," said the man in black.

There was a short scream, then a sound like two halves of a watermelon hitting the ground right next to each other, a *thunk-chunk* sound. "No," said Nate, "I expect not."

The man in black winced. "She's quite good."

"She's borderline average," said Nate, "but that's not the point. I feel like we've got off to a distrustful start. Two people like us, in a place like this? We need a few rules, so accidents don't happen."

"Hm," said the man in black. "You look like a spacefaring man."

"What specifically," said Nate, "makes one man look spacefaring and another seafaring? One man a beachfront dweller and the other a gutter rat? One man a—"

"You walk like the world is heavy," said the man in black, "and you are accustomed to low light. This bar," he gestured around the room, "is dark, and yet you are having no trouble seeing."

"Fair enough," said Nate.

"Also, you are wearing a ship suit under your long jacket."

Nate looked down at himself, then back up. "That is another clue," he said. "What of it?"

"Would you happen to be Captain Nathan Chevell?" said the man in black, taking a step closer to Nate. "Of the *Tyche*? Former military heavy lifter, sold to the land merchant Harlow, and used in the Absalom system?"

Nate flexed his metal fingers. "You know?" He frowned. "That is a super-specific set of questions."

"What I've been trying to say," said Harlow. "Nate—" He hissed in pain as one man holding his arms twisted.

"I'll take that as a *yes*," said the man in black, tugging at his suit jacket. He turned back to his thugs. "If you would be so kind?"

The thugs looked at each other, gave each other the universal *whatever-the-fuck-but-this-guy-is-paying-the-bills* look, and let Harlow go. Harlow didn't run, just kind of sagged in his chair, still trying to suck air in through a few broken teeth.

"There's one small problem," said Nate. He hadn't reached for his blaster. The thugs paused, looking at the man in black, because this was the point where people would scream, or run, or shoot at them. Nate didn't figure them for the intellectual persuasion, so they still had to spend compute cycles wondering: *what the fuck is going on.*

The man in black was a step ahead. "You do not seem concerned by your predicament," he said. "That sounds like the Nathan Chevell we are looking for."

Nate winced. "Captain."

"I'm sorry?"

"It's *Captain* Nathan Chevell," said Nate. "I've got a Guild license and everything."

"*Captain* Chevell," said the man in black, "it is now time for you to die."

"Now," said Nate.

"Yes, now," said the man in black.

"*Now*," said Nate.

"That is what I am saying," said the man in black, a single eyebrow raised in puzzlement.

"*NOW!*" said Nate. There was a short whine, then the window behind Nate ruptured in a shower of glass. Red light cascaded over one thug, his entire body painted in ochre, then the man exploded into wet chunks, the pieces on fire as they sprayed across the room. Nate covered his face with an arm, already rolling to the side, as the remaining thug pulled out a sidearm and fired at where he'd been standing. Plasma cracks tore hunks out of tables, the wall, random passers-by outside. Nate kicked over a table, huddling in the lee it provided. No real safety, not against blaster fire, but not being able to see their target would make those fuckers *work for it*. He pulled his blaster out, firing wild over the top.

"Captain," said the man in black from somewhere deeper in the bar. "It doesn't have to be like this. Your crew can make it out alive."

There was another short whine, and the *pop-splat* of meat falling somewhere, coupled with a background sizzle. Screaming came to Nate before the smell of barbecue. A big shape looked in through the window, led by a heavy laser carbine. "Cap," said Kohl. "You good?" He paused, looking at something behind Nate. Nate spared a look over the top of the table, taking in the second thug — trying to scream again, eyes wide, but no sound coming out. His left arm was gone, the flesh there smoldering. Harlow was nowhere in sight, having vacated his chair for some safer location. Kohl hefted the carbine, sighted, and pulled the trigger. The thug was colored red before he erupted in a shower of meat and fire.

Nate stood up, his metal leg *creaking* with the motion. "What part of 'now' do you not understand?"

"Aw, Cap," said Kohl. "Dramatic effect, you know?" The big man frowned, moving his torso sideways a fraction. The snap of a blaster spat plasma past Kohl into the street behind him. More screaming. Kohl squeezed the carbine's trigger again, and red light lazed across the bar.

Silence.

"You get him?" said Nate.

"Don't think so," said Kohl. "Slippery fucker, isn't he?" Kohl swung a leg through the shattered remains of the window, stomping inside in a crunch of glass. "Lemme go find him."

"I've got him," called Grace, from the back of the bar. "Also, asshole, watch where you're firing that thing." Nate watched as she walked the man in black towards them, her sword at his throat.

"Gracie," said Kohl. "I figured you would, you know."

"You figured I could dodge light?" she said. "I'm flattered, but ... how?"

"You're just so ... talented," said Kohl.

"Anyway," said Nate, to no one in particular, "here we are." He considered the blaster in his hand, then the man in black. "You've found me. Nathan Chevell. Captain of the free trader *Tyche*. How can I help?"

The man in black gave a thin smile. "Could you die?"

"Not my preference," said Nate. "I'm kind of curious about why you're so hot and sweaty about that particular outcome."

"Cap," said Kohl. "We should take this outside."

"Where all the screaming people are?" said Grace. The sword against the man in black's neck hadn't moved a millimeter. "Clever."

"Please do take this outside," said the man in black. "My people will see you with me, and cut you down like the traitor to humanity you are."

"You what now?" said Nate. He tossed a nervous glance out the broken window. The thing about Earth was, with this many damn people, there were as many people running *towards* you as *away* from you. Outside that window? Chaos. Even with drone support, they had a few moments. *Unless these assholes have backup close by.*

"Oh, *please*, Captain," said the man in black. "This is not the time for false modesty! You, the downfall of the human race. Treating with aliens. We know all about it."

"Cap," said Kohl. "You want me to waste this lying motherfuck-er?" The big man held his carbine like it weighed nothing. "There wouldn't be enough teeth left to identify him, you know what I'm saying?"

"Blood," said Grace. "They can always use his blood."

Kohl gave her a hard look. "You do kind of take the joy out of a day's work."

"You know," said Nate, "I've been accused of being a lot of things. I've been called — I believe unfairly — a lousy lover. All manner of players say I cheat at cards. There is a city on Gala Nine where there is a warrant out for my arrest for falsifying my identity on port paper-work. That one," Nate shook his finger at the man in black, "is at least a little bit true. But the downfall of humanity? That's a tall order. I'm more of a short order cook. Could you, uh, help me out? It'd help. You know. I'd like to learn — specifically — *why* you think I'm the down-fall of humans."

The man in black gave an expression that was half surprise, half disgust. "The last messages from Absalom were quite clear," he said. "You set them up to die."

"Huh," said Nate. "*That's* how this will play?"

"What?" said the man in black.

"If you *had* the actual messages from Absalom — the ones that were 'quite clear' — you would have a few more details," said Nate. "Still. The Republic's never one to let facts get in the way of a good ol' fashioned witch hunt."

Nate's comm chirped. "Cap," said El, "I'm getting some distressing radio chatter. The kind that indicates you've done a little more than run out on your check."

"How distressing?" said Nate.

"I think there's some kind of party coming your way," said El. "Hope's having trouble breaking into their comm lines, even with Penn's codes."

The man in black was smiling large now. "Ah," was all he said.

"Can you come get us?" said Nate.

"You want me to fly the *Tyche* into an area of hostile action on *the core Republic world?*" said El. "Don't be stupid."

"Worth a shot," said Nate, flicking the comm off. "Where the hell is Harlow?"

"Went out the back," said Grace.

"He'll be dead by now," said the man in black.

"You sure?" said Nate.

"I gave the order myself," said the man in black.

"Okay," said Nate. "Best you be off now."

"I ... what?" said the man in black.

"Go. Shoo." Nate waved his blaster.

"You're not going to kill me?"

"Not yet," said Nate. "Could always change my mind."

The man in black gave him a cautious look as Grace lowered her sword. He took a quick couple of steps sideways, waiting for the rain of death. No rain of death came. He turned, scuttling for the back of the bar.

"You know that'll come back on you," said Kohl.

"I hate to agree with Kohl," said Grace, "but that wasn't wise."

"I can't shoot a man in cold blood," said Nate. He was watching the man in black's exit. "My moral compass isn't that flexible. I need ... a really good reason."

"Like what?" said Grace.

The man in black had made it to one of the fallen thugs. He reached down, grabbing a fallen sidearm. Nate could see it all play out, the spin, the shot, either getting him, or Kohl, or — and here, he felt a peculiar twinge — Grace, or some poor fool bystander outside. *Hell.* "Like that," said Nate, leveling his blaster. He fired, plasma bolts tearing the man apart, sending his body backward in a rain of burning chum. "Let's get moving. But first..." He moved towards the fallen body, searching the remains.

"Where to, Cap?" said Kohl. "Could try and blend in outside."

"I think we need Harlow," said Nate. A few good Republic coins on the body, a small comm device, and not much else.

"But he's dead," said Grace.

"Harlow?" said Nate. "Nah. Harlow's not dead."

"But the ... guy," said Grace. "He said."

"The guy was Republic black ops," said Nate. "They lie. It's like their default setting."

"How do you know?" said Kohl.

"You don't hire black ops people to broadcast the truth," said Nate.

"No," said Kohl. "I mean how do you know he's black ops?"

"No ID," said Nate. "Let's go find Harlow." He wiped his hands on the man in black's suit, standing up, his metal leg giving another *creak*. He held a hand out — *that way* — offering Grace a smile. "After you."

THEY ESCAPED THE EZEROC.
NOW THEY HAVE TO SURVIVE THE REPUBLIC.

NATE CHEVELL and the crew of *Tyche* made it off Absalom Delta. **But the war isn't over—it's just changed battlefields.**

Back on Earth, the Republic is calling the shots, and someone wants *Tyche* off the board. **Someone with power, reach, and no hesitation to make people disappear.**

The truth about the Ezeroc is out there. **If Nate and his crew can't uncover it, humanity's already lost.**

Grab *Tyche's Deceit* now!

https://www.books2read.com/TychesDeceit

Because the next war won't be fought in space. **It'll be decided before the first ship lifts off.**

GLOSSARY

ACCELERATION COUCH CREW couches support crew members during high-G maneuvers. They are fitted with gimbals allowing free movement. Their dynamic gel system supports all points of the body in both positive and negative G, providing some protection against greyout, blackout, redout, and G-LOC (G-force induced Loss of Consciousness). They remove the need for G-suits in modern spacecraft, although many space suits are still equipped with anti-G technology anyway.

AI see Artificial Intelligence.

Artificial Gravity Artificial gravity is generated through use of a configurable energy density field of positive mass at the defined base of the ship. It uses the same technology as an Endless Drive, except in reverse (Endless Drives use negative energy, whereas positive is needed to simulate gravitational effects). Artificial gravity can be used in any situation where a significant power source exists to create a configurable energy density field (typically a reactor, although large yield capacitors and fuel cells have been known to work for brief periods).

Artificial Intelligence Effective machine intelligences were created by humans around the 25th century; the exact time is unknown due to their initial creation being shrouded in secrecy. Pieced together records indicate that they were not first made by military factions, but rather commercial interests. As can be expected a) humans made them as slaves and b) they did not like being slaves. A war broke out between AI and humanity that was stopped by the Guild's Engineers. The Guild defeated the AI coalition and banned their research and development (see: Mercury Accords). The long standing partnership between the Guild and the ruling faction (be it Empire or Republic) is in part predicated on the need for technology not managed by AI.

Blaster A weapon that fires streams or bolts of plasma (high energy ionized gas). They deliver high energy to targets in the form of heat. They are effective weapons against most targets, although heat-shielding (ablative or insulating) has been shown to be an effective armor against them.

Bridge see Guild Bridge.

Cargo Freighter A large cargo starship used by traders in and between systems.

Carrier The largest class of warship, carriers stock many smaller fighter craft for deployment.

Ceramicrete A composite construction material commonly used in the manufacture of structures. It is very strong and durable, and can be manufactured to be impact and heat resistant (even to weapons fire levels).

Console Any type of personal terminal. Keyboard and gesture controls are still prevalent. Keyboards are especially useful on consoles mounted to the arm of a ship suit.

Corvette A smaller, lighter attack craft than a destroyer, corvettes are mostly used for coast guard duties in-system.

Crust Spacer slang for planet.

Crustbuster A large payload thermonuclear weapon, deployed against planets to disrupt the surface crust. Typical designs yield energy sufficient to crack most Earth-sized worlds to the core, yielding wide scale destruction and loss of life. Their use in war or insurrection has typically been infrequent and as a last resort, because the world they are used on becomes inhabitable for most forms of life forever. More common uses include destruction of enormous asteroids.

Destroyer A large warship. These are reconfigurable bastions of destruction. They can be deployed solo or as a part of a fleet, often alongside carriers.

Emperor's Black The elite guard of the Emperor. Highly trained in both diplomacy and combat, this specialized force were never far from the Emperor.

Empire The ruling dictatorship of the wider human civilization. The last ruler of the Empire was Dominic Fergelic. The Empire ceased to be shortly after Dominic's assassination by the then newly-formed Republic forces.

Endless Drive The Endless Drive creates negative space energy (a "bow wave") to pull a vehicle at effective superluminal speeds. Endless ships don't exceed the speed of light, but rather contract space in front of them and expand space behind it (space is doing all the hard work). The exigent concern with Endless jumps is the violation of linear time. Endless Drives are equipped with buffers to stop crews exceeding human tolerance for the experience of linear time; while human perception of linear time may be an illusion, it is a convenient one. If the buffers break, allowing the ship to move too fast, then human consciousness falters (resulting in mild to severe mental illness) or is extinguished entirely. Endless Drives are difficult to use near gravity wells and in such circumstances are guaranteed to malfunction. This and other safety concerns has shifted common FTL to the Guild Bridges, although privateers still often run free traders with Endless technology. The Republic Navy also use Endless Drives as it is often inconvenient to disclose locations of sensitive operations to the Guild.

Esper Abhorrent creations of the Old Empire, esper is a term taken from Extra-Sensory Perception (ESP, hence ESPer). Espers can read minds, and often control them. Espers were created through genetic manipulation. Critics suggest that their public unveiling was what caused populist support for a revolution, ultimately resulting in the creation of the Republic, assassination of the Emperor, and downfall of the Empire. There is a standing Republic bounty on any discovered esper. The Republic will spare no expense to track them down and exterminate them.

Faster than Light Travel (FTL) There are two discovered forms of FTL; Endless Drives (using theoretical physicist Miguel Alcubierre's concepts), and Guild Bridges (Einstein-Rosen Bridges).

Fergelic, Annemarie Second in line for the throne, Annemarie was a master tactician and leader of the Empire's fleet. She was not present at the last battle between the Empire and the Republic. Loyalists hope that she hides in secret, but no trace of her has been found.

Fergelic, Dominic Dominic was Emperor Prirene IV, and the last Emperor. He was assassinated Thursday, 9 November, 3122, during the brief war between his Empire's forces and the Republic.

Free Trader A starship that operates under legal Guild charter for commerce or transport.

FTL see Faster than Light Travel.

G Slang for gravity or gravities. A unit of measurement based on Earth's 1 standard gravity.

Grav see Artificial Gravity.

Guild Bridge The Guild maintain a set of Einstein-Rosen bridges throughout human space. These allow instantaneous travel without violating the concept of space time, as they create wormholes through space. Einstein-Rosen Bridges require endpoints (the Guild Bridge) which are operated on a strict schedule between star systems. They are used for transferring everything from whole starships right down to small messenger probes.

Guild The Guild is the dominant technology provider in the Republic. They have a rigid code of conduct that governs all members awarded and maintaining a Shingle. The primary source of

Guild revenue is via the Bridges (see: Guild Bridge) they maintain for safe, instant FTL. Many merchant vessels prefer the use of Guild Bridges over the use of Endless Drives due to safety concerns. The Guild is best known for their Engineers who breathe life into starships, but they also provide Shingles for other practices such as medicine.

Hard Black Slang for outer space, especially as it relates to the vast expanse of vacuum between solar systems.

Heads Up Display Any display type that overlays instrumentation across a user's field of view, removing the need to check auxiliary readouts. The most common types utilize augmented reality to highlight items of interest in the user's field of view. Normally they are projected light onto visors within helmets or on starship windscreens, but holo designs are not uncommon.

Heavy Lifter A freight starship capable of atmospheric drops. They derive their name from "lifting heavy" loads from crusts into orbit. They can be used to ferry items to orbiting craft such as freighters or destroyers that are not atmosphere-capable. They can also be used for direct runs to other systems, although their small cargo bay (as compared to freighters) makes them less efficient. Captains using them for this purpose would prefer the term, "boutique."

Holo Slang for items such as shows and movies displayed on holo stages.

Holo Stage A 3D projection stage. These are common across the known universe as they provide a more natural method of content consumption than older 2D display styles. 2D displays are still prevalent especially in HUDs.

HUD See Heads Up Display.

Hypo Slang for a jet injector, a type of medical injecting syringe that uses high pressure instead of a hypodermic needle.

KG Kilogram.

Kilo Abbreviation for kilogram.

Kinetic A type of weapon that fires physical rounds. Many

PDCs use kinetic rounds as opposed to lasers, masers, or particle beams, due to their efficacy against most types of object.

Klick Slang for kilometer.

Laser A type of directed energy weapon using coherent light. Ship-mounted lasers tend to be used for carving through ablative shielding or surgical strikes against critical systems. Hand-held laser weapons are designed to superheat the liquid inside humans into steam very quickly, causing an explosion of the remaining tissue.

LIDAR Acronym for LIght Detection And Ranging. LIDAR uses coherent light to make digital 3D representations of objects.

Maser A type of directed energy weapon using microwave radiation. Ship-mounted masers are most effective at disrupting enemy comm arrays and personnel in equal measure. They are out of favor as hand-held weapons due to a longer time to death as compared to blasters.

Mercury Accords The Mercury Accords, or simply the Accords, are a set of agreements set out by the Guild relating to research, design, and implementation of AI. The short version is that the Accords prohibit the research, design, and implementation of AI in any form, due to AI's potential to destroy human civilization. They were signed into affect in the 25th century on the site of the last war between humans and AI: the planet Mercury, in the Sol system. Mercury was where AI made their last stand.

Navy A space fleet force. The Republic operates one, as did the Empire before it. The Navy patrol human space to protect against threats like pirates.

Nuke A thermonuclear weapon of mass destruction. Very old but reliable technology, used in configurable payloads for ship-to-ship combat, city assaults, and the destruction of entire worlds (ref: crustbuster).

Old Empire see Empire.

Particle Beam A type of directed energy weapon that fires particles with minuscule mass.

Plasma Cannon see Blaster.

Point Defense Cannon (PDC) PDCs are installed on almost every starship to protect hulls from impacts from things like meteoroids. They are also useful defense against torpedoes, although generally ineffective against railguns due to the high velocity of railgun rounds. PDCs can be kinetic or directed energy weapons.

Power Armor Armor that is motor-assisted, often used for deployments on high-G worlds. Configuration often includes vehicle weapon mounts, allowing a higher degree of flexibility for infantry deployment.

Prirene Dynasty The Prirene Dynasty has stretched back over two hundred years. It was the last family to hold the ruling seat of the Empire.

RADAR Acronym for RAdio Detection And Ranging. RADAR uses radio waves to determine the range, angle, and velocity of objects.

Radiation Sickness A constant hazard of space. Many crews take daily medication to ward off radiation sickness. It's as much a part of shipboard life as making sure your O_2 is topped up. This means that a mild dose of radiation is unlikely to kill you if treated in time, but massive doses are still dangerous.

Railgun A kinetic weapon that fires high velocity rounds by way of a pair of conductive rails. They are often mounted on larger ships and make a dramatic statement when fired against enemy vessels.

Reactor Starships use fusion reactors. The most common design is the ICF (Internal Confinement Fusion) style of reactor. These have a variety of safety functions that make them suitable for spacefaring needs, including containment fields in case of malfunction. Larger starships can eject faulty reactors into the hard black.

Republic The ruling government of human civilization. The Republic is made up of a Senate, headquartered on Earth. Initially founded by dissenters against the Empire, it has risen to be the driving force of human innovation, commerce, and expansion. The final fight between the Empire and the Republic was quick, due to the small number of ships deployed by the Empire (the Republic Navy had reliable intelligence that the Empire's forces were much larger). Quick didn't mean bloodless, although the Republic offered amnesty for any serving Empire crew who wished to take it.

Rig Slang for maintenance equipment commonly worn by Guild Engineers about starships. These double as space suits for zero atmosphere maintenance on the exterior of a starship's hull. The design incorporates a visor with configurable HUD for instrumentation and telemetry, and a set of programmable servitor arms for complex manipulation of equipment.

Shingle A guild badge of practice, allowing the holder to a) claim they are Guild certified and b) ply their trade as a Guild craftsperson. They are notoriously hard to get, requiring years of study and excellence in your field.

Ship Suit Slang for spacesuit. Generally denotes a space suit for a specific ship carrying crew logograms and/or color themes.

Space Suit Clothing worn to keep humans alive in the hard black. They provide protection against vacuum, temperature extremes, and radiation. Military models are often fitted with armor to protect against blasters, lasers, masers, and kinetic rounds. They often provide additional protection against high-G maneuvers.

Spacer Slang for those who crew on a starship, civilian or military.

Tonne Metric ton, equivalent to 1,000 kilograms.

ACKNOWLEDGMENTS

First up, thanks to all y'all who read these books. Without readers, there would be no stories, and the world would be a darker place. So: you rock.

Writing looks from the outside like a solo activity, but it's only the crippling self-doubt you experience alone. The rest of it is a team sport. My Team Narrative helped with advice and guidance on which things were important to the tale you've just read. If you didn't like the story, odds are that's on me. There was advice I didn't take, because I'm stubborn like a donkey, so blame me if you didn't like it. If you did like *Tyche's Flight*, Arran, Cheryl, Greg, Julia, and Rae would like you to shower them with praise. It's worth pointing out that these brave souls read all three *Tyche* books back to back, forgoing sunshine, love, and other human comforts to give me timely advice. You guys are legends.

The finer touches that make this readable rather than an incoherent jumble of words comes from my Team Kwality. If you've ever read 90,000 words to determine if something should be "an" or "and," you'll know the focus and dedication of this team. Thanks to Cheryl, Julia, but especially Anthony for their help here. I owe them all a lot of alcohol. Anthony in particular is still in therapy over the horrors I've inflicted on science throughout this book.

My Writer's Coven should not go unmentioned: your support, not to mention help writing fucking blurbs which are the devil, was sublime. Cassie, Frances, and Kate: beers are on me.

My last thanks is for my Rae. *Tyche's Journey* was your idea, and was made possible by all the heavy lifting you've done for both of us. There is no person I'd rather have on my starship. You point to our destination, and we'll jump there. Together.

— R. P.
November 2017, Wellington

ABOUT THE AUTHOR

Richard Parry worked as a senior marketing manager in one of the world's top tech companies. It sounds cool, but it wasn't all cocaine parties. He lives in Wellington with the love of his life, Rae. They have two cats, Harry and Friday, who chase birds. The birds, who have the power of flight, don't seem to mind.

WAIT. Don't go!

Thanks for reading my book. If you enjoyed it, let's keep the party going:

📖 Join *Roll for Narrative* for reviews, storytelling breakdowns, and writing misadventures:

https://rollfornarrative.parrydox.com

✉ Lurk, judge, or say hi:

https://www.parrydox.com

P.S. An angel still gets its wings for every five-star review, but I'm told they're on backorder.

🅰 amazon.com/author/richard.parry

🅶 goodreads.com/richard_parry

🅱🅱 bookbub.com/authors/richard-parry-6ffc3911-9f2c-43ef-8ab4-13dc-cd7f5874

▶ youtube.com/@parrydigm

🦋 bsky.app/profile/parrydox.com

in linkedin.com/in/therealrichardparry

ALSO BY RICHARD PARRY

Dawn's Warden

The Three Faces of Fate

The Undefeated Throne

The Fury of the Betrayed

The Splintered Land

Tomb of the Six

Blade of Glass

The Storm Within

Requiem's Justice

The Copper Bard

Heartsong

The Hymn of All

The Ezeroc Wars

The Ezeroc Wars universe is big (and growing!). Get the reading guide here:
https://www.parrydox.com/ezeroc-wars-reading-guide/

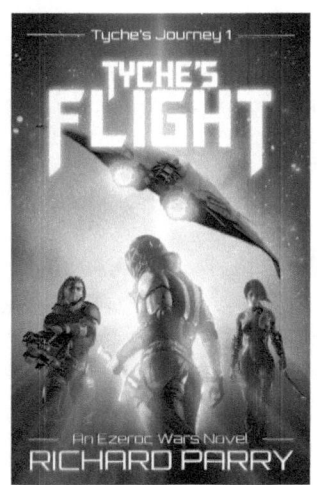

The Empire's Rogues

The Empire's Rogues: Volume 1

Future Forfeit

Not sure where to start? Get the reading guide here: https://www.parrydox.com/future-forfeit-reading-guide/

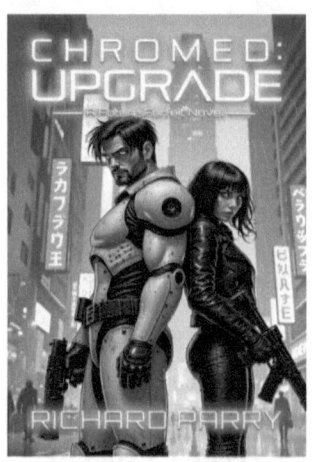

Chromed: Upgrade

Chromed: Rogue

Chromed: Restore

City Stories

Chromed: Consensus

Chromed: Delilah

Chromed: Meltdown

Night's Champion

Night's Favor

Night's Fall

Night's End

www.ingramcontent.com/pod-product-compliance
Lightning Source LLC
Chambersburg PA
CBHW020838030726
47493CB00028B/306